THE SWAN HARP

ELIZABETH
CREITH

THE SWAN HARP

WINGS OF VALENIA
BOOK ONE

ISBN 979-8-9878309-6-3 (paperback)

ISBN 979-8-9878309-7-0 (ebook)

Published by Type Eighteen Books

www.typeeighteenbooks.com

*This book is dedicated to the memories of Jennifer Bulman,
Larry Raney and Ted Remington— good readers,
great friends, gone too soon.*

ONE

When my father was newly King Tir of Valenia, he went hunting alone for wildfowl. He lay in wait along the shores of the lake but instead of geese, he saw swans on the water. As he watched, one drifted in, close enough to shore that he could easily retrieve the bird after he'd shot it.

As he trained his arrow on her, waiting for a clean kill, she began to glow. She rose up in the water, showing her breast, but the brightness around her dazzled the king, and he didn't shoot. When he could see again, a lovely woman stood in the shallows. She had pale skin, blue eyes, and black hair like midnight against the white feather cloak covering her. She smiled at him, hiding there in the reeds, and he forgot his bow and his hunting.

And that was how my father, Tir of Valenia, met my mother, Tianis of the swanfolk.

The day my mother brought three swanfolk to foster with me and my sisters was the day I knew I would never get my wings.

I was thirteen the day the swanfolk arrived. I looked like my father, with hazel eyes and curly, red-brown hair that tangled with the slightest breeze. My older sister Adana was almost sixteen, and my younger sister Orla was eleven. Both looked like Mother, with her fair skin, blue eyes, and black hair straight as rain.

And like my mother, both Adana and Orla could take swan form, a gift I envied with all my heart.

I remembered the day Adana first took her swan form as clearly as if it had happened to me. It hadn't started as something to envy. Adana was twelve. She woke up one morning in the bedroom we shared and immediately began scratching her arms.

"I'm itchy all over!" she exclaimed.

"Did you get into a patch of prickles yesterday?" I asked. We'd been out along the riverbank, where grass with prickly seedheads grew in large swaths.

"No, this is different," she said. "It's underneath my skin."

We dressed and went down for breakfast. By the time we arrived at the family table in the great hall, she couldn't sit still for itching. Mother took Adana's chin in her hand and turned her face, looking at both cheeks.

"You have a rash starting, swanling," she said.

Adana held out her hands. There were tiny, raised bumps on the backs. Mother took one look and stood up.

"Come with me," she said. She took Adana up the stairs to the solar, a room that was warm even on the coldest days, and they stayed up there all day. Elena, mother's lady-in-waiting, took food up and brought the dishes down, but nobody else, not even Father, was allowed in.

Father was worried and trying not to show it. In the afternoon, the smith reshod Father's big grey, Cloud, and Father took us over to watch. He held Cloud while Sylard removed each old shoe in turn and trimmed Cloud's hoof before putting on the new shoe.

When we came back into the hall, people were bustling up and down the stairs to Mother's solar. Elena met us halfway across the hall. She curtsied to Father.

"Sire, the queen requests you come up with your daughters."

"Is everything well?"

She smiled. "Yes, Sire."

Father took the stairs two at a time, and we ran up behind him. At the door we ran into his arm, braced to keep us from charging in. Mother sat in her chair, with a smile on her face and a finger to her lips. Resting on the hearthrug, looking at us out of one bright, black eye, was a swan.

"Gently, girls," she said. "Don't startle your sister."

"Adana?" I whispered.

"Yes." She glanced at Father. "The next Swan Queen."

"What do you mean?" I asked. "Adana is the oldest. She's going to be queen of Valenia after Father."

"No, swanling," Mother said. "I'm the only child of my parents. When your father and I fell in love, your grandfather, my father, made us promise that the first of our children to take swan form would become his heir in my place. Now Adana has fulfilled that promise."

"That means," Father said, putting his arm around my shoulder and pulling me to his side, "that you'll be queen after me, Kiar."

"And I'll be queen after Kiar!" said Orla, clapping her hands. Adana started back at the sound and Mother hushed her.

"It doesn't work like that, sweetheart," Father said.

"You'll have a destiny of your own," Mother added.

The next day, Adana came downstairs for breakfast with Mother, looking no different than she had the day before except that her rash had disappeared.

"You're not a swan anymore," Orla said. "You're just the same as you were."

"Not quite," Mother said. "Now she can be a swan whenever she wants to be."

"I want to be a swan, too!"

"All in good time," Mother said. "When you're ready, you'll know how."

"Me, too?" I asked.

"Of course, swanling. Tir, I'm going to the lake this morning. My father should know about this."

"I agree," Father said. "He'll be glad we've been able to keep our side of the agreement."

"I always knew we could," Mother said. She leaned over to kiss his cheek. "I'll also take Adana for her first flight."

Adana, who had been shoving bread and honey into her mouth like she was starving, stopped eating and looked at Mother.

"Today? Now?"

Mother just smiled. Adana finished eating quickly and bounced up from the table. When she and Mother had left the room, Father turned to me.

"Kiar, it's time for your first lesson in something new as well. A queen should know how to fight. Today you'll start learning to use a sword."

There were more changes in our lives after Adana gained her swan form. She moved out of our shared bedroom into a room of her own. She spent more time with Mother, and more time at the lake with our swan family and the flock. The lake was the nesting grounds for the flock, where they spent half the year. The other half was spent at the winter grounds, far to the south of Valenia.

We all visited our grandparents during their stay at the lake. They always took their human forms out of courtesy, but it was clear they were not at home in them. My grandfather in particular had a way of looking at us with one eye, with his head turned sideways. It was not his fault that his voice sounded harsh, but I found him a little frightening. After Adana's change, she and Mother visited much more often and occasionally stayed overnight on the lake.

They also went flying. Mother had never talked about flying before. She must have done it, at least when she visited her family. Later I thought she might have tried to put it aside, to be a good queen to her human subjects, and to fit into her new life. But after Adana fledged, they went out several times a week in good weather to let Adana practice and build up her strength.

"Is it necessary for her to spend so much time as a swan?" Father asked. "She won't go south with the flock for years yet."

Mother didn't answer him directly.

"It's a long journey, days of flying," she said. "Even with practice, it will be harder for her than for those who seldom take human form. The more used to swan form she is, the easier it will be."

It was the first time I'd seen them disagree about something to do with us.

Autumn came, and the flock left without Adana. We had the autumn festival, when the hard weather closed in, with bitter cold, snow, and wind, Mother and Adana no longer flew. Things returned to how they had been before. Except now I spent an hour every day with Dar, the captain of Father's guard, learning how to use a blunt, wooden sword, a shield, and a spear.

"Well done, young Kiar," Dar said one morning, when he'd knocked the sword out of my hand yet again and caught me a rap on the shield that sent it smartly into my shoulder.

"How can I be doing well? You always beat me!"

He took the shield from my arm and rubbed my shoulder with his hard palm.

"I've done this since I was younger than you are now," he said. "And when I started, my sword master beat me, every time. You're stronger and faster than you were a few months ago. Give yourself time."

"Why does everything take time?" It wasn't really a question I expected Dar to answer. He was a guard and a sword master, not someone I thought might consider other things, or even take my question seriously.

"If I told you everything I know about fighting all at once," he said, "you'd never remember it. You have to learn things little by little. Look at your right hand."

I held it out and he ran his finger over the stripe of callus starting at the base of my fingers.

"If you could do all the work in an afternoon that you've done in the last months, your hand would be raw and bloody at the end of it. But now you can swing a sword for a long time," he said, "Things have to happen when they're ready. The kingcups don't bloom in the winter, nor the lambs come before they're ready to be born."

I shook my head.

"Have some patience, young Kiar," he said. "Everything comes with time and work and patience. Or at least most things."

I thought of those words often as I learned the sword and spear and bow. Spring came, the flock flew back from the winter grounds, and Mother and Adana began to spend time flying again. Work improved my skill with weapons, and time brought me closer to my twelfth birthday—when I was sure I, too, would be able to take swan form.

Patience was hard. It became even harder when, late the next summer, Orla developed the same rash and bumps on her skin.

"It's not fair!" I said to Adana when Mother and Orla had shut themselves into the solar. "It was supposed to be me next!"

"I know," Adana said.

"I don't understand why!"

"Maybe it's because we—Orla and I—look more like Mother?"

"I'm almost twelve. In the autumn, I'll be the same age you were when you took swan form—but she's only ten."

"You'll have to ask Mother."

The next day, when Mother and Orla joined us for breakfast, Mother beamed with pride, one arm around Orla's shoulders. "Tir, our little girl is a black swan!" she said. "The first since Queen Amala, five hundred years ago!"

"What does that mean?" I asked. "A black swan?"

"Someday," Mother said, smiling down at Orla, "she'll be able to use powerful magic. Perhaps that's why she fledged early."

My heart sank. My older sister could fly, and now my younger sister could, too. And on top of everything, she would do magic. Compared to that, what was learning to use a sword or a bow?

I was Father's heir now, and one day I'd be queen. But when I looked at Mother, Adana, and Orla and thought of flying, somehow the thought of being queen didn't comfort me.

CHAPTER

TWO

That autumn I turned thirteen. I was stronger and faster than when I'd begun training with Dar. For my birthday. Father had Sylard make a sword the right length for me, and a knife with a bronze pommel and a sheath I could slip into my boot. Dar made me practice hard with a blunted sword before he let me try with my new one. When I finally used the new sword, I was surprised by how much lighter it was than the practice swords. It moved much more easily and felt almost like part of my arm.

"That's because it's made for your height and reach," Dar said, "and good balance. You'll improve quickly with a weapon made for you."

There was another gift, too—a sorrel mare. In the last few months, I'd outgrown my pony. The new horse was taller, with a narrow white blaze down her face and a flaxen mane and tail. I named her Kestrel.

But the gift I most wanted did not come. Morning after morning, I tried to convince myself that an itchy spot on my back or dry skin on my arms was the beginning of the rash that would end in flight. Morning after morning the itch faded, or the dry skin yielded to a salve, and I was still just Kiar, a human girl in a family of swanfolk.

During the winter, when the flock was gone, it was easier not to feel left out. Mother, Adana, and Orla did not fly. In the evenings, we sat in Mother's solar, listening to stories while Father sharpened knives, and it almost seemed the household was as it had been before Adana got her wings.

But with the first days of spring, Adana and Orla were eager to be in the air. As soon as the snow had melted and the ice was gone from the lake, I watched them from the door of the castle as they rode out to the lake. Mother came up behind me and put her hands on my shoulders.

"Don't be envious," she said. "You'll be a queen in your own right someday. That's a great responsibility and a great honour."

"I can't help it," I said. "I thought by now—" A lump rose in my throat.

"It will come, swanling. You have the swanfolk blood."

"I think Orla got my share," I said. "And I have her share of human blood, and Adana's, too."

"Is that such a bad thing? It will be easier to be queen in your turn if you are human."

"I know."

Mother sighed and rubbed my shoulders. "You're all growing up so fast. Dar says you'll be a great fighter in time. He's very pleased with you. Your father and I are, too."

"Thank you," I said. "I'd rather be able to fly. I want that more than anything."

"I know, swanling. Humans and swanfolk rarely marry and have children. There are stories, but I don't know of any others alive except your father and me. We didn't know if any of you would be able to fly."

"What about your agreement with Grandfather? If none of us could be swans?"

"I don't know, swanling. It was a worry, but I'm glad it worked out as it has." She bent and kissed my cheek. "So far. There is swan blood in you, Kiar. Give it time."

That evening, we sat in Mother's solar after supper. Father was putting an edge on the small knife Mother used to cut thread. I had torn the knee of my trousers on a nail and had a patch to sew on.

Orla played cat's cradle in the corner, while Adana watched the dance of the flames in the hearth. None of us were prepared for Mother's words.

"We need to consider who Adana will marry," she said.

The *ssst-sst* of Father's whetstone stopped, and we all looked at Mother.

"What is this, then?" Father asked.

"I'm not even sixteen yet," Adana said. "I don't want to get married."

"Not right away," Mother said. "Tir, you know she must marry one of the swanfolk."

"But we don't know any swanfolk," I said.

"You don't know any," Orla said. "We know some."

I stuck my tongue out at her.

"Girls!" Father said, then turned to Mother. "Adana is too young to leave us and go with the flock. She will stay with her family until she's grown."

"Of course," Mother said. "I thought that maybe we could foster some of the younglings here. That would give all of us a chance to get to know them. It would be good for relations between us."

"That's a good idea." Father turned to me. "Kiar, a king or queen needs to know their allies. Even if Adana will someday be queen of the swanfolk, having other friends among them will help."

"I'll speak to my father and choose some fosterlings to join us before the flock leaves for the winter grounds," Mother said.

When autumn began to set in my mother went out to the lake with a packhorse carrying a bundle of clothing and returned with three young swanfolk. We caught sight of them as they approached the castle, but Mother quickly shepherded them into the solar, and we didn't get a good look.

Elena took Mother's supper up to the solar that evening. Finally, the next morning, we were invited upstairs to meet the new additions to our household.

They were the first swanfolk we had met in human form, except for Mother and our grandparents. All three had blue eyes, pale skin untouched by sun or wind, and smooth, black hair that hung long down their backs. They wore the trousers and tunics we all wore for riding, but the clothing couldn't disguise what they were.

I looked from them to Mother, and then glanced sideways at Orla and Adana. It was as though they had all been made from the same pattern, or grown, like birches, from the same seeds. I was the odd one, the lone oak sapling in the birch grove, the pattern that didn't match. In that moment, I felt my difference keenly, like a physical pain in my chest. I was not a swan, not even a little bit, and I never would be.

I refused to show my hurt and distracted myself by looking at the three swanfolk. Each looked wary, and the girl braced her legs and held her arms away from her body, almost as though she expected a fight. The taller and heavier of the boys came forward a step, and the other, lighter and wiry, stood apart, watching us sidelong.

"These are my daughters," Mother said, "Adana, Kiar, Orla."

She put her arm around the girl and brought her forward a step.

"This is Willow, Gil," she said, and nodding toward the taller boy, "and Tuan." Tuan turned his head and looked at me steadily. I met his gaze and after a few seconds, he looked away.

We all stood unspeaking for a long minute. The girl Willow never moved from her braced stance. She looked nervous, I thought, but ready to take anything on, and I decided I liked her.

It was Orla who broke the silence. She skipped over to Gil and took his hand.

"I'm Orla," she said, tipping her head back to look up into his face. "You can ride my horse if you want to."

"None of us know how to ride," he said. "You'll have to teach me." He smiled down at her, and she smiled back.

The thought of little Orla teaching this tall boy to ride made me smile, and when I looked at Willow, she smiled back at me.

When we went down to the hall to eat, Orla walked close to Gil, chattering about horses and riding. She was seldom as talkative. Adana walked beside her, saying little, listening to her chatter. Willow peppered me with questions about horses. After a brief hello, Tuan hadn't spoken, but he trailed us into the hall and slid onto the bench next to Willow.

Everything was new to the swanfolk; none had slept alone, or indoors. On the second night, as on the first, they all stayed together in Mother's solar. On the third day, Mother spoke to me after breakfast.

"Kiar, would you share your room with Willow?" When I didn't answer right away, she continued.

"The boys can share, but she'll be lonely by herself."

"I don't mind sharing. She can stay with me." What I didn't say was that I found it lonely to have the room to myself. Since Orla had fledged and moved into her own room, I'd been alone, with nobody to talk to, in a bed that was colder with only me in it. Willow would be company for me as much as I would for her.

The first thing we taught the swanfolk was to ride. Even with the quietest horses we had, they fell off. Eventually, they learned to hold on with their knees. The first time we tried a gallop in the meadow, Willow whooped with excitement and barely stayed in the saddle. Her hair flew loose around her, and when she finally stopped the horse, she had to brush strands from her eyes and mouth.

"It's almost like flying!" she said, her eyes shining. When she discovered my sword, she wanted to learn that, too. I'd forgotten how much I'd practiced to control my weapon. More than once, she lost hold, and the sword went flying. I was glad that Dar gave her a wooden sword to start with.

It was Tuan, though, who really took to weapons. He never had to be shown anything twice and accomplished each move with a silent concentration. He was almost frightening, even in sparring, and I hoped I'd never have to face him in a real fight.

Willow and I were always together, and Tuan usually stuck with us. Gil and Adana took to each other at once. I remembered the story of how our parents had met and wondered if that was how people always fell in love. In the evenings, Gil and Adana sat hand in hand while others talked, and sometimes bent their heads close together in private conversation. Adana was the tallest of us sisters, but next to Gil she looked small and delicate. Orla was their faithful shadow. Gil teased and joked with her as though she was his own little sister and called her Mouse.

"Because she's small and quiet," he'd say and tug her braid affectionately.

It was true; Orla had a gift for silence. Often, she'd fade into the background. Sometimes when she spoke, you would realize she'd been there all along.

Gil laughed with Adana, too, but they were more often quiet, content just to be together. We all knew that this was one more step towards the day when Adana would leave us for good to join the swanfolk.

Within a few weeks, it seemed as though Gil, Tuan, and Willow had always been part of our family.

CHAPTER

THREE

In his council chamber, Father had a map, drawn on a single sheet of parchment and showing Valenia and the lands around us. To the east, far down the river that flowed past the hill where our castle stood, were the wide plains of the grasslanders. They didn't build houses but lived in tents and moved around all year, following the weather and the grazing. To the west was Dendale, where a distant cousin of Father's ruled. To the south, a few days' travel beyond the river, the land turned to sand, like a lakeshore that went on for miles. We knew the winter grounds were on the other side, but nothing about what else there might be.

To the north was Noermark.

Noermark was our enemy and had been for as long as anybody knew. Long ago, Valenia and Noermark had often fought, but since my great-grandfather's time, only rare skirmishes occurred when Noermarker raiders crossed our borders. The king of Noermark, Gythorn, was ambitious and greedy for land, and our pasture and farmland was better than his. For all that, their horses were the most beautiful anyone had ever seen. Small and swift, with slender legs and wide, dark eyes, they made ours look like plough horses. Noermarkers also made beautiful swords and knives, the blades patterned with waving lines.

Ambassadors traveled back and forth between us. Guthric was the ambassador from Noermark. He came once or twice every year, always bringing some gift for my sisters and me—sweetmeats or ribbons, tokens that made us believe he had daughters of his own. He was a kind and friendly man, although our father and King Gythorn weren't friends at all.

Well into the autumn after the swanfolk had come to live with us, Guthric arrived. Willow, Tuan and I were out riding when he reached the castle. Willow cantered wide circles around us on her white horse Whiffle, while Tuan on his bay Lightfoot and I on Kestrel walked. She only stopped when we had to climb the slope of the dun, the hill that led up to the castle. When we turned our horses into the paddock, I noticed the Noermarkers' beautiful animals.

"Whose are those?" Willow asked.

"Guthric's here," I said. "The ambassador from Noermark."

"A stranger?" Her eyes grew round. "And you let him stay?"

"He's not really a stranger," I said. "We've known him for years."

"But Noermark's your enemy!"

"It's hard to explain," I said. "It's how we talk to King Gythorn."

Willow shook her head. "If a stranger came to the nesting grounds, we'd drive him off."

"The king won't allow anyone who isn't part of the flock," Tuan said.

Willow leaned forward and lowered her voice. "Noermarkers eat swans."

"Not here. My father wouldn't allow him if he did that here." She looked unconvinced.

As usual when Guthric arrived, Father ordered a feast in his honour. The table where my family sat every day was near the door of the great hall, so the king could be first in defense of the walls. During feasts, a dais at the far side from the doors held a high table for the family. The rest of the trestle tables were arranged in long rows before the dais. The two thrones, one for my father and one for my mother, stood centered on the long side of the high table.

Mother sat on Father's left, with Orla next to her, and Gil between Orla and Adana. I sat on Father's right, with Willow and then Tuan next to me. Guthric sat at the far end of Adana's side of the table. I could almost feel Willow trembling next to me, even with Guthric as far from her as possible.

Father often said that Nias, the cook, could make a feast with a rabbit and an apple. While most of what we had was everyday fare, for dessert she had managed a custard, rich with cream and yellow with egg. I was finishing the last of mine when Guthric stood.

He was a tall man, and everything about him said he was a Noermarker. Our men wore their hair cut shoulder-length or shorter, and were either clean-shaven or had short, trimmed beards. Only women wore their hair long. Guthric's hair was red-brown, as long as mine. Both his hair and beard were plaited with bronze wire that glittered in the candlelight.

His feast clothes were russet trousers and a cream-white, thigh-length tunic. Although they were made of fine wool and embroidered in bright colours, they were cut the same as riding clothes, as though feasts were frivolous, and he was eager to return to the saddle.

Father seemed more at ease in the long, embroidered sleeveless robe he wore over his trousers and linen shirt. His crown was a circlet of gold set with garnets. Nothing about him looked warlike at all, except the sword hanging on the back of the throne.

"Your Majesties," Guthric said, "Your health. Waes hael!" He raised his cup and drained it. At the tables, his men echoed the toast and did the same.

"And yours," Father said. "What brings you to us so late in the season?"

"Your Majesty, my king has charged me with an errand that may prove beneficial to both our kingdoms. I have been sent to ask for the hand of your eldest daughter Adana for one of Gythorn's sons."

The entire hall fell silent; fire in the central hearth seemed to roar in the stillness. I counted three breaths before my father stirred.

"Thank King Gythorn for us," he said. He spoke to Guthric as though they were the only two in the room, but his voice carried through the hall. "We must decline the honour."

"We expected this answer," Guthric said. His glance at Adana took in Gil seated next to her. "Among us, it is customary that the eldest daughter marries before her sisters, and we thought it only courteous to offer for her hand first."

My breath stopped and for a moment, it seemed my heart did as well. Beside me, Willow sat very still.

"Our younger daughters are too young to be betrothed," my mother said. She, too, spoke as though to Guthric alone, but in the hush of the hall, her words carried.

Guthric nodded. "But girls as young as Princess Kiar may still take thought about a husband."

Father didn't reply immediately. Why didn't he say something? Had he waited this long to refuse Guthric's offer for Adana? It seemed an age before he spoke.

"One of his sons, you say. If I recall, two of Gythorn's sons are married, and two are still children."

"That is true, Sire. But there are two others, Othar and Hafor, who are of an age to marry."

"We do not know Gythorn's younger sons as we know his heir, Prince Beorn," Father said.

That was diplomatic; Beorn had led his men on a raid across our border not many months before.

"If we knew their qualities," he continued, "we could more easily give an answer. Let us speak of this tomorrow in private."

Guthric bowed again.

"Of course, Your Majesty. I have had a long day in the saddle. Might I have Your Majesties' leave to retire?"

"You have our leave," Father said.

Guthric bowed and left the hall, along with his men.

I glanced at Father, but he didn't return my look. Willow opened her mouth as if to speak, then thought better of it. I scraped at my bowl, although nothing was left in it, trying to look calm. Marry a Noermarker! Why had Father not simply said no?

As soon as possible, I excused myself from the table. Willow and Tuan followed me out of the hall to the foot of the double stairwell. The left side led up to my parents' room, and the rooms where the girls and single women slept. The right side curved the other way to the boys' and single men's rooms.

"The king wouldn't make you marry one of them?" Willow sounded shocked.

"Shhh, not so loud! I don't know. No, of course not." But I felt far from certain. If he didn't mean to let me marry a Noermarker, why not say so? And if he did—no, the thought didn't bear thinking.

We patrolled the northern border to keep King Gythorn from sending his men over to spy or to raid. I had gone out with Father myself this year, my first time to the border, and had learned firsthand about sleeping out and cooking on a campfire. Guthric might bring us gifts and treat my parents respectfully, but he was still King Gythorn's man and so, our enemy.

"Marriages make alliances," I said at last.

"An alliance with swan-eaters," Tuan said. His voice was low, and he and Willow looked sidelong at each other.

"The king won't like that," Willow said. I knew she wasn't speaking of my father.

"I don't think the swan king will get a say," I said. "I'm going up to bed."

I said nothing more, nor did Willow until we were in bed and the only light in the room was the flicker of the low fire in the hearth.

"Will you do it, if he says you must?" she asked.

"My parents agreed that the first of us to take swan form would join the flock and become Grandfather's heir," I answered. "Do you think Adana could say no to that even if she wanted to?"

Sleep was a long time coming.

CHAPTER

FOUR

The next day, Father took Guthric hunting. Guthric's dark bay looked tiny next to Cloud; the horse was only as tall as Kestrel, with much slimmer legs. I went along and if Guthric was surprised, he didn't show it.

We hunted nearly every day in the autumn. The deer were fat from summer, and venison was a welcome change from beef and mutton. We killed two young stags with only two prongs on their antlers. Then Father sent the rest of the hunting party ahead, keeping only Guthric and me back.

"No ears in the fields, Your Majesty?" Guthric asked.

"None but the ones I choose," Father said. "Let's talk about Gythorn's sons."

He looked past Father to me. "Before the maid, Sire?"

"Why not? Better for her to know ahead of time what kind of man he is. What of these two princes, Othar and Hafor? What sort of men are they?"

"Prince Hafor is closer in age to your daughter, eighteen last spring. He is a fighter by nature but also a thinker, and a great persuader of people.

"Prince Othar is the elder, twenty-two years. He is not warlike by nature, but he has been tried and is able. His men think well of him and follow him willingly. He is more inclined to thought than action and considers the opinions of those around him. I will tell you plainly, Sire—he has less favor with his father for it."

"I can well imagine."

"While both are of an age to marry, the king has been pressing Othar to do so. At his age both his elder brothers were married, with a child or two."

"If he's in a hurry, he'll have to look elsewhere," Father said. "Kiar still has much to learn about ruling and should be free to learn it."

"I believe my king would be satisfied if Othar made a choice. If he were to begin a courtship of Princess Kiar, we might say. With this alliance in the future, the heir, Prince Beorn, could be persuaded to seek excitement in other places than on our shared border." He looked at me, and his moustache twitched as he smiled. "Both are accounted handsome, as women judge such things."

As though a pretty face was most important to me!

"But can they read and write?" I retorted, and his smile disappeared.

"That is the work of scribes, not princes."

"Then he could never send, or receive, a private message?"

"I didn't say that, my lady. It is not usual for a prince to do such work, but both can read and write if need be."

"Good," I said, and smiled at him.

We stood in silence for a moment, before Father nodded to Guthric, then turned Cloud and set him galloping back towards the castle. I followed, and Guthric's bay came up behind me with light, quick hooves. When Father slowed Cloud to a canter, we caught up and rode home, not talking, which suited me. I had much to think about. Once inside the gates, Guthric took his leave and went back to his men. Two grooms came to take the horses.

"Come with me," Father said. "We'll talk in private."

His council chamber was a small room, with most of the space taken up by a large table with chairs for eight people. Father took his seat at the head of the table, and I sat next to him.

"What do you think?" he asked.

"If I let one of them court me, there won't be any more raids."

"I agree," Father said.

"So it's a treaty, not a courtship."

"Any marriage you make will also be a treaty, Kiar. When I married your mother, I swore for all of Valenia that we would hunt no large waterfowl of any kind—no swan or goose, not even herons."

"Shouldn't Mother be with us?"

"She would rather no Noermarker came near any of you girls. Refusing both would be her choice, but she will accept what you and I decide."

I sat and thought for a minute. "Othar is much older than I am," I said. "He has more experience. And Noermarkers don't have queens who rule. He might be difficult about not being in charge once I'm queen."

"He might, but Guthric also said he listens to others," Father said. "What of Hafor, then?"

"He's closer to my age. But he persuades other people to do what he wants. He might try that with me."

"Whether that's good or bad depends on his plans," Father said. "A persuasive man could be a useful diplomat."

Last night, I hadn't a thought of marriage, and today I was choosing between two men, neither of whom I wanted to consider. The speed of it unnerved me.

"Do I *have* to marry one of them?" I asked.

"A marriage would mean lasting peace, but I'd never force that on any of you. We will see if you like the man, no more."

"Whoever he is, he'll have a part in ruling Valenia, if only as a counsellor. Don't you have an opinion?"

"Of course I have. But that's your concern. When you come to the throne, remember, I'll be past caring."

I thought about it. In Valenia, girls and boys alike learned at least to shoot well with a bow, and many also learned the spear and sword. We were too few to waste fighters, and women as well as men needed to be able to defend themselves and their homes. Noermarkers didn't teach women to fight, and the queen was only the king's wife.

"Guthric said Othar was less in his father's favor," I said. "He didn't say Gythorn disapproved of Hafor. I think I'd prefer the one Gythorn didn't like as well. If it has to be one of them, then Othar."

"I'll tell Guthric," Father said.

When I walked into the great hall, Willow and Tuan were waiting for me. Willow's brow was furrowed, and she grabbed my hands.

"What happened?" she asked. "Do you have to marry one of them? Which one?"

"She can't tell you," Tuan said. "She was with the king. It's the royal family's business, not yours or mine."

I squeezed Willow's hands then let go and walked towards the door to the courtyard. In a heartbeat, they followed. We passed the gate, and the guard returned my wave. As we walked down the dun towards the river, Willow passed me and walked backwards in front of me.

"What happened?"

"You'll trip and roll right to the bottom. Calm down. I don't want to be overheard."

We walked in silence down the slope and then over to the riverbank. I picked a few pebbles out of the clay and tossed them into the water, one by one.

"You don't have to say anything," Tuan said. "You were in council with the king. We're outsiders, like Guthric."

I stopped throwing pebbles and turned on him.

"Is that what you think? Outsiders? You are not! The swanfolk are my family, too, and you, Willow, and Gil are part of this family. And my family has a right to know." I suddenly didn't want to tell them. What would they think of me? But they'd find out sooner or later.

"I agreed to let one of them court me. Othar. He sounded like the better choice."

"How could one swan-killer be better than another?" Willow's face crumpled, her eyes filling with tears. "I thought you'd say no! I really did!"

I looked at Tuan. He said nothing, and his face was wooden.

"If I do this," I said, "there will be no more raids across our northern borders. It's not only what I want. It's what's good for Valenia."

Willow turned away. I tried to put my hand on her shoulder, but she shook me off.

"If I marry him," I said, "and it's only *if,* it will be years away. And I promise, Willow, I *promise,* I'll make him take an oath that neither he nor any of his people will hunt swans, or any waterfowl at all, before I even think of marrying him."

Willow wiped her eyes, her back still turned, and nodded. I looked at Tuan, and he gave a brief nod as well. By the time we walked back up to the castle and went inside for supper, nobody could tell that any of us had been upset.

But that night in our room, Willow didn't want to talk. I heard her breath catch as though she might be crying. When I spoke, she stopped and refused to answer. For the remainder of the Noermarkers' stay, she was quiet and wouldn't come down to supper. She avoided Guthric and his men. Mother said nothing to me but had food sent up to our room for Willow.

Two days later, Guthric left for Noermark with my decision. I watched the party ride away, hoping I wouldn't regret my choice.

CHAPTER

FIVE

A few days after the Noermarkers left, two unexpected visitors arrived. Hollam was the travelling bard who came every year or so. He could have stayed with us, or in any other household he sang for, but he said he liked the change of scene. He was always welcome, and this time, he brought someone with him.

Hollam's apprentice was a boy slightly older than I was, fair-skinned and fair-haired, with green eyes. He rode a bay pony and carried Hollam's harp behind his saddle, in a case so dark it was nearly black. The cover of the case had an intricate knot worked on it in tooled leather.

"You are welcome here, Hollam," Mother said, smiling and holding out her hand.

He kissed it, bowing and flourishing his free hand in elaborate swoops as he bent. When he finished, his hand was far behind him, and higher than his bowed head.

"This unfortunate lad is Aren, who has his heart set on the life of a bard." Even when he wasn't singing, Hollam's voice was beautiful. He carried not only songs and stories, but also news, from court to court, and always spent an hour or two with Father in his council chamber.

"Welcome, then, Aren," said Mother. "You have a good teacher."

"Thank you, Your Majesty," Aren said, with a bow that was more a bob. His knees and elbows seemed to stick out every which way as he bent over. His cheeks flushed, and I thought he must know how much more graceful and polished his master was and feel embarrassment for his own ineptitude. Hollam was a very good bard, and it would be difficult to learn all he had to teach. I sometimes felt the same way about Dar and my swordsmanship. I felt a surge of sympathy for Aren. I tried to catch his eye, but he was looking at Orla.

Orla had a way of blending into the background. She liked to watch whatever was happening, taking everything in, listening to Dar instructing someone in swordwork, or Nias teaching a new kitchen girl which herbs to put in the dishes. She stood or sat out of the way, taking everything in, often completely unnoticed until she moved to leave.

Now, however, she wasn't blending in at all. In her blue feast dress and amber necklace, she stood out. She must have gone to change as soon as she heard of Hollam's arrival. Her eyes looked bluer because of the dress, and her hair was freshly braided. Adana and I still wore our tunics and trousers, from a day of work and riding. I knew we smelled of horse.

"She looks like a queen next to us," Adana giggled as we left to wash and change into dresses. "Of course he's going to stare at her. She's pretty, and she's going to be prettier. Poor Aren."

"Why?" I asked.

"Oh, Kiar," she said. "*You* know. He's looking at her as though she's a princess in a song. And she'll lap it up as a cat laps cream and forget all about him when he's gone."

After supper, Hollam and Father went to talk.

"Perhaps you'll join us in the solar," Mother said to Aren.

He bobbed his head again, making his awkward bow. "Thank you, Your Majesty," he said.

"'Lady' will do," Mother said, and led the way up to the solar. We three girls followed after.

"Like ducklings, quack, quack," Adana murmured.

I stifled a giggle. Aren bowed as we passed and came along behind us, still carrying Hollam's harp.

"Aren, sit with us. Elena," Mother said, "please bring some of the spiced ale the king is having."

"And we should have a song!" Orla said, looking at Aren.

He flushed; even his ears turned pink. "I'm not permitted to play or sing for people yet," he said. "Otherwise, I would be honoured."

"But we're not in the hall now," Orla said. "Who will know if you sing us a song? One little song?" She smiled at him, and he turned even redder.

"Orla, don't tease," Mother said. "If Hollam has said that Aren isn't to play, then he must obey."

Orla's smile faded. "I'm sorry." She seemed to shrink slightly, like a disappointed little girl.

Aren jumped up and took Orla's hand in both of his. He bowed, and his face was very close to hers.

"I'm sorry I can't oblige you, Lady," he said, "Please don't be sad. I'm honoured that you asked, and as soon as I'm free to sing, I'll make you a song. My first."

"Really?" Orla said softly. "Will you?" Something shimmered in the air between them, a ripple of heat over the land as on summer noons.

His eyes never left hers. "I promise, Princess Orla. My first song will be for you."

It sounded like something out of a ballad, a pledge of love. What a silly game! Orla couldn't really care for this boy. Adana was right, she only wanted the attention. I wanted to say something to Orla, or to Aren, anything at all, but nothing came to mind. The heat-shimmer between them faded. Hollam and Father finished their talk and joined us briefly in the solar before we all went up to bed.

We had the pleasure of Hollam's music and stories for three nights before he left.

"I am incurably restless, Sire," he said. "Only that prevents me from taking advantage of your hospitality."

They left on the fourth morning, with fresh supplies and generous payment. As they rode down the dun, Aren looked back over his shoulder, and Orla blew him a kiss.

With the Noermarkers gone, Willow quickly went back to being her old self, almost as though Guthric's visit, and my decision had never happened. It was still on her mind, though.

A few days later as we put our weapons away after practice, she suddenly asked, "Why does Noermark want your territory? They have their own."

"Our lands are better— richer farmland and wider pastures. Farming is easier here and grazing better. They'd start by trying to take a bit of borderland, maybe Stony Ridge, the northern farmstead. Then they'd move farther south, a bit at a time."

"Or their king could just fight your father for it. When a younger swan can beat the king, he can become the king."

"That doesn't happen often," Tuan said. "Mostly the king has a son, or a daughter's mate, who can beat any other swan who attacks the king. So anyone who tried would beat the old king, and then would get beaten right away himself."

"But it does happen sometimes," Willow insisted.

"I don't think Gythorn could beat my father in a fight," I said. "We don't do that, anyway. In Valenia, everybody fights, or at least most of the men and some of the women. In a fight people would get hurt or killed on both sides."

"Everybody?" Willow looked shocked, and even Tuan looked troubled.

"Not children, or old people, and most women don't fight with swords. They have bows. But those are useless once everybody's in close together. You'd hit your own people, too."

Willow shook her head, speechless.

"The lands to the east are full of grass," Tuan said. "Maybe you could go there?"

"The grasslanders live there," I said. "If we went there, we'd be raiding just like Noermark raiding us. Besides, this is our place. Would you leave your territory, the lake and the winter grounds?"

"So you have to marry a swan-killer to stay here," Willow said. "But if you didn't stay here, it wouldn't matter. Kiar, you could fly away with us, fly to the winter grounds!"

"I can't," I said. "I'm the heir. I have to stay, and Adana has to live with the flock someday."

"But Orla could be the heir," Willow said. "Come with us, Kiar!"

"You can't go now. The flock has left. You'd never get there on your own."

"Yes, we could! I know the way, and so does Tuan. The winter grounds are beautiful, Kiar. You'd love it there. Come with us."

"I can't," I said. "I can't fly."

Willow stared at me, her mouth an O.

"But Adana and Orla—"

"Yes, well, I don't even look like swanfolk, so it's no surprise I can't fly."

"Kiar, I'm sorry! I didn't think—you're royal blood. I thought you could do anything you wanted."

"I want to fly more than anything! But I'm never going to. There's no point talking about it." I turned my head to hide the tears I could feel pressing on my eyelids.

Willow patted my shoulder. "It's true what I said before. Riding is almost like flying."

"Is it really?"

She nodded vigorously. "Truly it is, Kiar. True as water and sky."

She was trying so hard to make me feel better. "Almost" was not what I wanted, but I hadn't the heart to say it to her.

After that day, she never mentioned Noermark, or marriage, again.

The weather turned cold, and the first light snow fell, sparse flakes that vanished almost as soon as they touched the ground. We culled the herds, killing the sheep and cattle we couldn't feed through the winter, and hanging the meat in outbuildings where the cold kept it sweet. Some we smoked or salted, and some we dried to use as travel food on patrols. The job lasted for several weeks, but when it was done, we had a feast, with all the meat we could eat.

A week after that, I turned fourteen. There was a feast, with all the things I liked best. Mother and Father gave me a new gown, and Adana and Gil a bronze cloak pin with a horse's head.

"We have something, too," Willow said. "We'll show you tomorrow."

The next morning, we rode out at first light, towards the forest to the northeast. As we went along, Willow and Tuan scanned the skies. I looked, too, but with no idea of what I was looking for.

At the edge of the forest, we stopped the horses.

"On foot from here," Tuan said. "We shouldn't be long."

We tied the horses, and he led us in under the trees to a small clearing. We stood quietly across from a large oak. As he stopped, something large and light glided overhead, swerving between the trees. We watched as a great white owl settled on a branch of the oak. I'd never seen one as close before.

She flipped her wings to settle them and began to preen her breast. I hardly dared to breathe. We watched until the cold began to seep through our clothes.

As we moved to leave, she stopped preening and turned her large yellow eyes on us. I thought she might take flight, but she only stared as we quietly backed away.

Once we were back with the horses Tuan said, "I saw her when we were flying a few weeks ago."

"We didn't find her tree until the day before yesterday," Willow said. "We didn't know about gifts on your birthday."

"She's beautiful," I said. "She's perfect."

CHAPTER

SIX

The next day, Willow woke me by bouncing on the bed. "Kiar, come and look! The air! It's full of down!"

I rolled over and rubbed my eyes. Willow jumped off the bed and pulled the curtain back from the window. Soft, white flakes of snow fell past the opening, layers and layers, making curtains in the air.

"You've seen snow before," I said. "It snowed weeks ago, remember?"

"Those were little speckles. This is turning the ground white!"

"That's what happens in winter."

"Can we go out in it?"

Outside in the courtyard, Willow might have been six years old. She stood with her head tilted back and her hands up, trying to catch flakes.

"Fog and feathers all at once," she said. "Watching it makes me dizzy. Look, there." She pointed at a dog trotting across the courtyard. He faded into sight as he neared, then turned and trotted into the curtains of falling snow. "He disappears, a little at a time." She watched the little flakes melt into drops on her palms.

"It melts on my hands, but not on the ground."

"The ground is too cold, and there's too much snow at once. If the sun comes out, it'll melt. And it's melting in the lake. There won't be any ice yet."

"Ice—what's that?"

"The water turns solid, and you can walk on it."

"Now you're teasing me! Water isn't solid!"

"I promise you it will be, later." I scooped up a double handful of snow. It was too dry to make a good snowball and fell apart before it hit Willow. She ducked and then scooped up a handful to throw at me. We ran around the courtyard throwing snow at each other. Willow refused to stop until she was wet and shivering. We kicked through snow all the way back to the door.

"That was fun," Willow said as we went back into the hall.

"Wait until we play the sheep game," I told her.

"What's that?"

"Father explains it best," I said. "I'll ask him to tell you tonight."

That night after supper all the family, including Willow, Tuan, and Gil, went upstairs to Mother's solar. Mother was sewing a gown for Willow. I had a patch to put on the knee of my riding trousers. Father honed Mother's small knife, the one she used for cutting thread. The whetstone made small shishing sounds as he rubbed the blade on it. Once we'd all settled, I spoke up.

"Tell us about the sheep game," I said to Father. "Willow's never heard it, or Tuan, or Gil."

"Kiar said you explained it best," Willow said. "Please tell us."

"We haven't heard it since last year," Adana added. Orla, leaning against Gil, nodded in agreement.

Father gave the knife a last rub on the whetstone and set it aside. He stretched his legs towards the fire and crossed his ankles. The firelight caught on the waves in his hair and beard, making them look even redder than usual. He folded his arms and leaned back in his chair.

"Well, then," Father said, "Long ago, we didn't live in one place but wandered all over the country with our flocks and herds, riding our horses. We didn't have gardens or houses, and we lived on milk and meat. Since we couldn't eat grass, the lambs made the grass into mutton for us. We let the sheep grow up, eating the wild grass, and then we ate them. Often, they were quite tough." He paused, looking around at us. "Now, we found that when we ate a tough, old ram, we had to chew and chew, and our jaws would tire, and the bards couldn't tell stories or sing. A dinner of tough, old ram, without even a song to wash it down, is a great hardship.

"One day, an old woman with few teeth became so angry at her piece of tough, old ram that she began to hit it with her cane. She beat it and beat it, and then, because she had nothing else to eat, she took a bite of it. And she found that it was more tender and easier to eat.

"For some time, it was the work of all the old women, and the old men, too, to beat the mutton with their canes to make it tender. When the old folk grew tired, we made the young folk take over. Of course, we always made sure to kick them in the shins, so they'd have an excuse to use a cane."

"That's not true!" Willow said.

"As true as true. Would I lie to you?"

Willow sat quite still, and I could see from her face that she wasn't sure whether Father was serious or not.

"After a while," he continued, "the young people got tired of being kicked in the shins. The old people were all worn out, and some had broken three or four canes. And then one, bright young woman had an idea.

"'Why don't we beat up the whole ram all at once?' she asked. Why indeed, we thought. So we started by tying a rope to the ram's leg—after we'd killed him, of course—and dragging the ram around the field. But that didn't work as well as the sticks, so the young people began riding past the ram on their horses and hitting it with sticks. And you know young people; if they can make a game of something, they will. They set up goal posts and split into teams, and each team tried to move the ram through the other's goal posts by whacking it with sticks. One day, somebody picked up the ram and rode towards the goal posts with it, and the other team set on him with their horses and sticks, and the other team set on *them,* and there were bruises and a broken bone or two, and so, of course, the game was better than ever.

"Eventually we settled down and grew grain for our sheep and made pastures with better grass, and now we have more sheep, and we can eat lamb when it's tender. But you know, we hate to give up a good game. Now we use a stuffed sheepskin instead, and we don't have to eat it afterwards."

"When can we play that?" Willow asked.

"As soon as the snow's deep enough," I said. "We'll tramp down a field with snow walls around it. Then you can't ride just anywhere, and it's harder to make goals, and the game is faster."

"Just try not to break any bones," Mother said from her chair.

The snow went on for four days. When it stopped, Willow and I walked out to the gate. Although the snow in the courtyard was stamped down and worn away from people going to the stables and storehouses, outside the wall it was knee-deep.

A dozen of us rode down the east side of the dun to flat ground, with staves for goalposts and the stuffed sheepskin. We marked out a playing space and drove the staves in at each end to mark the goals.

The sheepskin had been torn and sewn up again many times. Grabbing a leg could tear it. The sheep wore a harness made from straps of leather with loops to allow a proper tug-of-war between two or three riders.

We dropped the sheep in the center of the field, divided into teams, and withdrew to opposite ends. Then we charged in.

Because the snow was so deep, the game started slowly. Most of the time, two or three riders bunched together, tugging on the sheep. If somebody grabbed it, they couldn't get away fast enough to avoid someone else grabbing on, too. We trampled down a good portion of the field in these slow tugs of war. Cleared areas let the horses run more easily, and everything sped up.

Suddenly, Gil pulled the sheep away from another, and it flew over his head and landed on the ground. Adana, leaning low over the neck of her black mare, Lady, made a dash for the sheep. I thought I could beat her. Kestrel stretched her neck and her legs and picked up speed, kicking up sprays of glittering snow. We came in at an angle and got there first, but I missed the harness by a hair's breadth. Adana stretched down and snatched it away.

Then Tuan came up hard on Lightfoot and grabbed one of the legs. As he and Adana tugged, I saw my chance and rode straight between them. Kestrel ducked her head, and the sheep caught me full in the chest. I managed to keep from falling backwards and turned Kestrel towards the goal. Two other players galloped towards me. I swung the sheep at one and his horse shied. The second pulled away as Tuan cut past me, clearing my path. I threw the sheepskin into the snow at the end of the field, and we all bunched together, laughing and shouting, our breath steamy in the cold air. We fished the sheepskin out of the snow, took it back to the center of the field, and started over.

Back and forth we battled, first one team and then the other scoring. Nobody kept count. Our cheeks were burning, and the horses' breath frosted on their muzzles when we remembered it had been a long time since breakfast. Once we had stabled our horses, we were hungry enough to eat the table as well as the food.

As winter closed in, it became easier to ignore the swan half of my life. Nobody flew in the cold, and all I had to remind me that I was different was the way Mother, my sisters, and the swanfolk looked so alike, and so different from me. The familiar ache wouldn't go away, but I learned to ignore it, the way I ignored the pain of a blow on my armour in sword practice.

CHAPTER

SEVEN

S pring came, and the snow melted in a rush that made the river swell and roar. There was mud everywhere, and then fresh, new grass sprouting in the dry brown of last year's growth. Willow, Tuan, and I were on our way to the paddock when four Noermarkers rode up to our gates.

One of the guards came to the paddock shortly after.

"The queen says you are to come to her," he said. "You alone."

I wished, as I climbed the stairs to the solar, that my stomach wasn't full of birds and my throat dry. I knew without asking what this was about. Mother stood just inside the solar, hands clasped. Her mouth was set, and her face looked stern.

"Put on a good dress and comb your hair," she said. "Your suitor is here."

"Already?"

As I dressed, I wondered whether this early arrival was good or bad. Was he eager to meet me or looking for a weakness he might use? What if I really didn't like him? My hands trembled as I combed and braided my hair. Finally, I was ready. The dark green dress suited me and showed off the strand of amber I wore only on special occasions. I felt exposed and wished I could wear my sword. From downstairs, I heard the faint sounds of the hall being arranged to receive the Noermarkers.

When I came down, it looked as though everyone in the castle had dropped their work to come. Father and Mother were seated in the carved thrones they used to receive messengers and ambassadors, and a plainer one had been set out beside Father for me. Several men stood on each side of the row of thrones, and one behind each throne. To my surprise, Tuan stood behind mine, wearing his sword and carrying a spear. I saw that someone had hung my sword belt over the back of my chair. The knot in my middle undid a bit. I smoothed my skirt over my knees and laid my hands on the arms of the chair.

"Where's Adana?" I whispered to Father.

"Out riding," he murmured back.

Out flying with Gil was more likely; it would be impossible to say when they'd return.

Father nodded to a guard standing by the door of the hall. He left and returned quickly with Guthric and three other Noermarkers.

"Sire, the ambassadors from King Gythorn."

The men knelt bareheaded before my father and mother and then stood again. The two guards carried helmets under their arms and stood behind Guthric and the man who had to be Prince Othar.

I'd seen Guthric many times, windblown in old riding leathers. This time, however, he had clearly changed his clothes while I had changed mine. Under the plain bronze circlet on his head, his reddish hair was smooth and freshly braided. His beard had been freshly braided, too, and the bronze wires he wore in it glinted.

Prince Othar was also finely dressed, with wide, embroidered bands on the sleeves and hem of his tunic. He looked only a few years older than Adana. He was as tall as my father, better dressed than either Guthric or the guard. His dark brown hair and beard were also braided with bronze wire, and he wore a bronze circlet. He had glanced at my mother and me as he came in, but afterwards kept his eyes on my father.

"Guthric," my father said, "We haven't seen you for some months. How was the travel?"

"Chilly and damp, Sire. My bones are not as young as they were."

"King Gythorn continues well?"

"Indeed, Sire," said Guthric, "although the lung illness struck many of us this winter. The king was spared. This is Prince Othar, the king's third son."

"Prince Othar, you are welcome here," my father said.

Othar bowed to my father and mother in turn.

"Sire," said Othar, "I have wished to come since Guthric brought the news that Princess Kiar would accept my suit. I look forward to knowing her and to winning her good will. Will you give me leave to speak with her and learn her mind?"

I'd been looking at Guthric while Othar spoke, and something flickered across his face. It might have been annoyance—

perhaps Othar had not been supposed to speak? I looked directly at Othar's face then and caught his gaze on me before he returned his attention to my father and mother.

"If our daughter is willing, then we give our consent," Father said. He gave me the slightest of nods.

"As my father wishes," I said.

"Good. Prince Othar, Princess Kiar will meet you in our private chamber. Give us a short while to light a fire and warm it." He and my mother stood, and I followed their example. Both Guthric and Othar bowed. My mother turned to the guard behind her and said a few words. It was the first time she had spoken; she'd said nothing even to Guthric. The guard came forward.

"My lords, if you will follow me," he said. The four Noermarkers trailed him out of the hall. We waited until the sound of their footsteps on the stairs told us they were up in the men's part of the second floor.

"Kiar, come with me," said my father. I went with him to the council chamber. As people turned back to the interrupted work of the day, a buzz of talk rose behind us. When Father closed the chamber door, I saw that a fire burned brightly in the hearth. The room was already warm.

"Sit down," he said, pointing at the chair across from his. "What did you think of all that, Kiar?"

"I think Guthric really wants to make a good impression. He combed his hair."

Father chuckled.

"So he did. That was a pretty speech the prince made."

"Guthric seemed annoyed about it."

"Guthric is an ambassador who has learned to control his face as well as his words. It may suit his purposes—which are Gythorn's—to have us think that. If we think this prince is less like his father, it might make him more acceptable to you."

"Maybe he only hopes I'll like him."

"Do you honestly think so, Kiar?" Father's face and voice were both serious.

"I want to believe so. It would be nice to think he's more interested in me than the throne. But, no, I can't really believe that." I paused. "And Mother wasn't happy we agreed to let Othar come here. If I like him, well—she won't be happy about that, either."

"I know," Father said. "It's hard for her. The swanfolk think differently about strangers."

"But Mother's been living with humans for such a long time. She's nice to Guthric, I mean truly nice, not only polite."

"Guthric's been coming here so long, she's used to him. And Kiar, knowing something in your head isn't the same as feeling it in your heart. Your mother knows an alliance with Gythorn would make things more peaceful. The northern patrols wouldn't be as big, or as risky, and we wouldn't have to spend as much time watching that border."

He stopped, looking into the fire. "This is difficult for her, thinking of letting one of you marry an enemy. Othar may be a good-hearted young man, but he is still Gythorn's son. Gythorn's people kill swans. She doesn't believe that can be changed."

"But you do?" I asked.

"Marriage makes alliances. Dendale was not always our friend," he said, "and before your great-great-aunt married the king, we got along with them not much better than we do with Noermark. At one time, that western border was vulnerable. We weren't allies with the swanfolk before your mother and I married."

"You don't have to promise anything, Kiar," Father said. "If you enjoy his company, no harm in that. Keep things pleasant and polite. If he leaves thinking you wouldn't mind seeing him again, then we will probably have more peace on the border. That would be good."

"If you trust Guthric."

"I think we can. Gythorn knows he has to give us a reason to consider this match. That will buy us some time. And there's this, too. Othar will tell you more about Noermark than Guthric would ever tell me, especially if the prince thinks you look favorably on him. A woman who's going to marry a man is naturally curious about his family and home, and men will tell a woman things they won't tell another man."

"Like spying."

"Part of ruling is finding out what your enemy thinks without telling him what you think. Any ruse is fair. What you learn will be good for the kingdom and the people. If you do decide to marry him—well, then, you haven't cheated him." He stood up. "You'll have privacy for talking, but guards will be within call at all times."

"I'm not afraid," I said. "I don't need a guard."

"Even so, it shows your status." He smiled at me. "I'm not worried about you, daughter of mine. You've surprised Guthric, and I believe you'll surprise this prince as well." He kissed my forehead and left.

There was a knock on the door, and a serving woman came in with a pitcher of wine and two goblets. She set them on the table and went out.

A few minutes later, someone tapped on the door. I wanted to stand but didn't want this prince of Noermark to think I felt vulnerable sitting down.

"Come in," I said.

The door opened, and Othar stepped in. A guard closed the door behind him.

He was not quite as tall as my father, although I'd still have to look up at him, even standing. His hair and beard were pale gold-brown, and both were braided. His eyes were hazel, like mine, and crinkled a little at the corners as he smiled at me. The smile and his relaxed stance made me feel more relaxed, too.

"My lady," he said, bowing.

"Please," I said, "sit down. And call me Kiar."

"Kiar." He pulled up a chair beside me, at an angle to the table.

I turned my own chair to face him. His knees were a hand's breadth from mine. "I'm glad to meet you at last," he said. "We hear of the princess who rides her borders and wields a sword."

"Is that why you came?" I asked. "A woman who fights isn't unusual."

"Perhaps among you." He held out his right hand and I put mine out, too, expecting him to clasp it, but instead he turned it over. He looked at the stripes of sword-callus on my palm. "There isn't a single woman in my father's court who uses a sword."

He curled my fingers into my palm and let go of my hand.

"Gythorn said you resembled your father, and your sisters favor your mother. When I pressed him, he said you were fair rather than dark, and that your hair curled. He didn't tell me you were also beautiful."

Nobody had ever told me I was beautiful.

"Guthric made a point of telling me that you and your brother Hafor are both handsome," I said. "What he said, really, was that women thought you were handsome."

"Do you think he was right?"

I considered, looking at his face. He tried to keep his face straight but gave up and grinned at me. I had to smile back.

"I suppose you are," I said. "I like the way you look when you smile."

"I certainly won't become vain on your words," he said. Then he laughed and I found myself laughing, too. When we stopped, it was as though something had eased between us, and he didn't seem such a stranger.

"Guthric didn't look happy when you spoke to my father," I said on impulse.

"I had to say something for myself. If I'd let Guthric drag out his diplomat's talk, you'd have thought me boring past belief."

"I haven't found you boring yet," I said.

"Nor I you." He took a pouch of soft leather from his belt. "And there's something else, too. My father expects that we will marry. What we think of it doesn't matter to him. But I hope we can be friends, as well I brought you this."

He held the pouch out. When I took it, the contents slipped and slid over my hand. I loosened the drawstring and tipped out a strand of polished green stones, flecked with rose and darker green. It was long enough to loop twice around my neck.

"We call them moss-stones," Othar said. "Many ladies prefer brighter colours, but I've always thought these are the most beautiful. When I saw the colour of your gown, and your eyes, I knew I'd chosen well."

"They *are* beautiful," I said. "Thank you. Will you have some wine?"

By the time my mother arrived to interrupt us, Othar and I were speaking easily together of horses and hunting. He stood up when she came in.

"Your Majesty," he said.

"Prince Othar," Mother replied. "I trust Kiar has taken good care of you?"

"The best care, Majesty."

"Good. The king wishes to speak with you now. Kiar, will you come with me?"

"I will see you at supper, Prince Othar," I said.

He bowed to me and to my mother. As I turned, I glanced back, and his eyelid flickered in a wink. My cheeks grew warm. Whether or not I'd surprised Othar, I had certainly surprised myself.

Mother said nothing as we walked away from the council chamber.

"I think I like him," I said into her silence, brushing at an invisible spot on my dress.

"Why don't you and Willow go somewhere for the afternoon," Mother said. It wasn't a question, and her mouth looked tight.

When I got up to my room, Willow sat on the end of the bed, her eyes wide.

"Were you waiting for me?" I asked.

"The queen asked me to," she said. "She said we should take the horses and go somewhere. What did he say? What did you say? When is he leaving?"

I hesitated. Perhaps I should talk to my father first. I didn't know if I could tell him how Othar's wink had made me feel. Willow gave a little bounce on the bed.

"Well?"

"He brought me a gift," I showed her the necklace, and she ran the polished stones through her fingers, first singly, then in a doubled strand.

"Very pretty," she said, "and colours you like. I wonder how he knew?"

"I don't know," I said.

"Probably Guthric told him."

"I don't think so, Willow. He said when he saw my dress he knew he'd chosen well. I think he chose himself."

"He *would* say that," she said.

"You don't like him," I said. "Mother doesn't, either."

"He's here to ask you to marry him," she said. "Even if he's kind to you, he's still a swan-killer."

"He seems different."

"You've talked to him once and you think he's different?"

"You haven't talked to him at all, and you've already made up your mind! I shouldn't have said anything."

Willow sat very still. The necklace dropped from her fingers, into her lap, and slithered to the sheepskin rug on the floor.

"I'm sorry," she said in a small voice. "But look—he's coming between us already. I'm afraid that if you really like him, you'll turn your back on us."

"I'd never do that," I said. "You'll always be my friend, Willow."

"And Tuan?"

"Of course," I said. "I'd understand if you didn't want to be friends if I married a man of Noermark, but it won't change how I feel about you."

"You don't understand," she said.

I sat down and put my arm around her shoulders. "You'll see. He's different. He said he hoped we could be friends. He must know we couldn't be friends if he killed swans." I hugged Willow and slipped off the bed. As I bent to pick up the necklace, I remembered what my mother had said.

"We'll ride out to the lake," I said. "You can fly. You'd like that. I can look for mouse-willow." I loved the little grey catkins that clung to the slender brown stems early in the spring.

Willow shook her head.

"I wouldn't feel safe," she said. "There are men of Noermark about."

"Nowhere near the lake. Willow, you love to fly."

But she shook her head, and nothing I said changed her mind.

CHAPTER

EIGHT

O thar stayed a week. On each of those days, we went riding together with two guards—one of his and one of Father's—riding behind us, far enough away that we could speak without being overheard. Sometimes Tuan rode with Father's guard. Nobody had said anything to me about Tuan becoming part of Father's regular guard, but it looked as though he was training to do that.

"Tell me about your brothers," I said to Othar on the first day. The sun was bright, but the air was damp, and chilly enough to bring colour to our cheeks.

"Beorn is the heir. His wife died over a year ago and left him with a small son. He's a good man in a fight, and smart enough to take counsel when he doesn't know something. He'll be a good king—better than Ranfer would have."

"Who is Ranfer?"

Othar looked at me, his face serious.

"My eldest brother. I no longer know if he's alive. Fader banished him."

"Banished him?"

"Ranfer was stupid enough to criticize Fader's judgment, and also stupid enough do it where the wrong people could hear. Beorn helped escort him and his wife and child over the border and well into the mountains. That was—" He tapped his thumb on his fingers, counting, "a year ago last spring. Early spring. We haven't heard anything of them since."

I didn't know what to say to that. I couldn't imagine Father banishing one of us.

"Kett is nine, still a child," Othar went on. "He's Moder's favorite. Right now, he gets away with being cheeky, because he's the youngest, but he will have to learn better. Alfar is twelve. He's a smart lad and knows how to hold his tongue. He may live to grow up yet. With six of us, and all sons, you learn to watch out for older brothers. I'd have liked to bring Alfar with me, but Fader forbade it. I hope he stays clear of Beorn."

"Would he really hurt a child, your brother?"

"If it suited his plans." Then he looked at me and smiled. "Don't look so worried. Hafor will look out for him. I spoke to him about it before I left."

"I thought brothers would be friends. My sisters and I are."

"Maybe in some families. I've convinced Beorn that I haven't any interest in the throne, mainly by supporting him when I must and avoiding him when I can. Hafor is no threat, mostly because I've beaten him a few times he tried something. But he wouldn't grieve if I were to have a sudden accident."

"Strange. I don't agree with Adana and Orla all the time, but we'd never hurt each other."

"Only one could be king. Fader says you have to be strong to rule."

"My father says you have to be smart."

"Between us, maybe we could be both," Othar said. He looked around at the trees, leafing out in fresh green. "It's beautiful here, and your home is peaceful. I would like to live here with you."

I didn't know what to say. He turned to me and smiled. "Am I rushing you?"

I shrugged. "It's why you're here. You know you won't be king."

"I'm not interested in that."

"What *do* you expect?" I asked.

He reached out and took my hand. "To be your advisor and your helper. I want to live my life out from under my father's and brother's hands."

"I couldn't promise to always do what you or anyone —told me."

"No. But Fader would be happy with his grandson on the throne of Valenia."

"It could be a granddaughter."

"So it could," Othar said.

I slipped my hand out of his and shook Kestrel's reins. "Race you," I said.

In honour of Othar's visit and its purpose, there was music and dancing in the evening after supper. The tables and benches in the great hall were pushed back to the walls and for several hours, the musicians took turns and kept us all dancing. Othar was a skillful dancer, light on his feet, and a pleasure to have as a partner.

At the end of each evening, I met with Father in his private chamber and told them what Othar and I had talked about on our ride.

"And what do you think of him?" my father asked on the last night of our guest's stay. The dancing was over and almost everyone had gone to bed.

"I think he's truthful, and he could be helpful to me."

Father nodded.

"From what he told me," I continued, "he can stay out of trouble that he doesn't want, but if he can't avoid it, he knows how to fight. He takes care of his younger brothers, which Beorn doesn't. He knows his father doesn't think much of him, but that doesn't worry him. He wants to be out from under his father's control. That's part of why he wants to marry me. But he says he likes me, too, and I believe that."

"Do you like him?"

"Yes," I said. "I don't love him. I've only known him a few days. But—"

"But?"

"Willow is afraid."

"How so? Anyone who comes here, whether to visit or to stay will abide by our truce with your mother's family. Othar knows that; I made sure of it."

"I told her that, but she said it's not only about the hunting. She thinks I'll turn away from her and Tuan. How could I,

Father? But she said I didn't understand, and she's still afraid. And that makes a difference, too."

Father sat back in his chair and met my eyes.

"It's a hard choice, but not one you need to make immediately. If Othar goes home tomorrow feeling you're open to his suit, that may be enough to satisfy Gythorn."

"I can do that," I said.

After Father left the council chamber, I sat before the fire a while, thinking about Othar, the things he had said to me, that he thought me, and Valenia, beautiful. Sleepy and happy, I decided to go to bed.

When I reached the bottom of the stairs, Tuan was waiting for me, leaning on the balustrade.

"There's something you should know," he said.

"I'm tired, Tuan—can it wait until morning?"

"Othar's men are planning a hunt. They say they're going to get a swan."

For a moment I couldn't speak. Finally, I found my voice. "How do you know that?"

"I've been riding with the guard all week, while your prince courted you. His men talked among themselves."

"In your presence?"

He nodded. "They wanted me to hear. It's part of the game. Their Valenian is bad, but their meaning was clear."

"You know Othar would never let them! They wouldn't dare say it where he could hear."

"And yet they said it, and he didn't hear. If they do it out of his sight, his anger won't matter, for the swan will be dead.

They don't think of the swanfolk as people. Will you bring this down on us?"

"No! You know I wouldn't."

"But here they are, and that is what they said."

"It's only words!"

Tuan straightened up. The way he stood reminded me of my mother on the day Othar arrived.

"Words intended to make swanfolk afraid. Words foretelling deeds. Marry who you will, Princess Kiar," he said.

It was the first time he had called me "Princess," and the hair on my arms stood up.

"But know who, and what, you are marrying. Good night."

He was gone before I could answer.

I had to speak with Othar, now. Maybe he could explain what Tuan had heard in a way that would take the harm out of it and make everything all right.

One of Othar's men stood guard at the guest room door.

"Tell Prince Othar that Princess Kiar wants to speak with him," I said. For a moment, the guard stared at me as though he thought I would drop my gaze. I looked back at him without blinking until he nodded and entered the room.

Almost immediately, Othar came out with his tunic half-buttoned.

"Kiar!" he said, smiling. "I was on my way to bed. I didn't expect to see you again tonight." His fingers swiftly fastened the rest of the buttons on his tunic, and he held out his hand. I took it before thinking, and he stepped closer. I had to tilt my head back to keep my eyes on his face.

"I need to speak to you privately" I said, and his smile faded.

"Is something wrong?"

"Father's chamber," I said. "You can bring your guard, if you want."

"Do I need a guard against you?" he asked.

I couldn't answer.

"Never mind," he said.

We went down to the council chamber. The fire was only coals, giving off heat, but no light. I lit a couple of candles.

"Something's wrong," Othar said. "What is it?"

I told him what Tuan had told me. When I was done, he took my hand.

"It's only words," he said. "No harm done." He bent towards me, and I stepped back, pulling free of him.

"There is harm done," I said. "They meant to make Tuan afraid. Willow is afraid. I'm sorry, Othar, I'm so sorry. I wanted us to be—" I paused. "I wanted us to be friends."

"Friends," he said.

"Yes, but your men want my mother's family to fear you. I can't allow that. They would never trust us again."

For a few moments Othar didn't speak, just stood with his arms at his sides. Then he folded them and looked at me, his face serious. "Our marriage would be very good for Valenia," he said. "My father would leave us alone—in fact, he'd be an ally. In time, we might be able to persuade my people to see your mother's people as allies as well."

"We would need to convince the swanfolk. That will be harder. And some will never believe—they'll always be in fear.

They might even leave. I can't make a new ally who will cost me one I already have."

"I see." He stood silently for a few seconds, then took my right hand and turned it over. He traced the sword callus with his fingers then went on. "I thought that we, too, might be good for each other. I like your company. I want time to know you better, years of it. I thought you wanted that, too."

"I did," I said, and fresh tears welled up. I blinked hard. "I do, Othar. But—" I faltered, and a picture flashed across my mind: Willow sitting on our bed, looking stubborn and angry. Tuan in the darkness saying, "Marry who you will, Princess Kiar." I wanted to listen to Othar's arguments. I liked him, and I thought love might come in time.

But if I married Othar, Willow would leave, and maybe Gil and Adana. My grandparents could take their people away. The voice in the back of my head said *and Tuan?* I ignored it, and the little rush of anger it brought.

"I can't, Othar," I said. "I'm sorry. I wanted to tell you privately."

"That was thoughtful," he said. "I'm sorry, too, Kiar."

His kindness brought the tears welling again. I wiped my eyes, but they kept coming, although I kept control of my voice. "I thought you'd be angry," I said.

"No," he answered. "Only sad."

I took off the necklace of moss-stones and held it out. The strand heaped in my cupped hand, spilling over the side. "I can't keep this," I said.

He closed my fingers over it and pushed my hand gently back towards me. "Keep it from a friend," he said. "I hope that you will count me a friend, Kiar, whatever happens. I will think of you that way."

"Yes," I said, and held out my other hand. He held it tightly between both of his for a moment, then let go. "Good night, Kiar," he said. "Sleep well." Then he left, closing the door softly behind him.

I stood swallowing my tears, breathing hard with the effort, until I was sure he was out of hearing. Then I collapsed into my father's chair and wept until I had no more tears, angry at Tuan, angry at Othar's guard, and at my own stupid loyalty. Slowly, I went up to bed. Whether Willow was asleep or not, she had the wisdom not to speak to me.

It was almost dawn before I finally fell asleep. When Willow rose, I remembered that I, too, had to see Othar off. Neither Willow nor I spoke as I dressed. I hesitated over the moss-stones but in the end, put on my amber necklace.

Mother and Father were in the hall at breakfast, and I told them what Tuan had heard and my decision about Othar.

"I'm sorry, Father," I said. "I couldn't."

"Well, done is done," he said. "There will be trouble from this, but it seems there would be trouble either way."

In the courtyard, the formal words of leave-taking went through my head without meaning. I gave the parting drink to Othar, and he drank and passed the cup back, his fingers never touching mine.

They left without looking back. After the gates had closed behind them, I went back to my room and put the moss-stone necklace in the bottom of my chest before changing into my riding clothes. Once on Kestrel, I turned away from the north and didn't look in the direction Othar had taken. I rode along the edge of the forest, my mood as dark as the shadows of the trees on the new grass.

CHAPTER

NINE

After the Noermarkers left, Willow quickly went back to her old self. I couldn't be angry at her—she had been afraid—and I wondered if she had heard the Noermarkers speak of hunting. Once she said, "I'm sorry, Kiar. I know you liked him."

It was harder to forgive Tuan. I knew he'd done right in telling me what he had, but I was angry that he'd left me the difficult task of telling Othar. Soon, I wondered why I hadn't talked to Father and let him speak to Othar. I had no good answer to that, but the question itself eased my anger.

Ever since Orla got her wings, everyone knew she was to study with the wisewoman, Sianna. Black swans wielded powerful magic, but magic without discipline was dangerous. Sianna would teach Orla how to control it, and how best to use it. She knew how to treat the lung fever Mother's medicines couldn't touch, and how to call back a wandering spirit when someone was badly injured. She knew how to talk to spirits, work the weather, read the future, and all kinds of magic, light and dark.

She lived in the forest, some said alone, and some said with talking animals and water-spirits and wood-woses for company. The stories said her house was protected by a ring of magical fire that would burn up anyone who crossed it with intent to hurt her, and that she could call the eagles and vultures out of the sky and the wolves from the woods to attack her enemies.

It was unusual for her to leave her house, but late one morning a few weeks after Othar left, she rode up to the gates on her dappled grey horse, Night Wind. The guard didn't notice her until she came to the threshold of the gate. He sent word to Father right away, and news of her arrival went through the castle like fire through dry grass. We all came to the great hall to see her escorted in.

She was an ordinary-looking woman, neither tall nor short, with weathered skin and a plait of brown hair beginning to turn grey. Her clothes were the same as anyone else's—leather pants for riding and a plain woolen tunic, a sheepskin jacket with bone buttons, and leather boots.

Only her eyes were out of the ordinary. They were light brown, almost yellow, like a hawk's.

"You are welcome here, wisewoman," Father said.

"Most welcome," Mother echoed, smiling. "We wondered when we might see you."

"When the student is ready," Sianna said, and smiled at Orla.

Orla wasn't usually shy, but she smiled only briefly at Sianna before looking at the floor.

"Can you stay the night?" Mother asked. "We can have Orla's things packed to leave in the morning." When Sianna said nothing, she added, "Or as soon as you like."

"The morning will do." Sianna beckoned to Orla. "Let's you and I talk, Orla."

They went off to sit by the central hearth, where four pillars supported the great chimney and openings threw heat in every direction through the hall. There they sat talking, while the rest of us went on with our day. By mid-afternoon, Orla was over her shyness, and they looked like old friends.

At supper, to my surprise, Sianna came to me.

"May I sit with you, Kiar?" she asked. I hadn't even known she knew my name.

Willow and Tuan moved over, and Sianna took Willow's usual place. It seemed she brought a little quiet space with her, and the rest of the people in the room seemed farther away, their voices softer, or muffled.

"How is it with you, Kiar?" she asked. The hawk's eyes had little laugh lines around them. Sitting beside me, turning her winecup between her hands, she seemed surprisingly ordinary.

"I'm well, thank you," I said.

"But troubled, I think."

"No," I said, then, "Yes. Yes, I am. I had to do something that hurt someone."

"You are unhappy about that."

"I am. But if I hadn't done it, other people would be hurt. Why can't there be a decision that doesn't hurt somebody?"

"I'm sorry you had such a hard thing to do," Sianna said.

"I wish you'd been here," I said. "I'd have asked your advice. You can see the future, can't you? You could have told me what was best."

The space around us grew even quieter, almost as though we were in a separate room. Sianna looked very serious.

"Sometimes, yes, I can see the future," she said, "but it's a slippery thing that changes with every little act and decision. It's impossible to say, 'if you do this, that will happen.' If you had asked me to see the future for you, I would have said no."

"Why?" I asked. "I wanted to do what was best for everybody. If I could have done that—" *and still said yes to Othar*, I thought.

"It's easy to get trapped by the wrong kind of advice. Worse than trapped—weakened, corrupted. Magic makes things look easy, but if you rely on it too much, you begin to think it's good for everything. I don't use magic to keep the weeds out of my garden, or make it rain, or bake my bread."

"That's different from giving advice."

"But not from asking to know the end of a story before the beginning is written. And rulership has to be learned the same as gardening and baking. Do you see?"

"Yes," I said.

"If you knew how much work magic is," she said, "you might well think it easier to do things the ordinary way. Don't envy your sister her magic. Her path is harder than you imagine."

The next day Sianna left, with Orla trailing behind her on Star, her little chestnut horse. The things Sianna allowed her to bring fit into a roll on the back of her saddle, no bigger than what I took on patrol for a few nights out. Orla hugged all of us goodbye and clung to Gil and Adana until they pried her off.

"We'll miss you, Mouse," Gil said.

"Be good and study hard, my little black swan," Mother said to Orla. "Make me proud."

"I will," she promised.

We watched them ride through the gate, and when they were far enough down the dun that we could no longer see them from the courtyard, only then did Mother allow herself to cry.

That spring and summer passed as others had, in work and hunting, riding patrol and weapons practice. One day Dar brought a sword longer than the one Sylard had made for me.

"This is the king's sword, when he was your size," he said. "That dagger you're using isn't enough for you anymore."

I took the sword. As soon as I drew it, I could feel how perfectly balanced it was. The blade was straight and sharp, with silver leaves chased near the grip. The pommel was a polished yellow crystal as big as a hen's egg.

"It's beautiful," I said.

"And it bites like a demon," Dar said. "That is, if you land a blow. Time to work a little harder."

He'd had me sparring against the older boys, but today he waved over Corin, a guard nearly as tall as my father.

"You'll never be the size of most men, young Kiar," he said. "That's plain enough to see. You need practice fighting bigger foes. They don't square off by size in a battle, you know. Try not to kill her, Corin."

Dar was right about working harder. At first, I had more bruises and a few cuts, although I could see Corin wasn't doing all he could against me. But as the summer went on, I began to hold my own, and one glorious day in September, I managed to disarm Corin and send his sword arcing out of his hand to land ten feet away.

Dar cheered and clapped me on the back as if I'd been one of his own men. Willow hugged me—not the most comfortable, with both of us in armour. Tuan picked up Corin's sword and made as if to hand it to me before giving it to Corin.

We left our leather cuirasses and leg armour in the armoury and walked back towards the hall.

"I want a bath," I said. "I'm covered in sweat, and I itch all over." I wiped my forehead with the back of my hand and felt a pull on my skin, and a roughness that sent a shudder down between my shoulder blades.

I touched my forehead again, this time with my fingertips, and then ran my fingers down my cheeks and felt those same bumps, tingling and pulling as I touched them. I stretched out my hands and looked at the backs. Then I looked up at Tuan and Willow.

"I need to find Mother," I said.

As I reached Mother's solar, the itching was almost unbearable. I couldn't get out of my clothes quickly enough. Mother spread a cool green salve on my skin and the itch eased slightly. She sent for a soft linen shirt and my oldest robe and made me sit on the couch in her solar. Willow stayed with me for that first day, but I was too restless and cross, even with the salve, to be good company.

All through that day, and the two following, the itching persisted. On the third day, when I rubbed my neck, I felt down fluff out over my skin.

"Feathers!" I said.

Mother got up from her loom. "Get undressed," she said. "Quickly, now!"

As I pulled off my robe and shirt, the itching gave way to a bursting feeling all over my skin, and a ridge of feathers sprang up along the back of each arm. Feathers pushed out through my whole skin with pain I hadn't expected. My chest and stomach felt hot, my joints shifted, and my muscles flowed. The room swam around me. I gasped and cried out, hurting and confused. The cry began as my human voice and ended in a swan's panicked honk.

The pain faded, and with it the confusion. My mother spoke softly. I didn't understand the words, but her voice reassured me. My body felt strange, but it knew how to move; I found my feet and settled my wings. A wave of exhaustion washed over me, and I settled on the warm floor near the chimney and tucked my head under my wing. I was asleep quickly.

When I woke, the room was dark. For a moment I couldn't recall where I was, or why I was on the floor. Then I remembered, and a rush of joy went through me. I spread my wings again, and something in the way the air moved around me and whispered back along the tips of my flight feathers told me that I was enclosed.

Outside, I thought. It would be better out in the open. I turned; the movement of the air and the soft echoes told me there was an opening. I moved towards it and felt the change of entering a different space. Then my toes curled over an edge, and I flapped and backed up.

Stairs. I knew it would be easier to deal with them on human legs. All at once my whole body shuddered and a light grew from my breast and enveloped me. There was no pain as my feathers vanished. My muscles rippled like water, and the brightness around me faded. I was a human again, naked in the dark at the top of the stairs, suddenly chilled and exhausted.

I crossed the room towards the heat of the chimney. My foot touched a pile of fabric: my discarded robe. I pulled it on and felt my way to the couch. I was asleep again as soon as I lay down.

When I woke, I was ravenous, hungrier than I could remember ever being. I took the stairs two at a time down to the hall. Adana, Willow, Tuan, and Gil all looked up from their breakfast.

"There," Adana said, "I knew you'd get your feathers, didn't I?"

"You can say you told me so all you want," I said as I sat down. "I'm going to fly today!"

After breakfast, Mother and I rode out to the lake. I hardly noticed anything around me in my eagerness to get to the water, and then to the air. We tethered the horses and began to undress.

"I don't know how to make it happen," I said.

"Remember how it felt when you were a swan. Remember your wings. It helps if you stand in the water."

"Does it hurt?"

Mother smiled and put her hand on my cheek.

"Maybe a little. Last night was the worst, swanling. It won't feel like that again."

I undressed quickly. The air was cold, but the sun warmed my skin. Mother stood in the water, the glow of the change already starting around her. I stepped into the lake and gasped at the cold. Goosebumps sprang up all over my skin, and as though that was all it needed, the change began, a tug in my breastbone and a ripple in my flesh. The brilliance of the glow dazzled me.

When the world came back, Mother was already on her way out to the middle of the lake, bobbing as the waves ran under her. She called and I followed, paddling hard to catch up.

As I reached her, she turned and spread her wings. I swerved out of her way and watched her beat her wings and run forward on the surface of the water until her toes touched the tops of the swells. Then she was airborne. She called to me, and I spread my wings.

The first time I slewed sideways to the roll of the lake. A wave caught me off balance, and I fell back into the water. In that moment of falling, I panicked and forgot my shape, tried to swim with arms I no longer had. But my swan body floated, and I remembered and calmed.

Mother called encouragement from the air. I settled my feathers, then turned into the waves again and beat my wings hard, stretching my neck forward.

At first it seemed as though I was pinned to the lake while the waves lifted and dropped, and I went nowhere. Then, in an instant, I lightened. I felt the lake fall away from me, the water receding down my legs until my feet dangled. I tucked them up against my body and I was flying.

Instantly, it felt as though I had always known how to fly. The air bore me up as water does a swimmer. When Mother swept by me, I felt the rush of air behind her like a current, drawing me along me in her wake. Without any more effort, I was quicker, lighter. My swan body wanted to follow that current of air. She pulled ahead of me, and I beat my wings harder to stay with her.

I don't know how long we flew. There were so many things to learn—the way the air pulled on my feathers, the layers of it and its currents. There were no words; every part of flying seemed simply physical but learning all the same. Then, in one moment, it all fell together. I was at home in the sky, and it held me as securely as the ground.

I remembered that I was Kiar, that I had two shapes and could take either at will. If I had been in my human form, I would have wept from a joy I couldn't put into words. For so long I'd wanted this. I'd almost given up hope. Now I was here, in the sky, with all the world below me.

An impossible lightness filled my heart. I tucked my wings close and turned my shoulders, as I sometimes did when I swam in my human shape. The world spun as I corkscrewed, and I was dizzy. I felt myself falling, and then spread my wings to stop my fall. The lake was so near, I could feel the weight of wet air above it, but before I hit the water the air caught me and tossed me upwards again.

I repeated my spin, catching myself this time and doing it again. It was like dancing with the sky. Ravens came to my mind, and I dived and swooped, and spun again.

Mother circled and called to me, and in the sound of her voice I heard, "Enough." We glided down to the lake. My landing was rougher than hers, but she never turned to look. I paddled after her. When my feet touched bottom, I called the change to me without thinking, and when the bright flare of magic faded, I was Kiar again in my human shape.

I'd half-expected to be wet all over when I changed back, but my skin was as dry as it had been under my swan's feathers. The bubble of joy in my chest made me feel I could float, even in this shape. And I was hungry again. I pulled on my shirt and trousers.

"I'm starving!"

Mother handed me a knotted cloth. Inside were an apple and a piece of cheese. My cold toes didn't stop me from eating half the cheese before I put on my boots.

On the way back, I couldn't stop looking at the sky. It was no longer a blue bowl over the world, and the horizon where it touched the ground no longer a boundary. Why was it only ravens and crows who danced with the air? Why didn't every bird feel that joy in flight?

"It *does* take your skin off," I said to Mother.

"What do you mean, swanling?"

"All this." I looked around and back at her. "It's all new. I know you said Father's story, that you shed your swan skin to be human, isn't real. But it feels as though I've taken something off and yet, I feel *more*."

She smiled and said nothing.

"Does that happen for everybody?"

"I've never heard anyone put it quite like that. When you change back, it's not all at once. You know when Adana has been with the swans, she sees things as swans do for a while. It can take a little time to return to being human."

"I don't want to! This feels…more. Better."

"It will happen again, swanling.

It would happen again. I had my wings.

CHAPTER

TEN

After flying, I was sore and tired, and I fell asleep in the middle of the day. But after that, I took every chance I could to fly. I couldn't get enough of the sky.

At first I took brief flights, but as I gained strength and confidence in the air, Willow, Tuan and I flew farther afield. We usually travelled along the river that ran east past the castle. If I doubted where I was, I knew I could follow it home.

With every flight, my stamina and skill grew. In my swan form, all I knew was the joy of flight, but once back in my human form, I began to wonder how long it would take to fly around the borders of Valenia, or to reach the edge of the world, where the blue bowl touched the ground.

Harvest season began in late summer and there was more than enough work for all of us. We picked apples and wild berries and cut grain. The winter's hay had to be scythed, dried, and brought in. We picked beans for drying and pulled the root vegetables. The bee-woman pulled honeycomb from the hives and prepared the bees for winter.

When it was all done, we had the harvest festival. The trestle tables from the hall were set up in the courtyard, and the bronze fire bowl we used for the festival fires was brought out. It was big enough that two men's arms could just reach around the top edge and stood as high as a person's hip. Four men carried it out and set it up. On the sides of the bowl were patterns for air, fire, water and earth, set so that air faced east, fire to the south, water to the west, and earth to the north.

Everything was new to Willow and Tuan and seeing it through their eyes made it seem new to me, too. I imagined how everything would look from the air—the bonfire in the court, the patterns of the dancing, the people in their bright festival clothes.

Willow was full of questions. "Why do you have a fire?"

"Fire is sacred," I told her. "What we burn goes straight to the Otherworld, where spirits live. It's a way of saying thanks."

"But you did all the work! Why give anything to the spirits at all? What did they do?"

"We thank them for good weather. What if the spirits decided to make it rain for a week right after we cut the hay?"

"You don't know that spirits cause rain," she said.

"Well, we don't know they don't," I answered. "What if we didn't give them grain and wine and flowers at the harvest festival, or make birds out of grass for a funeral fire? The next harvest might be poor, and everybody would go hungry."

"We don't do that, and we still have good years and bad years."

"Maybe different spirits look after the swanfolk," I said. "But the important thing is, we've done a lot of work. Now, it's over, and we're going to have a lot of food, and a lot of music and dancing. You can dance all night if you want to."

"I think I might," Willow said. She loved to dance, I thought, as much as I loved to fly.

The bonfire in the courtyard was lit as the evening sun touched the horizon. By the time a few, red clouds marked sunset, the fire burned so high that the tops of the flames were twice the height of a man.

The courtyard was crowded with all the castle folk. Everybody wore festival clothes and bright colours. There were ribbons in the women's hair and in rosettes on the men's sleeves. The tables of food and barrels of ale and the platforms for those who played the flute and drums and harps made the courtyard look strange, like something from a story. The top of the castle wall faded from grey stone to a line in the dark where the stars stopped.

Mother tossed into the fire a wreath of faded, summer flowers and the first few stalks of grain cut on the king's lands, kept carefully from the threshing. Her voice was clear and sweet over the crackle of the fire. "Spirits of this land, of rain and wind and sun and moon, we thank you for the bounty of the summer. May the snow fall deep to warm the earth and the beasts who sleep on her, to feed the rivers and streams for the coming year. Let it be so."

"Let it be so!" we echoed. With all those voices, only the rhythm of the sound told us that all were saying the same words.

Father stepped forward with a jar of oil and wine in his hands. He held it easily, but I knew how heavy it was. I had tried lifting it myself. He flung the jar forward and then pulled it back in one smooth motion, sending the contents in a wave onto the flames. The bonfire blazed up where the oil and wine entered, gone before it touched the wood.

"We ask for comfort for loss, healing for hurt, safety from storms, and courage to meet what must come in the dark half of the year," he said. "Let us endure what we must and change what we can, take cheer where it is offered and give help where it is needed. Let it be so."

"Let it be so!"

Father and Mother kissed, the brief touch of lips the ceremony required, and everyone cheered. Then someone began to play a pipe and soon, the air was full of music that drowned the roar of the fire. People formed circles around the fire and pairs and squares away from it. Someone put on the Deer mask with its crown of antlers, and three others wore the Hunter masks and chased the Deer through the crowd.

The Deer Hunt reminded us that death came to everyone, and that all our lives were linked. But it was also a game of tag, more serious than a child's. If one of the Hunters touched the Deer with his spear, a stick tipped with a tuft of red wool, the Deer left the game, and the Hunter took the Deer's mask and gave his own mask and spear to the person nearest him. The hunter became the hunted, and nobody was safe. You couldn't refuse if a Hunter chose you.

People usually helped the Deer and hindered the Hunters. If the Deer was caught, everyone nearby scrambled not to be closest to the Hunter. Some people screamed in the excitement. The game went on throughout the dancing, although sometimes the Hunters and the Deer rested, especially if nobody had caught the Deer for a while. Mostly they rested by the beer barrels.

Gil danced with Adana. He wasn't a good dancer, but Adana didn't seem to mind his missteps. I didn't see Tuan among the dancers, but eventually caught sight of him with Mother in a circle dance near the edge of the courtyard. When the music near me stopped, I went over to that circle and waited for the dance to end.

"Did you want to dance with Father?" I asked Mother.

"I'd like that," she said. "Tuan, do you mind?"

"You can dance with me," I said. "I can show you the steps."

"Lady," said Tuan, bowing to my mother. Then he came over to me, and I took his hand. As the musicians started again, we moved into the circle.

"This one's simple," I said. "Forward three steps, then back, six left, three right, turn around. Then all go into the center and back out. Then you do it again."

After a couple of tries, he had the steps. It was hard to tell, because he always looked serious, but I thought he was enjoying himself. In a while, we stopped to have something to drink.

"What do you think?" I asked Tuan. He was watching the Hunters as he drank.

"It's loud," he said. "And people move so fast."

"Did you want to stop? You don't have to stay. The Hunt can be a little scary."

"Yes," he said. "But I like the dancing." He drained his cup and took my hand. "Teach me another." He looked around and said, "That one."

I followed his gaze and saw my parents in a dance where everyone circled, and the men lifted the women into the air.

I wondered if Tuan would find me heavy to lift. All the swanfolk were light-boned, and I was heavier than either of my sisters. When we began dancing, though, he picked up the steps at once, and when he lifted me into the air, I felt as light as if I were flying.

CHAPTER

ELEVEN

Over the next four weeks, we culled the herds, choosing the animals to be slaughtered and preserved for winter. When the ground was hard and the air cold enough to make our breath smoke from our mouths and nostrils, we began killing the sheep and cattle we'd chosen and hanging the meat in a stone building by the north wall. It was a long, bloody job. At supper every night we had as much meat as we could eat.

Father sent a rider to invite Sianna to the feast on the last night of the killing time. On the second-last day she rode in on Night Wind, with Orla following her on Star. Almost as soon as they arrived, Sianna rolled up her sleeves and began working at the cauldrons, rendering the fat to store in kegs.

For the feast, Nias roasted a whole beef, a sheep, and a pig in pit ovens outside the walls. There was plenty to eat and drink, and afterwards, music and dancing and a tub of water with apples in it. The children's game was to pick up apples using only their teeth. It was loud and noisy, and everyone got well-splashed, but the adults' game was noisier. Their apples were in a barrel of ale.

The second day after the feast, Orla put down her bread and honey.

"I'm going home with Sianna today," she said.

"We'll miss you," I said.

"I'll miss you, too." She looked around. "All of you."

Gil and Adana sat close together; she was saying something, and he was smiling.

"I'm going to be gone for *months*," Orla said.

"Yes, but think of what you're learning," Willow said. "That's worth missing us."

"Mm-hmm," Orla said, still looking at Gil and Adana.

Mother put her arm around Orla. "You listen well to Sianna," she said, "and pay attention to your lessons." Her voice trembled a little.

"I always do," Orla said.

"I'm so proud of you, my black swan." Mother was smiling, but her eyes were bright, and she was close to tears.

We had barely finished breakfast when Orla jumped up from the table. "Gil, come and help me saddle the horses!"

Gil glanced at Adana, and she nodded almost imperceptibly.

"All right, Mouse," Gil said.

As they left the hall, Orla skipped a little in her excitement and took Gil's hand. He swung her through the door and outside we heard his whooping and her laughter as they crossed the courtyard.

"I'll miss her," Adana said.

"We'll all miss her," Mother said. "But she has to learn. Being the black swan is a great responsibility." She wiped her eyes on her sleeve, and Father took her hand and squeezed it.

"She's not leaving forever," he said.

Mother nodded. "I should see about food. It wouldn't do for them to be hungry on the way." She stood and hurried to the kitchen. I knew there was already a large package of fresh meat wrapped for Sianna, along with a round of cheese, a jar of honey sealed with a waxed cloth over the mouth, and a sack of new apples.

"It's half a day's ride at most," I said to Father. "They won't starve on the way."

"If it comforts her to send half the kitchen with Orla, let her do it," he said.

When we went out to the courtyard to see them off, Sianna's Night Wind, and Orla's pretty chestnut Star stood together. Adana was leaning over and hugging Orla. Orla reached out with one arm to Gil, and he put his arms around both Orla and Adana in a bear hug. When he straightened up, Orla didn't let go, and her feet came off the ground as she put her other arm around his neck.

"I'm going to miss you so much!" she said.

Gil glanced at Adana and bent over again to let Orla stand. He unwound her arms from his neck. "We'll all miss you, Mouse," he said. "It won't be the same without you here."

"I'll come back as soon as I can," she said, looking into his face.

I wanted to smile at how serious she sounded, and how she looked at Gil as though he was the only one there to see her off. She looked so small. It was hard to remember she was nearly thirteen.

As Orla mounted Star, Gil stepped closer to Adana. Orla blew a kiss to Mother and Father, and as she rode out the gate behind Sianna, she turned and looked back over her shoulder. Her hand rose towards her face, but she passed the gate and was out of my sight before I saw what gesture she made.

CHAPTER

TWELVE

"We were lucky this year," Father said one morning. "I expected a raid on the northern border. I don't know what Gythorn is thinking, but if he stays on his side, that's good enough for me."

"I know," I said. "I thought there'd be trouble." I still felt uneasy about turning Othar down, and the lack of consequences was not reassuring.

Every morning after breakfast, the floor of the great hall was cleared for sword practice inside. We didn't ride patrols in the winter. Winter was peaceful, and nobody raided anyone. If you had enough food, you stayed home in comfort, and if you didn't, you probably didn't have the strength to leave home. My fifteenth birthday came and went. This time, instead of counting the years that my wings had not come to me, I held my ability to fly like a treasure, eager for the spring when I could be in the sky again.

As though Orla's departure had removed some constraint, Adana and Gil quickly grew closer and closer. A few weeks before the solstice festival, they met with Mother and Father in the solar. When they came out, all four looked happy.

"We're going to be betrothed at the solstice," Adana said. Gil put his arm around her and said nothing, but the adoring way he looked at her told everything.

"Orla should come home at solstice," Mother said.

"She'll only have settled in," Father said. "We shouldn't interrupt her studies. Travel is hard in midwinter."

I didn't think it was a good idea, either. But if Orla came home and the betrothal was done, she'd have to stop mooning over Gil. Nobody came between a betrothed couple.

The day Gil and Adana announced their betrothal, grey clouds rolled down from the north and settled over the whole sky, from horizon to horizon. The snow started falling sometime in the night, and in the morning, it was still coming down. It snowed for more than a week.

I loved the snow. I loved the way it fell, and how it covered the land like a white blanket. I loved the feeling of being snug and safe indoors while outside, the snow piled higher and higher. I loved riding out to the playing field and coming in after to hot drinks, and toasting cheese on the fire until it softened enough to spread on bread.

After a week of steady snow, we woke up to yet one more day of thick, white flakes coming down, and no end in sight.

"I don't see how Orla can get home for the solstice festival," Adana said at breakfast. "We thought, Gil and I, that we would put off the betrothal ceremony until the festival of lights. We could hold it then just as well."

"I think that's a good idea," Mother said. A tightness went out of her shoulders, and I saw how much it meant to her to have the family together for the ceremony.

Solstice marked the halfway point of winter, and the turn of the year. From now on, the days would grow longer all the time. We brought in green branches of pine and bright winterberry to hang in the hall for three days, then burned them all in the hearth. The fresh, sharp smell sweetened the air in the hall and promised an end to winter. Nias made the little round festival cakes with dried fruit and honey.

After the Solstice, the snow didn't fall as heavily or as often, and the snow already on the ground began to collapse on itself. Even so, most of the work was indoors, mending old harness, clothing, and furniture, or making new.

A little more than a month after Solstice, the guard on the wall called out.

"Two riders from the forest! Two riders!"

A few minutes later, another guard entered the hall, where most of us were working or talking. He looked around and then strode over to me.

"It's the wisewoman and your sister," he said.

I ran up to the solar. The news sent Mother into a flurry of activity, sending maids this way and that to air out Orla's room and prepare one for Sianna. She herself went straight to the kitchen to see what treat Nias could make to celebrate Orla's return. Then she put on her heavy winter cloak and went out to the gate.

She waited a long time. The snow was still deep enough to slow the horses, and they ploughed up the dun at a snail's pace until they came to the beaten path we used to reach the playing field. Once they reached the path, both horses moved faster. Even in her fur-lined cloak and winter boots Mother still must have been cold by the time Orla pulled Star to a stop and flung herself into Mother's arms.

"Swanling, you've grown!" Mother said when she finished hugging Orla and held her back at arm's length. "Are you well? Did you miss us?"

Orla was taller than when she'd left. Once she stepped back from Mother's embrace, she stood looked still and watchful. She'd always been quiet, and always watchful, but now she didn't seem as much like a mouse as a fox, or an ermine.

"I'm very well," she said. "I missed you, all of you. But there's so much to learn. I don't have a lot of time to miss home, or anyone." She looked around. "I don't see Gil, or Adana."

"Oh, they're off somewhere," Mother said. She let go of Orla and held her hands out to Sianna. "You're welcome here, Sianna. Thank you for bringing our daughter home."

Sianna took Mother's hands and smiled at her. "I'm glad to see you again. We can stay until after the festival of lights."

Then the horses had to be cared for and packs taken in and put away. When that was done, Mother had a little meal set out in her solar. Adana and Gil came in, flushed from a walk in the cold, and there was more greeting and hugging. Orla sat down next to Gil and leaned across him to talk to Adana. Mother said hardly anything but watched Orla as though she could never get enough of seeing her.

Sianna sat next to me. As before, it seemed she brought a quiet with her.

"How is it with you, Kiar?" she said, as she had done before, "and the consequences of your choice?"

"Better than I hoped," I said. "Things could still go wrong, but they haven't, at least not yet."

"And the ones you protected?"

I glanced at Willow.

"Safe," I said.

"Something has changed," she said. "You're at peace, as you weren't before."

"Yes," I said. "I can take swan form now. I can fly."

"And do you still wish to know the future?" She sounded severe, but laugh lines showed around her eyes.

"It still sounds like it would be useful," I said. "But you said it wouldn't, so, no."

"Then you are learning as much as Orla is," she said. "People long for power, but whether you hold it, or it holds you depends on the person. Magic isn't the only kind of power that needs discipline."

"I know," I said, "Or I know a little. It's harder than learning to use a sword."

"You know more than a little if you know that," Sianna said. "Training the mind and heart takes more work than training the body. Well done."

"Thank you."

"You're welcome, Kiar. And you're welcome to visit me any time, if you have questions, or want to talk."

I didn't know what to say. We often sent messengers to Sianna, but an invitation to visit her was a rare thing.

At the festival of light, halfway from solstice to equinox, we had a feast. Instead of a bonfire in the courtyard, we lit candles in the hall, one for every person living in the castle. When the castle was built, a ledge had been built into the wall of the great hall at shoulder height, and we put our candles there.

This year, just before the candle-lighting, Father stood up in his place. When the talk and laughter died down, he said, "We have a betrothal!"

Adana and Gil stood up. They stood with Mother and Father, where everyone in the hall could see them. A cheer went up. Of course, the betrothal was an open secret; everyone knew beforehand. No, not everyone, I realized. Nobody had told Orla. Her wide eyes and dropped-open mouth showed that she'd been taken completely by surprise.

"Gil of the swanfolk and Adana, our eldest daughter, wish to join in marriage. Adana," Father said, turning to her, "are you willing to bind yourself to this man in betrothal?"

"Yes, I am," she answered.

"Gil," my mother said, "are you willing to bind yourself to this woman in betrothal?"

"Yes, I am," he said.

My father took Adana's right hand in his, and my mother took Gil's. Then they joined Gil and Adana's right hands together and drew back, leaving them holding hands.

"Then let this betrothal be seen and witnessed among the people. Let none come between them unless they themselves declare the betrothal dissolved. Let it be so!"

"Let it be so!" we answered. A cheer went up, and Gil kissed Adana. There was more cheering and hugging as people rushed in to congratulate them. I watched Orla, whose face showed nothing. Then she smiled. I wanted to believe it was real, but at the moment we'd cried "Let it be so!" I thought I'd seen something else flash across her face. Anger? Disappointment? Whatever it was, it was gone. Maybe the flickering light of the fire had cast a momentary shadow.

Then we lit our candles.

In other years, Mother, Father, Adana, Orla, and I had placed our candles together. This year, Adana and Gil put their candles together a little apart from Mother's and Father's. Sianna placed her candle alone. I watched Orla standing with her candle, chewing her lower lip, before she set her candle near Sianna's. It was a choice that had to come for all of us, but I thought Mother would be a little sad it had come so soon for Orla, and that she had chosen as she had.

I put my candle nearer Mother's and Father's, but not next to them as I had done last year. There was no man I was interested in, and I knew I'd be staying in Valenia and taking the throne in due time. All the same, I didn't want to look like a little girl afraid to leave her parents, especially when Orla had already done it. Willow and Tuan set their candles near mine. It made me feel less alone to see our three candles flickering there together.

The candles flickered and twinkled during the dancing, a cheerful, festive glow we had only once in a year. Tuan danced with me several times, and with other girls, and I danced with anyone who asked me.

After the feast and the dancing, when everyone had gone to bed, I crept back downstairs, as I did every year, to stand in the middle of the hall and looked at all the candles in the dark, stars brought indoors. I loved the quiet, and the little points of light around the wall delighted me in a way I couldn't explain. As I stood in the middle of the hall, turning and turning to look all around, Father came out of his private chamber.

"Beautiful, isn't it?" he said.

"Yes. I don't know why, but they make me happy."

"We used to believe that each candle was the life of the person who lit it, and the first ones to go out told who would be first to die. Blowing somebody's candle out used to be good for duel."

"How do you know these things, Father? Nobody else tells them. Or—" I narrowed my eyes, "are you making them up?"

"I have enough to do without making anything up! When I was a boy, I listened to the old people talking. They knew the lore, and I liked to hear it."

"I like to hear it, too."

He sighed and put his hand on my shoulder.

"I've forgotten so much of what I used to know," he said, "and I don't know if anyone else thinks of the old customs or remembers them. It's our past, what has made us. It would be a shame if it was all forgotten."

We stood in silence for a little while, watching the flames dance.

"Time I went up to bed," he said, "and you, too. Good night, Kiar." He kissed my forehead and left.

Soon, I, too, went up to bed while all the candles were still burning. Most of them would be out by morning, and I didn't want to see which ones went out first.

CHAPTER

THIRTEEN

Afew days after the festival of lights, Sianna and Orla rode away. Mother pressed gifts on them—new blankets, a skin of wine, dried fruits. She held Orla close for a long time. Orla hugged and kissed all of us, but she seemed content to leave. Perhaps she'd become used to the quiet of being alone with Sianna; for the last couple of days, she had been more around the edges than in the middle of things. Sometimes, on a ride or during a conversation, nobody even noticed she was there until someone thought to ask, "Where's Orla?" and she'd say, "Right here." She was probably happy to return to her studies.

As though lighting all the candles made the sun come back, the days became longer and brighter. A few weeks after the festival of light, the sun was so bright every day that the snow quickly melted into a heavy, soggy layer. Overnight it froze again and made a hard crust that could cut the horses' legs if we weren't careful. That was the end of the sheep game for the winter.

I became impatient to fly. I'd been patient all winter about staying in my human form, but now I thought longingly of the sky again.

I was completely unprepared when Mother took me aside one morning right after breakfast.

"Kiar, your father and I want to talk to you," she said.

Together, we went down to Father's council chamber. He stood at the window, looking out, but he turned so quickly when we came in that I knew he'd been waiting for us. I felt my stomach sink. Had Beorn or that other son—what was his name, Hafor—come over our borders? I'd turned Othar down, and there'd be no promised peace between Valenia and Noermark.

"What is it?" I asked. "Is it Noermark?"

"What?" Father said. "Oh, no. Not that. Sit down, Kiar."

If it wasn't Noermark, or a raid, then what could be making him look this serious? He sat, and Mother took the chair beside me and put her arm around my shoulders.

"Swanling," she said, "we have something difficult to ask you. You know we made an agreement with your grandparents when we married. The first daughter who could take swan form would be their heir."

"Yes," I said. "Has something happened to Adana?"

"No, no," Mother said, and squeezed my shoulders. "No, it's only—well, nobody expected there would be more than one of you who could take swan form. Now, Orla has her magic, and she has no kingdom to be responsible for. But you'll be ruling human people, not swans."

"We've talked it over, your mother and I," Father said, "and we think it would be best if you didn't fly without talking to us about it first."

"You let me fly all the time last year," I said. "You never said anything, and I went whenever I wanted. I always had someone with me."

"I know," Mother said. "I wanted to let you have that time to remember."

"What do you mean, to remember?" I shook her arm off.

"We think it best," Father said, "that you be human as much as possible."

"If you want to fly, talk to us first," Mother said.

I jumped up. "You mean I have to ask permission, and you'll decide if I can do it or not! That's not fair! I waited longer than Adana or Orla to get my wings, and I've had only one summer! Now you want to stop me!"

"You were taking longer and longer flights," Mother said. "You know how Adana is when she's been with my family. She has trouble coming back and being human again. You can't do that, swanling."

"I've never had trouble coming back!"

"Not yet," Father said. "But we can't wait for trouble to come. We have to think about what's best for the kingdom."

"I don't see how me flying now and then is bad for the kingdom."

"Not yet," Father said, "but if the day comes when you do have trouble coming back, then what? It will be harder to stop flying if that happens. Believe me, it will be easier to stop now."

"You said I didn't have to stop. Do I, or don't I?"

"Don't get upset, swanling," Mother said. She reached for my hand, and I jerked it away.

"I'm already upset. You've told me I can't do what I love most."

"If you already love it most, then that's the very reason you need to control it," Father said.

"It's not fair! I waited almost fifteen years to fly—even Adana only waited twelve."

Father looked as he did when he spoke to Guthric – his face showed nothing. Was he even listening to me?

"Fair or not," Father said, "that is my command. Come to us to discuss it, and abide by our decision. You will keep it, Kiar, or suffer the consequences."

"What consequences?" I was almost shouting now. "Will you cut off my arms?" I turned and bolted out of the chamber, slamming the door behind me.

I ran out to the stables and buried my face in Kestrel's mane. I could hardly breathe, and my eyes felt hot and dry. I wanted to bite. I wanted to breathe fire like a dragon and burn everything around me. I wouldn't have been surprised if Kestrel's mane had crisped and curled from the heat of my anger. It pounded in my ears and pulsed in my temples and fists. When a hand touched my shoulder, I jumped.

It was Tuan, with Willow behind him.

"What's wrong?" he asked. At first I couldn't speak. I looked at him and saw nothing but concern in his face. Willow was wide-eyed.

"What's happened?" she asked.

My head whirled, and all I could think was that they could fly, and I was forbidden. I had to give up flying to be the queen. And Tuan had told me about Othar's men, and I'd had to send Othar away when I didn't want to.

"Nothing," I said. "Nothing that concerns you."

I shrugged my shoulder, but Tuan kept his hand there.

"What did we do?" Willow asked. "We were waiting for you in the courtyard, and you didn't even see us."

It wasn't fair to be angry at them, to punish them for what Father had commanded.

"Father and Mother have decided I can only fly if they give me permission. I waited so long, and I love it so much, and now I can't."

Willow's mouth fell open.

"That's a hard judgment," Tuan said.

"I've never had trouble coming back to being human. Not like Adana. She spends weeks with Grandmother and Grandfather. It makes sense she'd have trouble. But I never have. It's not fair."

"No," Tuan said. "It's not fair. Are you going to obey?"

"I suppose I must," I said. "He said there would be consequences if I don't."

"What consequences?" Willow said.

"I don't know." I looked from Willow to Tuan. "He could send you away."

"He couldn't!" she said.

"He would do it if he thought it best," Tuan said. "But I don't see how it would make things better."

"Maybe it's only a threat," Willow said. "Maybe he won't do anything."

"No," I said. "If he says something, he means it. I can't remember a time when he didn't do what he said he would." I sighed. "I'll have to obey him. Maybe they just want to know when I'm flying. Maybe they'll say yes when I ask. It might not be so bad."

I looked from Willow to Tuan and knew I wasn't fooling them. I wasn't even fooling myself.

CHAPTER

FOURTEEN

That was a hard spring for me. At least the work was some distraction. There were fields and gardens to plant. Gil and Adana spent most of their time with our grandparents. We hardly saw them.

I was too busy and too tired to fly. I didn't even notice if Tuan and Willow flew. Several times after supper, Mother suggested music and dancing instead of going up to her solar. I think she was trying to give me something else I liked to make up for flying.

At first, I was angry she thought I'd forget about flying that easily, then I considered how she'd left it behind. She didn't often fly herself and seemed quite content to be in her human form. But she loved Father. Perhaps if I'd married Othar, I'd be content to remain in human form, too.

I tried to think of the things I loved about being human: riding Kestrel, dancing, the little honey cakes Nias made, bonfires at the festivals, the candles all around the great hall, new songs when a bard came around. Newborn lambs in the spring. My room, and the blanket with horses woven around the edges. It was like trying not to think of food when I was hungry.

Being angry about not flying made me tired, and perhaps the worst was that some part of me agreed with Father, and I was angry at myself, too. I felt wrapped in clouds or fog; everything was dull and grey, and not really worth doing.

When the hardest work eased off, I went to Mother and Father and asked them if Willow, Tuan, and I could go flying.

I wasn't really surprised when they said no.

"Not yet, swanling," Mother said. "You want to fly so badly, we're afraid you'll stay a swan too long, and forget yourself."

"I wouldn't want it so badly if you'd let me fly a little sometimes!"

"You've always wanted to fly," Mother said. "You think too much of it. You need something else in your life, my darling. There's more than flying."

"What? What more is there?"

"That's something you need to find for yourself," Father said.

I went away without arguing, wondering if "not yet" really meant "not ever."

Shearing was a steady week of work. Each fleece had to be sorted, the dirtiest wool and tags of manure picked away. Then we sorted the wool into fine and coarse. The finest was spun for indoor clothing, and the coarser wool for heavy cloaks and blankets. Even the very greasiest and dirtiest wool was simmered for the oils in it, which were soothing to skin, and then used to stuff pillows or pad boots against the cold. Once the shearing was done, I asked my parents again for permission to fly, and again they refused.

The last of the rainy weather ended. Ploughing was done, and planting was well under way. Grass and wild greens were springing up everywhere. The fields where we grazed the herds showed lush, new grass that grew almost while you watched.

I was still in my shirt, braiding my hair one morning, when Willow finished dressing. She stood on her toes and leaned as far out our window as she could, stretching her arms wide and drawing a deep breath. Then she whirled, her arms still outstretched, and bounced across the room. Her cheeks were pink, and she hadn't seemed this excited since the Noermarkers left.

"Oh, Kiar," she said, "this is such a perfect day for flying. Can't you smell summer coming?"

"Yes, I can," I said, "just the same as yesterday, and the day before. You think every day is a perfect day for flying, Willow."

"Not every day," she said.

"Every day there isn't a thunderstorm." I pulled my tunic on and fished under the bed for my boots.

"Well, it's true. Almost every day is a perfect day for flying. I don't understand how your parents can keep you away from it. I'm twitchy all over from wanting to change."

"I don't know what to do to convince them that I can fly and still be human."

"Your grandparents look as human as anyone here, and they spend almost all their time as swans."

"They *look* human, Willow, but they don't *talk* and *act* like humans. They're somehow strange when they're people."

"But you've been human for weeks and weeks. And before that, all winter." She sat on the bed with a little bounce and pouted at me. "We could take a short flight today. Honestly, what could it hurt? Come on, Kiar."

I wanted to agree, but I remembered Father's words about consequences.

"I can't. You go. You can fly all you want."

"It's not as much fun alone. I like to be with someone."

"Tuan can fly with you."

But when we suggested it, he refused.

"The king said Kiar couldn't fly. It's cruel to do it when she can't."

"It's cruel to keep me from flying when I want to," Willow retorted.

"Nobody's keeping you from it," Tuan said. "I'll go with you, but I'm staying on the ground with Kiar."

Willow had no choice but to agree.

Father was out somewhere, but I found Mother in a storeroom, looking over the winter-stored vegetables with Nias.

"Willow is restless. She wants to fly. She and Tuan and I are going out somewhere to let her do that. Tuan says he'll stay with me for company," I said.

"All right," she said, "as long as you're back by dark."

When I returned, Willow was in the kitchen already, asking Nias for food to take along. She came back with a bulging leather pouch hanging by its strap from one hand.

We rode down the dun and towards the north. On our left, the grain fields rippled in green waves with every breath of wind. On the right, the open pasture gave way gradually to firs, hemlock and cypress in the increasingly wet ground. This way lay the bog, where we sometimes put cloth to dye, but where very little grew. The land rolled in two gentle rises, and as we walked the horses down the second, I looked back over my shoulder. Past Tuan I saw the walls around the castle, the slope of the dun.

"Are you coming or not?" Willow called from below. Then she whooped and ran down to the creek at the bottom. "Let's go look at the bog." The mists of the bog hung low to the ground, dark and heavy as thunderclouds. It was far enough away that I couldn't make out the stunted willows and alders that straggled around its edges, but I knew that nothing wholesome grew there.

"No," said Tuan and I together.

"Oh, come on," she said. "It won't take long."

Neither Tuan nor I answered. When I turned towards the woods, Tuan came with me. After a few steps, I heard Willow on Whiffle behind us.

"Aren't you even curious?" she asked.

"Why? I know what's in the bog. I've heard stories all my life. The marsh-feys lure you off the path to drown. They sound so much like people you know that you can't tell the difference. And the bog-walkers are ghosts with bodies. They're not dead, and they're not alive, and they hate anything that is."

"Anything that's dead, or anything that's alive?" Willow said.

"You're just being stubborn," I said.

"Those are stories to scare children. I bet there aren't any marsh-feys, or any bog-walkers, either."

"Stop it, Willow," Tuan said. "We have stories, too."

"Really?" I asked. "What kind of stories?"

"The lost king," Tuan said.

"What about him? It's an old story," Willow said. "A long time ago, hundreds of years, when humans still hunted swanfolk here. The king flew around his territory with some of the other swans. It was nesting time, and he was looking for danger. He was flying too low when he came on a group of people, and they shot at him. He only had one way to fly, and that was too near the bog. The story says the bog reached up and snatched him down, and he was never seen again."

We paused as we reached the woodland edge.

"So swanfolk believe the bog is dangerous, too," I said.

"It's an *old* story, Kiar. Haven't you ever noticed? All of those stories are old."

"Old doesn't mean they're not true," Tuan said.

We dismounted and let the horses graze while we sat in the sunshine to eat. There were dried apples in the bag, and we each had a few. I got up to give one to Kestrel, and Willow stood up and stretched.

"I'll go over there," she said, pointing. "Past where the trees grow out into the field. I think that would be a good place to take off. Are you sure you don't want to come?"

Tuan shook his head.

"I wasn't talking to you," Willow said. "Kiar, come with me. It'll be fun. Just a short flight, and we'll come back."

"You know I can't. Father commanded. He never does that."

"What's he going to do? He's not here to stop you. Nobody will know but us. Tuan won't tell, will you?"

Without even waiting for an answer, she hurried on. "A short flight won't do any harm. You can't possibly forget who you are down here if we only fly a little around here." She pointed around a circle that took in the field and part of the woods. "Tuan, tell her. She won't forget who she is for a short flight, will she?"

Tuan hesitated, looking at me.

"Will I?" I said.

He looked away and said nothing. Now it was my turn to hesitate.

"I don't know, Willow," I said. She slapped her arms against her sides.

"He's treating you like a child, and you haven't done anything to deserve it. You're not a child anymore, Kiar! Some queen you'll be if you can't even fly around a little field in daylight when you want to."

Her words touched my own secret thoughts, that I was all but an adult and supposed to be queen after my father, and yet couldn't do what I most wanted to do. I jumped to my feet.

"Let's go," I said.

She turned and ran towards the point of woodland, and I followed. I pushed down the thought of my parents and the threatened consequences. We were far enough away from the castle that nobody would notice us. There would be no harm done.

We stripped our clothes off quickly. The little breeze that had been barely noticeable when I was dressed raised gooseflesh on my skin. I rolled my clothes into a bundle and set a rock on it. I didn't want to have to chase my shirt across the field when I got back.

It crossed my mind that there would come a time when Willow would return to the swanfolk, maybe when Adana joined them. Gil would go with Adana, and Tuan would follow, because he'd be alone among humans. Orla would probably go, too—a black swan would be honoured among the swanfolk. I would be left behind, with my human throne and my human world. Who would I fly with then? I had to admit that Willow was right; flying with someone else was better than flying alone.

With that thought, my hesitation disappeared.

I spread my arms and closed my eyes. The one time I'd kept them open, the whirling light of the shapeshifting magic had made the earth and sky move so strangely together that I'd become dizzy and sick. It was better not to watch.

My skin shivered all over, and then everything in my body seemed fluid. My arms would no longer stay straight out from my shoulders. My muscles, bones and joints moved, shaping themselves around some small, still part that was yet me. Every hair on my body seemed to stand on end and then lie flat again. Through my closed eyelids the light flared, then faded. The breeze died away, and my skin no longer prickled. I opened my eyes.

The trees were taller than before, the clearing smaller. Nearby, Willow shook her feathers into place and preened her breast for a moment before spreading her wings to fly. I followed her into the air, beating hard to lift from the ground. Taking off from water was easier. Soon, however, I was in the air, and then I had no thought but flight.

The air flowed under me and pressed upwards against my wings. The air was like water, full of movement and currents, warm and cool places that bore me up or let me fall a little, making me work harder to stay level. I caught up with Willow and flew a short distance behind her, letting her break the air ahead of me.

We wheeled out over the woodland. It was different from above, a pattern of dark and light green, the tall pines piercing the rounded roof of maple and birch. The air, cooler and heavier over the woods, didn't bear us up as well. Our shadows flickered over the uneven surface, losing themselves between the trees. When we came back over the field, the rising warmth buoyed us higher, and our shadows took their own shapes again and echoed our flight on the ground. I rolled and twisted, and swooped, then came back to take the lead from Willow, letting her fly more easily in my wake while I broke the air.

Gradually something in me became uneasy. *Time to land,* said a small voice inside me, *time, before you forget.* I wheeled around again, gliding in a smooth turn that took me over the field. Down below, something stood in the field, looking up at us with the front-facing eyes of a predator.

"Kiar!" it cried. The word was predatory, too, the cry of the marsh hawk. "Kiar!" *Tuan.* The voice in my head said. *Time to go down.*

Willow came up beside me. She made a small, encouraging mutter. *A little longer. Just a little.* Then she slipped ahead of me and beat strongly through the air. My own way eased as she took the lead and I followed.

Time said the small voice inside me again. The word meant nothing. I forgot the creature below and reveled in the bliss of flying. The sun, slightly past its highest point, warmed my back as we circled around to the east. A billowing shape, soft all over, dark and wet smelling, loomed ahead of us. At first it seemed no more than just another part of the ground, but as we approached, the air seemed heavier. It became harder to fly, and I felt an urge to turn away from this place.

I called a warning to my companion and veered away. When she didn't follow, I circled to look for her.

She had skirted closer to the dark place than I. As she turned away, wheeling in a smooth arc on wide-spread wings, it billowed up and reached for her.

If she had been a feather's breadth closer, it would have had her. The edge of that darkness brushed the trailing feathers of one wing, and in a second she was falling out of the air, flapping desperately. She beat hard, pulling away from that grasping darkness, finding the air again only a few feet above the ground. As she climbed, she passed close by me, and I smelled the foulness trailing from the darkened edges of her wing, and her terror, and was suddenly terrified myself. Whatever had left that foulness on her had tried to fling her to the ground. The sky seemed the only safe place.

She flew away to the northwest, beating hard, and I followed her over the field, where the strange creature stood. It called again as we passed over, and for a moment I hesitated, wanting to land. But the terror still beat in my head, and my companion never slowed. I didn't want to lose her, to fly alone, hearing the creature on the ground calling to me in a swan's voice. I flew on after her, over the forest, leaving the voice behind.

The sun moved down in the sky, and no longer shone down on my back. My shadow ran over the ground, a little behind me now, and to my right. In time, my companion slowed, and I caught her up. *Turn back,* I thought. There was some reason to go back the way we had come, but I couldn't remember what it was.

She was flagging now, and we flew more slowly. I took the lead from her, and we went on, over forest, then fields. Some of the fields were dark and smelled of turned earth and young, tender green things. I was hungry, but I saw creatures like the one that had called to me and turned away. Water glinted a little way ahead. There would be tender weeds to eat, reeds to shelter in.

We landed in the water, and I folded my wings. I wanted to eat and sleep. My companion splashed and ducked herself under the water. The darkened ends of her feathers, the barest edge, crumbled and drifted away in the water, taking the odour of fear with it. We ate, reaching down for the underwater growth, and then we paddled to the reeds that grew up at the edges of the pond. Although the sun was still high above the horizon, I was tired from my long flight. I slept, nestled next to my companion, my head tucked down.

CHAPTER

FIFTEEN

I started awake at the sound of two swans honking in greeting. My companion was no longer with me—she was in the middle of the pond, where another swan had just settled. The ripples of his landing ran across the pond and broke in little sloshing wavelets against the reeds.

The newcomer was a cob, a male. He and my companion greeted one another with bending necks and gentle noises. I paddled out towards them.

As soon as he saw me, the cob's whole demeanour changed. He hissed, and his feathers rose a little on his head and neck; he fixed me with one eye, the pupil shrunk to a small dot. I hesitated and withdrew a little. Before I could change my mind, he swept across the water, his neck curved back as he hissed, beating his wings at me, trapping me against the thicket of reeds between me and the shore. I shrank back and he pressed closer, keeping me from swimming away or getting enough space to fly. He settled his wings and smoothed his feathers, but when I tried to slip by him, he ruffled up again and hissed.

The light brightened beyond him, and then I heard my companion's voice, a quiet, reassuring muttering, but somehow muted, less resonant. Then a heavy body moved towards me, pushing larger ripples that made me bob on the water's surface.

"Kiar." It was the same call, the same, almost-swan word I'd heard before. "Kiar, it's me, it's Willow. Come back, Kiar. You have to change back. You have to be human again."

The voice approached, and I saw another of those strange creatures, pressing through the water, only her shoulders and neck above the surface.

"Come on, Kiar," she said. "We have to go home. Tuan, what if she won't change back?" She began to murmur to me again, the comforting swan noises a mother makes to her cygnets, and moved gently closer until she was beside the cob. I circled, unable to move farther from her, somehow unwilling to attack her. The cob bent his head to hers and nibbled at the dark hair falling over her face to drift on the water. She raised a hand and gently pushed her hair aside. I saw her face, strange now, but still my companion's, and I—remembered.

I backed as far from the cob as I could. As I raised my wings to change, I saw him spread his as well and drift a little forward. I couldn't get by him, but that wasn't what I wanted. I beat my wings, once, twice, and then felt that shifting of muscle and skin, my bones moving, everything changing all at once. Then I fell from the surface of the water and my head went under before I could get my feet under me.

I surfaced, spitting water and snorting it from my nose. Magic flared before me as Tuan changed.

"Ow, that's *cold!*" I said, wiping my eyes. "Where are we, exactly?"

"You don't know?" Tuan said.

"I know northwest," I said, "but I don't know how far."

"Far enough," he answered. "We have to go back." He glanced at the sun.

"Can we get back in daylight?" Willow asked.

"Maybe," Tuan said. "But Kiar can't."

"I can fly back," I said, "I got here, didn't I? And can we get out of the water? I'm freezing."

Tuan pushed past me and pressed through the reeds.

"Go on," Willow said, "I'll follow you." I felt I was being herded, but I followed Tuan's path and came up to the shore of the pond as he climbed out. It wasn't much warmer in the air, but at least I had the sun on my skin and could dry off. I stood up to shake the water off, and Tuan grabbed my arm and pulled me down into a crouch beside him. When Willow came up, she crouched down, too.

"What is it?" she asked, whispering now.

"Hunters." He jerked his head towards the south, across the pond.

"How far?" I asked.

Tuan glanced at the sun again.

"Not far," he said. "They'll be here soon. We have to leave. Not straight back. We'll go around."

"But if they're coming from the south, they'll be from one of the farmsteads," I said. "They'll help us."

Willow and Tuan exchanged a glance.

"I'm sorry, Kiar," Willow said, "It's my fault. We're not in Valenia. Those are Gythorn's people. Swan-hunters."

CHAPTER

SIXTEEN

"How do you know?" I asked Willow.

"All swanfolk know. They feel different, sound different, from your people."

I didn't think we'd flown as far as the border of Noermark. But I'd never flown so long before, and time was different in swan form. If they were right, there was no time to argue.

"All right," I said, "Where now?"

"Sneak around them?" Willow said.

Tuan shook his head briefly.

"They'll see us," he said.

He was right. The cover here wasn't good, long grass and some scrubby bushes. To use it, we'd have to crawl. Even then, Tuan and Willow would show, all black hair and pale skin. I wasn't much darker myself. My hair would blend in better, but where my clothes usually covered my skin, I was nearly as pale as Willow.

"Mud," I said. "If we cover ourselves with mud, at least we won't show as much."

"Run to the trees?" Willow said.

"Too far," I said. "They'll catch us. We'll have to fly."

"You can't," Tuan answered.

"If we don't, we won't get back before dark," Willow said. "She'll forget herself again."

"I'm not a child," I said. "I can decide for myself."

Tuan turned on me, face flushed and eyes narrowed.

"You *did* decide," he said, almost through his teeth. "And here we are. You forgot."

I'd never seen Tuan angry before, and that shocked me as much as what he'd said. I had forgotten myself. I couldn't deny it.

"You go," I said. "Get help. I can hide."

"There's nowhere to hide," Willow said. "They'll catch you."

Gythorn would not have forgiven me for refusing Othar, and Othar wouldn't be able to protect me, even if he wanted to. "I don't want to be caught," I said.

"Nor do I," Willow said.

"Then we'll fly," Tuan said. He gripped my wrist again and shook it. "I lead. You do what I say."

I nodded. He glanced at Willow.

"Yes," she said.

We changed and went back into the pond; it was always easier to take off from the water. As we rose, I heard shouting. The hunters were directly behind us, close enough to shoot. I beat my wings hard, working for height as we flew directly away from them. As we wheeled southeast, still climbing, an arrow hissed past my wingtip. Weaving and turning to spoil their aim, we climbed higher.

Tuan set a course straight back the way we had come. We flew until we came to the edge of dark forest, and he angled down toward land. As soon as we landed, he changed, and Willow and I did, too.

"Why are we stopping?" I asked.

"So you will be Kiar when we get home," he said.

"I'm Kiar. Let's keep flying."

He shook his head.

"Why not?" I asked.

"Look at me," Willow said. I did. She took my chin and gently turned my head until I was looking at her with both eyes.

"You've been looking with one eye," she said, "ever since Tuan found us."

"So I'll have to stay human until I look at you with both eyes?"

"How else will we know you remember you're human?"

"We'll take forever getting home," I said, "How far is it?"

Both shook their heads.

"We know we're not there yet," Willow said.

"So are we lost?" I looked at Tuan, remembering to face him straight on.

"No," said Tuan. "We know where we are. If you've remembered yourself, let's go on."

I lost count of how many stops we made. Each time we changed I fretted over the lost time.

People would be out looking for us if we weren't home by dark. They'd find our clothes and know what I'd done. I was afraid to think of what consequences my father had in mind. Whatever he did to me would be bad enough, but what would he do to Tuan and, worse, Willow?

That flight was bittersweet; the joy of being in the air mingled with the knowledge that it might be my last flight.

The sun set before we reached home. In the last, fading light of day, we landed by a large patch of evergreens near a loop of river. Once out of our feathers, we found the air had chilled rapidly since our last pause. I was aching and tired, and Willow rubbed her arms and stretched her back.

"We could rest a while and then go on," she said. "We've flown at night before."

"Kiar hasn't," said Tuan. "And taking off in the dark is much harder. Either go on now, or rest until daylight."

"I want to get home, but I need to rest," I said.

"Then we'll go on in the morning," Tuan said. "There can't be more trouble waiting for us tomorrow than there will be tonight."

"We'll need shelter," I said, "under the trees. The branches go all the way to the ground, look."

We crawled under the skirts of one of the trees. The little shelter underneath smelled pungent and fresh, and the ground cushioned us with layers of shed needles. The air underneath was still, and seemed warmer than it was outside, although still too cold on my bare skin.

"We should sleep," Willow said, "but Kiar's going to be cold."

Tuan nodded and crawled back outside. I saw the flare of his change, and then his swan self ducked back through the branches and settled on the ground. He lifted one wing, twisted his neck to look up at me, and gave a soft, muttering honk. Slowly I sat, then lay down, curled on my side on the ground with one arm under my head. He shifted to nestle against me, his breast feathers just brushing my chin, and spread his wing over me. It covered me from my shoulders almost to my hip, warm, soft, and light.

"Good idea," Willow said. She went out human and returned in swan form. In a minute she settled in the crook of my knee, her wing covering my legs and feet.

Tired as I was, it was hard to sleep. If Tuan was right, it didn't matter now when we reached home. But I knew everything coming to us was not her fault, but mine. If I'd let Willow go when she flew off, if I'd listened to Tuan and come down when he called, I wouldn't be in trouble now. I dreaded seeing my parents. Finally, my tired body overwhelmed my worry, and I fell asleep.

CHAPTER

SEVENTEEN

I woke chilly and sat up. Both Tuan and Willow were gone, and light slanted through the branches of the fir. I sat up and brushed dry needles off my skin before crawling outside. Tuan and Willow were still swans, moving across the grass in a rolling walk, but as I watched they both beat their wings and took human form.

I saw Tuan's shoulders broaden and square into their human shape and turned my eyes away. The sight made me feel shy and uncomfortable, as though it were something I shouldn't watch. Then I felt foolish for the thought, and for the odd flutter in my stomach. We'd all changed back and forth in front of each other before, and even before the swanfolk came to live with us, I'd seen people without clothes. How else did anyone swim? Yesterday I hadn't thought anything of Tuan changing. I wondered what was different today.

"You're awake," Willow said, stretching her arms over her head.

"And ravenous," I answered.

"It's weeds for breakfast," she said, nodding towards the river, "and the sooner we get back, the better."

"I don't know about that."

"We should go now," Tuan said.

"You can't make us go without eating," Willow objected. "You can't make Kiar face her parents without something to eat first, even a little."

He turned to look at me.

"Eat, or fly?" he said.

Why was he asking me? Yesterday he'd made me agree to do what he said.

"Fly," I said. "It's not going to be good, and I'd rather get it over with." He nodded briefly and strode down to the river, changing on the shore and sliding down the bank into the water. Willow sighed and followed, then stopped on the bank to wait for me.

"Come on, then," she said. "It's cold standing around without feathers." When I reached the river, she stood waiting until I changed. Once we were all in the water, we took off.

That flight was over all too soon. It seemed to me we were hardly in the air before we were flying over forest, and then open ground, with the mist of the bog away east of us. Across that open ground a line of riders paced, spaced out, along with two men with dogs. The dogs strained, nose-down, against the leashes wrapped around their handlers' waists. Almost as soon as I saw the riders, they saw us. One pointed, and two or three called out.

Tuan led us around in a circle and came in to land ahead of the line of riders. I recognized my father on Cloud, his grey horse. As we changed, he dismounted, and when I was human again, he stood before me, holding out my clothes.

"Get dressed," he said. His voice sounded flat, more frightening than if he'd been angry. His eyes were dark-smudged. He turned to Willow and said, "You, too." Another rider came forward with her discarded clothes. I pulled on my shirt, damp from lying out overnight. As I dressed, Father turned towards Tuan.

"Thank you," he said. "Will you ride with us? We brought your clothes." Willow, her shirt half over her head, turned on Tuan. "You told!" she said. "You told on us!"

"Enough, Willow," my father said. "Yes, Tuan came to tell us what had happened. Then he followed you. We'll speak of this when we get home."

Willow said nothing, but the look she gave Tuan said there would be trouble later.

"I'll come with you," Tuan said. Another rider came forward and handed him his clothes.

"You take Willow," Father said, and the rider leaned to help her mount pillion behind him. Someone else brought Tuan's horse Lightfoot forward and held him while Tuan dressed.

I looked towards Lightfoot; riding with Tuan would be less shaming than being taken home behind my father, like a bad child.

Father dropped his hand onto my shoulder. "You come with me," he said.

I got up behind him on Cloud. The horse's back was so broad that I couldn't stay on properly without holding onto my father. I could feel from the tension in his back that he was angry, and in all fairness, I couldn't blame him.

"I'm sorry," I said, "I didn't mean to worry you."

"We'll speak of this later, in private," he answered.

We were back at the castle by midmorning. As we came into the courtyard, I saw my mother standing at the door, her hands clasped at her waist. I thought she might come to us, but she waited while everyone dismounted. Father sent Cloud off to the stables with one of the other men, and, to my surprise, Tuan did the same with Lightfoot.

Father walked so quickly that I trotted to keep up with him. Willow caught up behind me. As we reached Mother, I saw the same dark shadows under her eyes.

She watched me as I approached, then looked past me. "Thank you, Tuan, for bringing her home safely."

"Lady," he answered.

"Your mother and I will talk about this," Father said, "and speak to you later. You are forbidden to pass the gate until I say you may." Together they walked into the castle, leaving Tuan, Willow, and me standing before the door.

"What will they do?" Willow asked. To my surprise, her voice was trembling, and when I looked at her, there were tears in her eyes. "Will they send me away?"

"I don't know," I said.

"I'm sorry, Kiar, I didn't think we'd be found out. I didn't mean to fly close to the bog. I didn't know it could reach me—it was just suddenly there. I almost fell out of the sky."

"I know." I glanced at Tuan. "And you tried to call me back, Tuan. Thank you for that, even if it didn't work. I suppose I should thank you for telling my parents, too."

"They had to know," he said.

"What do we do now?" Willow asked. Her voice sounded thin, and she brushed tears from her eyes.

Was this the same Willow who had tempted me to fly, the girl who had wanted to explore the bog? I'd never heard her sound frightened. I wasn't happy either, wondering what my parents might have to say. I tried not to believe they would stop me flying. I didn't want to think of what they might do. Chain me up? Set a guard on me? Break my arms? Anxiety knotted my stomach, but Willow looked and sounded on the verge of panic.

I put a hand on her shoulder, and she gripped my fingers painfully. "We have to wait and see what they decide. It'll be all right. Nobody will hurt you. They'll probably never let me fly again."

She blinked, and tears slid from the corners of her eyes.

I looked at Tuan. "Why is she afraid?"

Tuan put his arm around Willow's shoulder, and she leaned her head against him. His thumb just touched my wrist. I wished he would comfort me, too. In spite of what I'd said to Willow, I didn't believe everything would be all right. Tuan looked at me, still holding Willow close with one arm.

"Waiting is hard," he said. "When I found you, I was angry."

I nodded.

"But then I stopped. We swanfolk, we're angry quickly, and then we're done. We never think of punishments for later. There's enough danger and fear in the future without that. Sometimes humans are hard to understand."

"Why does your father want you to be afraid?" Willow asked, her words muffled against Tuan's shoulder.

"He doesn't," I said without thinking. Then I realized it was true. "He doesn't want me to be afraid. He wants me to think about what I did, what might have happened. He's taking time to think so when he decides, it will be something fair."

All the possible consequences of our flight rushed in on me. We had crossed the border into the land of our enemies. We could have been shot down as we flew. If they'd found us as humans, they would almost certainly have made us slaves. If anyone had recognized me, Gythorn would have wasted no time in letting my father know I was a hostage, maybe forced me to marry one of his sons. Either one of those things would be cause for war. People would have died because I'd impulsively done what I wanted.

Swanfolk defended their nesting grounds, but they had no other territory to fight for. Willow had never needed to think of things like borders and diplomacy and war. She'd known I wasn't supposed to fly, and she might even have thought it was wrong to tempt me to do it, but she couldn't have predicted these consequences. But I, I knew, should have thought of them.

I knew what to do. I put my arm around Willow. "I'll go talk to Father," I said. "I can explain things. Don't be afraid."

Tuan put his other arm around my shoulders and pulled me in. The three of us stood in a small, closed circle, heads almost touching. My own arm slid around his waist before I realized it. Willow put her free arm around me, and we stood quietly for a few moments before I stepped away. The longer I put this off, the longer I'd have to dread it.

"Don't worry," I said to Willow, although I felt far from happy myself.

Tuan put his hand on my shoulder and squeezed. I looked at him, realizing how far back I had to tilt my head, when I stood so close, to look into his face.

"I'll come and find you when I'm done," I said.

"We'll be in the stables," he answered.

I nodded and went to find my father.

CHAPTER

EIGHTEEN

My mouth felt dry and sticky as I walked into the castle. I paused in the great hall and thought about where my parents might be. Either in the solar, I decided, or in my father's small chamber, where he met with messengers and ambassadors. Where he met with Guthric. My cheeks felt hot, and my stomach gave a queasy little flip as I imagined what kind of meeting Father might have had with Guthric because of my stupidity.

The chamber was closer. I decided to try there first. My boots seemed to be full of rocks, and I wanted nothing more than to run upstairs and hide in my room. But I'd told Willow I would make it all right. I couldn't run away now.

The door to the chamber was closed, but I heard Father's voice, too muffled for me to make out any words. I raised my hand and hesitated, then tapped on the door.

"Father?" I said. It came out a croak, and I tried again. "Father? It's Kiar. Can I talk to you?"

The door swung inward. Over my father's shoulder I saw Mother sitting curled in one of the armchairs. She looked small and young, almost like Orla. I often forgot how small Mother really was, because she stood so straight and moved so gracefully. When she saw me, she uncurled and put her feet on the floor and her hands on the arms of the chair, sitting upright as though she were on her throne to receive guests. Her eyes looked bruised, as if she'd been crying.

"What do you want, Kiar?" Father asked.

"I want to talk to you about what I did."

"I told you we'd talk later," he answered. "Your mother and I have to discuss what to do."

"Yes," I said, "I know. But Willow is really afraid, Father. Tuan says that swans don't save punishments for later. For her, waiting is worse than if you beat her right away. I said I'd talk to you."

He looked at me for a long minute, then stepped back and opened the door to let me in.

"Sit down," he said, pointing to a seat across from their chairs. When I did, he took his own seat again and leaned back, watching me, unsmiling. He didn't look angry; he looked more as though he was considering a difficult question. My tongue felt glued to the roof of my mouth, and I tried to work up a little spit to loosen it.

"What do you have to say, then?" Father asked at last.

"First, I'm truly sorry I flew off with Willow. I'm sorry I disobeyed you by flying at all. We were going to go around the field a few times and then land, but Willow flew too close to the bog, and she got scared and flew off." I stopped, but my father said nothing. Even Mother didn't speak. They both sat watching me. After a few moments, the silence seemed so heavy that I had to break it.

"When she flew away, I forgot myself and flew after her. Maybe I didn't really forget exactly. But I was afraid to let her go off alone. I thought she'd get lost."

"I see," Father said. "And what good did you think it would do if you were with her?"

"I don't know. I didn't really think of that."

"She would be able to find her way back, or she would not," he said, "but either way, Willow is much more used to flying and to finding her way, than you are. Do you realize where you landed?"

"No," I said, shaking my head. "At least, I didn't know where we were at the time. Tuan told us. I don't know if Willow knew."

Again, they sat silent, watching and waiting for me to speak.

"We were over the border," I said, "in Noermark."

"Oh!" Mother's exclamation was hardly more than a breath. Father leaned forward, hands on his knees.

"You were in Noermark," he repeated. His voice was flat, as though he didn't believe what he was hearing. I nodded, just once, and looked down at my hands, clasped together in my lap. The knuckles were white. I forced my eyes back up and looked at him.

"Did anyone see you?" Mother asked.

"They saw us fly over, but they didn't see who we were, only that we were swans."

"Did they shoot at you?" Father asked.

I nodded again. "But they missed. The only arrow that came close went by my wing."

"Are you certain they didn't see you?" Mother asked.

"I don't think they could have. When Tuan came, Willow and I were swans. Then we changed, because they wanted me to remember who I was, but people were coming. We stayed low in the grass, but there wasn't enough cover to hide, and no trees nearby. We had to change back to get away."

"You changed with people near," said Father, "Twice. Was that before or after they shot at you?"

"Before."

Father looked at Mother.

"Then they knew," she said.

"Unless they were blind or all looking the other way." He looked at me. "The three of you must have given off quite a lot of light changing. That means someone knew you were swanfolk, even if they didn't know who you were. You said the arrow went by your wing?"

"Yes."

He sighed and rubbed his forehead.

"You've been lucky," he said, "and so have we. It sounds as though they were trying to wing you. At least we can hope they couldn't tell who any of you were, and it was pure luck they nearly injured you. I don't think they can tell the swanfolk apart."

"None of my parents' flock have gone near Noermark for decades, maybe generations." Mother looked at me, and I'd never seen her face so serious and worried. "Any swan who does go near might be one of you—you, Adana, or Orla. Gythorn might have given orders to bring down any swan within the borders, but not to kill it."

"But if we didn't change—" I began.

"Are you sure you wouldn't?" Mother asked. "I'm not. Maybe the shock of being shot down would make you change. If they threatened to kill you, or you thought they would, you might change. Even if you didn't, Gythorn has a wiseman or wisewoman who could tell what you were."

"We're in an awkward position just now," Father said. "You refused Othar, and I've been putting off any courtship of you by one of his other sons." He sighed. "I think we can expect to hear from Gythorn sometime soon. Even if he doesn't know it was you, he may guess. He'll think, no doubt, that if you're old enough to fly, you're old enough to marry. He'd have married you to one of his sons by force, if he'd caught you, and only let you go home after you'd had a child or two."

I opened my mouth and closed it. It was too horrible to think of, but he was right, and there was nothing I could say.

"What might happen then, Kiar? What would happen to our long peace with the swanfolk?"

"I'd never let anything happen to it!"

"Could you be sure nothing would change? If you had a husband who thought of swanfolk only as animals? His folk would be swan-hunters, too. You can't control everything."

I said nothing. I knew what he said was true. Even Othar hadn't seemed to take his men's words seriously, frightening as they were. I doubted any of Gythorn's other sons would be as reasonable as Othar.

"You've put me in a very bad position. Only the greatest good luck, and Tuan spotting the hunters, prevented you from being taken captive. If Gythorn had captured you, we would have been at war."

"And if he'd captured Willow?" I asked.

Father's mouth hardened into a grim line. "I think from the way you reacted yesterday if they had captured Willow, they would certainly have captured you as well," he said.

I said nothing. He was right again.

"I don't understand what you were thinking," Mother said. "You're smarter than that."

"If you think I'm so smart, why didn't you let me fly, even a little?"

"You seemed to be happy," Mother said. "We didn't want to stir things up."

"You said that I could only fly with your permission, and I obeyed, but you never gave it, even once. It was only going to be a short flight. I know I have to be human. And Willow said what kind of queen can't fly if she wants to, but it's not her fault. It was my decision. She was right. Why can't I fly if I want to?"

"You've just shown why," Father said. "A queen can't always do what she wants, nor a king, either. I have to be able to take care of the kingdom and its people. It's up to me to see food is stored for bad times, the borders are defended, and the peace kept as much as possible. And when the peace can't be kept, it's up to me to lead the fighting. None of those are things I would always choose to do. But they must be done."

"Yes," I said. "I understand. I won't take off like that again. I remembered who I was coming home because Tuan made us stop and change. If you let me fly sometimes, I'll only do short flights close to the castle." It would be like riding a pony on a lead rein when I wanted to race across the world, but it would be better than nothing.

"It's too late for that promise, Kiar," he said. "You can't disobey me, not in this. You flew when I'd forbidden it, and you crossed our borders. You chose your own wishes over the good of your people and kingdom. Do you understand?"

"Yes," I said. "I understand."

"If I can't command you and keep you safe, how can I keep my kingdom and people safe as a good king should? A weak king usually dies suddenly. If that happened to me, what would happen to your mother and you girls? Or Gil, Tuan, and Willow?"

He paused then and took a deep breath.

"Worse than that, Kiar, the country would be without a leader. People will fight for the throne, make no mistake. We'd be divided, and Gythorn would be over our borders in a trice."

This was dreadful. My stomach seemed full of iron. There'd been border raids, but never a war, not in my lifetime, and not in my father's. The thought that I could have started one just by being careless terrified me.

"Now, I'm not ready to be killed," my father said, "or to see you girls left without a father or the country without a king. So everyone has to know that I'll keep them safe. Understand?"

"Yes," I said.

"We'd have had trouble with your mother's people, too, if Willow or Tuan were killed, or Gil, either. Everyone owes obedience and fealty to the king, especially my daughter and my heir. You have to bear some penalty for this, and it has to be seen."

"I understand."

"Good. Then tomorrow Sylard will make you an iron necklace."

"Tir," my mother said, but he held up his hand and she fell silent.

I realized my mouth was open, and I closed it.

"Kiar?" my father said.

"Yes, Father." I could hardly get the words out.

"You will wear it until it is my will that you remove it."

"Yes, Father."

"Go and tell Willow," said my father, "that her punishment is that you will no longer fly with her."

CHAPTER

NINETEEN

I stood in the hall, trembling. Wearing an iron necklace, I would be tied to human form. I heard my mother's voice inside the council chamber, but I couldn't make out her words. I hardly felt the latch of the door under my hand.

I walked out through the great hall. My head felt stuffed with wool. I tripped on the lintel of the door, stumbled forward and barely caught myself, then stood in the courtyard. An iron necklace, an iron necklace. My thoughts settled on it and flew up again as birds do when they see a cat; my heart thudded until I thought it would break my ribs.

People walked by, but they were like creatures in a dream. Finally I remembered—Tuan and Willow would be in the stable. I turned and put one foot in front of another. How would the necklace feel, how would it look? Not a collar like a dog's, please not!

As I stepped over the threshold of the stable, the sunlight fell behind me. Willow threw her arms around me.

"What did he say, Kiar? What's going to happen?"

Willow's voice, thick with tears, surprised me. I'd never seen her cry.

"Come over here." She pulled me by the arm and blindly, I followed. I couldn't focus on anything. The smell of leather told me we were in the harness room.

"Sit here." I felt a hand on my shoulder pressing me down. I sat down hard on a small stool, and Willow sat on the floor in front of me, leaning against my knee.

"What will he do? What *did* he do?"

I looked up, still half stunned by my father's decree, and saw Tuan cross-legged on the floor, leaning against the closed door of the harness room.

"I won't be able to fly anymore," I said.

"You mean that's all? But you already—"

"No. He said I'll have to wear an iron necklace. The smith is making it tomorrow."

"Oh, no," Willow whispered.

Tuan's brows drew together, and his eyes narrowed.

"He *can't*!" Willow said, her voice rising. "That's too cruel, Kiar. You don't deserve that. Nobody could deserve that!"

Inside, I agreed with her. How could my own father cripple me, take away my wings? But I remembered our conversation, and almost against my will, I said, "No, he's right. He has to do it."

"You *agree* with him?" Willow looked as though I'd struck her. Even Tuan was shocked into speech.

"He has no right to cripple you," he said.

"He has every right," I said. "We could have had a war."
Tears threatened, but I swallowed, and they stayed down. "The
swan-hunters—they were *waiting* for us. Not only those we saw
yesterday, but all of them. Waiting for swanfolk. They could
have shot better and hit one of us, but they didn't. They don't
want to kill us. They want to catch me, or Adana, or Orla. And
they almost did get me. Then I'd have been forced to marry one
of Gythorn's sons. And my father would have gone to war to
get me back."

"But even if they did make you marry someone you didn't
like, you could change and fly away," Willow said. She sounded
honestly confused.

"Willow," I said, "Gythorn has blacksmiths, too. He'd make
me a collar and chain, like a dog. I'd never get free."

"You're free now," Tuan said.

"Yes," I answered.

Willow looked from Tuan to me and jumped to her feet.
"Yes! You're free now! You can fly away with us, before the
necklace, and never come back."

Tuan shook his head. "No," he said, "she won't." He got
up from the floor. For a moment he stood, then dusted his
trousers, one leg, the other, and then the seat, as though he
had to think about it.

Willow slapped at one leg and left it at that.

I stood up, too, feeling a hundred years old. "Willow, you
asked me what kind of queen can't even take a flight around a
meadow if she likes. Well, what kind of queen would I be if I

ran away? I'd have no right to rule. And if Father doesn't punish me, everybody will know I can disobey him. He'd look weak, and he'd have no right to rule. I have to do this. I—" The words almost choked me. I breathed hard until my throat loosened and went on. "I want to do this." I looked past Willow at Tuan, still guarding the door. I had to blink hard to keep the tears down, and I wasn't entirely successful. He seemed blurry around the edges. But he nodded, his eyes meeting mine.

"She's right, Willow," he said. "She's going to be queen. And he's the king. We don't fight the king."

"You're also being punished," I told her. "Father said your punishment is that I can't fly with you anymore."

Her face fell. "Not even now, while you still can?"

I shook my head. "I have to think of—of the kingdom. I agreed to this, and I'm going to do it."

Willow pushed herself to her feet and blundered past Tuan to thrust the door open. She ran out, the sound of her footsteps rapidly fading.

"It's strange, being a human," Tuan said. He squeezed my shoulder. "You do it well."

I followed him into the court. Willow was running, but as we watched, she stopped with her arms at her sides and her fists slowly clenching.

"What's she going to do?" I asked.

"Share your punishment," Tuan said.

"Father wouldn't do that to her!"

"Not the necklace," he said. "But she won't fly if you can't."

For a moment we stood watching her, then Tuan said, "Sword practice."

We turned toward the armoury. I still had the whole day to get through, and all of tonight, without giving in to what Willow had asked, and what I badly wanted to do. Anything that kept my mind and body busy was welcome.

Sometime during practice, I heard Sylard's hammer from the forge. The taps were light, but each one went through my head. I knew I was fighting badly; Dar said nothing, which was worse than if he'd shouted. I took two solid blows on my helmet, and when practice finished, I had a headache that wasn't entirely from the hits.

 From the smithy, the tap-tap-tap of the small hammer on the anvil went on and on.

I wasn't permitted to go outside the walls; I knew better than to try. What chores I found to do inside didn't occupy my thoughts and left them free to bounce and chitter in my head like squirrels. Every moment was a temptation to take one last flight. What more could my father do to me than he was already doing? I wavered between thinking I should take the final chance to fly and feeling I had already consented to my penalty to stay human. By mid afternoon, between indecision, fatigue, and the terrible waiting, my body trembled constantly. It didn't help that I could hear the ring of the hammer on the anvil wherever I was within the walls.

I went up to my room, hoping to shut out the sound. But even there, the small, ringing taps echoed against the wall and traveled through the window. I looked out at the curtain wall surrounding the castle and the sky beyond. Anger rushed through me; how could my father take away my wings? I should change here and now and fly away forever! I imagined soaring through the window, over the walls, and away, flying until I found some lake or pond where I could sleep.

The fantasy collapsed. If I changed in this room, I didn't have enough space to get into the air. If I did get airborne and found a pond for the night, then what? I couldn't live on my own; I'd be as apt as not to stray into Noermark again, and this time I might not be as lucky. I couldn't join my grandparents, or they'd send me home in disgrace. I'd consented to my punishment, and flight would prove me a liar and a coward. I wasn't going to let anyone say either of me.

I dreaded supper, wishing both that it would never come, and that it was already over. Nothing looked different in the hall when I entered. I took my place, feeling like every eye was on me. Gil patted my shoulder as he passed by, and Adana stole sideways glances at me at the table.

I ate very little. Food stuck in my throat, and my stomach felt full of rocks. Willow sat on one side of me, silent and red-eyed. Tuan sat on the other, and I didn't know whether to be grateful or annoyed that he seemed unmoved by my punishment. I didn't dare look at Father or Mother.

My father stood up in his place and waited while the talk in the hall died away. "Kiar, come with me."

I followed him to the heavy, oaken outer doors, closed now for the night. When he reached them, he turned and stood to one side, where everyone in the hall could see him. He nodded to me, and I stood at his right, within arm's reach.

It has to be seen. It has to be seen. The thought didn't lighten the weight in my stomach or cool the blood rising in my face.

Sylard approached us. The smith stood only shoulder-high to my father and was lean and corded with muscle. He wore his hair, rusty-red and streaked with grey, cut to shoulder-length and tied back. In the forge, he tied a cloth around his head to keep sweat out of his eyes. He bowed and held out his hands, and across them lay my chain and a pair of pliers. Father took both things and nodded, and Sylard returned to his place. He didn't look at me.

Father held the chain high, one end in each hand, turning to display it to everyone in the hall. Close up, I saw that Sylard had made it pretty and delicate. The links were doubled spirals of wire, intertwined and hammered flat and yet subtly twisted to catch the light. If it had been silver, even bronze, any woman would have been proud to wear it.

It was open because it was too small to go on over my head. Such a chain needed a clasp, but this one had none. Instead, an open ring hung from one end. I wished Father would simply put it on me, get it over, but he faced the people and held the necklace out at shoulder height.

"Princess Kiar has defied the crown," he said. "She acknowledges her wrong and bows to our will. And our will is that she shall wear a necklace of iron until it is our pleasure she take it off."

Nobody in the hall made a sound. In the hush, the small clatter of dishes from the kitchen was clearly audible.

"Turn around," the king said.

I turned, and he slipped the necklace around my throat and lifted my braid over my shoulder to hang out of the way.

The chain moved a little, and the tiny hairs on the back of my neck stirred as my father put the loop through both ends of the chain and pinched it closed.

I'd expected to feel pain or some physical sense of loss, but all I felt was the cold touch of the metal. Even that faded as it warmed against my skin. He lifted my braid back into place, and for an instant, I felt his hand squeeze my right shoulder, the one facing the door. Then he turned me to face the people.

Some stirred in their seats. It was clear that nobody knew how to respond to my punishment. My mother sat straight and stiff. I remembered her outburst in the council chamber; whatever she felt, she couldn't publicly disagree with my punishment. I wondered what it cost her to do that. Gil's arm was around Adana, and she leaned into his shoulder. Willow's face was in her hands. Only Tuan looked at me as he viewed everything, with a calm, appraising eye. In that moment, it occurred to me he must have been very angry indeed, or very afraid, when he found me and Willow in Noermark.

My father said nothing more, only put his hand on my back and walked me to our table. In the hall, people began to talk again.

"Well done," he said softly.

CHAPTER

TWENTY

I slept that night, although sleep was long in coming. The necklace slid on my throat, changing position as I turned in bed. I could never be unaware of it. I woke early again and slipped quietly out of bed. Willow had cried a long time before falling asleep, and I didn't want to disturb her.

I dressed and walked boldly to the gate. As I approached, the guard swung the door open for me and stepped aside to let me pass. At least I could leave the walls of the keep. I walked around to the path that led over two rises and down to the creek and continued in the rising sunlight until I reached the water. Nobody could see me from the castle, but still I hunted out a clump of alder and hid behind it before taking off my clothes and calling the change. The light flickered up around me.

Instantly, I was on the ground, gasping with the pain that flared through my body. The necklace seemed red-hot, and I tore at it frantically, feeling my fingers burning, too. I rolled and twisted on the ground as my muscles spasmed, and bright lines of pain shot the length of my bones. My stomach heaving, I threw up on my hair and my hands, then collapsed on the grass in exhaustion.

Once I could move again, I crawled to the water and washed myself clean, then dried myself with my shirt. I shook from chill and the strain of throwing up; it was difficult to do even those simple things, and I had to rest briefly before I dressed. I felt my neck, but the skin was smooth, with no sign of blistering or burning. My fingers, too, were unmarked; the pain was only a memory.

The rise leading up to the castle had never seemed so steep. Once I was within the walls, I found Willow waiting for me in the hall.

"Where did you go?" Willow demanded.

"I tried to change," I said.

"Does it hurt?" Her voice was a shocked whisper. "The necklace?"

"Not now," I said. "It did." Tears filled Willow's eyes, but I felt that mine had all been burned out by the iron on my neck, and that I would never cry, or laugh, again.

The stairs took forever to climb. When I reached my room, I collapsed onto the bed, exhausted from my attempt to change and my battle with the iron necklace. I fell into sleep. When I woke, briefly, the slant of light through the window told me it was evening. I slept again and didn't wake until early morning.

When I turned my head, Willow was awake and watching me.

"Do you feel better?" she asked.

"I don't know. Maybe."

"What are you going to do?"

"What I always do, I guess. Weapons practice. I go out on patrol in a week."

"I'll come with you," she said.

"You don't have to," I said. "I know you'd like to go to the lake and spend time with your family. Isn't that what you always do when they're here and I'm not?"

"Yes," she said, "but not anymore. This is my fault, Kiar, and you shouldn't be the only one who's punished." She set her mouth.

"All right, then. I'll ask Father if you can come, too." When she frowned, I added, "I'd do the same for anyone else."

"You wouldn't have to. Anyone but me would just ask the king."

"You don't have to be afraid of him," I said. "He wouldn't put a necklace on you."

As we assembled for sword practice that morning, I didn't see Tuan. He was usually one of the first on the practice ground. I had fastened my shirt as high as it would go, but I still caught people glancing uneasily at my throat, and finally I undid the ties that held the neck of the shirt closed. Then they looked away, which was almost worse.

When Tuan arrived, everybody forgot about me.

"What did you do?" Willow said.

"Cut my hair. Can't you tell?"

Tuan's hair, which he wore tied back for practice, now came down barely to his shoulders. It had clearly been sawed short

with a knife. The ends were ragged and uneven, and he wore
a strip of cloth around his forehead to keep his hair out of his
eyes. His face was a different shape with the wings of hair falling
down around it.

"Why?" Willow asked.

"It's less work," he said.

She snorted but said no more. I couldn't help stealing looks
at Tuan and seeing him with his hair cut short made me feel
almost shy. It was an uncomfortable feeling, one I didn't know
if I liked or not. He seemed different, even though only his
hair had changed.

After practice, I fell in beside him on the way to the armoury.

"Mother would trim that for you, if you asked," I said. "She
could tidy it up."

"Could you?" He turned his head, and I barely avoided his
eyes. I felt my face grow hot, and it annoyed me. It was only
Tuan, and all he'd done was cut his hair!

"I guess I could," I said. My voice sounded sharper than
I'd meant it to. "I'll get the shears." Mother had a small pair of
shears, like the larger ones used for the sheep. I'd watched her
trim Father's hair often enough.

On my way up to borrow Mother's shears, I thought about
where we could go. I wanted a little privacy. Mother did Father's
in the solar. I didn't have any room but the bedroom I shared
with Willow, and I knew Tuan wouldn't be allowed there, nor
would I be allowed up to his room on the men's side. That really
left nowhere but the hall or one of the outbuildings. When I
came back out with the shears and a comb, I still hadn't decided.
Tuan waited for me at the door of the armoury.

"Where do you want to go?" I asked.

"Here will do," he said. He untied the cloth around his forehead and stood looking at me.

"Turn around," I said after a moment.

He did. I combed down his hair at the back, and then around each side. The comb ran smoothly through the straight black strands. The tiny hairs on the back of his neck rose, and I felt a shiver on my own nape.

"Stand still," I said, "and keep your head straight. I've never done this before, so it might come out crooked."

Once I started cutting, my uncomfortable feelings faded. Keeping the ends of the hair even was more difficult than I'd thought it would be. Clipping a little at a time, I tidied the ragged ends as much as I could. Once the worst was done, I combed his hair down smooth again and worked on making an even edge. Tuan stood quietly. I shielded his earlobes from the shears with my hand, and each time the hairs on my arms rose and I heard a catch in his breath.

When I was almost done, I asked, "Why did you do it? Your hair was beautiful. And now you look—I don't know —different from Gil. Different from yourself. Everybody was staring at you, and they're probably going to keep on staring."

"Yes," he said.

"That's not an answer." I snipped a last strand and brushed roughly at the clippings on the shoulders and back of his tunic.

He turned around and looked at me, smiling slightly. I couldn't meet his eyes for long and looked down at my hands, fiddling with the shears and comb.

"You didn't stare at me," he said. "And nobody stared at you. Don't cut yourself," he added.

I stopped fidgeting with the shears. "You did it so nobody would stare at me?"

He lifted one of the spirals of the necklace on a finger. "It's pretty," he said, "if it didn't stop you changing. Thank you for trimming my hair." He put one hand briefly on my mine, which still clutched the comb and shears, and walked away.

CHAPTER

TWENTY-ONE

I expected a messenger from Gythorn at any time, demanding what, I didn't know. Would he insist on one of us marrying a son of his? Would he accuse us of spying and demand something in reparation? Or would he simply attack? The fear disturbed my sleep, and several nights I started awake, certain I'd heard the shouts and clash of fighting. I dreamed of blood and of swans falling from the sky with arrows in their wings.

The days passed, and then the weeks, and no messenger came, either from Gythorn or from any of the farmsteads to say there was trouble. Father sent out two patrols to the northern border and left a small group of men at one of the farmsteads to keep an eye on the border between patrols. He said nothing to me, but I knew the farm folk were feeding extra men and horses because of my flight.

Adana wanted a little more time with us, so she and Gil had put off their wedding for an extra year. I knew I would miss her when she left, but part of me wished she would marry and go. If they were married and away with the swans, they would be safe from Gythorn. I was glad that Orla was safe with Sianna.

The summer passed with no word from Gythorn. My dreams of blood and war stopped, and I began to think the Noermarkers didn't know who we were. Maybe they hadn't seen our change and thought we were ordinary swans, not swanfolk at all. They might have said nothing at all to Gythorn.

Orla came home briefly and alone at the midsummer festival. Mother kept her close as much as she could, but she was often off with Adana and Gil, riding or flying.

"She must miss having other young people around," Mother sighed. "It's hard on the child."

I thought Orla wasn't really a child any longer. She was almost fourteen, the same age at which Guthric, Mother and Father had thought I was old enough to think about a future husband. Or maybe that was only because I was going to be queen. Wisemen and wisewomen didn't marry, after all. And Orla was Mother's youngest—still, in a way, her baby. The visit was brief, only a few days, although Mother had hoped for longer. Adana seemed relieved to see Orla go. When Orla wasn't with Mother, she was always around Adana and Gil, and if Adana had something else to do, Orla coaxed Gil to ride with her, or play knucklebones, or sit and talk. I tried to talk to Mother about it, but she merely smiled.

"It's a baby crush, swanling. She'll grow out of it. You worry too much."

I hesitated to say anything more, but one day Adana said to me, "I wish she'd leave him alone. She's as bad as a puppy, and I'm tired of it." She was mending a tunic and stabbing the fabric as though she was angry at it.

"Why don't you say something?"

"I have. I've said we want time to ourselves, and she gives me a hurt look and says she's missed us. I can't say she's doing something particular wrong. She holds his hand, rides with him, plays games, just like a little sister. And that's what Gil thinks, that she's acting like a sister."

"But you don't."

She sighed. "I don't. And I don't know why. Nothing she does is improper. But she's always there, always looking for his attention. Mother doesn't see it."

"I know," I said.

Adana looked at me, round-eyed. "You see it. You know what she's doing!"

"She's not *doing* anything that I can see, but, yes, I don't like it."

Adana leaned toward me. "I like it less when she's here, and I don't know where she is. It's as though she's nowhere, and everywhere.

"She's always been quiet, Adana. Mouse, remember?"

"Mice get into things they're not supposed to," she said darkly.

And, I thought, what they don't eat, they spoil. I hoped Orla's pet name didn't mean more than we thought it did. When she rode away to return to Sianna I was almost as relieved as Adana was.

By the time the harvest festival came around, I was able to sleep at night with the necklace on. Every time I moved, I felt it, but it became something to live with, like a bruise or a scar.

I missed flying worse than ever.

When I dressed for the festival, I pinned the neck of my underdress close to hide the iron spirals. I had a new dress of pale green wool with woven bands of blue and dark green at the hem and sleeves, and Othar's moss-stones looked beautiful over it.

This year, when Father asked for comfort for loss and healing for hurt, I hoped I would find those things. I'd given up Othar's courtship because of our alliance with the swanfolk, and now I was barred from what I loved most about that alliance. I couldn't think of anything that would comfort me for losing the sky.

When the ceremony was over, Willow turned to me. "Remember, you have to dance with the first man who asks you!" Then, she was off in a swirl of skirts.

A hand took mine and I gave a startled squeak.

"If that's the loudest you can scream, nobody will hear you," Tuan said.

"I didn't expect that."

"I know. First man who asks you, remember?"

He smiled, and I smiled back. We went looking for a dance to join.

The Deer dodged past us, and we stepped ahead of the Hunter who followed. He swore at us and laughed, then dodged around us. We chose the nearest circle, and Tuan swung me into the steps.

"You dance much better than you did last year," I said, when the music paused between tunes.

"Practice," he said as we joined another group. "The same as anything else."

I followed him from square to circle, through the swirls and grapevine steps and swingings and duck-and-divings of the whole harvest dance. Several times we stopped to drink. Dancing was thirsty work, especially near the fire. Once or twice we saw my parents in a circle dance. Once Tuan danced with Willow, and several times other partners claimed my hand, but Tuan was always there to take it back before we moved on.

The fire burned down to a glowing pile; the dancers slipped away until only a few circles remained. At the edges of the square, it was dark enough to see the stars overhead in a clear sky.

Tuan stood, head tilted back to look at the Chariot, as though he would be able to see the constellation wheeling around the north star. I thought how restful he was to be with. His silence had been disconcerting at first, but I was used to it now and sometimes felt that I knew what he was thinking. There was no need to fill the space between us with chatter. I looked at the sky, picking out the Hound and the Deer, and the curve of stars that marked the Hunter's bow. The chill of the autumn night crept through my clothes, and I yawned.

"I think it's time I went to bed," I said.

Tuan took my hand and together we walked back to the castle, skirting the dancers, keeping to the darker edges of the courtyard. We walked through the great hall, where the fire had been covered for the night. At the bottom of the double stairs, we stopped.

"Good night," I said, "Sleep well."

"Good night, Kiar," Tuan said.

I thought for a moment that he might try to kiss me, but he only smiled and squeezed my hand before going up the stairs to the men's side, taking the steps two at a time. I walked more slowly up to my room.

I took off my festival dress and unpinned my hair. I settled into the high, wide bed with its counterpane woven with prancing horses. Willow wouldn't come to bed until the last dance was danced. Music sounded from the courtyard, and I tapped my fingers on the cover and remembered dancing with Tuan and his hand holding mine. I yawned again and blew out the candle. I didn't even feel Willow come to bed.

TWENTY-TWO

As soon as we had finished culling the cattle that autumn, I went with Father and half a dozen guards on the last patrol of the year. We had perfect weather, dry and clear. The air was cold, but the sun was warm and made riding comfortable. Even the wind was no more than a breeze. It was too late for the biting insects, and we always managed to find a reasonably dry place to camp.

Whenever the chance offered, we took game to vary the bread, cheese, dried apples, and grain cereal that we carried. Most often it was grouse or rabbit, but once we killed a deer.

There were no signs that anyone had crossed the border, not the track of a lone hunter or one dead campfire. Bards travelled all during the spring, summer, and fall. On an earlier patrol, we'd found a bard in the midst of breaking up his camp and had invited him to come along with us. He was happy to take our offer; travelling with a well-armed group was safer than travelling alone. While nobody would attack or rob a bard, wild animals weren't as particular. We had plenty of food to share, too, including fresh meat.

This time we didn't see anyone. We moved slowly, making large camps and leaving signs that a group had been there, with horses and weapons.

"It's the same as dogs marking territory," Father told me. "If people know we're patrolling in large numbers, they're far less likely to trespass."

I enjoyed sleeping out, eating what Nias had packed for us, or fresh meat cooked in the open air, and making camp bread with dough wrapped around a stick when we stopped at midday. If Tuan or Willow came along, we shared a place at the fire and laid out our bedrolls near each other. Neither had come along on this patrol. I wondered how things were going at home, if Willow was helping out with my tasks, keeping an eye on things for me and whether everything would be all right when we got back.

The sun had already dipped halfway below the horizon as we approached the castle, and the night-chill had begun to cool the air. Dar swung the gates open for us and we rode in. I unsaddled Kestrel and brushed her down, fed and watered her and slung my bedroll over my shoulder. I felt tired to the bone, and happy to be back.

The happiness lasted until Mother came out to meet us. We knew right away that something was wrong.

"What is it?" Father asked.

"Lung fever," Mother said. "Shortly after you left, some of the little ones fell ill, and then, of course, the mothers, and then others. Half of the people in the castle are ill or recovering."

"You look worn out," Father said. "Did you send for Sianna?"

"She's here, with Orla. They've been working hard, making the medicines and nursing. Orla's hardly slept. I'm surprised she isn't sick herself. At least there's nobody left with a dry cough, and the fever is done. Everyone who is still sick can sleep; that and time is mostly what is needed now for everybody to get better. Almost everybody."

"Are you sick?" Father asked.

"No, but I'm tired. I'll sleep better now that you're home." She linked her arm with Father's. Her face was so drawn, I felt something must be very wrong.

"Willow," I said. "And Tuan? Are they all right?"

"Sleeping," Mother said. "Willow is still recovering. Tuan didn't catch it badly at all, and you'd never know he'd been sick."

"But there's something," I insisted.

She sighed. "A few still aren't doing well. Gil's the worst. I've spent more time with him to let Adana rest."

"How bad is he?" I asked.

"You'll see." Mother leaned her head against Father's shoulder, and he put his free hand on her hair. "Oh, I'm glad to have you back, but what a sorry welcome."

"I'll take Cloud," I said to Father. He handed me the horse's reins and I led Cloud and Kestrel to the stables while Father and Mother hurried into the castle.

After I'd seen the horses watered and fed, I wanted nothing more than my bed. At the foot of the stairs, I remembered Mother's worry about Gil. I ran up to the men's chambers. I didn't even think about not being allowed. I'd never been up there before, but it wasn't hard to know which room was Gil's. A bar of light lay across the floor of the hall outside one room.

Adana sat by Gil's bed, holding his hand. The fact that she was there, on the men's side, told me how serious this was. When she looked up, I was shocked at how pale and thin her face had become in such a short time. Her eyes were red from crying, and the shadows underneath were darker than the ones under Mother's eyes.

Behind her Father and Mother stood together. She leaned her head on his shoulder, looking wearier than I'd ever seen her.

I crossed the room to the near side of the bed and looked down at Gil. He lay so still, as though he were deeply asleep, but his eyes were open and moved aimlessly. I took his other hand.

"Gil," I said, "it's Kiar."

His eyes flickered towards me, then drifted away again.

"Where's Sianna?" I said.

"She's sleeping for a while. It's all right," said Orla's voice. I turned to see her enter, carrying a wooden cup. Steam curled out of it. "I'm making the same medicines she would. We don't need to bother her."

"He's better than he was," Adana said. Her voice was hoarse; she must have cried her throat raw. Still, she sounded calm. Orla handed me the cup, and together she and Adana lifted Gil while Mother packed cushions behind his back. Then Adana took the cup from me and held it to Gil's lips.

"Drink this, love," she said, tipping it so the liquid lapped against his upper lip. He opened his mouth and she let a little liquid flow in. He swallowed and she did it again, coaxing him patiently. We watched while Gil slowly drank the whole cupful.

"Thank you, Orla," Adana said, handing the cup back. She managed a small smile.

"I'll bring more of this in an hour or two," Orla said, "You should try to sleep, Adana. Are you drinking the tea I made you?"

"I'll go and lie down in a minute," Adana said, but she made no move to get up.

"You need some rest," Orla said, "I can watch him."

"I can, too," I said.

"I'll go when you bring the next cup," Adana said, "I promise."

Orla left, then, and I followed her out.

"What happened?" I said as we walked down the stairs. "He's really sick, and even the babies are better, Mother said."

"I don't know. I thought he'd recover more quickly. Tuan had a cough for a few days, that's all."

"Mother said some were sicker than the rest."

"Yes. There were a few." Orla wiped her hand across her eyes. "I'm sorry, I'm tired, too. Some of them had vomiting as well as a cough. The ones who could keep food down healed faster. There were only two this morning who couldn't get up, besides Gil. Both of them were up this afternoon and asked for water. Gil hasn't asked for anything." She rubbed her eyes again with her free hand. "My eyes feel full of sand. I wish I could sleep better but I'm—" She stopped, and her mouth worked a little. Finally, she said, "Worried." Her voice sounded small.

"That Gil might die?"

She nodded and looked away.

"Does Adana know?"

Orla shook her head. She sniffed and rubbed the back of her wrist over her eyes, then looked at me again.

"I haven't told her. She's frightened enough. Don't say anything."

"Isn't there anything else to do? A spell or something?"

"I've done a few little things," Orla said, her voice rising slightly. She stopped and took a deep breath before going on. She rolled the stem of the empty cup between her fingers. "Air spells to help him breathe and clear water from his lungs, water spells to keep the fever down. It's hard, though, trying to clear liquid with an air spell while you use a water spell to lower a fever." Although I had to look up at her a little, Orla seemed in that moment like a tired, small girl. I rubbed her back.

"That feels good," she said. "There's only one more thing I can think to try, something different. Then I can rest, at least for tonight. She peered out the nearest window at the sky. "I need to hurry. As it is, I won't be back until well after dark. No moon tonight."

"Will you need a torch? I know I can't help with the spells, but I could hold the light for you."

She smiled. "I can see what to do, even in the dark. The best help would be to get Adana and Mother to rest. If you watched beside Gil—"

"I wouldn't know what to do."

"Sit with him. If he wakes, give him water. The fever dries him out."

"I'll do that."

"Thank you, Kiar," Orla said.

I managed to get Adana and Mother both to promise they would go and sleep, then I sat by Gil's bed, watching his breaths come shallow and slow. He seemed to be more in a trance than asleep; sometimes, he opened his eyes and looked up at the ceiling. If I spoke to him, he'd turn his head towards me, his eyes would find me then slip away again. Twice he drank water, but more spilled on the blanket than got into his mouth.

While Gil was in one of his sleeps, Tuan came to the door. He carried a cup of wine with a piece of bread laid across it, and a bowl of something that steamed a little. In spite of everything, I smiled to see him.

"How are you?" I asked quietly. "Orla said you had a cough."

"I'm well now," he said, walking around the end of the bed. "I brought you something to eat."

I hadn't realized how hungry I was. Tuan handed me the bowl, and the smell of beef stew tickled my nostrils. My stomach rumbled. I picked up the spoon stuck into the stew and ate. Tuan found another stool and sat beside me.

"Bread?" he said.

I took the thick slice from the wine cup and mopped up the gravy with it. When I was done, Tuan took the bowl and handed me the wine.

We watched Gil breathing. His chest rose and fell hardly at all, and he looked long and flat under the blanket.

"There's always some that get sicker than others," I said. "I'm glad you're all right."

Tuan put a hand on my knee, leaning a little closer. I felt the warmth of him on my shoulder, or maybe it was only my own heat reflected back. When I put my hand over his, he linked his fingers with mine, and left them there while we watched Gil draw those slow, shallow breaths. Eventually Tuan disentangled his fingers and took the wine cup.

"You need to sleep, too," he said. "You've been riding all day, now this." He gestured towards Gil.

"Orla will be back in a while. I'll go to bed then, I promise." I leaned my head against his hip, and he stood there for a moment.

"Goodnight, Kiar," he said.

"Goodnight, Tuan." He stepped away and left quietly as he had come.

Sometime later, Orla came back. As she stepped into the sphere of light cast by the flame of the candle on the bedside table, I saw she held a tiny cup, not the larger one she'd brought earlier. Steam curled out of it and tickled my nose with a bittersweet, spicy fragrance. Even Gil turned his head as though he smelled it, too.

"Is that it?" I said, "that little bit?"

"Yes. It's strong. You don't need more than a little. Is there any water left?"

"Yes. Will that make him better, Orla?" The question slipped out before I could stop it. My poor, tired little sister.

" Yes, I believe it will. Help me sit him up."

I put my arm behind Gil and raised his head and shoulders. The swanfolk were always warm, but his skin felt frighteningly hot. Orla put the cup down on the table long enough to pull a pillow up behind him. His head rolled a little, and Orla steadied it with her left hand while with her right she held the little cup to his lips.

In a sing-song tone, she chanted some words I didn't understand, one phrase, then another, and he drank. As he finished, she chanted a few more words, and glanced up at me.

"Now the water," she said.

I passed her the half-full cup, and she held it to Gil's lips. He swallowed almost eagerly and finished all of it.

"Lay him back down," she said. "You should go to bed."

"I can stay. You're tired."

"No, I'll be fine. Besides, Tuan will kill me if I don't let you sleep." She smiled, a tired, one-sided smile.

Gil drew a deep breath for the first time and turned over, curling onto his side. His forehead shone. Orla wiped her fingers over his skin, and they came away wet.

"He's sweating," she said. "Finally." Gil's hand groped over the covers, and she took it between both of hers and held it still.

"Go on," she said, "Go to bed, Kiar. Thanks for your help."

I went down the stairs in the dark, my hand on the wall, then back up the stairs to the women's side and down the hall to my room. Willow lay fast asleep, and I listened to her breathing for a few minutes. It sounded a little heavy, but not wet, as the lung fever sometimes sounded.

As I pulled off my clothes, my stomach turned, the faintest beginning of queasiness. I stood, half dressed, wondering if I was going to throw up. Surely, I couldn't have the lung fever so quickly. After an uneasy minute or two, my stomach settled again. I finished undressing and got into bed. I was asleep almost as soon as my head touched the pillow.

CHAPTER

TWENTY-THREE

When Gil finally left his bed, Sianna and Orla went back to Sianna's house. Gil was still weak and improved only slowly. Maybe because he'd been sicker with the lung fever than anyone else, he was clumsy and dull-witted, like a man half-asleep. When we hunted or played the sheep game, Gil stayed indoors.

Winter wore on. We hunted as often as we could and rode out several times a week to our gaming ground. It snowed nearly every day. The deer were quicker in the snow than our horses were, and their grey, winter coats let them disappear among the grey trunks of the trees. Tracking them was easier, but actually spotting one was more difficult.

"If we had to live on what we hunted day to day, we'd starve," Tuan said as we headed home one afternoon. Dar and my father, riding ahead with the older men, laughed over something. We had taken four deer, winter-thin and little enough on them. I suspected this was the last we would hunt deer this winter.

"Well, there's potted meat, and smoked and dried," Willow said. "We won't starve."

"Cheer up," I said, "It's only ten days to midwinter festival. After that it will be warmer and brighter."

The day before the midwinter festival, we rode out to collect pine and winterberry to hang over every doorway in the castle. The bright red berries and green needles reminded me that even in the black, white, and grey world of winter, there was colour and life, waiting to rise again in spring. I loved the smell of the pine branches; they were fragrant even cold, and as they warmed, they filled the rooms with their pungent, sharp scent.

On the shortest day, we made the midwinter fire in the courtyard outside the castle. It was always a small fire of split wood, because we had to wait until it burned down to coals before going inside to the feast. In the afternoon, Gil, Adana, Tuan, and Willow and I went out to sweep the stone clean before putting down the fire bowl and laying the kindling and wood.

As we worked, the guard on the wall called out, "Two riders!" We weren't expecting anyone, but Willow looked up from setting curls of firebark among the kindling.

I knew right away it was Sianna and Orla. Both riders wore long, dark cloaks that fell over their horses' backs, but Star's chestnut colour stood out against the snow almost as brightly as winterberries.

They rode into the courtyard shortly after, red-cheeked from the cold. The horses' breath looked like smoke in the air. Mother was waiting at the hall door, and I went to the gate.

Orla flung herself off Star and hugged me. "Oh, it's good to be home!"

"I'm glad you're back," I said. "Mother's waiting for you. We can talk later."

Orla glanced up at Sianna. At the wisewoman's nod, Orla ran across the court to Mother. Sianna and I watched as Mother reached out for Orla and pulled her close. Sianna dismounted and pushed back her hood.

"How are you, Kiar?" she asked. "Orla told me about the iron necklace."

"I'm well," I said. "I'm not happy about it, but—" I trailed off, not sure how much to say.

"I'm sorry," Sianna said. "You waited a long time to fly, and I know you love it."

"I loved it," I said. "I don't know when I'll fly again. Maybe never, after this."

"I'm sure your father is wise enough to know that keeping you chained forever won't teach you anything," Sianna said. "You need to be able to make your own decisions."

"Didn't Orla tell you? They don't trust me to make my own decisions," I said. "I had to ask permission to fly, but they never gave it. When I did make my own decision, I made a horrible mistake."

"Yes, but maybe yours wasn't the first mistake," she said.

"You mean Father and Mother should have let me fly?"

"I mean that no one is perfect. We all have to make mistakes, or we learn nothing."

"Did you ever make a mistake?" I asked. Then I realized how impertinent my question sounded.

Sianna smiled at me. "Many, many mistakes," she said. "And I have more to make. Let's put Star and Night Wind inside."

When we went inside after stabling the horses, Mother waited in the hall and came to greet Sianna. "There's a room for you," she said. "After you've had time to wash and change, I have food and hot drinks in the solar. Come and join us there."

Later, we all dressed up for the festival, then put our heaviest cloaks over our clothes. Willow and I met Tuan at the bottom of the stairs, and we went out to the courtyard, where almost everyone in the castle had already gathered around the fire bowl. We threaded through the crowd to stand where we could watch everything.

Adana and Gil stood hand in hand. Gil looked pale, not as the swanfolk usually did, but with a greyness that showed he hadn't shaken off the effects of his bout of lung fever. They would have been getting married at this festival if Adana hadn't wanted one last year with her family. I wondered how they could bear the wait, or if Gil would live long enough for them to marry. Orla and Sianna stood together near Father.

Mother and Father faced each other across the firepit, wearing their best clothes under their heavy cloaks. A guard stood on the wall, watching the sun set. As it touched the horizon, he waved to Father, who threw off his cloak and stood in his trousers and shirt. Over it he wore a sleeveless blue robe embroidered with suns and flames. Mother's dress had sleeves and was darker blue embroidered with the same suns and flames. Father raised both arms. We fell silent to hear.

"Tonight, the sun takes her longest journey. Tonight we reach the coldest, darkest night of the year."

"But tomorrow," Mother answered him, "the sun returns, and returns sooner every day."

"We have lived into the heart of winter," said Father.

"Now we return to summer," said Mother.

They spoke together. "May all who have lived to see midwinter live to see summer come again. Let it be so!"

"Let it be so!" we answered.

Then Orla glanced at Sianna, who nodded. Orla took off her cloak and stepped forward. She wore a plain white wool gown, and a white shawl wrapped over her head and around her neck, covering her hair. Nothing showed of her but a pale face and hands, no colour but her blue eyes and her lips and cheeks, flushed with the cold. She might have been a winter spirit; in the snow, she would have all but disappeared. Against the dark cloaks of the people around the fire, she stood out like a young birch in a pine forest. She held her arms out, palms down and fingers spread, over the pile of firewood.

For a few minutes she stood there. Nobody moved or spoke. Then, far down at the bottom, under the split pieces of yellow-brown maple and pale ash, something snapped, a sound as sharp and thin as the cracking of cat-ice on a puddle. A thread of smoke spiraled up out of the pile. The small flames licked up, the dry kindling of twigs and bark crackled, and the fire caught with a sound like a breath blown out. All around the circle, people gasped.

For a minute more Orla stood, and then a branch popped and flung sparks, and everyone cheered, even as she jumped back. The fire blazed up as though it wanted to chase her.

Orla tried to look solemn, but her lips twitched, and she smiled in spite of herself, ducking her head to hide it, looking almost shy as we cheered. The shawl slipped down, revealing her hair, and she put her cloak back on and stepped back to stand beside Sianna.

Mother and Father each took a small round cake from a plate and tossed it into the fire. We all cheered and clapped. Some people tossed small things into the fire, wishes for the coming year written on the thin, white firebark or scratched onto slips of wood.

The fire snapped and danced and burned up quickly. Children ran around throwing snow at each other, and people talked in groups. Someone started up a tune on a little metal whistle, and a few couples began a ring-dance, but the musician stopped halfway through the tune. Someone always tried music outside at the winter festival, but it was too cold for anything but a metal whistle, and that was too cold for the musician's lips. The real dancing would be inside, after the food.

Mother kept Orla close all through the feast. Afterwards, Sianna came to speak to her, and Orla slid out of her chair and came to sit by me.

"It makes me tired, sometimes," she said. "All that attention, all on me. It's bad enough that Mother hardly leaves me to myself. I know she's proud of me. Sometimes it's too much."

"I didn't know. But as for tonight, what did you expect?" I said. "That was startling, lighting the fire that way. I've never seen it done before."

"It's not terribly difficult," she said.

"Tell that to somebody who can't do it," I said. "You impressed everyone tonight, my wisewoman sister."

She looked at me and smiled, the same half-shy smile she'd given when we'd cheered her fire.

"Not a wisewoman yet. I still have years of work, even after Sianna has done teaching me. I've lit small fires before. I wasn't sure I could do it with everyone watching—it's easier when you're alone. No distractions, you see. But I wanted to try, and if it didn't work, there's always the regular way."

"I had no idea wisewomen carried a flint and steel," I said.

"Oh, yes," she answered. "Magic is hard work, and sometimes the hardest part is knowing when not to use it."

"I wanted to ask you something," I said.

"What is it?"

I gnawed my lip, unsure how to start. How could such a simple question be so hard to ask?

"Well?" She looked amused. "Kiar, this isn't court, and I'm not Guthric. You don't have to pick your words with me. And Tuan may always know what you're thinking, but I don't."

I felt my cheeks heat. I saw Tuan watching me from across the hall, and I quickly looked back at Orla.

"He does not! Anyway, what has Tuan got to do with anything?"

"Oh, Kiar, everyone knows he loves you!"

"Really? At practice the other day he nearly took my leg off!"

"And would you expect him to go easy on you at practice? Not everyone in love behaves like Gil and Adana. Look at Father and Mother."

"That's different. They're our parents and older."

"From the color of your face, I think you love Tuan, too."

I didn't know how to answer. I didn't feel about Tuan the way Adana seemed to feel about Gil. That brought me back to what I'd meant to ask her.

"Orla, I wanted to ask—are you all done with Gil? He and Adana are betrothed, and you being there won't change that. You know it's no good, not for him or for you."

She looked down.

I waited for her answer, hardly daring to breathe.

"Yes," she said at last. "And also, no. He loves Adana, and I have to give up any idea that he'll love me. I'm trying to consider him a brother, because he's never thought of me as anything but a sister."

"I'm sorry," I said.

"So am I," she answered, straightening. "Sianna says a wisewoman needs balance," she said. She held her hand out and tipped it side to side. "Everyone with power must keep the balance between good and evil."

"I'd think it would be better to do magic for good, instead of keeping a balance."

"I know. You'd think that *would* be better. But if you force things to act differently from their true nature, even if you do something for good, it may cause something bad to happen. I could bring rain for our crops, but the rain would have to come from somewhere, and that place wouldn't get rain. And maybe that would mean deer would starve, and then people would starve because the hunting was bad. So to them, what I'd done would be evil."

"I see."

"I have to be very careful. Doing something that looks like good and feels good can be bad."

As Orla said this, she looked so sad, and I remembered how my joy in flying had brought the iron necklace on me.

"Isn't there a spell you could do to help? To make you not love him like that?"

She shook her head. "I wish there were. I hate the way I feel. But such spells, they're not real. You can make someone feel something, and act like the feeling is real. But it's an illusion, even to them. Deep down they don't really feel it."

"But it might make you feel better, at least for a while."

"That's true," she said, "but you need control, too, and being under a spell takes that away. Who knows what would happen?" She smiled, and I could see she was trying hard to be cheerful. "I might start with a spell to stop loving Gil and end up with a pig's nose."

"Oh!"

"That was a joke."

"Oh," I said again.

"Eventually, I'll have to get over it. I'll have to love him like a sister, because that's the only way he thinks of me. But sometimes, when I'm really tired, I feel like I'd do anything to make him love me. Let's talk about something else."

I did my best to distract her, but even in the midst of our talk her eyes turned again and again to Gil, sitting out the dancing with Adana.

CHAPTER

TWENTY-FOUR

The day after the festival, we took the branches down again. We threw the winterberry out on the snow for the wild birds and boiled the pine to make a tea against winter disease. That was another thing we seldom saw now, the winter illness that made people's teeth bleed and fall out, and their fingers and toes blacken and rot. Still, Nias made the pine-needle tea all winter. We all drank it once a day, a sharp, pungent drink that smelled of the pine boughs it was made from and made me think of the midwinter festival.

Orla and Sianna stayed for three days. After what Orla had said about how tiring Mother's attention was, I thought she would be glad to leave. She hugged us all, and this time she had nothing extra to say to Gil. I was sorry to see her go for Mother's sake, but glad for her own, and for Gil's and Adana's.

We had two more blizzards after midwinter, and then a long stretch of cloudy days with no snow. At this time of the year, it seemed spring would never arrive, until the morning we woke to sun and melting snow. After that, although it froze over each night, and even snowed a few more times, we could foresee the end of winter. We were all hungry for fresh greens. The pine-needle tea couldn't stop that.

As the last snow melted away, the river's voice became a roar you could hear day and night. Between the flattened stalks of dried grass, shoots of green poked up. We turned the horses and sheep out to pasture again, and the ewes began to have their lambs. There were four mares in foal, and the calves would come after the lambing was done.

Nias sent the children out to look for the first bitter, young edible leaves of the starflowers that grew all over the pastures.

Willow, Tuan, and I were on our way back from looking at a new foal one morning when we heard the dogs yelping. We followed the sound and saw a half dozen horses near the gate, already saddled and bridled. Men were tying bedrolls and packs to the saddles.

"I didn't know anyone was hunting today," Willow said.

Someone came out of the armoury with four spears over his shoulder, and then I saw the two kennel-men, and the hounds leashed to their waists. I counted eight dogs, the biggest hunting hounds we had.

"It's a boar hunt," I said. "Where are they going?"

"Why not here?" Willow asked.

"We haven't seen any signs of boar." I ran after the guard with the spears.

"Where's the boar?" I asked.

"Near Fellstead. Messenger this morning." he said. "Are you coming?"

"I— " I said, but my father's voice cut me off.

"Kiar, I want you to stay here," he said. "We have six going, and that's enough."

I knew what he meant; with too many horses in the woods after boar, someone would get hurt because they couldn't get out of the way fast enough. The horses used for boar were chosen to be light and fast. Father rode a rangy bay with a white foot for boar-hunting. Cloud was strong and willing, but the bay was nimble.

"We could go along, stay back, and watch," Willow said to me. "It looks exciting."

"That's one word for it," I said. "I don't think there's any safe place in a boar hunt. You've never seen how they come at you."

"They're taking a pack horse," she said.

"That's for the meat and hides, afterwards." I crossed my fingers behind my back for luck; sometimes, the pack horse carried back an injured hound or man, or a dead one.

As the last bedrolls were tied into place and the spears settled, Mother arrived to see Father off.

"Keep my place warm," Father said, and kissed her. He looked at me. "I'm counting on you to support your mother."

What support could she possibly need, when the only danger was a boar in the west at Near Fellstead?

"I'll do that, Father," I said.

Willow elbowed me. "You could ask if we could go. It's not fair that you miss all the excitement."

"To tell you the truth," I said, "a boar hunt is more excitement than I want right now. I've seen what those tusks can do. I'll take a couple of quiet days instead."

We could count on Father being gone for at least week. It was two full days' ride to Near Fellstead farmstead. They'd give the horses a day of rest before going after the boar, and another before the two days' ride back. It was very likely the oats at Near Fellstead had brought out the boar. With any luck, they would kill it before it did too much damage to the crops.

In the mornings, Dar put us through sword practice, but Willow, Tuan, and I spent afternoons riding around the fields, tying trimmings of hair to stakes set at the edges of the planting. Most of the men had trimmed their hair and their winter-long beards. We kept the trimmings carefully wrapped in cloth and took them out in small amounts to set around the fields. Deer smelled the hair and stayed clear of our crops, but the clippings had to be renewed every couple of weeks. It was light work and let us get away from the castle for a while.

On the evening of the third day, while we lingered by the fire after supper, Dar entered the hall. He came straight towards us. Behind him a boy jogged, vainly trying to keep up.

I felt my heart jump. Was this the same messenger who had brought word of the boars? Had something happened to my father?

"Lady Kiar," Dar said, stopping in front of us. "A message for you."

I looked at the boy, and he gave me the salute people gave my father.

"Princess," he said, "I'm Donel, from Stony Ridge." I recognized the name of the farmstead, one of the two where we rested on our way to patrol the northern border. "Yesterday we found the remains of a sheep in the outer pasture. At first we thought it was wolves, but this sheep was butchered with knives. When we looked around, we found a ring of stones and a dead fire."

"How many people?" I asked.

"We've seen nobody, Princess," he said, "but someone had picketed horses, driven stakes in the ground. We counted five. There wasn't much left of the sheep but bones. A small one, but still more than one man could eat."

"Bandits, maybe," I said.

"I don't know, Princess. They left a trail, but we thought better of following it."

"If it's armed men, and a band of them," Dar said, "they might be trying the water, so to speak."

"How would Gythorn know the king's away?" I asked.

"He has wisemen and wisewomen," Dar said.

"Whoever it is, I'll have to do something about it." I looked at the boy. "Thank you, Donel." I waved one of the women over and asked her to get Donel something from the kitchen. "Dar, come with me to Father's chamber."

"Yes, Lady Kiar," Dar said.

"If you're going, we're coming with you," Willow said. "Tuan and me. Right?" She leaned around me to look at Tuan. He nodded.

"It's probably nothing, only some wanderers who'll need to be shown off," I said. But I felt a knot in my stomach. Could

Gythorn really know Father was away? Maybe I should ask Mother what to do.

No, Dar had brought Donel directly to me, not to Mother. I could deal with this myself.

"Ten fighters," I said. "If we outnumber them enough, they may leave peacefully. We don't want to look like we think they're a serious threat, but we want them to know we can defend ourselves."

"Bows and spears?" Tuan said.

"Yes. Three or four really good archers. Spears for everyone, as well as swords. I hope it won't come to a fight, but we need to be prepared." I chewed my lip, thinking. "We'll be sleeping out one night, maybe more. We'll leave early tomorrow."

"I'll talk to Nias about food," Willow said.

"Thank you. Tuan, can you get a party together?" I gave him half a dozen names of men, and he went to find them.

"Lady Kiar," Dar said. "Your orders for me?"

"You don't have to be formal, Dar," I said, "Nobody can hear but me. You were calling me 'young Kiar' this morning at practice."

"Your pardon, Lady, but you're the leader now, not only the king's daughter. What are your orders?"

"I'm going to leave you in charge of the castle. My mother has no idea how to defend anything, and she'll need you."

"Begging your pardon, Lady, but Cole is younger than I am, and faster at getting up and down and about if it comes to a brisk defense. I'd prefer to leave him here and come with you." He clasped his hands behind him and stood waiting. I'd just told him what I wanted, and instead of agreeing, he was proposing something different.

"You said ten," he said when I didn't speak. "You have nine in your party now, counting your two shadows. I'd make ten. Will you fight?"

"I hope I don't have to. Whoever it is, they'll have more sense than to take on a larger force on our own ground. We'll track them and find out what they're up to, then get them across our borders. But, yes, I'll fight if I have to. And Donel will probably come back with us, and that's ten."

"He's a boy. Willing and all, but he hasn't had your training," Dar said. "I'm asking to come with you."

"It's five men. They probably won't give us any trouble. Besides, you know what patrol is like, Dar. It's sleeping on the ground and looking for people we can't find."

His eyes glinted. "Right up until you do find them, and then it's apt to become interesting. You know I couldn't face your father if I let you go off alone and get hurt."

"I'm not going *alone*, Dar," I said. "I'll have a party, and well-armed at that. Nothing's going to happen to me."

"Nevertheless, I'm answerable to the king when he comes back, and there are questions I'd rather he didn't have to ask me."

"Someone has to stay here. All the guard are answerable to the king, and I can't take them all."

"Lady, I'm not asking you to take them all."

"No, you aren't. You're just asking me to take one of the best."

"You'll leave lots of guards behind, and some of the best among them. Cole is one. But if it's a small party you're taking, you need skilled and experienced fighters to back you up. One of the best would be a good idea."

I threw up my hands. "Fine! Come, then, and don't blame me if they turn out to be a bunch of ragtag wanderers who just need seeing off. You'll be bored, uncomfortable, and cold, most likely, with nothing to tell for it."

Dar bowed. "Thank you, Lady."

"Get your things. Be ready to leave at first light."

"As you wish, Lady." He bowed again and turned.

"And if my mother comes around with questions, send her to me."

"Yes, Lady."

"And Dar. Stop calling me 'Lady'!"

"Yes, Lady Kiar." He grinned and left.

"As you wish, Lady," I muttered to myself. It hadn't gone as I'd wished at all, but if things didn't go smoothly, I knew I'd be happy to have Dar with me.

I left the council chamber and took the stairs to my room two at a time. I knew I'd have to talk to Mother before I left, but it would be easier to do when I was ready to go. With the horses saddled and the men assembled, she would see I couldn't be talked out of going. I wanted a good night's sleep if I'd be camping tomorrow night.

I was sitting on the bed, taking my boots off, when Mother appeared at my door. She paused only a moment, then swept in and stood before me.

"What's this, Kiar?" she said. "Elena tells me you're going after a raiding party."

"That was quick. And it's not a raiding party, Mother. So far, all they've done is take a sheep. It's nothing I can't handle." I had to look up at her, and it irritated me. I dropped my boot and stood up in my bare feet. Now she had to look up to me slightly. That surprised me. When had I become taller than my mother?

"You could get hurt, swanling. Let the men take care of it. Dar could lead a party, or Cole. There's no need for you to run into danger."

"Unless you're going to ride out yourself, this is my responsibility!" I put my hand on the iron necklace. "I'm not a swan-woman, to stay with the nest and let the cobs fight!"

I'd never spoken as sharply to her in my life. She recoiled as though I'd bitten her.

"Of course, Kiar. I'm sorry." she stopped abruptly.

"I'm taking Dar, if that makes a difference," I said more quietly. "I'll have ten fighters with me, Mother. Now, we're leaving at first light, and I need to sleep."

For a moment I thought she would argue, but she gave me a small smile.

"When did you become so fierce, swanling? Good night, then." She kissed my cheek.

"Good night, Mother," I said.

She turned and left.

In the morning, I wasn't surprised when Mother came out to see us off. Some of the men were mounted already, and I'd just put my foot in the stirrup when I saw her. I took it out and waited for her to come over, braced for a last-minute argument.

"Be careful, Kiar," she said. "Send word on your way back, and I'll have Nias prepare a feast."

"What, for throwing out a bunch of strays?"

"Never you mind. Just send word."

"All right," I said. If it made her feel better to give me a feast, I could let her have that. I hugged her and kissed her cheek in return, then mounted and led the men and horses out in the grey morning light.

There were eleven of us, with Donel on a cobby brown horse that looked more used to pulling a plough than carrying a messenger on urgent business.

"You should rest," I said. "You've done enough, and someone at the farm can show us where to start looking."

"It'll save time if I come with you, Princess." He set his jaw. I thought about how I'd feel, being made to stay behind if my home was in danger.

"As long as you can keep up," I said.

He nodded.

"We'll take it steady today," I said. "We'll sleep out tonight and catch them up tomorrow. I want to spare the horses, and save our strength, especially if we might have a fight."

Nobody said anything, but as I turned Kestrel to ride her through the gate, the guard gave me the king's salute.

We rode north throughout the day, alternately walking and trotting. Willow, Tuan, and I rode together, slightly ahead of the main party. Nobody talked much. Donel rode off to one side, sometimes ranging ahead. We all took turns scouting, looking for anything out of place. I was glad of Donel's presence. He'd ridden this way most recently, and as we travelled farther away from the castle and our daily territory, he'd be the most likely to discover something out of place. Late in the afternoon, when the sun had fallen low, but the sky wasn't yet red, Dar came up beside me.

"Young Donel's spotted our usual camping place," he said with a smile. "Says there's a little hollow on top of the next ridge where the ground is dry. A nice little firepit, all ringed with stones."

I smiled back.

"I suppose this is what Father would call 'leaving our mark,'" I said. "Let's stop here. It's a short day's ride to the farmstead tomorrow, call it midafternoon when we get there. We'll have time to find our friends and deal with them, unless they've left already. Oh, and Dar," I said, "thank Donel, and tell him I hardly ever bite, will you? He could have talked to me himself."

Dar grinned and flicked his fingers to his forehead.

"I'll tell him," he said, and dropped back.

"What about tomorrow?" Willow said. "What are you going to do?"

"Get to Stony Ridge in the afternoon. Find the camp and track them from there. Five or six people are going to leave signs, especially if they're hunting."

"Or killing sheep," Willow said. "If they wanted to go unnoticed, why kill a sheep? Someone was bound to realize it was missing."

"Maybe they want to be noticed," Tuan said.

The same thing had occurred to me. All day I'd been thinking about that sheep, and how the fire and picket marks had been left for anyone to find. If they wanted to sneak in and out quietly, they would have avoided the farmsteads, or left the sheep alone, or at least buried the evidence.

The more I thought about it, the less certain I was we'd be dealing with scavengers and strays, outcasts living around the edges and hiding when they could.

I wasn't completely certain of who was waiting for us at the end of our journey, but I was sure that whoever it was had meant for us to come and find them.

CHAPTER

TWENTY-FIVE

T he night was quiet. We kept watch, but nothing disturbed the camp, save for some owls and hunting foxes. At first light, we rode on, and towards mid-morning, Donel rode up. He saluted me as he'd seen the men do.

"Lady. We found the remains of the fire a bit farther along."

"Then you lead," I said. He nodded and nudged his horse forward. After a while, we saw a patch of moving black through the grass, and then five ravens flew up, their wings flashing in the morning sun.

"Nothing to worry about there," said one of the men. "Looks like a common thief, Lady." A chuckle went around.

"What does he mean?" Willow asked.

"Ravens tell the future," I said. "We have a verse. *One for peace, and two for war, three for the stranger at the door. Four for the lover, five for the thief, six for joy and seven for grief.*"

It didn't take us long to reach the abandoned campsite. Even if the ravens hadn't shown us the carcass, the air stirred by their wings brought the smell of rot. The sheep carcass had been well picked over, but there were still enough scraps for that.

There were too many bones for one sheep, and then I saw the small skull, kicked to one side.

"They killed a ewe in lamb," I said. That was doubly wrong—to steal a sheep was one thing, but these thieves had stolen a piece of Stony Ridge's future. Dar and I walked over to the fire pit, and he bent down to feel the coals.

"Well cold, but not too scattered. I'd say this was last night's fire. With any luck, we'll find them today and get them sent on their way." He stood up again.

We didn't need a tracker—the horses had left a beaten path across the grass, curving north and west.

"It's as if they don't care if we find them, Lady," Dar said, "Or else they want us to."

"That's what I think," I said. "Maybe testing us, with Father away."

"Too bad for them, then." Dar grinned at me. His confidence made me feel both better and worse. If a seasoned fighter thought we were up to this challenge, we probably were. On the other hand, I'd never had to fight outside of practice, and I'd never had to be the leader.

Dar put his hand on my shoulder.

"Every warrior has to strike a first blow, Kiar," he said. "If you do it today, well, sixteen is earlier than many."

I forced a smile. "Did you have birds in your stomach before your first fight?"

Dar grinned back. "No, Lady. I heaved them all onto my horse's neck. And I wasn't the first nor the last to do that. None of us would think the worse of you."

"So before the fight, I get to heave my guts out. I'm looking forward to this more and more."

When we returned to the horses, Willow reined Whiffle over. "I could fly ahead and scout. It would save time tracking them," she said.

"No," I answered. "They're probably from Noermark. I don't want you shot."

"You know what the queen said. They probably won't shoot to kill."

"Worse. Then they'd have a hostage."

She opened her mouth, then closed it and nodded.

We followed the track at a trot all through the afternoon. When the sun was midway down the sky, Tuan pointed. To the west, a trickle of smoke curled up through the clear air beyond a small copse of oaks.

"Bold beggars," someone said. "Sneak up and surround them, then?

"No," I said. "We'll ride in openly. This is our land, not theirs. I want archers on both sides, ready to shoot on my word. Spears ready, too, but no attack until I give the signal. Dar," I waved him over and reined Kestrel in close to his brown horse Dancer.

"What is it, Lady?"

"If anything happens to me, or, I mean, if I can't—" I let the words trail off.

"Lady, if you fall gloriously in battle, I will take command."
He flickered me a salute.

"This is serious," I said. "I could freeze or forget how to use my sword."

"So you could, but you won't." He turned away and waved the archers out to flank us. I put on my helmet and slipped my little round shield with its central boss of rough crystal over my left forearm. Behind me, I heard the men arming. Tuan and Willow rode up to flank me, both looking strange and serious behind the nose and cheek guards around their faces.

"Let's go," I said, and kneed Kestrel forward.

They had built their fire in the shelter of the oaks. Four men squatted around it, and a fifth stood with the horses picketed a few paces away. I couldn't help admiring the horses. Even the plainest of them was beautiful. The horses alone said the party was from Noermark.

The men were a contrast to their fine horses. I had thought Guthric looked warlike and even rough in his feast clothes, but he was nothing next to these men. Their clothes were smudged with smoke and dirt, as anyone's would be after days camping out and hunting, but their hair looked as though it had been braided weeks before and neither washed nor combed since. Three had dark hair, one red; the fifth was grey as a rat, and his face seamed with wrinkles. Every head turned as I rode in, Dar on my right, Tuan on my left, and Willow beyond him, three others spread out behind. One man spat into the fire.

"You look for something?" another said. His accent would have told me his country, even if I hadn't been able to see him.

"Yes," I said, "I'm looking for the shortest path back to Noermark to put you on."

The one who had spoken turned to the man among the horses.

"Hey, Hafor?" he called, "King Tir sends girl to chase us!"

"Are no men in Valenia?" another muttered. Behind me, I heard a stir among my own men. Then the one among the horses stepped forward.

He looked as rough as his fellows, but better dressed, his clothes a little finer. I knew who he was immediately. He had a look of Othar about him, but grey-eyed, and fairer in color. His hair was pale as flax, and he had a sharp look. If he were a dog, I thought, he would bite. I ignored the men at the fire; if they needed dealing with, Dar would be watching.

"You're out of your own lands, Prince Hafor," I said. "Perhaps you missed your way. We'll be happy to escort you back into it."

"Princess Kiar," he said, dusting his hands on his pants. "The gosling among swans. Fine words to say to guests on your land on first meeting." His accent was fainter, and he seemed comfortable with our speech. I understood some of the language of Noermark and spoke a little, but I couldn't match his skill with ours.

"Guests don't lurk around the walls," I said. "They come to the door."

"Well, as you say, we lost our way." He tilted his head and looked at me, smiling faintly. "Or perhaps not. My fellows and I think this looks very much like Noermark, and it might be you, Lady, who has strayed out of her way."

There it was. If I showed doubt or indecision, Gythorn would have his first foothold in Valenia. One of the men at the fire chuckled, and my nervousness disappeared.

"You are wrong," I said. "These are my lands, and I will see you off them today. There are enough of us here to kill you all twice over. Take your warning and go now."

"Does King Tir think we take girl's order?" one of the men said.

Hafor looked past me at Dar.

"I will fight you for this piece of ground," he said. "The winner stays, the loser goes home. Agreed?"

Dar said nothing. I saw Hafor's brows rise.

"Or maybe you're afraid to fight?"

"Speak to Lady Kiar," Dar said. "We're under her orders."

"I see," Hafor said. He paused, then said to Dar, "I don't fight women."

"You're afraid to fight me?" I asked.

His head snapped around, and he looked at me as though Kestrel had spoken. Then he grinned. But there was no humour in it.

"Fierce words, Lady. Perhaps not a gosling after all, but a wildcat," said Hafor. "Very well, then. Will you try your claws on me? Your men and mine will stand aside, and you and I fight."

"Agreed." I said. His eyes widened the tiniest bit; he was surprised at my answer. "Sword and shield only," I added, "on foot, no one else to interfere. In the circle."

"It need not be to the death," he said.

A cold rage filled me. "In a quarter of an hour," I said, then turned Kestrel and trotted her out of earshot of the camp. All my doubts fell away, and the birds in my stomach came to rest. He thought I was afraid, and I was. I'd never fought outside of practice, and the peace of Valenia might rest on how I did now, in my first real fight. But Hafor thought I was afraid because I was a woman.

Willow brought Whiffle up beside me. "What are you doing?"

"He started by ignoring me and challenging Dar," I said. "Then he thought I wouldn't fight. Now he thinks he's being generous by saying it's not to the death. He's trying to make me look weak. He's trying to make me *feel* weak!"

"Get down," Dar said, dismounting.

I obeyed, and he brought Kestrel around to shield us from the eyes of the men of Noermark. He gave Kestrel's reins to Willow and put his hands on my shoulders.

"Is there anything you need to get rid of beforehand? Now would be the time."

"No, the birds have settled," I said.

"Good. Let's get you ready." He squeezed my shoulders and dropped his hands.

"He doesn't want to kill you," Tuan said, and Willow nodded agreement.

"No, he wants to beat me in front of my men on my own ground," I said. I shook out my legs to get the feel of riding out of them.

"Lady, there's a level spot over here," said Donel. I walked over and looked. A few tussocks of grass bumped up from the earth. I kicked one or two, and they parted without resistance. I nodded.

"Tuan, you get the men around this half of the circle," Dar said. "Lady, where will you start?"

I looked at the sun, falling away to the west.

"In the south," I said. "He can have the north. Nobody starts with the sun in their eyes."

"Good." He tugged at my sword-belt. "Get rid of this. You won't need the scabbard. Lose anything you don't have to carry. Take off your tunic and wear your body armour over your shirt." He started to unbuckle the strap over my left shoulder, and I undid the one on my left side.

"Should I cut off my braid?" I'd never thought about my hair in practice, but maybe Hafor would use it to get hold of me. I pulled the tunic over my head and the air felt chill through my linen shirt. I slid my body armour back on. Dar fastened the shoulders, tugging to snug the boiled leather tighter against my body, taking up the slack for my missing tunic.

"No, tuck it down your back," he said. "Turn your head to get some slack. Better?"

"Yes." I felt absurdly happier. I hadn't wanted to cut my hair off.

"Good. Don't watch the sword; you'll see it soon enough if it moves. Watch the eyes—that's where he'll give away his blows."

I drew my sword, and we walked over to the circle.

"Good luck," Willow said as she took her place. Tuan squeezed my shoulder as he passed behind me, his thumb and forefinger touching my neck above my shirt. My folk, including Donel, stood ranged around the south half of the circle. Hafor's men came to stand around the north. I waited, ignoring the gooseflesh rising on my arms and back in the chill.

Hafor took his time coming into the circle. He, too, had taken off his tunic and wore his armour over his shirt. He stood a head taller than I; his reach and his sword were longer. I'd have to be quick.

He swung his sword loosely in a circle and smiled.

"Are you ready to dance, Princess Kiar?" he asked.

"When you're done talking," I said.

His smile disappeared, and he stepped forward and to his right. I moved to stay opposite him, but also stepped forward, and for a few paces we spiraled in. He flicked the tip of his sword in a small circle, and I glanced at it, then back to his face. As he lifted his foot again, I charged.

I was inside his reach before he could react. I thrust with my shield and saw the tip of his sword swing wildly away. My own sword bit into the top of his shield and as he stepped back for room to swing again, I pressed forward. I caught his next two blows, but on the third stroke, the tip of his sword slipped under my shield and sliced across the top of my boot. Pain flared up my calf.

A cheer went up from the men of Noermark. I faltered, and Hafor stepped forward and leaned into another blow. I caught it, but over his shield he grinned.

"First blood," he said. "Are you hurt, lady gosling?"

He snapped blow after blow. I returned them, even as I caught them on my shield. In the middle of the ringing rhythm of sword-on-shield the battle feeling came over me, where the body makes decisions and frees the mind to pay attention to the adversary. Hafor wanted me to back up, to become used to backing up. If he didn't step away and take advantage of his reach, he could still force me to step out of the circle, which would mean he'd won.

My skin no longer felt chilly, and my shirt clung a little to my back and shoulders. A strand of hair stuck near the corner of my left eye, an irritation I couldn't do anything about. Hafor's blows were falling high, then low, as he forced me to protect my head, then my leg with the small shield, making a rhythm like a dance. I couldn't fall into that rhythm; if I did, he'd break it and catch me off guard.

Pressed as close as I was, I still had room to stab. It was a small advantage, and I used it where I could. Every time his shield moved, I tried to get the point of my sword past it. I couldn't stay here forever; his greater weight and strength would wear me down. Already, it was harder to breathe, and I could hear Hafor's breath rasping, too. I had to finish this while I still had strength.

The next time he struck, I punched with my shield, aiming the rough crystal boss in the center at Hafor's wrist. The tip of his sword slid over the top of my shield and rang against my helmet, then skittered across the face guard. Something touched my brow, over the eye. Instinct said to step back; instead, I shoved forward as hard as I could and turned my right shoulder into Hafor's chest.

He gave back two stumbling steps, and I followed, keeping the gap closed between us, drawing back just enough to use my sword, hammering blows and feeling nothing on my own shield. A red haze clouded my vision, and my own blood beat so hard in my ears that I heard nothing else. I felt a fury that had nothing to do with anger, only the drive to keep up the attack until my enemy disappeared. I couldn't even feel his sword on my shield anymore.

I twisted my blade and shoved, felt it slide and ring against the metal that bound the edge of the shield. The point of it caught, slid down, then pulled free again. It was only later that I remembered hearing Hafor suck in his breath.

Then he disappeared, and there was a wall of shields in front of me. A bearded face shouted words I didn't understand, angry and urgent. I pressed forward and stabbed again, but my sword struck only leather over wood. Then the noise in my ears became voices.

"Lady, enough! It's done!"

"Kiar, stop!"

I sprang back, shield raised and sword at guard, panting. Something tickled my left eye, and my nose under my helmet. I blinked, feeling liquid running into my eye. I shook my head impatiently.

"Kiar, you've won!" Willow shouted.

Slowly, I lowered my shield and sword, then shook my shield from my arm, wiped the hair away from my left eye and rubbed at the tickle down the left side of my nose. My fingers came away bloody, and it was only then that I felt the sting of a cut on my eyebrow.

Hafor stepped out from behind the shields of his men, gripping his right wrist in his left hand. His leather body armour was sliced across the right ribs, angling down to his hip, and blood showed on the brown leather. If I'd been a little quicker, or he a little slower to jump back, I could have gutted him.

"A good fight, Lady," he said.

"Leave now," I said. The battle rage was ebbing, but it left me no patience for courtesy.

"Yes." He walked towards me, but his eyes were on something beyond me on the ground. I turned and saw his sword lying near the edge of the circle. Tuan stepped forward to stand between Hafor and his sword.

"Princess Kiar," Hafor said, "tell your man to give me my sword."

"No," I said. "I think we'll keep it. You owe me something for trespassing on my land, and for the killing of a ewe in lamb. I'll consider your sword payment enough."

"That sword is worth more than ten sheep," he said.

I said nothing. He hesitated, and I thought for a moment he would try to take the sword, but he turned away. A cheer went up from my men.

Dar came forward and gently took my sword from my hand.

"Well done," he said. "Your father will be proud of you, which is more than can be said of *him*." He glanced over at Hafor. The prince stood aside from the campfire. One of his men kicked earth over it, while two more saddled the horses. The grey-haired man stood with Hafor, one of his hands on the prince's shoulder, and spoke while Hafor looked aside, not meeting anyone's eyes, and worked at the shoulder strap of his armour.

"Let's look after those cuts," Dar said.

"When they're gone," I said, nodding at Hafor's men. Dar stood with me, and we watched as everybody mounted but Hafor and the grey man. The grey man had bent to examine the prince's body. He poked gently at the wound and Hafor winced.

"The border's that way," I said, jerking my chin to the north.

The grey man said something to Hafor, who shook his head. For a moment nobody spoke, then the grey man came towards me. He held up his empty right hand and stopped a few paces away.

"Lady Kiar," he said. His voice was rough, but he spoke courteously. "We go—we will go to our king. We tell him your valour, Lady Kiar. Maybe no more raids, if Valenia women are so, yah?"

"Go in peace," I said.

He nodded and turned back to his companions, already on their horses. He mounted and the five rode off without a backward glance.

"Someone needs to follow them," I said.

"A good idea," Dar said. "You, you, and you. Three archers, two other swords. Make sure they cross the border. Catch up with us after."

"As good as done," someone said. Two of the men staying behind handed extra food to those leaving. They'd be a day getting to the border and another day back to Stony Ridge.

"Come and sit now," Dar said.

I bent to pick up my shield and thought for a moment I'd fall, but someone grabbed my left arm and pulled it over his shoulder. I turned my head and looked into Tuan's eyes. He put his arm around me and walked me over to a large stone. By the time I reached it, I was trembling all over and ready to sit. My leg hurt, and my brow, and a wide stain of blood had spread down across my boot and seeped up my trouser leg. I pulled my helmet off and pressed my fingers to my face, feeling the cut edges of my eyebrow and the welling blood.

"Tuan, when I get her boot off, press on the wound," Dar said. "This will hurt, I'm afraid, Lady." He pulled the boot off in one quick movement, and I gasped. Beneath the boot leather, my trouser leg was slashed and soaked with blood. Tuan pushed the fabric up to my knee and put one hand on my calf, holding the edges of the wound together. His fingers, pale against my bloody leg, were warm on my skin. With a wet cloth, he wiped the blood away from around the wound, then held the wound closed for a minute or two. When he lifted his hand from my leg and wiped carefully around the cut, the blood barely seeped. The cut was much shorter than I'd thought it would be.

Dar handed Tuan a wineskin. He squirted something from it over the cut; I jumped and cried aloud.

"Spirits of wine," Dar said. He was grinning. "Stings, doesn't it? Now you know why we're so careful not to get wounded in battle. The doctoring hurts worse." I grinned back, then winced as Tuan put a cloth wet with spirits of wine on the cut. I gritted my teeth, and Tuan looked up at Dar.

"Not too bad. I won't have to sew you up," Dar said. I must have made a sound, because he grinned. "What, didn't you know I could sew, Lady? It's a useful trick in the field. Not much to look at, but it does the job. However, you're spared my needlework today, at least. Have some of this. You'll feel better." He passed Tuan a roll of bandage, then took the wineskin from him and handed it to me.

I took a swallow. It burned my mouth and throat and made my eyes water.

"Take another," Dar said, "it'll do you good."

I obeyed. In spite of my shaking hands, I hardly missed my mouth at all.

Tuan wrapped my leg snugly and set my bare foot on the ground. He stood up.

"Look up," he said.

I turned my face up and closed my eyes as he gently wiped the blood away from my forehead and face. When he examined the cut, I felt again how warm his hands were. This time I was ready for the sting of the spirits of wine across my eyebrow. The pain ran in a line up onto my forehead and touched my cheekbone. To my relief, it completely missed the eyelid.

"Good work, Tuan," Dar said. "That cut's not so much bad as messy. Head wounds bleed a lot, even little ones. He missed the eye. You'll live, Lady."

"Good," I said. Then I threw up. The spirits of wine burned as much coming up as they had going down.

When I'd finished and rinsed my mouth, Willow stepped forward.

"Do you want to rest, Kiar?"

I shook my head. I was tired, but now that it was over, I didn't want to stay here. The wet cloth Tuan had used on my injuries lay beside me on the stone and I picked it up and slowly wiped my own blood from my left hand.

"Here," Tuan said, and poured water over my hands.

When I'd wiped them again, there was only a little blood clinging to the places around my nails and the lines of my knuckles. "I want to go home," I said. Only after it was out did I realize how childish it must sound, and I felt my face go hot. I bent over and eased my boot up over Dar's neat bandage. When I stood up and put my weight on my foot, the leg hurt. I bent my knee and put most of my weight on my right foot.

"You can rest at the farm," Donel said, "We have room to sleep all of you. If you wish, Princess."

"That sounds good," I said. "I promised Mother I'd send word. She wanted to have a feast ready."

"I'll go," said Willow. "I'm the lightest, and Whiffle wants a run."

"You won't make it tonight," I said.

"I'll make it most of the way. We can rest a few hours and go on when the moon rises." She pulled off her helmet and shook her dark hair loose around her. She hugged me, mounted and was gone, Whiffle's hoof beats fading as she galloped away.

Dar boosted me into my saddle as though I were a child. "You try to lift yourself on that leg, you'll be bleeding again," he said when I objected.

We rode back towards the farmstead. My body ached, and my hands trembled. I'd been bruised and cut before in practice. We all had little scars, and the blood didn't bother me. But Hafor had hurt me and gloated over it. Perhaps he could have killed me, if he'd wanted to. Now that it was over, the thought of how it might have gone otherwise shook me.

When we came within sight of Stony Ridge, Donel galloped ahead.

"I suppose they'll need to hear it all," I said.

"You won't have to say a thing," Dar said, "We'll tell the story."

I shook my head. "I'm not sure it's wise of me to let you do that."

"Ah, but you have no choice, Lady, because every one of us will be telling it out of your hearing anyway." He sounded unnecessarily cheerful about it.

As we rode up to the farmstead, people ran in from outbuildings. Donel rode ahead of us at a gallop and shouted something, and we heard the cheering.

When we reached the farmstead, it looked as though everyone on it had gathered to welcome us.

"This is my mother, Marin, and my father, Rafe," Donel said to me.

"You are welcome here, Lady," Rafe said. Then his face crinkled into a smile. "I look forward to hearing your story."

"Let the girl get a change of clothes first, and a meal!" Marin said, then flushed and looked at me. "No disrespect meant, Lady."

"I'd love a change of clothes," I said. My trouser leg was brown and set into stiff crinkles of dried blood. The smell annoyed me.

Marin took me to a room with a bed and helped me out of my boots and trousers. She clucked over my leg and eyebrow. Some blood had soaked through the bandage and Marin clucked over that, too.

"Let me get you a fresh bandage," she said.

"Thank you, but this will do. I'm afraid if I take it off, it'll bleed again. My mother will look after me when I get home."

"Do you need something for the pain, Lady?" she asked. "I have a tea that helps. Bitter enough to curl your tongue, but it takes away the pain, and you'll sleep easier."

"Yes, I'd like that," I said. "Mostly I need rest, I think, and something to eat. And to make sure the men aren't making more of this than they should."

A shout of laughter went up outside the door.

"Too late for that, Lady," Marin said. "Do you want your boots?"

"No," I said. "I'll leave them until I have to put them on."

She found me another pair of trousers to wear and helped me with them.

"I'll rinse these out," she said, gathering up my bloody trousers before I could object. She hurried out the door, and I took a couple of deep breaths and walked out barefoot to the main room.

For a few seconds, nobody noticed me at the door between the two rooms. I saw the men who had followed me seated around the table among the farmstead folk. There was already food on the table; the smell of meat and fresh bread made my mouth water and my stomach growl.

It was Tuan who noticed me first. He stood up from his place beside Dar, and then everybody fell silent.

"...greybeard was the only one to show her..." a voice trailed off. Everyone turned and looked at me.

"Lady Kiar," Dar said. Then he poured something into a cup and brought it to me.

"Come and eat, Princess Kiar," said Rafe.

"Thank you," I said, taking the cup from Dar.

"Water first," he said. "I imagine you'll want it."

The water tasted sweet and fresh. Three men jumped up from the table to make a place for me. I sat down between Dar and Tuan.

Someone brought me a plate heaped with meat and vegetables, and bread still warm enough to melt the butter spread over it. Donel's father put a cup of ale at my place.

"This smells wonderful," I said.

Rafe bowed. "Thank you, Lady Kiar. And thank you for driving off the raiders."

"It's probably not as good a story as the men are making of it," I said. There were things they wouldn't know to put in—the birds in my stomach, my fear of throwing up in front of Hafor, and of losing.

"I doubt that," he said. "Eat now, Lady, and let us enjoy your victory."

I spent several minutes eating steadily and ignoring the talk around me. Neither Tuan nor Dar interrupted me with conversation. When I'd finished my first plateful, Marin appeared with another helping of everything, and a cup of the hot, bitter tea for pain.

"I put some honey in it," she said. "It's still not the most pleasant drink."

"Thank you," I said.

When I couldn't eat any more, I slid my plate to the side. Someone took it away, and Dar stood up.

"You'll want to see this, Lady," he said. Another of the men came forward with something long wrapped in a piece of cloth. He laid it on the table in front of me. I pulled the ends of the cloth back to reveal Hafor's sword.

"The smiths of Noermark make good blades," someone said.

It was true. The blade was a long, bright tooth, as wide as three fingers at the hilts, and tapered evenly to the point. Even lying on the table, it looked dangerous. It had bitten me twice. The grip, wrapped with leather, looked well-used. A smooth-polished oval of dark-red stone, veined in white and black, was set in the pommel.

I picked it up. Although it was a little too big for my hand, and too long for my reach, I could feel that it was well-balanced. The light slipped up the blade and revealed waved lines in the metal. I'd heard of their watered-steel swords before, but never seen one close. I heard breaths drawn in all around the table.

"How do they do that?" asked one of the farmstead folk.

"I don't know," I said. "Dar? Do you?"

"No, Lady. Sylard might. That's a lovely thing."

"It is," I said, and laid it back down on the cloth. Then I looked around at the farmstead folk. "I took that in payment for their trespass, and for your sheep. Shall I leave it with you?"

Rafe thrust his hand out and waved the offer away.

"Don't leave that here, Lady," he said. "I'd never sleep sound with that thing around the place. Take it back with you."

"Very well, then," I said, "I'll do that, and send you sheep from our flocks instead."

He looked relieved, but past his shoulder Donel stared at the sword.

"We owe Donel something, too, for his quick warning. Can you spare him to come back with us for a few days? He could choose the sheep we send."

So it was that when we left the next morning, Donel of Stony Ridge came along with us.

CHAPTER

TWENTY-SIX

We rode home gently; there was no need to tire the horses, and I still ached from the fight the day before, both in body and mind. In spite of my victory, I was sad. I'd heard the men talking of this on patrol, how after a fight it seemed for a while as though the colour had gone out of the world, but it was the first time I'd ever felt it myself. By mid-morning, the feeling had passed. My leg still ached badly around the cut, and my eyebrow felt puffy. Even with Marin's tea, my leg had made it hard to sleep steadily. I knew that once Mother saw my injuries I would be in for some fussing and doctoring.

We'd been away only four days, but when the walls of the castle came into sight, I was as glad to be home as if it had been a year. As we rode through the gate, the guard saluted me again as he would have my father. Mother, Adana, Gil, and half the house folk waited at the castle door. To my surprise, Orla stood beside Mother. She must have come home after I left. I saw Mother's eyes flicker over me, but I couldn't tell whether she was relieved to see me back whole or alarmed about the cut on my face and the blood on my boot.

I dismounted awkwardly to the right, and Tuan supported part of my weight as my left leg came down. Someone took Kestrel's reins. Then I walked forward, feeling the jar of my left foot hitting the ground with every step as I tried not to show it.

Mother stepped forward and put her arms around me. "Welcome home, swanling," she whispered. Then she stepped back, gave me a formal kiss on the cheek, and said, "Welcome back, Princess Kiar. When you've rested, we'll have a feast and hear your story."

"Thank you," I said, then assumed formality as she had done. "Thank you, my lady Queen. I look forward to it." I saw Mother's mouth curve up slightly; she squeezed my shoulders and let me go.

Orla rushed to hug me. "You're hurt!"

"Nothing much," I said. "Why are you here?"

"Too long to tell now. You need some stitches, I think."

Orla reached to touch my eyebrow and I caught her hand. "I'll let you hurt me later, all right?"

"It might sicken," she said. "There could be something in it."

"Only half a skin of spirits of wine. Tuan poured at least that onto it, I'm sure."

"No, he didn't," Willow said, coming up beside her. "I haven't told them anything, Kiar, except that you won and were coming home."

Adana put her arms around me. "I'm glad you're home safely," she said, and kissed my cheek.

I hugged her back, noticing I was as tall as she was now. She felt little and fragile, but her arms were strong, and when she hugged me hard, I couldn't breathe.

Adana let me go and hugged Tuan. When he returned her embrace, the width of his shoulders hid her.

"I'm glad you were with Kiar," Adana said. "I knew you'd watch her back."

The stairs up to my room seemed longer and steeper than I remembered. When I finally sat on the bed I shared with Willow to ease my boots off, Orla entered with her healer's bag. She put a double handful of something into the steaming water basin, laid a white cloth on the bed beside me, and placed a threaded needle on top.

"Don't touch that," she said to me. "I've boiled the thread, so it's very clean."

"Dar said I didn't need stitching up."

"That's Dar's opinion. That much blood on your leg means you need stitching. Any cut will heal better if it's closed up properly." She put a hot, wet cloth on my leg, and in a few seconds, the crusted blood softened, and the cut began to sting.

"Ow. What is that?"

"Just salt. It'll draw out any dirt. You make an awful fuss about a little water."

"This is worse than the fight," I grumbled, but my heart wasn't in it. After I'd had three hot saltwater cloths on my leg, Orla smeared a gooey white salve on the edges of the wound.

"This'll numb it a little," she said. Then she picked up the needle and poked it through my skin. The salve didn't numb the pain of the stab completely. I clenched my hands in the blanket, gritting my teeth as she put three neat stitches into my leg. By the last, I had tears in my eyes and my nose was running.

"There," she said at last, and peered at my eyebrow.

"It's not too bad," she said. "I won't have to stitch it."

"Thank you."

"I'll shave the bit of your eyebrow that's cut, so the hairs don't grow into the skin."

Then there was more hot water and salt, and I kept my eyes closed while Orla soaped and scraped with a sharp knife. Finally, she was done. She smoothed a pungent, pale green salve over the eyebrow and finished with a clean bandage on my leg.

I watched as she packed her things back into her little bag.

"Can I have a bath before dinner?" I asked.

"You shouldn't get your leg wet," Orla said.

"If I hang it over the tub?"

"All right, then," she said, smiling. "If you get it wet, let me look at it again."

After I was clean, I soaked in the hot water until my fingertips wrinkled, then sat in the warm bathhouse while Willow had her bath. It was worth the chill of walking across the courtyard with damp hair to feel clean and relaxed. Almost everyone we saw touched their foreheads to me in the same salute they gave the king. As we came into the hall, the tables were being set up for the feast Mother had promised.

"I know I told her not to bother," I said, "but now I'm happy she did. Nias will make something I really like, and I think I deserve it."

"So you do," Willow said. As we went up the stairs to our room, we met Adana coming down.

"Father's back," she said." He rode in a little while ago."

"Did he get the boar?"

"He got two. The hides are enormous, Kiar! And there's a barrel of salted meat, and the men say they left as much with the farmstead. One of the dogs got slashed on the leg, but he'll be all right. They broke two spears getting the boars."

"I guess he had as much excitement as we did," I said.

"Everybody's talking about your fight," Adana said. "They're saying if you hadn't gone to chase Hafor out, Gythorn would be invading by now."

I snorted.

"It was five men. You were there, Willow." I stopped and looked her in the eye. "What did you tell them?"

She held up her hands and looked to Adana for support.

"I promise, Kiar, all I said was there was a small group of invaders, and you fought the leader and won. I didn't say anything else, did I, Adana?"

"Really? Then how does everyone know it was Hafor?"

"Be sensible, Kiar." Adana said. "All the men are going to talk about it. Dar went straight to Father when he got back. Tuan might be the only one who hasn't said anything. And Willow. And you."

"I'm sorry. Of course people are going to talk." I hadn't thought much about the feast. I'd been to so many, what was one more? This one, I realized now, would be different. I'd be the one everyone was watching. The birds in my stomach fluttered up again.

I dressed for the feast in my favorite dark green gown. I pinned closed the collar of my underdress to hide the iron necklace and wore my amber one. I liked the way the chunks of clear, golden-yellow amber caught the light and glowed against the dark wool. Adana came to do my hair. She was gentle, and the pleasure of having my hair combed and braided soothed me, making me relaxed and almost sleepy again. When I looked into the mirror, my left eyebrow, shaved in the middle and divided by the thin line of the cut, gave me a questioning look, as though I didn't quite believe what I was seeing.

I sighed and stood up. "Let's go, then."

Adana patted my shoulder. "Kiar, anyone would think you're going to be punished instead of praised."

"Maybe I'd rather have neither."

Nobody noticed me when I first stepped into the hall, but then someone cheered and clapped, and in a few moments, everyone was cheering. My face felt hot, but I kept my head up and walked straight to the dais where the high table was set up. Something about the chairs wasn't right; I saw Mother sitting on Father's right, on her own throne, and the chair on Father's left was also carved and inlaid with bronze, like theirs. Father stood in front of the dais, and as we approached, he held out his hand to me.

Willow gave me a little push on the shoulder as she and Adana slipped away to their places. I bowed to my father and took his hand. For a moment, I thought he was going to make a speech, but he smiled and drew me close enough to speak quietly.

"Well done, Kiar," he said. "I'm proud of you." It was then I noticed that over his shirt and trousers he wore the same embroidered sleeveless robe he wore when Guthric visited.

"Thank you." I couldn't trust my voice with anything more. He smiled more broadly and squeezed my hand.

"We've made a few changes," he said. "You'll sit on my left tonight, and from here on."

"That's Mother's place," I said.

"No, that's the heir's place, or the regent's. After tonight, it's yours. There'll be a fuss about that, too. But for tonight, we'll just celebrate your victory."

"Thank you," I said again.

"Come, now. Anyone would think this was worse than the fight, from the way you look. Give us a smile, Kiar. People want something to celebrate, and you've given it to them. Now you have to enjoy it, too, whether you want to or not. It goes with the job, daughter of mine. You're not allowed to sneak away and hide."

"I wish I could!" I said, a little more loudly than I'd meant to, and he laughed out loud.

"I know how you feel. Come up and keep me company."

Once the food was served, and people had their attention on their meal instead of me, my shoulders relaxed. I hadn't even realized how tight the muscles across my back had been.

"What do I do now?" I asked my father.

"Well, when we've eaten, you will stand up and tell everyone what you did. Then we'll drink a few toasts, and do one or two other little things, and then you and I will talk in the council chamber."

"Everybody knows what I've done," I said.

"Yes, but this is your only chance to tell your side of it. Believe me, you won't get another. After this it will all be about how you bravely rode out with banners flying and routed an army alone."

"That's not how it was!"

"Then you'd better say what you will tonight because that is how it will be remembered. In the meantime, enjoy your feast, or you'll have Nias to answer to."

That made me smile again, because Nias took feasts very seriously and expected those who ate them to do the same. She wasn't afraid to tell even my father if she thought he hadn't done her meal justice. She'd made everything I liked that she could manage with her springtime stores: meat pasties and a chicken stew with herbs, roasted vegetables and fresh bread with butter and honey. There was a dish of grain cooked in milk with spices and dried fruit, and plates heaped with tiny cakes. She must have used all the eggs the hens had laid for several days to make them.

Finally, we had eaten everything we could eat. I couldn't have found room for even one more of the tiny, sweet cakes. Father refilled his wine cup, and Mother's, and mine. Around the hall, other people refilled theirs, too. Then Father stood up, and the hall fell silent.

"I'm glad to be back home," he said. "We killed the boars that threatened Near Fellstead and brought back the hides to prove it."

A cheer went up, and he waited for the hall to fall quiet again.

"But while we were gone, another threat came into our borders, one that could have done more harm than a herd of boars." He was using formal speech now, speaking for the people and not only himself. "Our daughter Kiar rode against it and has come back victorious. We will hear her story from her own lips."

He turned to me, and I stood, although my knees trembled. Father's face was serious, but he winked at me. I stood up straight and faced the hall. I'd heard Father and others address the people often enough, but it was different doing it myself. Where should I start? Oh, yes, the messenger.

"Donel of Stony Ridge farmstead brought us word of a sheep-killing. The wolves that did it rode horses and wore swords. We rode out with spears, swords, and bows and tracked them to their camp. In the circle, I fought their leader, Hafor of Noermark. I wear the marks of his sword," I continued, "but he left his sword behind and went back to his own country."

There was a moment of silence, then everyone cheered and yelled, and banged on the tables. I heard my name cried out around the room. Father gestured to someone behind him, and then turned back to me.

"Turn around, Princess Kiar," he said, "and undo your collar."

I did as he said. I heard a light step behind me and felt someone lift the links of the iron necklace from my nape. The necklace pulled gently at the front of my throat, then slipped down and was lifted away.

I put my hand to my neck, and for the first time in months, touched only my own skin, without the linked spirals of iron over it.

"Princess Kiar," said my father, "take back your freedom to wear whatever form you will. You have shown yourself a true princess and a warrior, who will care for her people."

Once again, the people cheered, and Willow whooped and cried, "Kiar! Kiar!" over the noise. I turned around and bowed to my father, blinking away tears. I didn't want to cry here, now.

"Good work," my father said softly, under the cheering. He turned again and gestured with the hand that held my necklace. Sylard, who had brought him the pliers, came forward again with Hafor's sword, still wrapped in its cloth, across his hands. He leaned past me to lay it on the table. Then Sylard bowed to me, took the pliers and necklace from my father and stepped back. Father looked at me.

"This is yours," he said, "to keep or bestow."

I unwrapped the sword and held it up. As the torchlight slid over the watered steel, the hiss of indrawn breath ran around the room. Someone whistled long and low in admiration. I turned to my father.

"Sire, I cannot use this sword. It was made for someone taller. Such a blade deserves better than to hang on the wall as a trophy."

"Then give it where you will," he said.

"Dar of the guard, come forward to me," I said.

Dar stood up and walked to the dais, bowed to my father and then to me.

"For your support and wise counsel on my first fight, Dar," I said, "I give you this sword. Will you accept it?"

Dar looked at my father, who nodded, and then to me.

"I will, Lady Kiar."

I walked around the table, holding the sword upright, and came to stand before Dar. Carefully I laid it across my palms and offered him the hilt. To my astonishment, he knelt.

"I accept this sword, Lady Kiar. My sword, my honor, and my life at your command above all others." He took the hilt of the sword and gently lifted the blade. I realized my mouth was open and closed it. He knelt there still, as though waiting. Finally, I regained my wits.

"Rise, then," I said, and he stood. Was there something else I was supposed to say? I couldn't think.

"First man of the Princess's guard!" my father shouted.

I stared at Dar, who smiled at me.

"What did you expect?" he said, under the noise of the cheering and pounding. "You can't give arms without getting fealty, my lady."

"I didn't mean— you're my father's man!" I said.

"No more," he answered, "or at least, only after you."

Then the words of my half of the oath came back to me.

"Then be of my household and guard," I said, "Bear your arms in honour to protect the land, and answer to the law, to me, and to the king. I should have said that before."

"Never mind," he said, "It's said now, Lady."

"You don't need to stand behind my chair," I said. "You should sit down again."

"As you wish, Lady," he said, smiling.

I took my place again and looked at my father. "I didn't mean to take Dar away from your guard," I said. "I only meant to give him the sword because—well, because he could use it."

"It's time you had your own guard," Father said. "I imagine Dar will have some suggestions for it. Hafor's little raid came at a very good time."

After the meal, Father turned to Mother.

"Kiar and I will be in my council chamber," he said. "We won't be long." He kissed her and we rose and left the hall. Already the benches were being cleared back, and there would probably be dancing. I loved dancing. Maybe it would still be going on when Father and I were done. There would likely be much more of the council chamber in my life from now on, and less time for riding, or for flying.

As usual, there was a little fire burning in the chamber, and the room was warm against the damp chill of a spring night. A small table held wine and two cups, and someone had put an armchair across from Father's usual seat. We sat down, and he poured himself wine and passed me the jug.

"Your mother says you didn't ask her permission to go," he said.

I finished pouring and set the jug down before I answered. "No," I said. "I didn't. She wanted to send some of the guard."

"But you didn't think the guard could take care of it?"

Why was he asking me these questions? In the hall, he'd seemed proud of me. Now it sounded as if I might not have done the right thing after all.

"I suppose they could have. I'd have sent ten, and there were only five Noermarkers in the end. I didn't do anything Dar couldn't have done. He gave me very good advice."

Father sat back and looked at me over his wine cup for a few seconds. "No, Kiar. You did something Dar couldn't have done.

You showed Gythorn that my heir is ready to fight, herself, to protect her borders and not simply to send her men. What your mother advised is more likely what he thought would happen.”

“You think Gythorn sent Hafor to see what would happen if you were away?”

“I think he’ll deny knowing that Hafor crossed our borders. You did Hafor more damage than you know, Kiar. To be defeated is one thing, to be defeated and lose his sword is another. But to be defeated by a woman, someone he thought shouldn’t be able to stand up to him, that will be hard to live down.”

“He challenged Dar first.”

“Interesting. What did Dar say to that?”

“He told Hafor to speak to me. Hafor said he didn’t fight women.”

“But he obviously fought you.”

I couldn’t help smiling now. “Well, I *did* ask whether he was afraid to fight me.”

Father laughed out loud.

“You cornered him properly,” he said, when he’d finished laughing, “and then you beat him! I doubt his father thinks much of him right now.”

I remembered the grey man.

“One of Hafor’s men said there wouldn’t be any more raids. He said he’d tell Gythorn that the women of Valenia would fight.”

“And that’s something he wouldn’t have said if you’d sent out your men, or if Dar had fought Hafor, or even beaten him. You’ve saved me a lot of trouble, Kiar, and yourself as well. I’ve worried whether Gythorn would make war as soon as you became queen, because you’re not a man.”

"Did you ever wish I was a boy? I mean, that you'd had a son instead of three girls?"

He paused before he answered. "It would have been good to have a son, yes, but if I'd had all boys, I would have wanted a daughter, too. I've never wished you were a boy, Kiar. You'll be a fine ruler. You've done everything a queen, or a king, should do when the land is threatened."

He put down the cup and leaned forward.

"I meant everything I said out there. You can be a swan or a human as you wish, and fly whenever and wherever you like. I know you'll do what's best for Valenia, no matter what. You might find that's a heavier collar than the one you just lost."

I didn't know what to say to that, and even if I had, I didn't think I could get the words past the lump in my throat. We sat in silence, and then Father finished his wine and set the cup down with a little thump.

"I hear music, and I think there might be a young man or two who wants to dance with you. I certainly have someone who wants to dance with me."

CHAPTER

TWENTY-SEVEN

The next morning Willow asked me, "Do you want to fly today?"

I put my hand to my throat, where the iron necklace had lain for all those months.

"There's nothing to stop you now," she said. "You even have the king's permission."

"You didn't see what happened when I tried to change," I said.

"That was different. You tried with the iron on."

I said nothing. The memory of that horrible wrenching sickness was still sharp.

"You have to fly again sometime," she said. "You can't just stop, especially now."

"No," I said, "you're right."

"Then we'll go flying today? We can ride down to the lake and change there, and then ride back when we're done. You lead, and I'll do whatever you say. I promise."

I looked at her; she stood with her hands clasped together, the fingers twined and clenched. I could see how much this meant to her. She hadn't flown, either, since our trespass into Noermark.

"All right, then." I smiled to show her it *was* all right. "We'll go, this afternoon when it's warmer."

"Good," she said, as though I'd agreed to a ride or some other, ordinary thing. But her smile lit up her face.

Tuan caught up with us at the stable.

"Going without me?" he said.

"We don't need you to come after us this time," Willow said. "Kiar is going to lead. I'll make sure everything is all right."

"Good," Tuan said, and went past us into the stable. He brought Lighfoot's saddle and bridle from the harness room.

"You don't lead," Willow said. "Kiar leads."

Tuan said nothing.

"Come on," I said. I almost said, "Let's get it over with." My stomach felt tight, and I wasn't sure I'd be able to bring myself to change. I rubbed my fingertips together, remembering the sensation of blistering from tearing at the necklace.

We rode out to the lake without talking. Even Willow had nothing to say. We picketed the horses and went down to the beach. Willow stripped off her clothes so quickly I wondered she didn't tear them, and she called up the change immediately. She ran down to the water with a swan's rolling gait and flung herself in.

Tuan, tunic off and shirt in his hands, looked at me. I hadn't made a move to undress.

"I don't know if I can," I said. "You didn't—you don't know how much it hurt. What if I can't change any more?" My eyelids felt stiff, and I blinked them hard.

"But what if you can?" Tuan said. "The necklace is gone. There's no iron, Kiar."

"I still remember how it felt."

"And you still remember how flying felt."'

"Yes," I said. "Yes, I do."

"If you could fly again, would it be worth the pain?"

"Yes!" I said, without thinking.

"You think too hard," he said, smiling. He folded his shirt and set it on his tunic, then bent to pull off his boots. "Don't think," he said. "Just change."

I pulled my tunic and shirt off over my head, kicking my boots off so quickly I nearly tripped, then pulled off my trousers, closed my eyes and called the change.

The flare of light on my eyelids came immediately. I felt the familiar roll and shift of muscle and bone, and when I opened my eyes again, I was myself, my other self, the half I'd missed for the last year. I ran to the water and paddled after Willow. Then my shadow stretched across the water as Tuan changed behind me, and the three of us took to the sky.

It was as though I'd never left, as though the long flightless year had never happened. The sky took me back and held me up, showing me the world below.

My two companions dropped behind and let me lead. I tucked my wings and rolled and heard Willow's alarmed honk as we nearly collided. I wanted to laugh. I wanted to weep with relief and joy and the bliss of being back in the air.

I lost any idea of time. Sometime it came to me that I had another shape, and it was time to take it. I wheeled until I saw the shore where three horses waited and angled down towards the water. When I landed and drifted in, I raised my wings without thinking and called back my other shape. Then I waded out of the lake, wet to the knees and dry above. I touched my neck, where I'd worn the iron, and I knew it was really gone. My own magic was still mine.

Willow threw her arms around me. "You did it!" she said.

Tuan stood behind her smiling.

"You can say you told me so," I said to him.

That spring and summer, I flew every few days, always with Willow and Tuan.

I spent more time with Father, too, learning how to rule. I saw that the men obeyed him cheerfully, and he never seemed to force his will on anyone. When he asked for a thing to be done, it was done.

Years before, Mother had told me that learning to run a household was practice for learning to rule. I hadn't believed her. Running the household was no more, I thought, than telling other people what needed to be done. Now I saw that Father did the same, only for the kingdom.

When Father rearranged who went on patrols, he knew who had been on which border, who needed rest and who could go out again. He knew how many spears or swords needed sharpening or repair, what horses needed to be rested or trained. Nobody argued with his orders because they trusted his knowledge.

"How do you keep all that in your head?" I asked. "I don't know half of it!"

"Time and practice, Kiar," he said. "I didn't learn it all at once. You'll learn it, too, if you pay attention." Doubt must have shown in my face because he laughed and patted my shoulder. "You will! Just give it time."

I hoped I would. As I rode on patrol and did my share of the work and practiced my skills with sword and spear, I tried now to observe what others were doing, what their strengths and weaknesses were, how they worked. Someday, I would be responsible for them; I wanted them to trust me as they trusted my father, especially if I ever had to deal with Gythorn or his sons. With all of these concerns, summer seemed to pass very quickly indeed.

At the end of it, Guthric rode in from the north. He came alone, without a guard or any fanfare. Father sent someone to get me, and I came straight from the paddock to the council chamber.

"Princess Kiar," Guthric said as I came in. "I'm glad to see you well." He glanced at my throat, and I wondered what Noermark knew of the iron necklace.

"I'm very well, indeed," I answered.

"But not yet betrothed, I think," he said.

"Not yet, no."

"In time," he said. I held his eyes, unsmiling. He stood as straight as when he addressed my father, and for all both of us were in riding clothes, I had a sense of armour and shield, and two adversaries looking for weakness. Father spoke before either of us blinked.

"Guthric has brought us a letter," Father said. "Tell me what you think, Kiar." I took the letter over to the window. As I passed Guthric, I stole a glance at his face, but it showed nothing. Neither did Father's.

The letter was brief, almost terse, and said that Gythorn understood the younger daughters of King Tir were still neither married nor betrothed, and that he still hoped for an alliance by marriage between our two countries. The last sentence said, "Should either wish to visit Noermark again, we would be delighted to entertain them." I folded the letter and handed it to Father.

"Someone wants to come courting," I said to Gythorn. "It can't be Alfar. He's younger than Orla."

"You have a good memory, Princess Kiar," Guthric said. "I'm sure you remember all the comings and goings between us, and anything Prince Othar told you about his family."

"Prince Othar was easy to talk to," I said. That was two veiled references to my trespass into Noermark.

"Prince Hafor is also easy to talk to."

"Prince Hafor wants to court me? That seems unlikely."

"Ah, no," he said. "I am sorry, so clumsy to mislead you. No, he wishes to court your younger sister, Princess Orla. Of course, he would like leave."

"What do you think, Kiar?" Father asked.

I stood thinking. Orla was unlikely to want Hafor as a husband, and I certainly didn't. Still, allowing this attempt might smooth things over a little. Let him try. Orla would refuse him, and we would be back to the beginning again.

"Let him come, then," I said.

"Good!" Guthric said. He smiled widely. "You are a generous victor."

"We'll need time to call my daughter back from her studies," Father said. "She is hard at work and needs a great deal of solitude."

"There are yet three weeks before the harvest festival. Prince Hafor can be here in ten days, with your leave," said Guthric.

Father raised an eyebrow and thought for a minute. "I believe this can be done. I will send a message."

"Thank you, Sire," said Guthric. But as he bowed, he looked at me.

CHAPTER

TWENTY-EIGHT

Father went himself to talk to Sianna, and three days later, he came back with Orla. There wasn't much time to prepare for Hafor's arrival. Harvest was a busy time to be courting. It occurred to me that while most of us did some kind of farm work, probably none of the princes of Noermark ever had.

When the guard announced riders from the north, I hurried to change into court clothes. Willow ran up a few minutes later. "He's brought cattle!" she said. "And sheep! Why would he do that? Othar didn't bring anything like that when he came courting."

"I don't know," I said. "'I suppose we'll find out."

This time, Father had three extra thrones put out, one for each of us girls, and a plainer chair, although with arms, for Gil. He and Mother sat in the center two thrones, Mother on his right. Adana sat next to Mother and Gil next to her. I sat on Father's left, in the heir's place, with Orla on my left. Dar stood behind my throne, and to my surprise, so did Tuan. But I was even more surprised when Willow stepped up to Dar's other side, also with her sword.

"What are you doing?" I muttered over my shoulder.

"King's orders," Dar said. "Allies stand together."

Usually Guthric entered the hall first, and his guard followed. Even when Othar had come courting, he had allowed Guthric to enter ahead of him. This time the man who came first wasn't Guthric. It was Hafor, striding as though he were entering his own hall. I glanced at those following him, but the only one I recognized was the grey-haired man.

Hafor stopped in front of my father and knelt, then bowed his head briefly.

"King Tir," he said, then bowed his head to my mother, "Queen Tianis." Only then did he look at me.

I wasn't certain, but it seemed to me he hesitated just a bit before bowing his head to me. "Princess Kiar," he said, "we meet again."

"I'm glad to see you in better company," I said. And better dressed, I thought. His clothes clearly his best. Unlike Othar, Hafor had braided bronze wires into his beard, startlingly bright against the pale hair. He looked finer than he had at Stony Ridge, but no less willing to bite.

"And hoping for better yet. Sire," he said to my father, "I have something I must say to you and to Princess Kiar. May I speak?"

"You may," my father said.

He hadn't yet said that Hafor was welcome in the hall, and from the wary looks of the other Noermarkers, they'd noticed, too. Hafor was not yet an acknowledged guest with a guest's protection. Only Guthric's face was as calm and unrevealing as always.

Hafor looked at my father.

"Sire, the last time I crossed your borders, I trespassed both on your lands and on your people. We stole from your folk, and I offered both discourtesy and violence to Princess Kiar when she came to show me the road home. I am heartily sorry for my actions and ask your forgiveness."

"I can forgive your trespass on my borders," my father said, "but the theft of the sheep must be amended to those you stole from, and only Princess Kiar can forgive your offences against her person."

"As to the first, I have brought sheep and cattle from my own flocks and herds to replace what I stole and to make amends."

My fingers curled on the arms of my chair. Was this the same man who'd protested that his sword was worth more than ten sheep? What did he, or Gythorn, want so badly that he would pay again where he thought he'd already paid? Then Hafor turned to me.

"Princess Kiar," he said, putting his hand on his heart, "I am relieved to see that you've taken no lasting hurt from our fight. I am sorry for my discourtesy to you on our last meeting, both that I spoke as I did, and that I did not speak after. What Warulf said to you of the valour of Valenia's women, I say also. Her borders are well defended when women fight as fiercely as you, Princess."

The hair on my neck prickled against my robe, but I kept my voice calm. "I see you also took no lasting harm, Prince Hafor. I accept your apology."

"As I have come as a guest should, openly to the front door, am I welcome here?"

"You are," said my father. A tension went out of the room when he spoke. "Rise, Prince Hafor. We offer you and your men shelter, food, and our protection for your stay."

"Thank you, Sire," Hafor bowed again and stepped back. He nodded to Guthric, who came smoothly forward.

"Sire, we thank you for your welcome, and for your generosity and understanding in forgiving a young man's impetuous nature. Princess Kiar," he said, bowing to me, "you are truly your father's daughter, in courage and understanding." I remembered Guthric bringing me ribbons when I was a small girl and bit my lips to avoid smiling at his formality. Behind him, Hafor cleared his throat.

"We have another matter to discuss with you, Sire," Guthric said. "Concerning your daugh "

"There will be time to talk when you have rested and eaten," Father said.

I couldn't remember ever hearing Father interrupt Guthric before. Even Guthric was taken by surprise, I thought. But there was nothing he could say but "As you wish, Sire."

After the party from Noermark had been escorted out, Guthric and Hafor to rooms in the castle, their guard to bunks in one of the guardhouses, Father turned and looked past me to Orla.

"It seems it's your turn now to be courted by Noermark," he said. "Shall we go to the council chamber? Kiar, you come, too." He took Mother's hand, and the four of us went to discuss this new development.

"He hasn't said he wanted to court me," Orla said before anyone else spoke. She sat very straight in her chair, her hands folded neat and quiet in her lap. "Maybe he wants Kiar."

"He can want me all he likes," I said. "If he has any sense at all, he knows I wouldn't have him if he brought all of Noermark."

"Maybe he doesn't have that much sense," Mother said. "And after making a raid, why come courting? I don't trust him."

"He has to make up for getting beaten," I said.

Father nodded. "That's the truth. Gythorn has tried every way he knows to get a foothold in Valenia. He sent his sons to court Kiar, and he initiated a raid to see if she could defend the borders on her own. Both of those have failed, and I don't think he's prepared for out-and-out war. Hafor needs to show his father that he's still useful. The best way to do that, I think, is to make any kind of alliance with us. But Hafor knows marriage to Kiar isn't a possibility. And I think Gythorn could be satisfied with an indirect connection."

"Orla will be the most powerful wisewoman born in centuries," Mother said. "Wisewomen never marry."

"Yet she is the heir once Kiar comes to the throne, until Kiar has children."

"I don't like this," Mother said. "Orla, you need not think of courtship at all. You have your magic. The black swan isn't a woman of Noermark, to be traded for peace and goodwill."

"Nobody is going to trade Orla for anything," Father said. "When have I ever said a daughter of mine should marry for any reasons but her own?"

"You allowed Othar's courtship," Mother said.

"Kiar allowed that," Father said, reaching for Mother's hand. She folded her hands together in her lap, and he drew his back.

"The swan-hunters have tried three times, now," she said. "First soft words, then blows, and now words again, from the very one who invaded while you were gone. How often will you put up with this, Tir? And Orla, of all people, to be married to one of *them*."

"That is unkind, Tianis. I've never forced any suitor on any of our daughters. I'll put up with it, as you say, because it's better than war."

"No, you've never forced it, only permitted it, instead of protecting our swanlings."

"This is not the time, Tianis!"

"Then when *is* the time?"

I looked from Father to Mother. Had they fought when Othar offered for me? I hadn't heard of it, only that Mother was unhappy about an alliance with Noermark. She hadn't made a fuss about the alliance coming through me. "Orla, of all people," she'd said.

"What does it matter?" I asked. "She's not going to accept him." I turned to Orla. "Are you?"

"I don't know," Orla said, looking at Mother. Her face was calm, and her hands remained in her lap, the right laid over the left. Still, I saw her hidden left hand moved a little, as though her fingers were twisting in her gown. I remembered the uneasiness I felt when Guthric had first broached a courtship for me. Orla was still young. She hid it well, I thought, but she was as scared as I had been.

"I can't say I'm happy about Hafor being in the family," I said. "I don't trust him, for all his pretty words."

"It isn't you who gets to say if he's in the family or not," said Father. "Orla, it's up to you whether you're willing to be courted, let alone marry him, or anyone. What do you say?"

"Maybe it's not courtship at all," she said.

"What do you think?" I asked. "He wants you to be his court wisewoman?"

She flushed. "Why not?" Her hands curled into fists in her lap, and she scowled at me. "I'm good—Sianna says I'm the best student she's ever had. Maybe that's exactly what he wants."

"Hafor has something to prove," I said. "If he wants to be king of Noermark, having a wisewoman on his side would help. And he might want you to use your power against us. Did you think about that?"

"Now, Kiar, nobody could expect her to use power against her own family," Mother said. She turned to Orla. "Nobody wants you to marry if you don't want him. You don't have to agree to let him court you."

"He hasn't said he wants to," Orla said.

"Not yet," Father said, "but we need to expect that tonight, or tomorrow at the latest. We should be prepared."

"You mean you want to know what I'll say before I say it." Orla was still frowning. "The way you do with Kiar."

"Yes," Father said. "This isn't only about my daughter, either of you, and who she might want to marry. This is about the throne and Valenia, as well as the family. So, Orla, what do you say?"

"This is meaningless," Mother said. "Wisewomen never marry."

"Just because they don't," Orla said, "doesn't mean they can't."

Mother looked as though a mouse had roared in her face.

"Swanling—" she began, but Orla interrupted.

"I could listen to him."

"You can't mean that!" The words were out of me before I thought.

"Well, why not? Adana has Gil, and you could have married Othar, and this is the first time anyone's even thought about me like that! Why shouldn't I listen to him?"

"Because he tried to take us over. And do you know why I didn't take Othar? His men talked about hunting swans! Just talked!"

"Well, lucky for me I don't have to be queen!" Orla said. "I can have who I please!"

"Lower your voices," Father said. "There's no need to tell the whole country, you two."

"Sorry," I said.

Orla said nothing.

"But it's true," I said. "And Hafor's apology was nothing but diplomacy. A cat who purrs still has claws."

"A generous apology," Father said. "If he expects to mend fences, he's certainly not doing anything by halves."

"We should beware of them," Mother said. She looked at Orla again, and a line appeared between her brows. "You have great magic and power, swanling, and a great destiny. You don't have to take any man for policy or do anything you don't want."

"Tell that to Kiar," Orla said. "She has me married and traitor already for thinking about it."

"Of course I don't. But I don't understand how you could even think of marrying Hafor. It makes my skin crawl to look at him."

"Then don't look!" Orla said. She turned to Father. "If he wants to court me after all, I'll listen to what he has to say. Maybe I'll learn something useful, even if I don't want to marry him. And who knows—he might really be sorry for what he did. He might have changed the way he thinks. People do sometimes."

I remembered her saying of Gil, "I'll have to love him like a sister, because that's the only way he thinks of me," and I held out my hand to her. She'd been so good about trying to forget her love for Gil. If being courted, even by Hafor, made that easier, it would be unkind of me to object.

"I'm sorry, Orla," I said. "Maybe he has changed. He's a nice-looking man, and well-spoken. Guthric says he's a thinker, too."

Orla stopped frowning and took my hand. "You can't make me believe you really think well of him, but thank you."

"You'll leave him nothing to say for himself," Father said. "Enough, now. We'll see what Guthric, or Hafor, has to say tonight." He reached again for Mother's hand, and she let him take it. But she wouldn't look at him, only at Orla.

Hafor had to wait on Father's pleasure to speak of courting, and it pleased Father to make him wait until supper the next day. Even then it wasn't Hafor who spoke first. It was Guthric who spoke, as he had when Othar had come courting the year before. He stood before the head table, facing all of us. Orla sat at my left; Hafor sat beyond Gil and Adana, to the right of Mother, and I wasn't going to crane my neck to see him. I glanced down at the end of the table and caught Willow's eye. From her spot on the short end. she could see at least some of Hafor's reactions. When I turned my head a little towards my right and then looked back at her, she dipped her head the tiniest bit. Whatever she saw, I'd find out afterwards.

"Sire," Guthric said, "My lord King Gythorn asks you to consider permitting his son Prince Hafor to court your youngest daughter, Princess Orla. He hopes you will forgive a young man's rashness and poor manners in his conduct earlier this year."

"We have dealt with this already," my father said.

"Most generously, Sire, and Princess Kiar, too." Gythorn bowed to me. "King Gythorn was ill-pleased to hear of his son's behaviour, and of his fight with you, my lady."

Probably mostly because he lost, I thought, but said nothing.

"Your great courtesy to Prince Othar," said Guthric, "and the prince's report of the princesses, particularly Princess Kiar, makes my lord bold to ask if you would grant this favor."

"Princess Orla is too young to marry," Mother said. "Also, she is not yet done her studies with the wisewoman."

"Agreed, Lady," said Guthric, "Your Majesty is a careful mother. Still, courtship is not marriage, as Prince Othar has shown."

That was a slight on Othar, and I watched Willow's eyebrow rise.

"King Gythorn does not expect an early marriage," Guthric continued. "Indeed, he is willing that Princess Orla complete her studies before a marriage is considered. But these are future things. For now, he would be well content if you allowed a courtship."

"What do you say, Orla?" my father asked.

"I'll listen to his suit," she answered." Then we will permit it," Father said. "Prince Hafor, you are welcome to court our daughter as long as she pleases."

Hafor stood up and bowed.

"You are very kind, Sire," he said. He looked at Mother. "Lady, I understand how important Princess Orla's studies are. I am eager for her to complete them, certainly before considering marriage."

"Then it's settled," Father said.

After the meal, Willow came over to me. "He watched whoever was talking, all the time," she said, "And the only time he even looked in your direction was when Orla spoke."

"What about his expression? Was he happy, or surprised when Father said he could court Orla? Anything?"

She shook her head.

"He never frowned or looked surprised. He looked as though everything was interesting."

"I'm sure it was," I said. "But he wants something. I know he does."

"Maybe he wants Orla," Willow said. "She's beautiful and she's clever, and she does magic. And she's your sister, which means he would have a connection to you."

"To the throne, you mean." The music started up. "I don't know what else he's thinking, and I don't like that."

"He didn't give anything away that I saw," Willow said. "Maybe you'll have to ask him. I'm going to find someone to dance with."

I stood aside and watched for a while, refusing one or two offers. Hafor danced well; he didn't know all our steps, but he picked them up quickly. Eventually he came over to me.

"Princess Kiar, will you dance with me?" he said. "I would like to be friends with you. For your sister's sake, if not my own."

I wanted to refuse; there was nobody I wanted to dance with less. For Orla's sake, and because Father and Mother had consented to the courtship—even though Mother was obviously unhappy about it—I smiled and took his hand.

I was happy that the quick steps of the dance, and the circling and changing partners, left no time for talk. I didn't know what to talk about with Hafor. Everything I thought of touched on our last meeting, and it seemed better not to speak of that.

At the end of the dance, he bowed low over my hand. "Thank you, Princess Kiar. It's a pity my brother missed his chance with you, and a pity for me that I did, too. For all that, I hope I may someday say Sister Kiar."

"How is Othar?" I asked.

"My brother has gone over the mountains," Hafor said. "You understand that Father wasn't best pleased with him." He paused, and the corner of his lip turned up a little.

I thought that maybe he hadn't been sorry to see Othar leave.

"Othar found it wiser to make himself scarce. I see that's not welcome news." He glanced over my shoulder and smiled.

"Ah, your man is here to claim you." He winked at me, which I didn't like at all, and then walked towards Orla, who watched him with a calm, grave face.

Tuan arrived by my side and took my hand. "I thought you wouldn't want another dance with him," he said.

Hafor now held Orla's hands in his own and was talking to her. His back was to me, but Orla suddenly laughed.

"He's being charming," I said. "I hope he doesn't charm her out of her senses."

"It would take more than Hafor to charm a black swan," Tuan said.

Then the music started up again. For the rest of the night, I managed to avoid Hafor. It wasn't difficult. He seemed to be setting himself to win Orla, dancing mostly with her, talking and laughing with her between dances. All the same, I noticed that Father didn't offer the use of his council chamber to get acquainted, as he had Othar and me. I was glad that he wanted to keep Hafor under his eye.

CHAPTER

TWENTY-NINE

"He looks like a weasel," I said to Willow and Tuan as we put our swords away after practice the next day.

"He looks like his brother," Tuan said.

"Yes, a little, but I don't think Hafor has a kind bone in his body."

"It's what Orla thinks that counts," he said.

"Did you know Othar has left Noermark? Hafor told me last night it was because Othar and I weren't betrothed. I think it was dangerous for him to stay."

"I'll bet if Hafor doesn't get Orla, he'll have to leave, too," Willow said.

"I hope she turns him down."

"She's the black swan," Tuan said. "Maybe she can control him."

"You mean by magic? That doesn't sound practical," I said. "Orla told me spells take power, and you can't make someone change deep down. Any change is only an illusion."

"Maybe," Willow shrugged. "But who cares if it is? As long as they do what she wants? I'll see you in the bathhouse, Kiar." She left, and I hung up my shield.

Tuan turned his sword, looking along the blade. He took a whetstone down and ran it along the steel. For a minute or two I stood and watched. I couldn't tell whether he was angry about Hafor being here, or worried, or if he simply didn't care.

"What do you think about Hafor?" I asked.

He ran the stone down the blade again and sighted along the edge of the sword before speaking. "He can be trusted," he said, "the way you trust a fox around cygnets."

"Not at all, you mean."

"No. You don't leave the cygnets alone when the fox is around. You know what he'll do. It means you should be prepared."

"That's not trust. Trust means you know someone won't betray or hurt you."

He shook his head. "That's only half of it." He put the whetstone away and sheathed the sword, but slowly, as though he was thinking of something else. Finally, he spoke again. "When you hunt, you know what the deer will do. You prepare for that. You want to kill the deer, and the deer wants to live. If you don't kill the deer, you go hungry. If the deer doesn't outrun you or outwit you, it dies. Each of you knows what the other will do. How is that not trust?"

"Because we're—fighting, sort of. Not working together, like a dance."

"But you know what to expect and so does the deer. You know what to expect from Hafor, too. You think he wants to marry Orla to use her power for Noermark's good."

"Well, don't you expect that?"

"Yes. I trust him to be a fox. If I had a nest, I'd guard it while he was around."

He put a hand on my shoulder and looked into my eyes.

"You don't have to think too hard about it," he said. "Just watch the fox, because you know what he'll do."

I could feel the warmth of his hand through my tunic and shirt. I didn't know whether I wanted him to stand closer or move farther away, to keep looking into my eyes or stop. What if someone came in and saw us? *What if they did?* said a voice in the back of my head. Hafor had called Tuan my man twice, but that meant nothing. If it did mean nothing, though, why did I keep thinking about it?

"What if Orla marries Hafor?" I asked. "Would you—you and Willow—go back to the swanfolk?"

"Willow might," he said. "But probably not."

"And you?"

"Not if Orla marries Hafor, no."

"What if I'd married Othar? Would you go back then?"

He frowned a little, but he looked puzzled, not angry.

"You didn't marry Othar. What does it matter?"

"I want to know."

The silence stretched between us.

"Kiar," he said, finally. He took my right hand and turned it palm-up, then ran his thumb over the calloused pad at the base of my fingers. "You think too much about things. You make it difficult for yourself. Among the swans, it's not so hard. It looks like you have more choices, but that might not be true at all." He stroked the palm of my hand again and a shiver went up my back.

"No," he said. "Not if you'd married Othar."

He let go of my hand, hung up his shield, and walked out of the armoury. I stood there, my skin prickling uncomfortably with drying sweat, my hair sticking to my face, and unreasonably happy, happier even than the moment when Father removed the iron necklace.

I still didn't like Hafor any better, but whenever I saw Orla laughing with him as they came back from their ride, her face bright and her eyes shining, I thought that if he made her happy, I would be able to stand him as a brother-in-law. *I* didn't have to marry him and put up with him.

Over the next week, I seldom saw Orla and Hafor apart. They ate together and rode together, and much of the time had their heads close in conversation that seemed to please them both. I expected that Orla would want some time apart; she had grown used to the quiet during her time with Sianna. The talk and bustle of the castle and Hafor's constant company didn't tire her. Instead she seemed to thrive on it.

Hafor found Willow, Tuan, and me in the stable on his third morning with us. I wanted a quiet ride, and perhaps to fly. We were saddling our horses when he came in. He stood outside Kestrel's stall, leaning his arms on the top of the half-door.

"Princess Kiar," he said, "May I speak with you?"

"Of course," I said, putting on a smile. "I'm glad to see you and Orla getting along so well."

"You're kind, Princess. I would like to get along with you, if I might."

Willow snorted. "Come on, Tuan. Meet you at the gate, Kiar." She led Whiffle out, crowding Hafor a little. Any closer and Whiffle would have trodden on his heels. Tuan gave him a little more room, but not much.

"You foster sister doesn't care for me," Hafor said, "Nor does your man."

"Tuan is one of my guard," I said. "And as to what he, or Willow, thinks of you—it's what Orla thinks that matters," I said.

"But what her family thinks matters, too. It helps to be friends with the family of one's betrothed. We got off to a bad start, Kiar. I'd like to make amends, if you'll tell me how."

"You've settled that quickly," I said. "Have you spoken to Father and Mother?" I knew he hadn't; they would have told me.

He waved a hand, brushing the matter aside as he would a fly from his horse's head.

"I have their permission to court her. What outcome would they expect?"

"You can't be that sure of her so soon. For one, your people are swan-hunters. That's hard to ignore."

"You know how diplomacy works, Princess Kiar. Each side gives a little. It's much the same in marriage, I think."

"You mean, I don't kill your people and you don't kill mine? Even if they happen to look like swans? That kind of diplomacy?"

Hafor smiled as though he were genuinely glad.

"Yes, exactly! I see you and I will get along after all. Your foster sister will be impatient to start, so I won't keep you longer. Have a good ride, sister Kiar."

He walked out of the stable with a bounce in his step, and I heard him whistling as he crossed the courtyard.

Tuan and Willow waited at the gate. We mounted up and rode out. Halfway down the dun from the castle, Willow asked the question I knew she was dying to have answered.

"What did he want?"

Tuan said nothing, but he watched me.

"He said if I'd kiss and make up, he wouldn't kill swans. I'm not sure if he meant it. I'd hate to be friendly to him and have it make no difference."

"You could pretend to be friends," Willow said. "It won't be easy, but it might help."

"You mean lie to him?"

"Diplomacy," Tuan said. "Your father does it. Says things he doesn't really mean, or says them in a way that might mean two things."

"Yes," I said, remembering Father telling Guthric that we knew the older princes better, instead of saying they'd raided our borders.

"You don't have to tell him you like him," Willow said. "You don't have to tell a—a straight-on lie."

I laughed out loud. "Only a sideways one? It's still lying, and I've never been good at it. Hafor knew from my face last night that I wasn't happy about Othar. Do you think I can fool him?"

"Maybe he wants to be fooled," Tuan said.

"What do you mean?"

"Maybe he'd rather court you," Willow said. She glanced at Tuan, who nodded. "Maybe Orla was second choice."

"That's stupid," I said.

"Not really. What if you hadn't gone out to meet him yourself in the spring? If you hadn't seen him then, the way he acted, then maybe you wouldn't dislike him quite so much now." Willow said.

"How can you say that? He wanted to take part of Valenia!"

"Young males always challenge older ones," Tuan said. "Everything does it—deer, swans, people. What good is a mate who can't fight?"

"But stags fight stags, and cobs fight cobs. A stag doesn't fight a doe."

"Oh, Kiar!" Willow said, "Hafor didn't know he was challenging you! He thought he was challenging your father, and that all he'd get was your father's men. I'll bet he never thought he'd have to fight anyone in the circle, one against one."

"Father said something similar. But I'm the heir, and I can fight. It's my responsibility."

"You know that, but Hafor doesn't. And if his men could beat your father's men, he'd stay."

"We took more men than they had."

"Yes, but say they'd won," Willow said, "the king would have challenged him for that bit of Valenia."

"That's what males do," Tuan said. "They fight for territory."

"You almost sound as though you think I should like him! Do you think marrying him would be a good idea?" I asked.

Tuan shook his head, and Willow huffed out her breath. "I didn't say that," she said. "I said he's being a proper male. He fights for territory, and he courts a mate. They aren't the same thing. But when he had to fight you, they got mixed together. It tangled things up, and now he's trying to untangle them."

"Is that what you think?"

"I don't have to like him," Willow said. "In fact, I don't like him. But he'd probably be a good mate."

"Not for me!"

"That's because things got tangled," Tuan said.

"That's what I mean," Willow said. "You might think better of him if you hadn't fought him in the spring." She looked at me one-eyed. "In fact, if you were both swans, you'd probably find him very attractive."

"But I'm not," I said.

"But you're *like* the swanfolk," Willow said, "because you're the queen's daughter."

We rode along in silence while I turned over the idea that Hafor might really prefer me, and that Willow might be right about why I distrusted him.

"You're pretty, too," Willow said. "I know you don't believe it because you look different from Adana and Orla, and they're both so beautiful. Especially Orla."

"He called me a gosling," I reminded her. "And he wasn't being nice when he said it."

"Yes, but then he said 'wildcat.' Wildcats are beautiful in a different way from swans. Maybe he prefers wildcats. He probably meant to ask for you. Didn't you tell me that in Noermark, the oldest marries first? And nobody's courting you now."

"Well, it's too late for me to say anything. Besides, I don't want him. And he's courting Orla. How would that look, me trying to take my sister's suitor?"

Nobody spoke; we'd all seen already how that looked.

"All I meant," Willow said, "is just make it easy for him to change his ways, if he wants to. If he's married to Orla, then he's on our side, and he *is* a proper male. If you make him feel unwelcome, it only makes things worse."

"This is strange talk from you," I said. "When Othar was courting me, you were jealous and wanted him gone. Now you don't seem to mind the idea of Orla marrying Hafor."

She shrugged. "Your father is still king, and you'll be queen, and Hafor would have no power to disobey you. And you don't trust him, so you'll give him no chances."

"Didn't you think I would do that if I married Othar?"

"Maybe not," she said. "People do strange things when they love someone. The queen left her own people. Not many of us marry human folk. You might not have seen Othar clearly if you loved him. Hafor you see clearly. You'll protect us from him."

'You have a lot of faith in me," I said.

Her smile lit up her face. "Yes," she answered. "But we know you, don't we, Tuan?"

"All right," I said. "I'll be as friendly as I can, if you think it'll help." I looked at Tuan. He was smiling, too.

"It's not you who has to marry him," he said.

"True," I said. "That's something to be thankful for."

We returned to the castle and put the horses in the paddock. As we took our harness to the stables, Orla came out to meet us.

"Can I talk to you, Kiar?" She glanced at Tuan and then at Willow. "Alone?"

"Let me put my saddle away first," I said.

"It won't take long, what I want to say," she replied.

"Come on," Willow said to Tuan.

Orla watched them until they were out of earshot, then turned to me.

"Well?" I said.

"It's about Hafor," she said. "I wish you'd try to be nicer to him, Kiar. He really is sorry about the spring. He wants to start over, especially if he's going to be family. He told me about the fight, and how he said it wouldn't be to the death. He wouldn't have really hurt you." Her glance never flicked to my brow, where a few hairs grew crooked over the scar.

"He drew blood," I said.

"Even in practice, you sometimes get cut. And you drew blood, too."

"Did he show you the scar?" I asked, and to my surprise she flushed and frowned.

"There's no need to be nasty," she said. "And he's been proper and kind. He brought me a gift. Look." She pulled at a fine chain around her neck and showed me a strand of small blue glass beads. Hanging in the center was a silver pendant, a serpent curled and knotted back on itself, with its tail in its mouth.

"It's very pretty," I said.

"He says the serpent is for wisdom and dreams. He had it made for me especially." She looked at me, her eyes wide and sparkling. Orla was proud; she never asked for help, or favors. No wonder she'd wanted to talk privately.

"You like him, then?"

"I know you think it's odd. He makes me laugh, he's interesting to talk to, and he's charming and kind to me. Maybe I won't love him the way Adana loves Gil, and maybe Hafor won't love me that way, either. But it's pleasant to have his attention. He treats me as though I'm important, and not only because I can do magic."

"I see," I said.

"I know Mother's proud of me and thinks I'll be a great wisewoman. But I get—" She hesitated, "a bit tired of it. As though that's the only important thing about me. Even you said Hafor might want me because I'd be a tame wisewoman. And he hasn't said anything about that, not a thing. It's restful and fun to be around him."

I remembered how much I'd enjoyed Othar's company, and how Willow's jealousy had hurt me. I'd never imagined that Orla might be tired of being the young wisewoman or want my approval.

"I'm sorry if I've made things more difficult," I said. "I really am. I'll be nicer to him, for you."

Her smile lit up her face and warmed my heart.

"Thank you, Kiar!" She flung her arms around me and kissed my cheek.

"Go on," I said. "You and Hafor sit with me at supper. I'll be nice. Now let me go put my saddle away."

She turned and half-ran back to the castle, giving a little skip as she reached the door. I thought it took so little, still, to make her happy.

Willow almost pounced on me when I got to the stable. "What did she want?" She took Kestrel's saddle and put it in place.

I found a rag and wiped down the bit, then began to rub at the buckles on the bridle. "Only for me to be nice to Hafor. She likes him."

"Really? Probably only because she didn't see how rude he was to you."

"You said yourself I'd like him if I hadn't seen that," I said. "She knows what happened, and Gythorn apologized formally. And Orla thinks Hafor really does want to make up." I hung up the bridle and looked from Willow to Tuan. "If it takes her mind off Gil, that's good."

"I don't know if that's better or worse than being in love with Gil," Willow said.

"Better," Tuan said quietly.

"I think so, too," I said. "Look, she's happy, and Adana will be happier without Orla mooning after Gil."

"Gil, too," Tuan said. "He doesn't like it."

"He could just tell her so," Willow said.

"He doesn't want to hurt her feelings."

"Well, he'll have to hurt them sometime," Willow said. "When he marries Adana, if not before. He's too soft with her."

"It doesn't matter now," I said. "Orla is trying to forget about Gil. She told me so, months ago. I want both of you to be nice to Hafor, too. Especially you, Willow."

"Me?"

"Yes. You crowded him deliberately this morning. Whiffle almost stepped on him. Just—I don't know, smile a little, or don't say everything you think. Be polite."

"Believe me, I don't say everything I think! What about Tuan, then? Does he have to smile, too?"

I sighed.

"Willow, please, just try, all right? For me and Orla, and Adana and Gil?"

She turned her head away and stood silent for so long, I thought she wouldn't answer. Finally, she looked at me.

"All right," she said. "I'll be nice."

The next three days seemed the longest I'd ever spent. Hafor was near me at every turn. At least a dozen times a day, I had to speak with him, and once, he came riding with Tuan, Willow and me. We'd planned to fly, but with Hafor along we couldn't. Willow seemed hard-pressed to keep her temper and took the excuse of racing us home to break away from him.

The morning came when Hafor left with Guthric and their guard. He kissed Mother's hand, then Adana's, and reached for mine. I didn't want him to touch me, but with everyone watching, and remembering my promise to Orla, I couldn't prevent him. He curled his fingers into my palm and kissed the back of my hand. When he let go, he let his fingers slide across my hand. The touch felt furtive, like a secret between us, and it made the skin on the back of my neck crawl. I resisted wiping my palm on my clothes when he released me.

Hafor held Orla's hands as he said goodbye and kissed her cheek. She kissed his in return, and I saw Guthric smile. Then the party from Noermark mounted up. The grey man caught my eye and nodded to me. I remembered his name, and I went over to him.

"Travel safely, Warulf," I said.

He smiled broadly, a gap-toothed grin that crinkled his eyes and looked genuinely friendly. "Thank you, Princess Kiar," he said. He nodded again, and the party from Noermark rode out.

CHAPTER

THIRTY

After Hafor left, we had the harvest festival. Then I went out with Father and some of the guard on a patrol of the eastern border. We were gone two weeks, riding in the shadow of the denser forest that grew along the long, eastern border of Valenia. Beyond that forest were miles of grassland. It was good grazing, but the borders of the grassland people were less than a mile from the forest. Sometimes they grazed their curly-horned red cattle and their horses near enough to see from the edge of the trees, but we didn't approach each other.

Besides High Moor, the easternmost farmstead, there were several small farms of single families near the forest. They were spaced half a day's ride apart or so. We stopped at each one and were welcomed with meals and, at night, beds. Even if the beds were in the hayloft, it was warmer than sleeping outside, and I loved the sweet smell of the hay.

Despite the cold weather, it was the merriest of the patrols I'd been on. Every farm had a bit of ale put by for mulling with honey and herbs. The nights were too long to sleep through, and we stayed up late, telling stories and singing songs. The day we started home, a light snow fell, foretelling the winter to come.

When we arrived back at the castle, I was surprised to see Orla still there.

"Shouldn't you be studying with Sianna? You've spent a lot of time at home this year."

"Yes," she said. "I meant to say something earlier when you came back from your fight. But then with everything happening, I forgot. Hafor, and the harvest festival. And you've been on patrol. There never seemed to be a moment."

"I've got a moment now, if you have," I said.

"I'm building a house," she said.

"What? Where?"

"Down the dun, by the river. About a mile away. Don't look like that, Kiar. It's hardly a castle, only a dozen alder staves in a circle with willow woven through them for walls. I covered it with clay to keep out the weather. I bent the tops together for a roof, with more willow and clay. It's almost finished."

"Why do you need a house? You have a room here."

"It's for my work, for magic. A place to keep my tools and do magic where I can't be interrupted. I wish I'd had it when I was treating the lung fever. Trying to keep the spells from leaking all over the kitchen was difficult."

"The potions?"

"No—the spells. The words and the power, they get into things if you can't contain them properly. It's hard to explain. Having my own place will help."

"Why haven't I seen your house?" I asked.

She tipped her head. "Partly because I don't want anyone to find it," she said, "and partly because it's in a clump of alders. Ordinary, I know, but easier than the spells of hiding. It's temporary. When I'm fully trained, and when I've had enough practice, I can make one like Sianna's, with gardens and wider grounds and protection spells that stay in place by themselves."

"So you'll be staying here?"

"For a while, anyway," she said.

"Then we'll see more of you," I said as I turned for the stairs and my room.

She nodded. I didn't know what to think of Orla coming home, even for a while. I'd expected that she would live with Sianna for longer, and then make a place for herself away from people, as wisewomen usually did. I wished I knew what Sianna had told her to do.

At supper, I was shocked all over again at how Gil looked. It had been almost a year since the lung fever. He had gained some weight and a little colour, but he was still not his old self. His skin was pale and gray. He didn't dance at feasts, and I couldn't remember seeing him on a horse all year.

I noticed that now he watched Orla whenever she was in the room. Sometimes he even followed her around, although it clearly annoyed her.

"What's the matter with him?" I asked one day when Willow, Tuan, and I were out in the stable. "Can't he see she doesn't want him around?"

Willow looked up from the bit she was cleaning. "He almost died, and Orla saved him."

"I know, but he's well now, or better, anyway. It was Adana who looked after him most of the time."

Willow put down her work and chewed on her lip, thinking. "Have you had the lung fever?"

"Of course. Everybody gets it once, some more often."

"And you thought you were going to die."

"I coughed a lot, and I had a fever. I was in bed for several days. But I never thought I'd die. Hardly anyone dies from the lung fever."

"I thought I'd die," Willow said. "Tuan, too."

"But you were over it by the time I returned! Tuan, you brought me something to eat the first night, remember?"

"Yes, but Willow's right. At one time, I didn't know I'd get better."

"We usually don't," Willow said. "A swan sick enough to lose his appetite mostly dies."

"A predator finds him," Tuan said, "or the flock leaves, and he can't fly. Sometimes he drowns, especially if the water is cold. Or he just dies."

"You don't take care of each other?"

"We do, but not like you do. We don't have medicines, or a safe, warm place away from foxes and wildcats. It's easier for us to die."

"I feel a bit like following Orla around myself. She might have saved my life. And I wasn't nearly as sick as Gil," Willow said. "But maybe I was just as scared."

Now I understood why Gil wanted Orla nearby. If I'd been that sick and afraid, I would have felt the same. Still, it became harder and harder for Orla to break away for time alone in her house, and although she was patient, she was clearly not happy. After a few days, her irritation broke out.

"I have to get out of here!" she told Mother. "I want to go back to Sianna."

"The feast is the day after tomorrow," Mother said. "I sent a rider to Sianna early this morning to invite her. Wait and go back with her, swanling."

Orla grumbled a little but agreed. With the culling done, she took the opportunity to escape to her little house. Adana helped her shake Gil off.

We'd been slower than usual with the cull, but still we'd managed to beat the first snow. It began in the afternoon, fluffy, white feathers drifting down from a gray sky. When Orla came back after spending most of the day alone in her house, with her cheeks red from the cold and her braid sparkling with snow, she looked like a little girl.

The messenger returned late in the evening. Sianna had accepted Mother's invitation and would arrive the next day.

But overnight, the snow changed from drifting white feathers to a driving blizzard. The castle door was drifted in up to the latch, and when anyone had to go out or come in, it took all one person's strength to push the door closed against the wind. It was clear there would be no travel that day, and maybe not for days to come. If the blizzard went on long enough, nobody would travel again until spring.

THIRTY-ONE

"I don't understand why he's following her around," Adana said to Mother. The three of us sat by the fire in the solar. She and Mother were finishing the embroidery on her wedding dress, and I threaded needles and pretended to be useful.

"I don't know either, swanling," Mother said. "You know she's not happy about it."

"I think the lung fever did something to his mind. He doesn't seem himself anymore." Adana put down her needle and looked at Mother. "He wants to break our betrothal."

Mother stopped in the middle of a stitch. The needle trembled like a hovering dragonfly, sunlight from the tall windows sliding and dancing over its polished surface.

"That is serious. Did you agree?"

"No! But, oh, Mother, he said he doesn't love me anymore. He said he loves Orla."

"Swanling, that's nonsense. He treats her like a little sister."

"Not anymore," I said.

"He says she saved his life, and he loves her."

"That doesn't make any sense at all, Adana," I said. "You've been betrothed for over a year. How can he stop loving you because Orla cured him?"

"I don't know," she said.

"This is the last of the illness," I said. "He nearly died. You can't expect him to get better all at once. Anyway, he's not getting anywhere with Orla."

"Ye—es," Adana said, her voice breaking in the middle of the word.

"She's betrothed to Hafor, or almost. She wears that necklace he gave her all the time."

"I know, I know! But it doesn't matter what Orla feels or how she behaves," Adana said, "It's Gil—it's how *he* acts, and what *he* wants. It just feels useless," she said, "doing this embroidery. But if I keep doing it, I can pretend everything will be all right, and we'll get married at midwinter, as we planned.""

"You could ask Orla about it," I suggested. "She might be able to think of something to do."

"Swanling," Mother said to me, "if she knew something to do, don't you think she'd have done it by now?"

"Then we should send for Sianna," I said, "or at least, ask if there's something else, something Orla doesn't know about."

"In the winter, with the snow so deep, and nobody ill? Swanling, a messenger would take days to reach her. I'm sure Orla's doing all that can be done." Mother went back to her embroidery, and her face was smooth and calm. "She managed beautifully during the lung fever. I think we can trust her to know what needs to be done with this, too. Give Gil some time, and I'm sure he'll be himself again."

I opened my mouth to protest, then glanced at Adana. She was looking at Mother with an expression of wistful hope on her face. I closed my mouth, not wanting to destroy that fragile hope. Perhaps Mother was right.

The problem was, I didn't really believe it.

As winter wore on, Gil's new devotion to Orla seemed, if anything, to grow stronger. He recovered himself in every other way, but he no longer teased and joked or, it seemed, loved Adana. Within the castle walls, he was almost always at Orla's heels. Adana refused to break the betrothal, and as long as she would not consent, it couldn't be broken. Betrothed or not, it seemed to make no difference to Gil. Even Orla's carefully masked impatience with him made no difference. I couldn't imagine Hafor would be pleased, either.

The midwinter festival came and went. Adana, pale and thin as the ghost of some winter-starved woman, folded away her wedding dress. The long nights gradually shortened, and spring came on.

Halfway between midwinter and spring equinox, we held the festival of light.

We had a small feast, and Nias made a cake with dried fruit, and sprouted some of the grain. We were all so hungry for something fresh and green that we gobbled up the small sprouts more eagerly than the sweet. After the feast, we lit the candles and placed them on the ledge around the hall.

This year, I again put my candle apart from Father's and Mother's, and as I finished settling it firmly in place, Willow set hers beside it, and Tuan put his on the other side.

Adana and Orla lit their candles and placed them side-by-side. In the soft, yellow light, they seemed almost twins, but when they turned away, the shadows under Adana's eyes and in the hollows of her cheeks made her look years older. Orla could have been her daughter.

After Orla lit her candle, Gil placed his next to hers, and not next to Adana's as he had the year before. After everyone else had gone up to bed, I stood watching the family candles. Mother's and Father's candles, taller than the rest, stood over ours, casting their glow in a wide, double circle. Tuan's, Willow's, and mine burned in a row, the puddle of wax that formed around each running together in the middle. Adana's candle was dimmer than Orla's, but then I knew Adana was sad.

Gil's candle burned brightly, and unevenly. As I watched, one edge slumped and poured a stream of molten wax down the side. The wax flowed up against the base of Orla's candle and hardened there.

In the middle of the night, I woke up and remembered Orla's face in the light of the festival candle. Not this evening's candle but another one, a single flame casting a sphere of light in a darkened room. Orla giving Gil a cup and saying words I didn't understand. Orla hesitating before saying a final phrase that didn't seem to belong with the other words she'd said.

"Willow," I said, nudging her back.

"Mmf."

I poked her again, but she only snuggled further into her pillows.

Gil and Adana were still betrothed. Orla was as good as betrothed to Hafor. It was my imagination.

CHAPTER

THIRTY-TWO

Before the festival of light, I had seen what everyone else saw. Afterwards, I couldn't stop seeing Gil's infatuation and Orla's behavior differently. The thought niggled at me that she was acting, pretending she didn't care about Gil, pretending to be irritated with his adoration. Even to myself it didn't make any sense, but I couldn't let the idea go.

The days grew longer and warmer, and the snow began to melt away. Just before equinox, Guthric came with a message from Hafor. We received him in the hall. I sat on Father's left, with Orla beside me. She wore the necklace and bracelet that Hafor had given her. Adana sat on Mother's right, Gil beside her. Adana sat calm and straight, but her thinness and the lines around her eyes betrayed her unhappiness. Whatever Gil thought of sitting next to Adana, he still had sense enough to take his official place; he had not yet come to open defiance of my parents.

"Sire, Lady," Guthric said, "Prince Hafor asks you to give your blessing for his betrothal to Princess Orla. He would ask that the betrothal take place here, among her family, as soon as may be."

"We have not changed our mind," Father said. "If our daughter agrees to this match, we will be glad to accept Hafor as her chosen husband. But she will not wed until she is eighteen."

"The prince knows this," Guthric said, "and asked me to tell you that he will respect your wishes. He understands also that Princess Orla wishes to complete her studies in medicine and magic, and he is eager for her to do that as well before their marriage."

"Does this match suit you, daughter?" Father asked.

"It does, Sire," Orla said.

"Then you may tell Prince Hafor that his visit will be most welcome, and we will be prepared to celebrate his betrothal to our daughter."

"Both he and my lord King Gythorn will be most pleased," Guthric said, bowing. "Prince Hafor has sent a gift for the princess, although I'm afraid it's not fitting to bring it into the hall. If you would indulge me, Sire, in coming outside?"

In the courtyard a groom stood holding the bridle of a horse. The animal was bright, golden yellow, like butter in the summer when the cows eat fresh grass and wildflowers. Her mane and tail were pale as moonlight.

"Prince Hafor hopes this is an acceptable gift," said Guthric, smiling at Orla. "She is from a line bred for both speed and surefootedness."

"Oh, she's lovely!" Orla cried, her face lighting like a little girl's. "What is her name?"

"That," said Guthric, "is for you to decide, Lady."

Orla clasped her hands to her chest. "Come and speak to me before you leave, Guthric. I have a gift prepared to send back to Prince Hafor."

Guthric left the next day with messages of thanks for Hafor, and assurances that the betrothal would be prepared.

Orla put a small, embroidered leather bag into Guthric's hands. "Please see this goes straight from your hand to Prince Hafor's," she said.

Guthric smiled and bowed and tucked the bag into the inner pocket of his shirt. "No other will give it to him."

Orla's obvious delight in the golden mare, and her clear happiness with her upcoming betrothal, cheered everyone but Gil. Even my certainty that Orla had somehow stolen Gil wavered.

I'd always admired the horses of Noermark, but the thought of having one had been a faraway, impossible dream. My only chance had been when I bested Hafor in the circle, but I hadn't thought to take the horses. I'd only wanted Hafor and his men out of Valenia as quickly as possible. Mixed with my happiness at Orla's betrothal, and her pleasure in the golden horse, was a thread of envy.

"Cheer up," Willow said, "Maybe you can ask Hafor to give you a horse, too. I'm sure he'd be delighted. Look how easily he gave you his sword!"

Even Tuan smiled at that, but I sighed.

"I should have taken his horse when I had the chance," I said. "Even if Orla breeds that beauty, no stallion of ours will get a colt that looks like one of theirs."

"Too bad," Willow said. "Maybe we can talk his little brother into raiding and this time Tuan, and I will remind you to take the horses instead of the swords."

"Or we could raid Noermark and steal horses," Tuan said.

I scowled at him. "That better be a joke."

I wasn't the only one who was fascinated with the new mare. It seemed that every time I went to see her, whether in the stable or the paddock, there were several other people around her. I wanted her to myself, even for a few minutes, and could never manage it.

Nearly two weeks after Guthric left I woke one morning early, while there were still stars in the sky. The only people up would be the guard and some of the kitchen staff. Nobody would be going in and out of the stables on little errands. Nobody would be going out to hunt, or coming to look for a leather strap, or passing by. This was my chance.

"Willow," I whispered, shaking her shoulder gently.

"What? 'S too early."

"I'm going to look at Orla's horse."

"Mmmm."

That could mean anything.

I got out of bed, my feet curling as I tried to keep as much of my soles off the stone floor as possible. Willow sighed and got up, too, and we both dressed and crept out.

I felt a twinge of disloyalty to Kestrel, but I couldn't help it. I'd never seen a horse that colour, never imagined one could exist.

There were a few people about; the castle never slept completely. There were guards, but as I crossed the court towards the stables, I saw nobody but the men on the walls, darker shapes against the slowly lightening sky.

I pushed the stable door open gently, and we walked quietly down the aisle. As we passed each stall, the horse inside came into sight between the high wooden walls. Kestrel put her head over the door, and I stroked and fussed over her quietly for a few minutes. Willow did the same for Whiffle, two stalls down. Then we tiptoed quietly down to the golden mare. She looked out as we neared her and blew down her nose.

"So beautiful," I whispered, stroking her face.

Willow petted her neck, running her fingers through the fine mane. "Like the moon and the sun together."

I nodded, and wished I had an apple or some little treat for the mare. She wasn't mine, but I wanted her to like me.

Just then, I heard something rustle in the straw of an empty stall farther down the aisle. *Mouse,* I thought, and went back to petting the horse. Then I heard it again, something larger. Willow and I looked at each other. I put my finger to my lips, and she nodded.

I crept along the line of stalls, with Willow close behind. As I came to the second from the end, I saw a flash of blue fabric and drew back quickly. I peered quietly around again and saw Orla and Gil.

They were kissing. Orla stood pressed against the back of the stall, and Gil leaned down to her. Their arms were wrapped around each other, their bodies pressed tightly together, and Orla's fist was clenched on Gil's tunic.

The shock of it held me motionless. Willow leaned around me, and I heard the intake of her breath. Without thinking, I grabbed her arm. I put my fingers to my lips and shook my head. She frowned, and I pulled her away and hurried from the stable.

"What are you doing?" Willow said.

I jumped as though she'd shouted in my ear, although she'd spoken quietly enough.

"Ssh!"

"They were kissing," she said. "We have to tell Adana."

"No! I mean, yes, but I should talk to Orla first."

Willow stared at me. "Talk to *Orla*? What for?"

"I don't know. Tell her to stop?"

"The time for that was back there. Why did you drag me out? You've thought for years that Orla wanted to steal Gil, and now we've caught her at it, and you're acting like it's you who's done something wrong!"

"I know, I know. Ever since the festival of light, I've thought she did something, put a spell on him. But she's getting betrothed to Hafor, and I thought I must have imagined it. But thinking it's happening is different from seeing it. I couldn't say anything."

"Well, I could."

"And what would that do?" I tried to organize my thoughts, to explain to Willow. "It would upset Mother. It would make people angry. Orla and Hafor will be betrothed. If this came out in the open, that would all stop."

"I think that would be better," Willow said.

"Yes, but then it's an insult, and there might be fighting, and people getting killed. It would be better to settle it quietly, pick our time, and talk privately."

"Everyone will know anyway," Willow said. "I suppose they weren't caught before because you could hardly see them in the shadows, in those clothes. I wouldn't have noticed if you hadn't been staring. I only saw them because I looked where you were looking."

"What shadows? What clothes? Gil's shirt is blue. It was light enough to see that."

"That's not what I saw," Willow said. "But that's not important. We have to tell Adana."

"No," I said. "We can't just wake her up and tell her."

"You're right. She'll have to fight Orla for her mate, and she needs to be properly awake before we tell her. Let's wait until after breakfast."

"Willow, she's not going to fight Orla!"

"No? How will she get her mate back, then?"

"Sssh!" I said.

"We need to stay out of sight until breakfast. One look at your face, and Orla would know you saw her."

"Good thinking." Anything to get Willow away from the stable. We almost ran back through the hall and up the stairs. Once in our room, we watched the light bloom in the window and listened for the sounds of people passing our door. When we finally went downstairs, almost everybody was there.

Willow sat down beside Tuan, leaving room for me to slip in between them with my bread and cheese. Tuan often saw things differently. It would comfort me to talk to him, find out what he thought we should do.

"Meet in the stables after breakfast?" I said.

Willow kicked my ankle.

"Maybe we can avoid a fight," I said.

"A fight?" Tuan said.

Willow snorted and reached for her cup.

Tuan glanced down the table at Gil. Although Adana sat next to him, he acted as though he were alone.

"Where's Orla?" I asked, "Has she come down yet?"

"Gil said she went to her house before daylight." Tuan replied.

Then there was no danger Orla would overhear us. We could decide how to tell Adana, and what should be done. The knot in my stomach loosened a little, and I found it easier to swallow my food.

After breakfast, we went to the stables. Down at the other end, three people admired Orla's new horse and paid no attention to us.

"Ask him, then," Willow said, "but let's *do* something!"

Tuan turned to me.

"We – we saw Orla and Gil, kissing in an empty stall," I said in a low voice.

"When?"

"This morning."

"We have to tell Adana," Willow said. "I don't know why we're whispering. Everyone's going to know sooner or later."

"Diplomacy," I said. "We don't want Hafor to find out before we know what to do."

Willow shook her head.

"Nobody will believe me," I said to Tuan. "Mother's never believed Orla would try to take Gil. Orla's been acting angry with him all this time."

"I believe you," he said. "You don't lie. And Willow saw, too. That should be enough."

"See?" Willow said to me.

"Why is she doing this?" I said. "It doesn't make any sense."

"Not to you," Tuan said. "Maybe to them. Do they know you saw them?"

"No. If Orla knew, she'd do—something."

"Tell Adana," he said. "Gil is hers, her mate. It's her right."

"I can't," I said. None of us had ever told on each other. I could see this was far more than missed chores and filched apples, but it felt the same.

"If you don't," Willow said, "I will. She's going to be the Swan Queen. It's disloyal not to tell her."

"She won't fight," I said.

"She will," Willow said. It sounded like a promise.

I looked at Tuan, and back to Willow. Both waited for what I would say. I took a deep breath. "I'll do it, but this stays among us until Adana decides what to do. Don't say anything to anyone else. Promise?"

"I promise," Willow said. "As long as you tell her."

I looked at Tuan.

"I promise," he said.

He put his arms around me and pulled me close, and I leaned against him. I reached out and pulled Willow into our hug, glad to have allies. Then I straightened up. "I'll go talk to Adana now. Then we can go hunting, or something. I'll be back soon."

"Good luck," Willow said.

CHAPTER

THIRTY-THREE

I found Adana in her room, a little frown of concentration on her face. She had laid a tunic out on the bed, the front of it folded into pleats.

"Adana?"

"Oh, Kiar." She smiled, a ghost of what her smile had once been. "I'll have to take this in. It's so loose on me, it might have been made for Father."

"Adana, I have to tell you something."

She turned to me, her right hand still absently fingering the fine wool.

I took a deep breath. "I saw Gil and Orla this morning. They were in the stables, and they were kissing."

Her fingers stopped moving.

"They were— what? Are you sure?"

I nodded.

"I didn't mean to spy. Willow and I were looking at Orla's new horse, and I heard them."

"Kissing Gil?"

I nodded.

"And he was kissing her?"

"Yes. I'm sorry, Adana."

"She's agreed to marry Hafor!" Adana brought her hands to her sides, and her fingers curled into fists. "She's been *angry* with Gil for following her around!"

"I know what I saw, and, Adana, I think I know when she did it."

She looked at me with bewilderment on her face. I blundered on. "I don't know for sure, but when Gil had lung fever, the night I came home from patrol, she said she was going to try something different. She went down to her house, and when she came back, she gave Gil a drink. She said some words—I thought they were healing words."

"You let her do it!"

"Adana, I thought it was a healing spell! And Gil got better after that, he did!"

She stood trembling, her hands clenched at her sides. "Thank you, Kiar," she said. "You can go."

"Adana, I – "

"Just get out!"

I ran down the stairs and back out to the stables.

Lightfoot was saddled, and Tuan stood smoothing Kestrel's blanket carefully over her back. I ran into the stables and fetched up against Kestrel's door. The men at the other end of the stable looked up, then went back to their talk.

Willow peered out from Whiffle's stall. "What did she say?" she asked. "Is she going to fight?"

"She's really angry," I said, but softly. "She told me to get out."

I went to get Kestrel's saddle. My hands shook so badly, I nearly dropped it. Willow took the bridle. Back at Kestrel's stall, Tuan took the saddle and laid it carefully over the mare's back. As I bent to get the cinch, I heard footsteps outside, and Adana flew into the stables dressed in her riding clothes. She paused at the door, and then ran straight to Lightfoot's stall. I tried to open Kestrel's door, but Adana kicked it back hard, and I had to jump to avoid being hit. Kestrel shied and danced, throwing saddle and blanket onto the ground, and Whiffle flung up her head and whinnied. The men looking at Orla's golden horse stopped talking.

Willow managed to catch Whiffle's reins while Tuan and I tried to calm Kestrel. Adana flung Lightfoot's door open and slipped in. She had mounted him before we knew what she was doing, and rode him straight out, crouched low over his neck. She was out of the stable and clattering across the courtyard before we had Kestrel under control.

"She's going after Orla," I said. "No, leave the saddle, I'll do without." I heaved myself over Kestrel's back and rode after Adana. The guard at the gate stepped out of my way and I clucked to Kestrel as we started down the dun.

Adana still lay low over Lightfoot's neck, and he seemed to barely touch the ground, even downhill. I took the slope more slowly. I couldn't catch her now. Besides, whatever she had in mind, I thought Orla deserved a taste of it.

Lightfoot fairly flew down the dun and across the flat ground, angling towards a clump of alder by the river. At first I didn't see the little house, but suddenly it was clear as day, even among the bushes. Adana pulled Lightfoot up so sharply his haunches nearly hit the ground. She flung herself off his back and ran around the house. She stopped with her back to the river and screamed Orla's name. Her voice rose above the rush of the river, swollen and swift with melting snow.

"Come out, Orla!" she screamed, "Come out right now!" I caught up with Lightfoot, who came towards me, trailing his reins. Adana kicked at the door, and I heard the crunch of breaking willow.

"Come out here!" Adana screamed again.

Orla stepped out. She was bare to the waist and streaked with black and with ochre in red and yellow over her arms, face, and breast. Her hair was loose, crackling like silk in winter. Even from a dozen paces away, I felt my throat clench at the magic that poured off her skin in waves, like heat-ripple over rocks at midsummer. I turned sideways to it, my stomach lurching.

"What do you want?" she said, as though it were an ordinary question.

"You know what!" Adana shouted. "Whatever you've done to Gil, you take it off! Now! Right now!"

"I don't know what you're talking about."

"Do you think I'm a fool?!" Adana said. "Kiar told me! She saw you in the stables this morning."

Orla laughed. "You believe her, do you?"

"Yes! You've always wanted Gil. You tried before to take him from me!"

"It's not my fault he chose me," Orla said. "I can't help that."

"You were helping it this morning," I said.

Orla turned her head to look at me over her shoulder. She smiled, the barest curve of her lips. "You didn't see anything," she said.

The ripples of magic came faster, and I thought *back away*, but it didn't feel like my own thought. I turned my head, then looked back at her and brought the mare a step closer. My gorge rose. I spat a foul mouthful into the grass and wiped my mouth on my sleeve.

"I did," I said. "I saw you— and Gil—the last stall—" She raised her hand, and I thought again of backing away, without intending to think it. I shook my head and felt the magic break around me and flow by.

"Poor Kiar," Orla said, but there was no sympathy in her tone. "No lover, so little power. Maybe she's the jealous one. Did you think of that?"

I had never seen anyone move so fast. Adana hit Orla across the face. The force of the blow spun Orla around, and Adana flung her face-first against the hut and pinned her there. She wrenched Orla's right arm up behind her until she gasped.

"Take it off," Adana said. "Whatever you did, take it off *now*!"

She pulled up on Orla's wrist again, and Orla cried out. The ripples of magic slowed.

"Don't!" I said, "Adana, stop!" I slid off Kestrel and ran towards them. My feet didn't want to go where I wanted to put them. I staggered as I ran, but the waves of magic didn't press me back.

"Stay out of it." Adana's glare stopped me, a cold wall different from the heat-ripples of Orla's spell.

I stopped out of arm's reach. "You'll hurt her!"

"Good!" She twisted a handful of Orla's hair and jerked her head back. "Take it off."

For a few seconds, I thought Orla was choking; then, I realized she was laughing.

Adana pulled back and then slammed into her again, and Orla's breath came out in a grunt.

"Now you know," Orla said. It was almost a wheeze. "Now you know."

"Know what?" Adana said between her teeth.

"What it's like to want something so badly you'll do anything to get it. Will you kill me, sister? Will you kill me to get Gil back?"

"Do I have to?"

Adana jerked Orla's arm up again, and Orla cried out, then sucked in a gasping breath and closed her eyes. In a few seconds, she opened them again and strained to look back at Adana. She managed a smile.

"Careful," she said, panting. "If you break it, I won't be able to help him at all."

"So you did it."

"Oh, yes. I wanted him so much, and he didn't want me. You'd have done it, too, in my place."

"You knew he was mine, betrothed to me," Adana said.

"He would have died." Orla panted for breath. "You would have lost him anyway. I saved him. He's mine by right."

Adana jerked Orla away from the hut by her hair. In a flash Orla twisted her arm free and seized the hand Adana had in her hair. I had to jump back as they kicked and punched at each other.

I grabbed for Orla's arm, but the power still clinging to her skin turned my stomach again. She threw me off, and I stumbled away. It couldn't have been more than a few seconds, but when I looked back, Adana had Orla on her knees, and again had her by the hair, her own knee on Orla's shoulder.

"Take it off," Adana said, "and we'll see who he really loves!"

"If you want it done, do it yourself. There's my house. There are my books and my potions. Go on and try."

Adana gave a wordless cry. She jerked Orla to her feet and shook her, then threw her hard against the little house. Orla pushed off and charged at Adana, and Adana stepped aside and thrust hard at her back as she passed. Orla stumbled. As she fought to recover her balance, she stepped onto the slippery clay bank above the river.

Time slowed, and she hung suspended on the bank, flailing her arms. I thought I could catch her before she fell, but my movements took forever. With my foot still in midair, I saw Adana lunge forward in slow motion, hands open to grasp.

Then time snapped back into place and Orla slipped, both feet on the slick red clay, and disappeared head-first down the bank. Adana landed hard on her stomach. When I reached her, all she had in her hands was clay, and the only sign of Orla was the mark of her boots in two long, shallow gouges that ended in the river at its spring flood.

"There!" Adana said, pointing. In the middle of the river a pale arm rose above the swift-flowing surface and submerged again. In the flash of time it took to appear and disappear, it swept along the river faster than I could run.

I couldn't move; I couldn't speak. A moment before, Orla had been there, and now she was gone. Adana broke our stunned silence.

"I couldn't catch her," she said. "Where is she?"

"Downriver." I shook my head, trying to think. "We have to go after her. Come on!"

I looked around for the horses. Kestrel stood almost where I'd left her, Lightfoot a little farther away, both watching us. I clucked to Kestrel, and she blew down her nose and let me come up to her. I mounted and caught Lightfoot. When I turned, Adana stood by the hut, her hands over her face.

"Adana, come on!" I said. She looked up, and I saw she was crying.

"I didn't mean to push her in!"

"I know. Maybe she can get out farther along. I'll ride down to the rapids and work up. You look from here down."

"Yes." Adana rubbed her sleeve across her eyes and took Lightfoot's reins. Without waiting for her to mount, I turned Kestrel and put her into a gallop.

I rode parallel to the river, watching for the rapids a mile or so down. Orla would have to get out before she reached them, and she'd have to be quick and lucky. We were all good swimmers, but not in the cold, swift water of the river in spring flood.

I looked at the river more often than at the ground ahead

of me, trusting my horse's sure-footedness. I saw nothing of my sister Orla.

When I reached the rapids, I scanned the rocks. Perhaps she had managed to catch hold of one and hold on. Getting her out before the water tore her loose or pounded her under would be hard, cold work. I saw no sign of her, nothing that looked like a person in the foam and rush of cold water on cold rock.

I walked back up the river, close to the bank, leading the mare. At every snag, every eddy, every clump of willow, I leaned out and looked. I called her name, but without hope.

Something bobbed in the water, in a little eddy where the bank had fallen away and made a curve. The current tore by, but a little pocket of calmer, swirling water reached in below the undercut earth. Bare strands of root dangled from the clump of willows on the bank. Ahead of me, I heard Adana calling Orla. I must have come farther than I'd thought on my way back.

I found a place where I could get down the bank without falling in myself. As I slid down, clinging to the willow roots, Adana galloped up.

"Have you found her?" she cried.

I didn't answer, too occupied with my footing and keeping half an eye on the bobbing thing. It was smooth, paler than the water around it, though not as white as Orla's skin.

As I reached the water and leaned down, the thing turned, and I saw a neat patch stitched onto it. I knew that patch—Orla had put it on her boot over the winter. I felt a stab of hope; people who drowned in cold water sometimes came back to life. Someone with Orla's power would surely be harder to kill. If I could get her out quickly, we might still revive her. I grabbed at the boot.

The moment my hand closed on it, the sides collapsed. There was no foot in the boot, no ankle to seize, no Orla to pull out of the water and restore to life.

"Have you got her?" Adana asked from above me. I straightened up and showed her the boot.

"No," I said. "She's gone, Adana." My hand shook, and I had to clench my fingers on the sodden boot to keep from dropping it.

"Don't say that," Adana said. "Don't say it."

"She's not here," I said. I began to cry, my feet braced against the bank, a muddy willow root wrapped around my left hand, pinching the skin below my fingers, and Orla's waterlogged boot clutched in my right. Terror, grief, and remorse hit me at once; I howled until my throat was raw while tears ran down my face, only barely aware that Adana was crying, too, as noisily as I was.

When I could finally stop my legs ached from the strain of standing on the sloping undercut. Cramps ran up my left arm from knuckles to shoulder.

"We have to go home," Adana said. Her voice was hoarse from crying. "Can you get up the bank?"

She took the boot out of my hand and helped me back up onto the grass. The palm of my left hand was scraped and sore, and every muscle in my legs and back hurt. I bent over to ease my back, with my hands on my knees. When I straightened and looked at Adana, a dark bruise had bloomed on her right cheekbone, and that eye looked bloodshot.

We rode towards home, not talking. As we approached Orla's house, Adana pulled up.

"She had a fire going. I'll put it out," she said. Without waiting for an answer, she dismounted and went into the hut. I sat waiting, wishing I was back in my bed, that I'd never gone to the stables that morning to look at Orla's golden horse, that all of this could somehow be a bad dream. The sun was only halfway to noon.

When Adana came out of the hut, she propped the broken door back against the opening. We rode up the dun, much more slowly than we'd ridden out.

"What do we tell them?" Adana's voice trembled. She had always been the calm, sure one. Hearing her sound uncertain was almost as big a shock as seeing her in rage. I thought about my answer for a minute.

"As much of the truth as we can," I said at last. "And no lies. We'll say that you came down to beg for help with Gil. You interrupted her work, and she was angry and hit you. While you were fighting, you pushed her away and she fell down the bank. All of that is true. Then I rode down the river to look for her and didn't find her. That's true, too."

"What's the use? Why not just tell the whole truth?"

I leaned over to take hold of Lightfoot's bridle with my right hand and pulled Kestrel to a stop. Lightfoot stopped, too, turning his head towards me.

"Adana, they think she was their good, youngest daughter, studying to be a wisewoman. And Mother's so proud of her being the black swan, the first one in hundreds of years. It's bad enough that she's dead. How can we tell them she was selfish and cruel and used her power to steal Gil? I don't think they'd even believe us. You know how Mother feels about Orla. Remember when we were working on your wedding dress? When you told her Gil said he loved Orla? She'd never believe this."

Adana said nothing, her mouth set in a stubborn line.

"All right," I said, "What if they do believe us? It will break Mother's heart."

She twisted Lightfoot's reins in her fingers.

"You can't tell them the whole truth, Adana. I don't like it either, but it would be worse, whether they believed us or not. It wasn't your fault she fell into the river. You tried to save her."

I waited while Adana stared ahead, as though the answer to everything lay in the grass bending and rippling in the breeze, in the sound of the river.

Finally, she looked at me. "All right." She sounded as tired as if she'd had a long day at harvest. "We can't bring her back. At least let them go on thinking well of her. And Gil will be free of her spell. So I'm glad! I'm glad she's dead!" Her voice rose on her last words.

I put my finger on my lips. "I know. Just don't say it out loud, ever again."

She nodded.

"We should ask Sianna what to do with her things."

Adana said nothing. She turned Lightfoot away from me, and I let his bridle slip from my fingers. Together, we rode up to the gate. Dar said nothing when we came in. Surely he'd heard all the noise or seen something amiss? His brows drew together a little at the sight of us, Adana with her bruised face and hair torn loose from its braid, and me muddy from the riverbank.

We took the horses to the stables. Sword practice was happening across the courtyard, and when I glanced over, I saw someone leave and come towards us. While we were still getting the horses into their stalls, Tuan came in, sweating from practice. He took Lightfoot's reins from Adana.

"I'll do that," he said. "What happened?"

"She's dead," I said.

"Who?" he asked. Then, "Orla. Are you certain?"

"She fell into the river. We couldn't find her. I'm certain, Tuan. I wish I wasn't."

"We have to go and tell Mother and Father," Adana said.

Tuan put his free hand on my shoulder.

"What do you need?"

"I don't know," I said. "For this not to be true."

He squeezed my shoulder and reached for Kestrel's reins.

"Leave the horses," Tuan said, "I'll look after them."

"Thank you," Adana said.

I followed her out of the stable.

"You don't have to come," she said.

"Yes, I do," I answered.

Together, we went in search of our parents.

We found Mother in the dairy, and she sent a man to find Father. A short while later the four of us stood in Father's private chamber.

"What's happened?" Father said.

I opened my mouth, but Adana cut me off. "Orla's dead," she said. "She fell in the river and drowned. The current—we couldn't find her. She's gone." Then she began to cry, burying her face in her hands and sucking gasps of air between her sobs. Father stood as though he'd been turned to stone.

"Kiar," Father said. "Is this true?"

"I wish it wasn't," I said. "We looked for her all the way down to the rapids. All we found—" I had to stop and choke back my own tears. "All we found was her boot."

Then a shriek drowned out Adana's sobbing. Mother fell to her knees on the floor, tearing at her hair and raking her fingers down her face. She screamed again and beat her fists on the floor.

"Tianis, my heart, don't!" my father said. He bent down to lift her up, and she thrust out her arms and pushed him so hard, he stumbled back and fell half into his chair. Then she bent over again, rocking and wailing, her arms wrapped around herself, before she beat her fists on the stone again.

I couldn't move. Was this my mother? Even Adana was shocked out of her tears, and for a few, eternal seconds, we simply gaped. Then Adana knelt beside Mother and tried to hold her hands.

"No!" Mother shouted, her voice hoarse and strange. She struck Adana twice across the face and then pushed her away, too. "You were always jealous! She's the black swan, she can't be dead, not my Orla. She can't be dead!" She shrieked again and pulled at her hair. Broken strands clung to her fingers, and a thin line of blood showed below her left eye, where a fingernail had torn the skin.

"Mother," I said, and she glared at me. "Mother, don't please. Nobody was jealous, nobody wanted this to—"

"You!" she screamed, pointing at me. "Don't speak to me! You were the most envious of all! You're glad she's dead. Don't pretend you're not!" I looked at Father, still sitting where he'd landed when Mother pushed him. His face was in his hands, and his shoulders heaved.

Slowly, as though Mother might attack her if she moved too quickly, Adana pushed herself up off the floor. She stepped back and groped for my hand.

"What can we do?" she whispered. I shook my head. I'd never seen Father so helpless, or Mother so wild. I didn't know whether to leave or stay.

"Let's go," Adana said, tugging at my arm. I shook her off and edged around Mother, who still wailed and rocked on the floor. I put my hand on Father's shoulder.

He didn't look up. The sounds he made were too soft to be heard over Mother's clamour, but I felt his body shake, then pause, then shake again as he tried to strangle his sobs. I knew how that tearing pain in the chest felt, when you had to breathe, and breathing hurt. I patted his shoulder, the way I would have patted Kestrel, and he seized my hand in one of his own, holding so tightly I clenched my teeth as my fingers ground together.

If there was ever a time to cry, it was now. Orla was dead. Mother had said things I could hardly believe I'd heard, and my father, the king, was shaking with sobs. Yet I felt no tears in my eyes, no lump in my throat. The room, Adana, Mother, and Father all seemed small and far away, and Orla the farthest away of all. Even my own body didn't feel quite real to me, except for the pain in the hand Father clutched. I waited in a dazed, remote calm for something to change, for some reason to move.

I don't know how long I stood there. Mother's voice became hoarse, and she collapsed onto the floor and moaned. Father stopped crying at last and let go of my hand. My fingers were numb, and I shook them and rubbed them with my other hand. Adana was gone—I hadn't noticed her leaving. Father ran his hands through his hair and turned his face towards Mother.

"Tianis." His voice was a croak. She never gave any sign she'd heard. "Tianis," he said again, then looked at his own hands.

"It wasn't anyone's fault," I said. "Adana wanted her to help Gil. She interrupted what Orla was doing, and they fought. Orla slipped down the bank. We tried to catch her, Father, we did, and we searched all down the river to the rapids—"

"Not now, Kiar," Father said.

I'd never heard him sound tired. He never looked up at me.

"Just go, for now," he said. "Give your mother time to calm down."

I didn't see Adana when I stepped out. I stood for a few seconds, wondering where to go. My knees trembled, and my hands. I looked at my sore left palm, smeared with mud and blood. The root had rubbed the skin away on both sides of my hand.

Nobody was in the corridor outside the council chamber; nobody was in the great hall. Even the kitchen was quiet. Curious, I looked in and saw two of Nias's helpers cutting vegetables, moving slowly and quietly, not talking. When they saw me, they stopped what they were doing and looked. Everyone in the castle must have heard Mother screaming. I walked quietly upstairs to my room and washed my hands in the basin there. I found a strip of cloth and wound it around my hand, but I couldn't tie it properly one-handed, and I tore it off again. A little thin blood seeped along the creases of my palm.

"Kiar?"

Willow stood in the doorway.

"What happened, Kiar? Is it true, Orla's dead?"

I nodded my head and felt tears in my eyes again. I wiped at them with the back of my hand.

She came and put her arms around me. With one hand, she stroked my hair, and I leaned my head on her shoulder.

"I'm sorry," she said. "But whatever happened, it's not your fault."

"You don't know that," I said. "I could have pushed her in. You don't know I didn't."

"All right," she said. Her voice was soft, not the voice of the Willow I knew. "If you tell me you killed Orla, I'll believe you did." She pulled away, her hands on my shoulders, and peered into my face. "Tell me you killed her, and I'll believe it," she said again.

I said nothing.

"See?" she said.

"I'm afraid," I said. "I'm afraid of what's going to happen now. Mother was so..."

"We heard," Willow said. "What about the king?"

I shook my head.

"I don't know, Willow. He cried. He *cried*. And Mother pushed him away. What's going to happen?"

"I don't know," she said, putting her arms around me again.

Willow bandaged my hand, and we went back downstairs. It was still quieter than usual in the hall and kitchen, but outside, we heard horses. When we got out, we saw Adana talking to one of the guard while three others waited, already on their horses. When she finished speaking, he bowed and mounted, and the whole group rode out.

"There you are," Adana said as we reached her. Her voice was hoarse; my own throat ached in sympathy. Her eyes were red, but dry. The bruise had puffed out her cheek; her right eye was hardly more than a slit.

"What are you doing?" I asked.

"Organizing a search. Someone has to." She glanced at the walk along the wall, where Gil stood looking towards Orla's house. For a moment, her brow furrowed, then her face cleared. She looked almost happy.

"He'll come back to himself now, won't he?" she said. Before either of us could speak she hurried on. "If we can find Orla, Orla's body, maybe it will help. Gil, I mean, and Mother."

"Where are Mother and Father?" I asked. "Have they come out?"

She shook her head.

"I want to go and look," I said. "I have to do something. One of us should go, someone from the family. I thought Father, but—"

"I'll go with you," Willow said. "Adana, will you be all right alone?"

"I'm not alone," she said, glancing at Gil again. "And I'll keep away from Mother."

"I don't know how you can be so calm," I said.

"Nor do I," she answered. "I feel far away, like it happened to someone else. Or it's a story, and if I do the right thing, I can bring her back."

"Those are only tales," Willow said. "Nobody comes back from being dead."

"But we must look. You can take Lady," Adana said to me. "I won't be going anywhere."

"No," I said. "I'll fly. I can cover the other side of the river. It'll be faster."

"I'll go with you," Willow said.

On the far side of the castle, by the small back gate, we undressed. As we tucked our clothes against the wall, I looked at the sun—it was barely noon. That morning I'd seen Orla kissing Gil in the stable; now she was dead.

Willow changed, and I shook myself from my distraction and did the same. In a moment we had left the earth behind and flung ourselves into the sky. Willow dropped behind, letting me take the lead. I circled once, then flew across the river and turned along it, with the sun on my back. We left the castle and Orla's house behind us and flew as slowly as we could down the river.

For the first time I felt no joy in flight. The air held me, and I pushed through it, with every stroke feeling as though I flew against a headwind. Orla would never fly again. Orla would never dance again, or light her candle at the festival of light, or eat a honey cake or ride Star. She would never grow up and marry, or live to be wisewoman for the kingdom, or have children with any man of the swans or the human people.

If I hadn't told Adana what I'd seen, Orla would still be alive. I'd told Father it was nobody's fault, but in my heart, I felt it was mine. I didn't know how to judge Adana; I'd seen her grieved, afraid, and angry about Gil. But I judged myself. I didn't know what would have happened if I hadn't told her, but it couldn't have been worse than this.

We flew down the river and back, passing the riders on the other bank, circling around and weaving above the water, looking for anything that didn't seem right. We saw no sign of Orla anywhere in the water, or on the shore.

When we came back to the castle and landed, I fumbled my clothes back on. Willow was dressed while I was still tying my belt. My shoulders ached, and my hands were slow and clumsy. My head felt stuffed full of wool. I wanted to curl up in my bed and never come out again. Even the thought of seeing my mother made my stomach flip and my throat tighten.

As we came to the door of the castle, I looked for Tuan.

"He was with the men," Willow said, as though she'd read my thoughts. "Didn't you see him?"

"No," I said. My disappointment surprised me. I hadn't realized how much I'd wanted to see Tuan, to have him nearby. Willow put her arm around my shoulders and hugged me briefly.

"We were faster, as you said. He'll be back with the others." She didn't say "He'll find her."

If he did, I thought he'd be just as likely as not to leave her wherever the river had dropped her. Swans didn't bury their dead.

Adana was up on the wall with Gil. She was watching his face, and their hands were joined, although Gil didn't seem to be paying any attention to her. It seemed a hopeful sign that he was letting her hold his hand. Perhaps some good would come out of this after all.

"This morning seems like a year ago," I said. "Everything that's happened. Mother. Father. I feel like there are no walls. I feel alone."

"The walls are still here," Willow said. "Your people are here. The flock goes on, even if one swan dies. Even if the king dies, and the queen, the flock goes on. There's another king. or another queen. You're not alone."

She meant to comfort, but her words chilled me. I wasn't ready to be queen.

CHAPTER

THIRTY-FOUR

The first thing I did when I went into the castle was go to Father's chamber. The guard at the door saluted me; his face was grim. I couldn't hear any sound through the heavy planks of the door.

"Are they still in there?" I asked.

"The king came out shortly after you left, Lady," he said. "The queen is still there. Did you want to go in?" He put his hand on the latch of the door.

I did not want to go in, but Mother was alone. She might not want my help, but she might accept it from her lady-in-waiting.

"Send someone for Elena," I said to the guard. He nodded and opened the door.

The fire had died down, and the air felt cooler than when I'd left. Two of the candles had gone out; new shadows lay across the floor and furniture. The sharp after-scent of burned hair stung the back of my nose.

For a moment I didn't see Mother. I was looking for her on the floor, where she'd been when I left. And when she spoke, I jumped.

"Did you find her?" Mother's voice was hoarse, hardly more than a whisper. She'd never looked so small. She was curled into her chair, her feet tucked up and arms around herself. Blood and ash streaked her face, and her dark hair fell down around her bare shoulders.

"Did you find her? We will send for Sianna. She'll know what to do."

"No. We didn't find her. The men are still out looking." I whispered, too, although I didn't know why.

"Look again. She wants to come home, I know it. She wants you to find her."

I said nothing.

Mother turned her head and looked at me out of her left eye. "You don't want to find her. You're afraid."

"No," I said. But she was right. I was afraid, not of finding Orla, but of her, of my mother. She stood up, and her robe and chemise, both torn, slid off her right shoulder. She shook her arm out of the sleeve on that side. She stooped to the dying fire, rubbed her hands in the ashes, and picked up a double handful. Smoke trickled between her fingers, but her face never changed. She raised her hands over her head and dropped the hot ashes and black coals on herself. The smell of burning hair sprang up again as the coals fell onto her hair and glanced off. She dragged her hands over her hair and face and rubbed them down her dress on the left and her bare skin on the right. She fixed me again with one eye and turned her hands towards me. Even in the dimmer light and through the rubbed-in ash, I saw the oozing burned spots.

"Mother, Elena's coming. Let her look after you. You need to sleep."

"Not until Orla comes back," she said.

"She's not coming back." As soon as the words left my mouth, Mother shrieked and tore at her clothes. I tried to put my arms around her, but she fought me, beating at me with her arms and head. I shielded my own head and turned my shoulder while she struck me again and again. Then she stopped, and I heard her breathy rasp and the sound of cloth tearing.

When I looked up, she was naked. She threw herself against me and knocked me to the floor. Before I could rise, she was through the door and gone, her bare feet slapping against the stone floor.

"Lady!" That was Elena's voice, then the thud of flesh hitting stone and Mother's footsteps fading.

I pushed myself up and ran after her. The guard was helping Elena up. I dodged past them and ran to the end of the short corridor. Raised voices from outside told me where she'd gone, and then I saw the bright flare of the change. When I reached the door, it was already too late.

The swan beat into the air, ash falling from her feathers as she rose. She called out again and again as she flew away downriver. I heard nothing of what people shouted around me, only my mother's voice fading as she flew away, seeking the only thing that mattered to her.

I don't know how long I stood there, watching Mother until she dipped in the sky and disappeared behind the castle walls. I stared as though staring would bring her back. Nobody spoke to me or touched me; I couldn't have said what I was thinking. The world had turned upside-down, and I didn't know how to right it.

Someone must have found Father and told him what had happened, because when I came back to myself, he was leading Cloud across the courtyard. I caught up with him as he mounted.

"Where are you going?" I asked.

"To look for your mother." He looked over Cloud's head to the river.

"The sun will be setting soon," I said. I reached up and tugged his arm, trying to make him look at me. "Do you think you'll find her out there in the dark?"

"What if she's hurt or hiding somewhere? I have to look."

"You won't find her if she's hiding. Please, Father," I said. "Orla's gone. Mother's gone. Please, don't you go, too."

"Maybe she wants me to find her. Maybe she wants me to come after her. You can't understand, Kiar."

"I can, too! She pushed us all away and flew off. She wouldn't even let you touch her!"

"She's hurting. She was proud of Orla." He looked down at me at last. The lines on his face shocked me. He looked years older than he had that morning. "It's hard on your mother, Kiar, to lose Orla. She'll need me when she—she'll need me."

"What about the people?" I asked. "What about me? We need you, too! When are you coming back?"

He clucked to Cloud and rode away. I tried to hold on, running to keep up with the horse, but his arm pulled free of my hand. I stumbled, almost falling in the grass.

I watched him canter Cloud down the hill and turn towards the lake. It occurred to me that Mother might have gone to the lake, to her family.

As I entered the hall, I smelled food cooking. Supper would be on the table soon, and my knees and hands began to tremble again. When had I last eaten? Not since breakfast, and I had thrown that up. My strength deserted me, and I stumbled over to a bench and collapsed onto it. I folded my arms on the table and put my head down, closing my eyes and waiting for the whirling feeling to stop.

I woke to a hand on my back, gently shaking me. A man's voice spoke, dragging me up through the layers of exhaustion. I heard only the voice, no words. I didn't want to wake—something terrible waited for me. The voice came again.

"Kiar, wake up." At first I thought it was my father, and the feeling of dread lightened a little. What was I afraid of?

"Wake up. Have some supper." Not Father's voice at all, then, but Tuan's. The sense of dread sharpened again. I wanted to swim back down into sleep, but I smelled something savory. Hunger dragged me up the last little bit to wakefulness and I sat up, rubbing gritty eyes. The bench joggled as someone sat down next to me. When I looked, there was a plate of food—slices of meat, roasted roots, bread, in front of me.

"Here," Willow said from my left, setting a wooden cup on the table. Steam rolled up from it. "Nias thought you'd better have this. It'll help you sleep."

"I *was* sleeping," I said. The hall was almost empty. A few torches burned around the walls, and some candles on tables where people leaned together in talk, hunched and tense. One voice rose enough for me to hear.

"Not really dead. Who knows, with wisewomen? And she was in the middle—" Someone else said "Shh!" and everyone in the hall looked around at me, then turned away, their voices falling low again. Tuan watched me, his face grave.

"You didn't find her, did you?" I asked.

He shook his head.

"No. She didn't come out of the river."

"So she's gone," I said. "Has Father come back? Did he find Mother? Did she—did he bring her home?"

"No," Willow said. "I flew over the lake. She's there, Kiar, I saw her. The king was on the bank, calling her, and she wouldn't come. He was still there when I left. I don't know if he'll be back tonight."

I cut a piece of meat and put it in my mouth. It was tender and juicy, and I felt guilty for enjoying the taste, for even thinking about eating. What was the point?

"It doesn't seem worth it to eat," I said.

"You can't just give up and die," Willow said. "The flock needs a king, or a queen, no matter what happens. One person dying shouldn't make all this trouble!"

The small sounds of other people talking stopped, and every head turned towards us.

"Willow," Tuan said. "It's Kiar's sister."

"I'm sorry, Kiar," she said. She went on, but in a softer voice. "People are saying she might not really be dead."

"She is," I said. "She couldn't survive the rapids."

"She is—was—a wisewoman, or learning to be one. What if she can use magic against them, even now? That's what they're saying. And the king is no help. He's lost his mate, and he's grieving. You saw him—he went out to find the queen. He left you and Adana behind. He abandoned the flock."

"When he went to hunt the boar, he left us. That came out all right."

"Exactly," Willow said. "You looked after things then, even when the queen was here, and Orla was alive. What's different now is that the queen is gone, and the king left without saying anything about who was in charge. It's more important for you to look after things now than it was then."

"What about Adana? She organized the search."

"Adana isn't going to be queen here. Anyway," Willow said, "she'll have her hands full with Gil. She had a hard time getting him down from the wall and into his room. It took two men. He keeps trying to get out."

"Eat," Tuan said. "It does no good to starve."

I took another mouthful. My stomach growled, and for a few minutes I was completely occupied with eating. Even Willow said nothing. The quiet of the hall bothered me. Nobody laughed, and the people spoke in hushed voices. It felt all wrong.

"People are afraid," I said. "If this gets out, Gythorn will be on us faster than you can think."

"Maybe not," Tuan said. "You beat Hafor. The men followed you and took your orders."

Before I could answer, Adana came down the stairs, every step as slow as an old woman's. When she entered the hall, the people at the fire greeted her. A woman stopped on her way out to put her hand on Adana's shoulder and speak to her. I couldn't hear what she said, but Adana smiled and answered her before coming over to our table. She slid onto the bench across from me and sighed.

"He's stopped trying to get out, at least," she said. "I have a guard on the door, and one inside to keep him from hurting himself. I suppose all we can do is wait. This has to wear off, doesn't it? Now that she's dead?"

None of us had an answer for that—even Willow was silent.

"What about the fire?" Adana said. Willow glanced at the hearth and back to me, one eyebrow raised.

"Not that fire," I said. "The funeral fire. If someone doesn't come back, if we can't find them, we burn something of theirs and say goodbye."

"We should have that," Adana said. "Say goodbye, the same as we would for anyone else. I don't suppose we're going to find her body." Her face crumpled, and I thought she would cry, but she didn't.

"No," I said. "This is different. Look at them." I nodded at the group by the fire. "Orla was special. Magic. That scares them. You did the right thing. You sent people out to look for a body, the same as we'd do if anyone else drowned."

"But we didn't find her," Adana said.

"Then we have to find her, I said. "It's the only way we can prove she really died."

"We know she died. We were there when the river took her. Do you think she could have hidden from us?"

"I don't think so," I said, but it doesn't matter what we know, Adana. What matters is *them*," I said. I used my spoon to gesture at the people in the hall. "They don't know if she's really dead. They're afraid of her. Other people's children have died, and the mothers don't go mad. Fathers don't leave everything without a thought. Maybe they think she caused their reactions."

"And you think finding her body will reassure them?"

"I don't know," I said.

"We should wait until Father comes back before we make a decision," Adana said. "If we do this too quickly, it will look like we don't think he can rule."

"It's Kiar's decision," Willow said, "not yours. Kiar will be queen here." This time she kept her voice down.

Adana glared at her.

"Not yet," I said. With everything in pieces, I didn't need Adana and Willow at odds. "But we need to think about it soon. How long, Adana? How long do you want to wait?"

"It hasn't even been a day," she said. "We should wait until morning. In fairy tales, the time of day something happens is important. Maybe she has to be dead a whole day for the spell to wear off Gil. Or for her body to come to shore. We could wait that long, couldn't we?"

Willow shook her head but said nothing. Even Tuan looked away. Tears glittered in Adana's eyes. She'd been brave all day, through everything, and she was afraid for Gil.

"One day, then," I said. "Until noon tomorrow. If Father is still the same, and Mother hasn't come back, we have to do something."

"The longer you wait, the harder it's going to be," Willow said. "Right now you could probably put her over a horse and bring her home. In a couple of days—"

"I know," I said. "I know."

CHAPTER

THIRTY-FIVE

I didn't want to be in the hall, but I didn't want to be alone, either. We sat on while other people drifted off to their beds. I took my bowl to the kitchen after everyone had left, and on the way back brought a couple of candles from other tables.

"I should go and see how Gil's doing," Adana said.

After she left, the hall seemed to close around me. My chest felt tight, and I couldn't breathe properly. "I need to go outside," I said, pushing away from the table. I heard Willow and Tuan get up and follow me, but I didn't look back.

Outside, the air was cooler, and my chest loosened a little. I walked away from the torches and into the shadows by the castle wall. Out of the corner of my eye, I saw movement at the door, but neither of my friends came closer. I slid a little farther along the wall, leaning against the stone and letting the cold seep through my clothes.

Maybe it was because I'd slept, but Orla's death seemed to have fallen into place in my mind. Now the world had changed, and I would have to change with it. On the wall, the guard walked slowly back and forth. They never looked in, where torches would have ruined their night vision, but only out at the dark. One of them called out.

"A rider!" he shouted. The sounds on the wall told me other guards had moved to look. A few minutes later, the same voice said, "The king! Open the gate!"

In the quiet night, the sound of the hinges told me the guard had opened one wing of the gate. A horse walked slowly in. Even without the torchlight, Cloud's pale coat would have shown up on any but the darkest night.

"The queen, Sire?" someone asked. My father didn't speak, only dismounted and walked slowly towards the hall.

I waited for him to come into the light of the torches. His face was closed and told me nothing of what he felt, but I'd never seen him look so tired and old. He was alone. I wanted to know what had happened, what my mother had done or said, whether she would ever come back or would stay a swan forever. I wanted to know if she still loved me. But his face looked like stone, and I couldn't imagine him hearing me, let alone answering.

He went inside, pulling the hall door shut behind him. I closed my eyes, and the world seemed to spin around me again. I couldn't bear the dizziness and tried to open my eyes. They wouldn't open, and I felt as I did in nightmares, when I tried to run from horrors, and the ground grabbed at my feet. Now, however, I knew that something terrible would happen if I didn't open my eyes. It was coming closer, ready to seize me, and my heart began to race. My head whirled.

"Wake up," a voice said. It chuckled, then said, "Open your eyes, Kiar. Look at me." It was a whisper that turned my knees to water, and I felt myself beginning to fall. My eyes flickered open as the thing grabbed me. Willow stood by me, her hand on my shoulder.

"Kiar," she whispered, "did you fall asleep?"

"I must have," I whispered back. "There was something after me. It almost got me but then you told me to wake up."

She frowned, and then looked around at Tuan, standing at her shoulder.

"I didn't say anything to you until you opened your eyes."

There was nobody left in the hall when we crossed it to the stairs. The distance to my bedroom had never seemed so long. I fell asleep as soon as I lay down.

I slept deeply that night, except for waking once when I heard something outside my door. I opened my eyes and lay there for a few seconds before sitting up.

"Go back to sleep," Willow said in the darkness. "You need to rest."

"Why are you awake?"

"I'm keeping watch. Tuan's outside the door."

"What? Why?"

I heard movement in the darkness. Willow put her hand on my shoulder and gently pushed me back down.

"Protection," she said.

"From what?"

"From anything or anyone trying to get in. Anyone trying to catch you in your sleep. Go back to sleep, Kiar."

I closed my eyes again. Although I was sure I wouldn't be able to sleep, when I next opened my eyes, the light of dawn showed against the wall. I turned over and saw Willow by the window, peering out.

"Did you not sleep?" I asked.

"No. I'll sleep now. The king rode out a little while ago. I think he's gone back to the lake." She pulled off her boots, tunic, and trousers and shook out her shirt.

I sat up and rubbed my eyes. The day seemed to stretch ahead of me, and I didn't know what I was going to do. I washed and dressed. By the time I was ready to leave, Willow had curled up on the bed and fallen asleep. In the hall, Tuan sat on the floor beside the door. When I came out, he looked up and got slowly to his feet.

"You didn't need to do this," I said. "You should go and sleep, too."

"For a while," he said.

"Did you think someone was really going to try to hurt me? Here?"

"People do strange things when they're afraid."

"But you'll let me go down to breakfast alone. What if Nias tries to poison me?" I meant it to be teasing, but he looked serious.

"Then eat only what you see others eating, nothing specially made for you."

I shook my head and smiled against my will. Nias wouldn't poison me, even if only because adding poison to food would offend her to the heart.

I went down the stairs and chose a different table than the one we usually used. In the center of the table was a half loaf of bread on a plate. I tore off a piece, put some honey on it, and poured myself ale from the pitcher. Adana came in, moving only a little more quickly than she had the night before, and sat with me.

"How is he?" I asked.

"I don't know," she said. "He hasn't eaten or drunk since yesterday. He's lying in his bed. Oh, Kiar, he won't look at me, and he doesn't answer when I speak to him. He just lies in bed. He's watching someone moving around the room, someone I can't see. You don't think he's mad, do you?"

"I honestly don't know," I said. "Father went out this morning, Willow said. Do you think he can get Mother back?"

"I don't know. What are we going to do? We can't just wait. People are afraid."

"Yesterday, you wanted to wait."

"Yes, but Gil is worse now. I'm afraid if it goes on much longer, even a few days—" I knew what she meant. People could live a long time without food, but not without water.

"Make him drink," I said, "even if you have to get the men to hold him while you pour the water down his throat. I'll wait until noon—one full day. Then I'll go to Sianna. If this is magic, we need someone who knows magic to deal with it."

"All right," she said.

At mid-morning, Father rode in, carrying Mother in his arms, wrapped in his cloak. I slipped back inside where she wouldn't see me. After everything that had happened, I was afraid to go near her and didn't want to upset her.

Mother's hair hung in a long tangle, and as Father stepped into the hall, she struggled in his arms, kicking her legs free of the cloak before he hushed her. At first glance I thought her feet were black with mud; then I saw the wide webs, and long, sharp nails on her toes. It took a few seconds before I understood what I was seeing. Her human feet splayed out wide, with the webbing and nails of her swan's form. A few small feathers stirred on her ankles before her calf curved up into the shelter of the cloak. When she lifted her face to look at Father, her neck curved back, just a little too long for a human neck.

I couldn't think. I thought if Father brought Mother back, things would be all right, or at least better. But this was not my Mother. She was someone strange and frightening, caught between her two forms.

Neither she nor Father noticed me, or the few other people in the hall, all of us standing still as stones. He carried her up the stairs to her solar. When he came back down shortly after, I called to him, and he came over and slumped into a chair. His eyes looked bruised from lack of sleep, his face almost grey.

"Have you eaten at all?" I asked. He shook his head.

"Just wait here a minute." I ran to the kitchen. Everyone stopped what they were doing and looked at me, still as deer. My chest felt tight, and I opened my mouth, but no words came out. Then Nias wiped her hands on her apron and came forward.

She was a little round woman, bright-eyed as a wren, and brown as one, too. She'd been in charge of the kitchen all my life, as constant as my parents or Dar. Now eyes were red, but she spoke calmly.

"What is it, Kiar?"

At the sound of her voice, speaking to me as usual, my own voice came back. "The king is here," I said. "He needs food."

"And the queen?" Nias asked. She sounded so quiet and kindly. The kitchen staff took up their tasks again, and everything felt normal. Nias stood waiting for me to speak, nothing in her face but kindness and concern.

"She's in her solar," I said. I didn't know how to say what I had seen.

"I'll bring something out for your father," Nias said.

"Thank you. Thank you, Nias."

At the table where I'd left him, Father stared at his folded hands.

"What happened?" I asked.

"The swans won't have her," Father said. "Your grandfather says she's mad, that she disturbs the flock and attacks anyone who comes near her. He drove her up onto land and told her never to come back. She changed, but it seems she can't be one thing or the other now."

I couldn't speak at first. I'd never heard of the swanfolk driving anyone from the flock, and for Grandfather to drive out his own daughter was beyond my understanding.

"*Is* she mad?" I asked. "Will she always be that way?"

Father sighed and shook his head. "I don't know, Kiar. I don't know. Mad with grief, maybe. It will pass." From the sound of his voice, he didn't believe it. "She looks more like herself now than she did when she first changed."

"What can we do?" I asked. I wanted him to tell me that she would get better, that we'd have the fire for Orla, and people would know she was merely a girl who had drowned. I wanted him to change things back to the way they had been. Instead, he shrugged.

"I don't know what we can do, Kiar. I knew she was proud of Orla, but I didn't realize how deep her pride went, how much more—" He stopped, but I knew what he didn't say. Mother had loved Orla more than Adana, and certainly, I thought, more than me. Orla, and what Orla was, meant more to her than Father did, or anyone else in her life. It wasn't losing her daughter that had broken her—it was losing the first black swan in hundreds of years.

"We have to do something," I said. "Adana and I talked while you were gone. I'll visit Sianna this afternoon, and she'll know what to do. If anyone does," I amended.

"I don't want to lose you, Kiar." He took my hand in his. "I've already lost one daughter, and Adana will leave, too. Let someone else go and get Sianna. Don't you disappear on me."

It was an echo of what I'd said to him yesterday, when I'd begged him not to leave. Anger rose up in me. I pulled my hand back and showed him my palms, hard and striped with callus from sword work. "Look," I said. "I'm a fighter. You taught me to fight. You've taught me to think and make decisions. Someone has to look after the people, Father. They're afraid, and I don't know how to stop it. You need to stay here and be the king.

That's all. Just do that, and I'll—" I didn't know exactly what I was going to do, but something had to be done.

Nias came with a tray and set it down.

"I'll have something taken up for the queen," she said to Father. "Now you eat that." She glanced at the ceiling over the hearth, where Mother's solar was. "It does her no good to have you look like Death come calling."

Father nodded, putting his elbows on the table. "Yes, Nias," he said.

She gave a nod and hurried back to the kitchen.

THIRTY-SIX

Just before noon, I went up to my room. Willow was still curled up as I'd left her. I hated to wake her. I'd have to send someone to wake Tuan, too. In all the distress and confusion around Orla's death, only Willow and Tuan seemed to be calm and sure. I couldn't leave them in charge, but I wanted them on watch while I was gone.

When I touched Willow's shoulder, she jumped awake.

"What is it?" she said. She rubbed her eyes and pushed her braid over her shoulder. "How long did I sleep?"

"It's almost noon. I'm going to talk to Sianna. I'm leaving in a few minutes."

Willow swung her legs off the bed and reached for her trousers. When she'd pulled them on, she stood up, tucking her shirt in. "I'm coming with you."

"No, I need you here, you and Tuan."

"What for?"

"To keep an eye on things, on people. On Father."

"He's back?"

"Yes," I said, "and he brought Mother. Grandfather drove her out." Willow stopped and stared, one arm in the sleeve of her tunic.

"I've heard of that. But never in our flock. He really drove her out?"

"That's what Father said. And, Willow, she's—I don't know how to tell you. She's changed back to human, but only partly. Father says it was worse at first, that she's more human now."

"Oh, Kiar!"

"Grandfather said she was mad. Father said it was grief, and she'd get better. I don't know who to believe, Willow."

She pulled the tunic over her head and tugged it straight. "It doesn't matter which it is now. Maybe Sianna can help her, too."

"Maybe."

"I'll get you water for the trip. Don't leave without saying goodbye."

"I won't."

When she'd gone, I took my bedroll, and the two woolen blankets I used on patrol. There was nothing else I needed but my sword. If things went well, I'd be back tonight or tomorrow. If they didn't, I couldn't imagine what I might need.

Father had left the hall when I got back downstairs. He'd left some of his meal—half a loaf of bread, some cheese, a few slices of apple—on the plate, and I bundled them together into the cloth on the tray.

Willow and Tuan waited at the stable. As I saddled Kestrel, Dar stepped in.

"Leaving again, young Kiar?"

"Don't try to stop me," I said.

"Don't try to leave without giving your guard orders," he answered. "What do you want us to do while you're away? What are you expecting to happen?"

"I don't know what I'm expecting," I said, "but nothing good."

"Magic?"

"Maybe," I said. "Orla was the only one who knew how to fight that."

"Word is she was using it against your sister and her young man," Dar looked serious. "Is that true, now?"

"It is, Dar. I wish it wasn't."

"So could it be Orla's magic you're thinking we'll have to fight? That doesn't sound good, her against us."

"No," I said. "I'm going to Sianna."

"If you're going for help, send me. I can fetch Sianna here as well as you can."

"But I can't command the guard as well as you," I said. "In case someone finds out what's happened to Mother and to Father, I need you here to keep them safe. And I don't know when I'll be back. Tonight or tomorrow, if all goes well."

"Those are your orders, Princess? To keep things safe in case Gythorn takes advantage?"

"They are," I said.

He saluted me. "I'll see it done. Are you taking these two?"

"No," I said. "They can be your eyes, to let you know where I am and if anything's happening on the border. Will you do that?" I looked at Tuan and Willow.

"Yes," Tuan said.

"We'll watch," Willow agreed.

"Then you're under orders as well as Tuan," I told her.

"Be careful," Dar said. "I don't know much about magic, but I know about enemies. If there's mischief about, *she* might be watching you. Keep your wits about you."

"I will," I said.

We didn't speak as I saddled my horse and tied on my bedroll and food. I hung my sword from the saddle. "I don't know how much use this will be," I said.

"I'm still glad you have it," Tuan said. "Kiar."

He stood looking down into my eyes without speaking.

"What?" I said. "What are you thinking?"

"Foolishness," he answered.

It was nothing I'd ever expected to hear Tuan say.

"What foolishness?" I asked. "Everything is so grim, Tuan. I could stand to hear something foolish."

"Not that kind," he said.

"What kind, then?"

"When you come back," he said, "come back yourself. Don't come back changed, like the queen. But even if you are changed, come back."

I felt a lump rise in my throat.

"You're right," I said, trying to sound light, "That is foolish. Don't come back changed, but come back even if you are changed? What—"

Tuan put his arms around me and pulled me close. I hugged him back. I wanted desperately to take swan form, to fly away and leave everything. All seemed poisoned by Orla's malice and her death, and fear and uncertainty overwhelmed me. I wondered if I shouldn't say to Tuan, "Come with me," and fly away to join my grandparents' flock, or make one of our own. The thought of that freedom was like cool water after hard work.

Tuan let me go and took my face between his hands. I noticed again how warm his hands always were. He stroked his thumbs over my cheekbones.

"Go safely. Return safely," he said.

I nodded, and then mounted and rode through the gate and down the dun. I didn't look back.

CHAPTER

THIRTY-SEVEN

As I passed Orla's house, I stopped. What had she been doing? The hairs on my neck rose at the thought of going in, but Sianna might need to know.

The brazier held bits of charred wood and a puddle of sooty water. Light from the doorway showed me herbs and bundles hung from the ceiling. I saw a bag of books, and then, hanging below it, a doll made of soft, thin leather, faceless, with a blue tunic and trousers. Over the left breast, a heart embroidered in rusty-red wool stitched the tunic to the body, and a strand of the same wool stretched up from the center of the heart and twined around one of the rafters. At the other end of the strand, with another embroidered heart, was a second doll, dressed in a piece of one of Orla's old robes. I didn't need to be a wisewoman to know what I was seeing.

Two more dolls, neither one dressed, lay on the floor. As I stepped forward, I felt something hard under my foot. I picked it up and turned it in the light; it was one of the beads from the necklace Hafor had given Orla. It suddenly seemed hot in my fingers, or burning cold, and I dropped it. In the light from the door, I looked at my fingertips, expecting to see blisters, but they were unmarked. I turned back to the dolls and saw that one had long hair of brown wool, and a strand of the same beads wrapped tightly around its throat. Between the two dolls, as though they had been dropped there, lay the remains of the broken necklace, a knife, and a needle threaded with rusty-red wool.

A cold lump formed in my chest. Whoever the other doll was, one was me, wearing Hafor's necklace. I backed out of the hut and leaned the broken door across the opening as well as I could, then mounted Kestrel and rode away.

I came to Sianna's house in the late afternoon. She was working in the garden as I rode up, stooping and pulling. When she saw me, she straightened up, one hand shading her eyes and the other holding the weeds she'd pulled. I galloped the last few hundred paces and pulled Kestrel up outside her ring of garden beds. She dropped the weeds and hurried towards me as I slid off Kestrel's back.

"Kiar! What's the matter?"

"Orla's dead."

"How? When?"

"Yesterday. She and Adana fought, and Orla fell into the river."

"They fought. What about?"

"Orla put a spell on Gil. Oh, Sianna, it's all mixed up! Orla agreed to marry Hafor—she was going to be betrothed in a few days. But I found her kissing Gil in the stables, and now she's dead!"

"Kissing Gil." It wasn't a question. She stood in thought for a moment, hands clasped before her, tapping her forefingers together, then sighed and shook her head. "I thought she had more sense." She rubbed her hands over her face and let them drop to her sides. "You're certain she's dead?"

"She fell in the river. She was swept away before we knew it. I'm sure she went through the rapids, and she couldn't have survived that."

"It might be possible," Sianna said. She sounded far from certain. "Put your horse in the paddock, and come in. You can tell me everything calmly, in order."

She took Kestrel's reins from my hand and led both of us around to the shed she used as a stable. When I'd put Kestrel into the little paddock and given her water and hay, Sianna took me into the house and made me sit down.

She poked the fire up and set a kettle of water on it to boil.

"Now," she said, "Orla's dead, but that's the end. Start at the beginning. She put a spell on Gil?"

I told her of the lung fever, and the final potion Orla had made for Gil. I told her how Gil had turned from Adana and followed Orla around, and her seeming annoyance with him. I told her how I'd found them in the stable, and what Orla had said to Adana, and how they had fought, and Orla had fallen. I told her about Mother. She sat listening until I finished. The kettle of water steamed on the fire, and she made mint tea in two wooden cups and handed me one.

"Did anyone else act as though the fever might have hurt their minds?"

"No," I said. "Everyone else got better. I thought I might get sick, but I didn't."

Sianna's cup stopped halfway to her lips. "Why did you think so?"

"I thought I was going to vomit when I got back to my room. But I didn't. I didn't think any more about it. I was tired and worried about Gil. That's all."

"Did anyone else who returned from patrol get sick?"

"No, I don't think so."

Sianna looked at me, waiting quietly, at ease in her chair with her hands wrapped around her cup. When I didn't speak, she said, "Maybe nobody else got sick because there was nothing to make *them* sick." It took a few seconds for me to put her words together with my memories.

"I was right!" I said. "She did it right there in front of me, gave Gil a love potion. And it was the spell that made me feel sick. I thought it was a healing spell."

"I'm sure she counted on that. She has the strongest raw magic I've ever seen. It was exciting to teach her, to see that talent develop. But your mother's pride in her—she absorbed that and thought it freed her from the rules other people follow."

"If it wasn't for Orla, Mother said, people would have died from the lung fever. When I saw her, she looked as though she hadn't slept for days."

"I'm sure that's true."

"She told me that wisewomen have to keep the balance between good and evil."

"Yes. But she lost her balance," Sianna said. "To use magic to get something you want is one thing, but to use it to take something that isn't yours." She shook her head. "I thought she had learned that stealing love was as wrong as stealing a horse. I believed—I hoped—she'd be able to resist."

"But you weren't sure," I said.

Sianna nodded once.

"Then why did you let her come home?"

"Kiar, if I kept her here forever, she might never get a chance to do wrong, but she would also never get a chance to choose to do right. Everyone faces that test. Orla had to face it, too, without me there to watch her."

"Then she failed," I said. "And whatever she did to Gil isn't coming undone. He isn't eating or drinking. He just stands on the wall, watching for Orla. We thought, Adana and I, that the spell would come undone when she died."

"That depends on the spell. Some have to be worked again and again or refreshed by whoever cast the spell. Some of them are fixed, but fade over time, like colours in cloth. Some are like words cut in stone and fade so slowly they last a whole lifetime without seeming to weaken at all. If I knew what she did, I might know why it isn't unravelling."

"I looked into her house on my way here. There were two dolls, joined together. One was Gil, and the other was her. And there were two more dolls. One is me, I think."

"Joined how?" Sianna asked.

I told her everything I could remember about what I'd seen in Orla's house. When I finished, Sianna put her chin in her hand and sat without speaking. I drank my tea and watched her while she thought.

Finally, she straightened up. "I think I know what she did."

"Can you undo it?"

When she didn't answer right away, my heart fell.

"You're her teacher. I thought you could make it all right again."

Sianna sighed. "It's not that simple, Kiar. Orla was very strong. She used her blood, and maybe Gil's, to bind him to her. It will wear off in time, but Gil won't live long enough for that. I can guess what words she might have used, but I don't know them precisely."

"Can't you just try things until you get it right?"

She smiled. "Have you ever tried to take out a bit of embroidery you wanted to rework?'

"Many times," I said, "I'm not very good at it."

"And how do you do it?"

"Take the thread out of the needle and then pull out one stitch at a time, in order."

"And if you try to take out a stitch before you've undone all the ones ahead of it?"

"Sometimes it just pulls a bit, and you can find the right one to take out first. Sometimes it breaks. Sometimes you have to cut it."

"But you have to know which order to take them out neatly."

"Yes," I said.

"You can undo your own spells with a word. They unravel very rapidly. Trying to undo someone else's magic is like undoing embroidery. It has to be picked out one stitch at a time, in order. And you know the little holes left where the stitches went in? You have that with magic, too, even if you take it out very carefully."

"Is there no way to help Gil?"

"There may be. But what about you?"

"What about me?"

"She was doing another spell when Adana interrupted her. It seems she was trying to bind you to someone. Who would that be?"

"I think maybe Hafor. At least, the doll I think was me wore beads from the necklace Hafor gave Orla. But why? I don't understand that."

"Nor do I. Let me think about this, Kiar. Give me until morning. Now, you need something to eat. Finish your tea while I get a meal for us. After that, I will need to be alone and undisturbed. Take some food and blankets and stay outside and away from the house. Don't go too far—the protections don't extend past the gardens. You can sleep in the stable tonight with the horses. In the morning, we'll see what may be done."

"Thank you," I said.

"Don't thank me yet," she answered. "I don't know if I can give you any help at all."

After the meal of bread, cheese, and apples, I couldn't stay still. I weeded the outside edges of the gardens until the light faded.

As the sun went down and the afternoon's warmth gave way to the chill damp of evening, I put Kestrel with Sianna's horse, Night Wind, in the stable. He was still dappled, but the dapples were fading into his coat, now more grey than black. I took my food and blankets to the stable as well, and sat eating as dark fell, giving bits of bread and apple to the horses Then I fluffed up a bit of straw under the mangers and out of the way of the horses' feet and rolled myself in the two blankets. I fell asleep in the comforting smell of horses and hay.

Sianna's voice woke me. "There, there," she said to the horses, slipping in between them. "Kiar, are you awake?"

"Yes." I sat up and rubbed the sleep out of my eyes.

"Come and eat. I have a task for you."

I shook the straw out of my blankets and picked as much of it as I could out of my hair, wishing I'd brought a comb. I folded the blankets over my arm and went to Sianna's house. The morning air was chilly, the sun barely up.

Inside, the house was warm and dry, and smelled of fresh bread and stewed meat.

"Drink this," Sianna said, handing me a steaming cup. The ale was spiced and hot enough to chase the morning chill away. Sianna nodded to the chair, and I sat. She handed me a bowl of stew and a spoon and placed a loaf of bread on the stool between us.

We ate in silence, and when we were done, Sianna took the dishes away and set them in a bucket.

"Last night," she said, "I looked for Gil to see if the spell might be loosening, even a little. It isn't, so it will have to be undone. We'll have to make Orla undo it."

I stopped the spoon halfway to my mouth. "But she's dead."

"There is magic that is worked while the spirit walks outside the body. Someone with strong reasons can work it even after the body has died. Orla has some very strong reasons. First, she'll be angry about dying suddenly. Second, she has bound herself to Gil with blood magic, and even death will take a while to unravel it. She'll be close to her body, at least for the next few days, and maybe longer. You have to find her body and take three things from it."

"What three things?"

"To do magic, you need knowledge, passion, and action." She touched her head, then her breast over her heart while holding out her hand.

"Do I have to bring you her head and her heart?"

"A lock of her hair, a finger from her right hand, and a piece of rib from over her heart. Can you do that, Kiar?" She folded her hands in her lap and sat without speaking, giving me time to consider.

I thought about that. I'd helped bury people who'd died. I'd butchered game and seen wounds doctored, but I'd never cut a piece from a human body or thought to do it. And this wasn't any body; it was my own sister.

"I don't know if I can," I said. "Isn't there any other way?"

"There is not. I know it's a terrible thing to ask." She sat quietly while I thought. Orla was dead, and I couldn't hurt her. I could find the finger joint easily enough, and her hair would be easy, too. The rib was the hard part. I could cut open a dead deer without a qualm, but cutting into a human body would be harder.

"How big a piece of rib?"

"A sliver will do."

A sliver from near the breastbone; it could be done quickly. I took a deep breath. "Do you have a shovel I can take? I'll need to bury her afterwards."

"Of course. But come back as quickly as you can. I'll use fire, water, salt, and air to make her undo the spell."

"How do I find her?"

"Follow the river. She's somewhere downriver from here, caught on branches or roots sticking up in the water, close to the bank."

"How far down?"

"I saw her late last night. No farther than the river could take her in a day and a half."

"All right," I said. "I'll start now."

"I'll get you some food to take along."

She filled my saddlebags with bread, dried meat, and apples, and I rode out to find my sister's body.

CHAPTER

THIRTY-EIGHT

I took the straightest southeast route I could, angling through the forest towards the river. Once I caught a glimpse of a doe with her twin fawns before they disappeared among the trees. Another time, a hawk swooped down through the canopy and away again. I saw nothing else. I stopped long enough to gather some dry branches for the night's fire and rode on.

Shortly before noon, I came out of the forest. I stopped to unsaddle Kestrel and eat while she grazed. I was sparing with my meal; the food would have to last two days at least. If I didn't find Orla's body today, it would have to last longer than that. Water we would have in plenty once we reached the river. I swallowed a few mouthfuls from my waterskin and trickled water into my palm for Kestrel. Then I saddled her again and turned south and east.

As the afternoon faded to evening, I came to the river. Looking upstream to the west I didn't see anything sticking above the surface that could catch a body and hold it. There were no clumps of trees along the bank.

I piled a few stones into a cairn to mark the spot. Leading my horse, I walked downriver, stopping at every stand of willow or alder to duck under the branches and search along the bank. Sometimes I clung to branches one-handed and leaned far out over the water to peer into undercuts and among roots. I saw nothing, not a flash of skin or clothing that might betray where Orla had come to rest.

The light faded, and I could no longer see clearly. I found a place where Kestrel could get down to the water, hobbled and unsaddled her, then rubbed her down as best I could with her saddle blanket. I cleared a firepit and ringed it with stones. With flint and tinder, I made a tiny fire. As full dark fell, I rolled myself into my blankets and hoped the damp ground wouldn't soak through before morning.

I woke chilly, just before dawn. The fire was no more than hot ashes. Burying the fire and rolling my blankets helped me warm up, and we were soon on our way again.

I followed the river all day. Late in the afternoon, I crossed another stretch of forest. These were old, tall trees, whose leaves made a canopy that let very little light through. There was almost no undergrowth, and the little noise we made sounded loud in that space. I was glad when we came out onto the grassland again. Now I was beyond the borders of Valenia, and I still hadn't found any sign of Orla. I'd never been this far from home alone.

I spent some time looking carefully eastwards for any sign of people. The tawny, black-haired folk who lived on the grasslands travelled in bands on horseback, carrying all their goods with them. They made tent villages wherever they stopped and wore leather clothes embroidered in bright colours. Most of what I knew of them came from the traders, who went everywhere and knew everyone. I wasn't eager to find out how they'd treat a lone trespasser, but I had to go on.

There were more clumps of trees, and I stopped more often than I had the day before. Once I thought I saw an arm, but it was only a bleached branch curving up out of the water. I made camp again and ate another scant supper before sleeping.

The next day, the river became broader, with rocks and pebbly shoals rising in places. In the middle it was still deep, but the banks sloped gently to shallow edges. There was no chance of anything washing up on my side onto the wide, pebbly shallows. At mid-morning, I saw a clump of willow on the other shore. As I considered whether I should cross to search there, I saw movement.

On the bank a few paces above the willows and almost hidden, a person bent over something. He was fair-haired, dressed in faded brown, and alone. I couldn't see a horse. Whoever it was, it was not a grasslander.

He pulled at something on the ground, and his arm moved in a sawing motion. Without any reason, or any doubt, I knew that he had found Orla. I turned Kestrel's head and sent her into the water.

The water came up to my knees at the middle of the river. The man turned as we scrambled up the far bank. I drew my sword and looked at him. He stood staring at me over my sister's body, both bloody hands hanging by his side. The last time I'd seen that face had been years ago, leaning towards Orla, a heat-ripple of magic between them as he promised her his first song.

"Aren?" I said. Of all the people I might have expected to find carving pieces out of a dead body, the bard's apprentice was not one.

"Princess Kiar," he said. He stood very still, like a deer trying to avoid the hunter's notice.

He was taller than I remembered, and he'd grown a short beard and a moustache, both sun-bleached, like his hair. Except for that, he was brown all over—weathered brown clothes, tanned skin. His green eyes were startling in all that brown.

"What are you doing?" I brought Kestrel a few steps closer, and Aren jumped back. His right hand hung down, holding his knife tightly. The fingers of his left hand curled around something.

Orla lay at his feet, face-up and so still. Black smeared her face, neck, and right arm, but the rest of her skin shone pale against the dead grass. Smears of blood showed where Aren had cut into her chest, on the left near the breastbone.

"What have you done?" My sword hand came up, and I brought Kestrel a step closer.

He dropped his knife and raised both hands, the left one still clenched around whatever he held. A wave of rage rose up in me and clouded my vision. I kneed Kestrel and charged at him.

Aren jumped back. I heard a splash as I turned Kestrel, and saw the ripples in the river where he'd gone in. Right below the bank, the water swirled deep and brown. In a few seconds he surfaced, sputtering and coughing. He clambered partway out of the water, clinging to the dangling willow branches with his right hand. His left was still clenched.

"Damn!" he said. "I almost lost it!" He held his closed left hand to his breast.

"Good," I said.

"No!" His voice cracked a little. I noticed for the first time the dark rings under his eyes.

"I can explain," he continued. "Will you let me explain? Or should I just drown myself now and save you the trouble of killing me?"

"Out," I said.

When he was on dry land again, with his hands where I could see them, I said, "Now talk. What else have you taken? Have you cut off a finger yet? Or her hair?"

His mouth dropped open.

"How did you know?"

"Who told you to do it?" He opened his mouth, then closed it again.

"You won't believe me."

"Tell me anyway."

"*She* told me." He jerked his chin towards my sister's body. "She told me where to find her. She told me what to do. She wants me to take her home. That's the truth."

"What have you taken?"

"Her finger. A piece of rib. Some of her hair."

"She told you to do that?"

"I know it sounds crazy."

"Dry off," I said. "We have to talk."

A pack and harp case lay on the ground a few yards away. While Aren pulled clothes from the pack, I unsaddled Kestrel. I tried not to look at Orla's body, but I found Aren's bloody knife on the ground and wiped it on the grass.

When Kestrel was hobbled and grazing, I built a little campfire. I put water on to heat in a small, three-legged pot and got out some of Sianna's herbs to make tea. All the time, I kept half an eye on Aren.

He'd turned his back to undress; he moved like an old man, or an exhausted one. The dry shirt he changed into was patched and had been made for someone much bigger. I noticed the trousers, tunic, and shirt on the grass had been patched, too. I'd never seen Aren in patched clothes. Even his travel clothes had been finer than these. He wasn't doing well at all. And he was alone.

"Where's Hollam?" I asked.

Aren stopped shaking water from his boots.

"Dead," he said.

"What happened?"

"His horse stumbled and threw him. Almost a year ago now." He put the boots down on the grass and sat down across the fire from me. In his hand was a small, cloth-wrapped bundle. He tucked it behind him, well out of my reach.

"I'm sorry," I said, "Have you been on your own since?"

"Yes. I'd only begun singing for people when he died. Now I have no master, no name, and no work. I sold the horses months ago."

"You should have come to us," I said, "You know you'd be welcome."

"I didn't want—" He paused. "I didn't want *her* to see me like this. I didn't want her to pity me. You know."

"Yes, I know." Orla hadn't cared about Aren; it made me sad how much he cared for her.

"What happened to her? Why is she here, like this?" he asked.

"It's a long story. And I have to ask you the same thing," I said. "What brought you here, now? I've been following the river two days, looking for her. How are you here ahead of me?"

"When did she die?" he asked. "And who killed her?"

"Three—no, four days ago," I said, "She fell into the river and drowned."

Aren stared at me, his eyes wide, then slowly shook his head.

"That's not what she said," he told me.

CHAPTER

THIRTY-NINE

"What do you mean, she said? She's dead!"

"I know! Of course I know. But she called me," He tapped the center of his forehead. "Her voice was inside me. She told me where I'd find her."

"When was that?"

"Three nights ago. Maybe. I'm so tired. I was sleeping, and I heard her calling my name. She sounded real. Alive. She was close, like she was lying beside me. But I couldn't touch her. Then I thought I was dreaming, but she said no. She was there, but not in her body."

"Go on."

"She didn't tell me she was dead, just that she needed my help. She said she knew I loved her, and she could trust me."

"And she told you where she was."

"Not in words. She showed me—led me here. She made me hurry. She only let me sleep when I couldn't walk any more."

"So when did you find out she was dead?"

"Early this morning, when I found her." He put his forehead down on his knees and wrapped his arms over his head.

I poked the fire under the pot and waited for him to continue. The water bubbled, and I threw herbs into it—mint, mugwort, sweet grass.

Finally, Aren looked up. He drew a deep breath and blew it out.

"She told me your sister murdered her. Pushed her into the river and left her to drown. And she said I had to help her tell King Tir about it."

"How can she do that?"

He smiled, only one side of his mouth turning up.

"Don't you know? A lock of her hair to string the harp, a finger from her right hand to make tuning pegs, and a piece of bone from over her heart for the belly of the harp. When the harp plays, she'll speak. She'll tell the king what happened. Didn't you come to retrieve those same things?"

"Not for that! I need them to break a spell she cast."

"Maybe if she tells the truth, the spell will break."

"I doubt that very much," I said. "And I doubt she's going to tell Father the truth. She didn't tell it to you. Did she tell you about Gil?"

"The tall boy Princess Adana's in love with?"

"Yes."

He shook his head. "She never said anything about him."

"She cast a spell on Gil, to steal his love from Adana. When Adana found out, she told Orla to take the spell off. But she wouldn't. They fought, and yes, Adana pushed her, and she fell into the river. But it was an accident. I was there, I saw. Adana tried to save her."

"She was so beautiful, so smart. Maybe he loved her without a spell."

"I know you want to believe that. But it's not true. I wish it was, but it isn't."

He sighed and rubbed his face.

"She did an evil thing, putting that spell on Gil, and it didn't break when she died. Now he's dying of it. The wisewoman sent me to get the hair and the bones. She can break the spell. She can save Gil's life."

He cocked his head to one side, his eyes unfocused.

"She says there's more. She says, why don't you just take what you need from her body?"

"She? You mean Orla?"

"Yes," Aren said.

A cold shiver touched my neck.

"She knows better than that. So do you—you know the songs. The wisewoman who brewed a potion to let her understand the language of the animals and left her maid to stir it while she slept. The maid tasted the potion, only a drop, and got the power."

"And there was nothing left for the wisewoman."

"Yes. I could cut Orla into little bits or take back her whole body, but there's no magic left. You took it."

It was on the tip of my tongue to say that I would take what Aren had, by force if necessary. Then I remembered that cold shiver on my neck. Orla was listening. Aren, too, sat silently.

Maybe he had had the same thought. I poured the tea into two cups, and we drank.

When I finished my tea, I picked up the shovel. I walked towards Orla's body, dreading what I might see.

She was bruised from the rocks, and bone showed through a ragged-edged wound on her head. She wore only her trousers, the boot that had not come off in the river and, on her left wrist, the blue bracelet. Her flesh was puffy from the water and sagged on her face, making her nose and cheekbones pointed. She looked, perhaps, as she might have looked if she'd lived to be old.

I crouched beside her and saw that the mud on her skin wasn't mud. Tiny black feathers sprouted sparsely over her right cheek and jaw, more thickly down her neck and shoulder. Along her forearm, the flight feathers must have barely begun to form before she died. They made a ridge of thin, overlapping blades, stiff and rippling.

When I lifted her left arm, the hand flopped down from a bend higher than the wrist. It felt lighter, too, and looked the wrong shape. She was trying to take swan form as she drowned. If she had succeeded, she might have lived. She reminded me frighteningly of Mother when Father carried her home. I hoped that she only looked like Mother had. If I had to deal with her ghost, I didn't want it to be mad, too.

The cold water of the river had slowed decay, but she smelled of death. I found a spot for the grave away from the riverbank, where the soil was softer, I stripped the turf off and began to dig. It was hard, physical work, and it kept my body busy and numbed my mind.

I dug the grave north to south. After a time, Aren came and took the shovel from me. The earth was light and easy to move, but we were sweating and tired before we'd dug deep enough to keep scavengers from Orla's body.

"Do you have something I can wash her with?" I asked. Aren brought me a cloth dripping with river water. I knelt and wiped the dried mud and flecks of weed from Orla's face, arms and body. Traces of the colours she'd painted onto herself still clung to her skin. I wiped everything as clean as I could, careful to smooth the feathers the right direction.

Then we picked Orla's body up between us, carried her to the grave, and lowered her as gently as we could. I stepped into the grave and straddled her to straighten her arms and legs and turn her face towards the west. As I climbed out, Aren came over with a small bundle in his hand. He held it out to me, and I took it; something small, squashy and loose wrapped in the wet cloth I'd used to wash Orla's body.

"I cleaned up her finger bones," he said. "This is what's left." I nodded and squatted to drop the package on her right hand.

I cried while I shoveled earth over her. Whatever she had done, she was my little sister, and she was dead. I'd never see her or speak to her again. The tears came at intervals, once so wracking I had to lean on the shovel and gasp for breath. When I finished, I sang the mourning chant through a throat and nose clogged with weeping. By the time I was done, the sun had dipped below the horizon and the air was chilly. I felt wrung out with weariness and grief, but at least I was calm again.

Aren took me by the elbow and led me over to the fire.

"Sit," he said. He handed me a wet cloth, and I wiped my face and hands of the worst of the dirt. He gave me a cup of something hot and a piece of bread, smeared with toasted cheese. I hadn't even noticed the smell of it as he cooked.

"I need to put her into the harp," he said after I'd finished eating. "It's going to take me most of tomorrow."

I said nothing. Orla was listening.

"But you said you were taking her back to the wisewoman."

I looked at him across the fire. "It's been a bad day. I don't want to talk about it." I hoped he'd take the hint. "Right now, I'm going to sleep." Then I rolled myself up in my blankets, with my back to the fire, and lay listening to the river. I watched the light fade until night covered the sky. At last, I slept.

CHAPTER

FORTY

I woke when the birds began their dawn chorus. For a moment, I couldn't remember why I was sad, and then the memories of the last few days flooded back.

Aren was no longer lying by the fire. The harp and his pack were there, so he hadn't tried to sneak off in the night. Kestrel shook herself and nickered at me. As I stood and stretched, Aren appeared from beyond the willows with an armload of dead wood.

"This will do us today," he said. "We'll have to move to find more."

"We should leave now," I said. "This is the grasslanders' country. We can be back in Valenia by tonight."

"Then go. I have to put her into the harp. The grasslanders won't bother me. I'm still a bard."

"I'm not leaving without you," I said. It was as close as I was willing to come to what I really meant. I didn't want to mention Orla's name. "Are you coming?" I said.

He shook his head. I walked around the fire and stood over him.

"If you won't come, then give it to me, all of it. Now."

"I can't."

I drew my knife.

"You can. Where is it?"

He reached into his shirt and pulled out a small bundle. His fingers were closed tightly around it, the knuckles white. I held out my left hand.

He reached towards me. Before his hand had covered half the short distance to mine, he gasped, and his elbow jerked back. His hand twisted up behind his back, as far from me as it could, and he fell backwards and cried out as his weight landed on the twisted arm.

"Please!' Aren gasped. "Stop! I won't! I promise!" His arm relaxed, and he lay on the ground with his eyes closed and teeth clenched. When he could speak again, he looked up at me.

"You see?" he said.

"If you can't give her to me, then you're coming with me."

"She wants me to fix her in the harp."

"She'll have to wait. I'm not staying here, and I'm not leaving without her. Are you coming?"

"It hurts," he said. "It hurts when I don't do what she wants."

"We'll be as quick as we can. Half a day to Valenia if we leave now and go quickly. You can start this afternoon."

He pushed himself to his feet and tucked the bundle back into his shirt.

"Put your things together," I said. When he was ready, we crossed the river, Aren on Kestrel and me clinging to the saddle. On the far bank, we rearranged the packs. I mounted and pulled him up behind me. He refused to let go of the harp and carried it strapped over his shoulder.

I turned away from the sun, now well over the horizon. Once I was safe inside my own borders, I'd take Aren by the shortest route possible to Sianna.

From time to time, I dismounted and led my horse at a walk while Aren rode. We stopped once for water for her, and food for ourselves. Aren barely managed to remount and said no more than a word of thanks for food or water. Early in the afternoon we passed the border into Valenia.

In spite of his silence most of the day, I was shocked at how drawn he looked.

"She's angry," he said. "It hurts."

"I'm sorry. You should sleep."

He shook his head. "I have to do this." He pulled a soft leather roll out of his pack and opened it to lay out some short, slender knives and a small, lidded pot.

"What do you need?"

"Water, and a fire to warm the glue."

I gave him our water-skin and built the fire. He set the pot beside it. I left him head-down over the harp and went to tend to my horse.

I ate and gathered wood for a fire for overnight. Aren never looked up from his work; he might as well have been alone. Finally, he laid the harp down and lurched to his feet.

He devoured bread and dried meat as though he hadn't eaten for a week. I know he was still hungry. I was, too, but we had two more days of travel, and the food had to last.

"Is it done?" I asked.

He gestured at the harp, and I bent to look. Two tuning pegs were capped with fresh bone, and a strand of black hair lay close to every bronze harp string, held top and bottom with glue. Aren had gouged a narrow slip of wood from the body of the harp and glued in the slender fragment of Orla's rib. He'd done a skillful, workmanlike job, and it filled me with horror.

I tore my eyes away from the harp and looked at the case. The dark brown leather was carved with intertwined bands, an endless knot that covered the whole surface.

"Who did that?" I said, tracing a strand of the knot with my finger.

Aren looked up. "A wiseman. It's to keep water, mold, and insects out, and the harp in."

"A spell."

"I suppose so. Hollam said the case has never come open accidentally."

He went back to staring again at nothing, humming a tune I didn't recognize. I would have asked him about it, but he looked worn to a thread.

"You need sleep," I said instead.

Just then a breeze came up, and the harp strings sang. I couldn't think of another word for it. "Aaaaahhhhhhhhhhh," they sang, like a woman's voice singing a dozen notes at once. The sound sent shivers up my back. Then it changed, as though the strings were shaping a word, but before the word was formed, Aren picked up the harp. The note stopped. He settled the harp in his lap and plucked the strings.

It sounded like ordinary harp music, but I couldn't forget that other sound.

When he finished playing, he laid the harp in its case, but left it open.

"I want to make sure the glue is good and dry," he said. When we lay down, he slept at once.

I turned my back to the dying embers of the fire and thought about the voice in the harp. It was only when I could no longer keep my eyes open that I allowed sleep to claim me.

"Kiar!" Somebody bent over me, whispering my name. "Kiar!"

I turned over and kicked off my blankets. Before I stood, the voice whispered, "Wait. Kiar, wait. Listen." I stopped, sitting up, one hand on my knife. I could see nothing. I couldn't hear Aren breathing, or any movement from Kestrel, or the sound of the river.

The voice laughed, and the hairs on my neck prickled as they stood up.

"Your knife is no good. You can't kill me twice." Orla said. Her voice grew softer, then louder again in waves.

"Where are you?" I whispered.

"Here," she said, "here, here, here." With each word, the voice came from somewhere new—over my head, behind my back, close by my cheek. "I'm here, sister."

"What do you want?"

"To do what I will do."

"Blame Adana for your death!" Anger got the better of my fear for a moment. "You know it was an accident!"

"She wanted it, even if she couldn't do it."

"What you did was wrong! You have to release Gil."

"Ahhhhhhhhhhhhh...." The voice died away on that word, and I thought I was alone again. Then she returned. "I love him."

"He doesn't love you. It's only the spell."

"I don't care."

"He'll die."

She sighed.

"And we'll be together."

"Will he love you then?" I made a wild guess. "When he dies, and he knows what you've done?"

A shiver went up my spine, as though a cold finger had been laid on my neck.

"Sianna will make you let him go," I said.

"She sent you. My hair, my finger bones, a piece of rib. The mind, the hand, the heart, joined together to make or break. How would you like Prince Hafor?"

"I wouldn't."

"He wants you."

"He hates me—I beat him and took his sword."

She laughed, and it was the ugliest sound I'd ever heard.

"The more reason to own you. We planned it. My spell, his revenge. Marry you and put his own son on the throne. And there will be a son. When the spell is done, you will want Hafor the way Gil wants me. He'll own you, body, soul, and spirit."

"You can't do that!"

"Half done, already."

"But you're a spirit. You can't sew those dolls together."

She was silent a while, but then she spoke, almost in my ear. "I still have power. I can complete the spell. Hafor will help me. Cross me and we'll do it. You will wed Hafor, willingly, eagerly." She chuckled. "Everyone will believe it. Even our parents. Even Tuan. Let this harper do what I want, and I will let it unravel. Marry Tuan, if you like. Rule Valenia. Adana will go to the swans and find another lover. Sianna is not here to stop me. You cannot stop me. But if you try, sister, if you try—"

The voice faded, or maybe the rush of the river drowned it out. The stars looked down again from the sky, the voice of the river rose beside me, and on the other side, across the banked fire, Aren snored.

I lay down again, hoping it had been a dream and knowing that it hadn't. I knew one other thing, too: whatever her threat, and even if I couldn't stop her, I had to try.

CHAPTER

FORTY-ONE

If Aren slept any better than I did, it didn't show. In the morning he still looked exhausted. I didn't feel much better. I had a length of line and a hook in my saddlebag and managed to catch a couple of small perch for breakfast. After we ate, I led Kestrel while Aren rode. I still hadn't thought of anything to stop Orla. It worried and frightened me that she might be able to make me love Hafor.

I counted the days since her death on my fingers. The day she died—one. The day I rode to Sianna's—two. The day I searched along the river—three. The day I found her and buried her—four. Yesterday travelling with Aren—five. We had another day's travel to Sianna, almost two to the castle. How strong would she be, six or seven days after her death?

Every day, every hour we travelled brought us closer to home and to Orla getting her will. If I could deliver Aren and the harp to Sianna, she'd know what to do. Aren might even be protected from Orla within the circle of Sianna's house and gardens.

I angled northwest, and our path took us under the trees. Aren dozed in the saddle, and when he was awake, he hummed to himself. Good. With his mind on his song, he wouldn't pay attention to our path. We should come out only a short way from Sianna's house.

It was late afternoon, and we were perhaps halfway there when Aren spoke. "Slow down! You'll run us right into a tree!"

"What do you mean?"

"You can't possibly see in this fog" He waved his hand through the air.

"What fog? What are you talking about?"

He clenched his eyes shut and gripped the saddle bow. Sweat beaded on his forehead and trickled down his face. Then his feet were floating up in the stirrups, and he rose slowly from the saddle. He kicked loose of the stirrups and flailed with his arms. His legs floated up, and he kicked and clawed at the air above him. Kestrel shied and stepped aside, and Aren floated higher, drawn by some invisible force.

I dropped Kestrel's reins and grabbed at one of his feet. When I tried to pull him down, he fought and kicked until I had to let go. His legs twisted back towards where the castle lay.

All around me, the air was clear and calm. A crow called somewhere in the distance, and Aren hovered above Kestrel, jerked by currents I could neither see nor feel, his whole body now angled feet-first towards the castle. He strained his head back, clamping his mouth shut. His body convulsed, and a stream of water gushed from his mouth, and then his nose.

"Stop!" I shouted into the air. "Stop it! We'll go back!"

Aren hung drowning in an invisible river.

I took Kestrel's bridle and turned her head towards the castle. In an instant, Aren fell from the sky and landed hard on the ground, retching. He struggled to his hands and knees, the harp swinging around to bang against him. He threw up a gout of water and then another, and hung his head, panting for breath.

I knelt by him. Although his face and hands streamed with water, when I put my hand on his back his tunic was dry under my palm. He retched again and wiped his mouth on his sleeve.

"Are you all right?" I asked.

He nodded. "I was drowning," he said. "It was a river. How could it be a river?"

"It was Orla," I said. "I'm sorry. I thought I could get you to Sianna."

"She noticed," he said. "And now she knows how to get to the castle. She threatened to kill me, and you turned back. You should leave me here. Take the harp and go to your wisewoman."

"And leave you to drown? No. There has to be some other way."

"It's the only way. Take her and go."

"I won't! Get up and mount or I swear I'll tie you to Kestrel's tail and drag you."

I walked Kestrel, with Aren sagging on her back, out of the woods and into open ground. In the warm sunshine, Aren slid off the mare's back and sat down abruptly. I put his pack on the ground, and he laid his head on it. Before I'd covered him with my blanket, he was asleep.

He wasn't going anywhere, and I would never get a better chance. I unsaddled Kestrel and hobbled her, then stripped off my clothes and called the change to me. If I couldn't take Aren to Sianna, I would have to bring Sianna to him.

From the air, I saw Sianna watching the sky in front of her house surrounded by gardens. She raised a hand in greeting as I landed.

"Do you have what we need?" she asked when I'd changed.

"Yes and no. I found her, but I wasn't the first. Aren, the harper—he'd already taken the things you need."

"Will he give them up?"

"He can't. She's strong, Sianna! She almost killed him, and she says she'll make me marry Hafor. I don't know if we can beat her."

"Slow down and take a deep breath. Good. And another. Come inside."

Seated by her hearth, wrapped in a blanket and with a hot drink, I felt calmer.

"Tell me everything," she said, "calmly and in order."

I told her all about the last few days, and afterwards, she sat thinking.

"Orla is strong, no denying that," she said at last.

"Can we defeat her? I don't want to be a puppet for her, or for Hafor."

"I don't want that either. We have to make her do three things: tell the truth, undo her magic, and leave. The first is up to you."

"How can I make her tell the truth? I have no magic!"

"You don't need it. You saw her cast the spell, and she knows that. You know something she wants concealed. If you tell the truth of what she did, she cannot deny it."

"All right," I said, though I felt doubtful.

"You said she spoke when the air moved the strings. If Aren puts the harp on the hearthstone, a rush of air up the chimney would make her speak. If you could control the air somehow—but how?"

"I don't know."

She put her hand together, forefingers touching her lips. After a moment or two, she shook her head.

"Something may come to us. Making Orla undo her magic is a task for me. I'll need all four elements close to her. Air and fire at the hearth, those should be close enough. Salt water on the harp, and on the bones and hair will be earth and water. I'll have until the water dries. It will be long enough, if I'm quick."

"How do you make her leave?"

"That's for the king to do. He holds Valenia against all enemies. When she brought Noermark into it, she overstepped and made herself an enemy of Valenia. That will allow the king to banish her. You must get to Tir ahead of time, tell him what's happening and what you'll do."

"I don't want her to overhear me."

"Ride ahead and leave Aren to follow on foot. She wants to go to the castle—you don't have to see to that. We'll prepare to fight her there. Make her tell the truth, undo her magic, and leave."

She made it sound so simple. Could it really work? I set my empty cup down. "We'll win—won't we?" I asked.

"I didn't expect her to be this stubborn, or this strong. And she's brought the bard into it, which is another kind of magic. I'll have to be secret. A wisewoman's power centers on her house. I'll be far from mine, and she'll be close to hers. I can't show myself until I must, and you can't tell anyone I'm there. Once we start, we'll have to be quick. How long until you get home?"

"Tomorrow afternoon. Can you be there?"

"Night Wind can still run, and I know a trick or two to shorten the road. Now go and be hopeful."

The way back seemed longer. From the air, I saw Aren still sleeping, lying as I'd left him. I landed and changed to human form. We still had a few hours of daylight, and there was a spring not far away where we could drink and camp. I hated to wake Aren, but now that I knew we'd have to fight Orla at the castle, I wanted to get there as early tomorrow as we could.

"Wake up," I said, shaking his shoulder gently. "We have to get moving."

I led Kestrel, with Aren on her back, across the plain towards the spring, the castle, and tomorrow's battle. I tried not to think about the fact that Sianna hadn't really answered my question. She hadn't said we would win.

CHAPTER

FORTY-TWO

s I walked, I puzzled over how to get salt water onto the harp, and how to control the wind. If only I had some magic of my own!

"There's a swan," Aren said, pointing into the air, "alone and far from water. That's strange."

The swan circled and landed a dozen paces in front of us. Then the bright flare of light rose around her as she changed form. When it died away, I was already running forward to embrace Willow.

"Hafor's on his way to your father's castle," Willow said.

"But the betrothal's not for several weeks. Are you sure?"

"Yes. I recognized his horse, grey with a black mane, remember? And he's not alone. There are six of them."

"But why now?"

Willow shrugged and looked at Aren. He sat open-mouthed on Kestrel. Knowing a swan could become a woman was not the same as seeing it happen.

"Aren, you remember my friend Willow, don't you?"

"Oh. Yes."

Willow nodded briefly at him and turned back to me. "He'll be there tonight," she said.

"Hells. Someone's going to tell him about Orla, and he's in on it."

"In on what?" Willow said.

"Orla *did* put a spell on Gil," I said, "right under my nose. And she started another, to make me marry Hafor. We have to stop her."

"She's dead," Willow said. "That should stop anyone."

"Not as dead as we thought," I said. "She's in the harp." I told her briefly what had happened but skipped over my visit to Sianna. If Orla could hear us, I didn't want to tell her more than she already knew or guessed.

"When you die, you fly away from your body, fly forever," Willow said. "If a piece of it could hold you back, every shed feather would keep you here."

"What if you wanted to stay, and knew magic?" Aren asked.

"Then why not come back in your body? It seems easier than all this!"

"Maybe there isn't enough magic in the world for that," I said, thinking of Orla's battered body. "But there might be enough to let her stay, if she found something to hold onto."

"If she's trapped in the harp," Willow said, "you should burn it."

For a moment, nobody spoke.

"Can she get out of it?" Aren asked.

"I don't know." I saw the same thought on his face: was Orla riding the harp, or was she stuck in it?

"If we burn it, it might destroy her," I said.

"Or set her free," Aren said.

"And if we try, she could still kill you, even if she's trapped."

"We have to think of something," Willow said. "What about Sianna?"

"We couldn't get there," I said. I held my finger to my lips before she could say more. "Thanks for the warning. Tell Father I'll be there tomorrow. Meet me in the stables."

She looked puzzled but nodded. She kissed my cheek, changed to swan form, and in seconds, she was in the air.

"I need to stretch my legs," Aren said. He tied the harp case behind the saddle, and we walked together, each in our own thoughts. He was the first to break the silence.

"You're very different from what I thought," he said.

"What do you mean, different?"

"Well, you don't look like a swan princess. Your sisters look like your friend Willow, but you look more human."

I didn't know if that was a compliment or not, so I said nothing.

"But you are. A swan princess, I mean. And you're brave, and clever. I thought Princess Orla was clever."

"She was. Is."

"But to fight a wisewoman, when you don't know magic—"

"I wouldn't call that clever, or brave, either. Foolhardy, more like. We don't even have a proper plan."

"You'll think of something."

I wished I felt as sure as he sounded. Ahead, I saw the little clump of bushes that marked the spring.

"We can stop there," I said, pointing. "We need water and sleep. We'll start early tomorrow."

We divided the last of the food. There was enough for a scant supper, and an even smaller breakfast. Then we slept.

As I saddled Kestrel in the morning, Aren said, "I think you should know—I'm writing a song."

"Maybe you need to keep your mind on what we have to do."

"Don't you want to know what it's about?"

I said nothing, fastening the straps and buckles of the bridle. When it was clear I wouldn't answer, Aren sighed and slung the harp case onto his back.

"It's about a quest to defeat an evil sorceress, free a swan prince from his enchantment and reunite him with his true love."

I clenched my teeth. I knew where this was going and didn't like it. We had dangerous work ahead of us, and he was playing around with a song.

"It's about you," he said. It was the last straw.

"I haven't done any of that!" I said, more sharply than I'd intended.

"You're doing it now."

"Hells, Aren! This could all go wrong! Gil isn't a prince, and Orla isn't an evil sorceress. She was just in love with the wrong man." Even to myself, that didn't sound convincing anymore.

"He'll be a prince when he's married to the Swan Queen," he said. "And it won't go wrong. You beat Hafor of Noermark in a fair fight—everyone knows that. You'll win this one, too. All I need to decide is whether to make you a swan princess or a great warrior. In the song, I mean."

"I'd settle for living through this and not falling under a spell myself, if it's all right with you."

"You will," Aren said.

"I hope your confidence in me isn't misplaced." I mounted and looked down at him. "See you at supper. Good luck to you, Aren."

"Good luck, Princess Kiar." He took my hand and snatched it down to his lips before I knew what he was doing.

I couldn't think of anything to say to that. I cantered away, only slowing down when I had left Aren well behind.

There were too many gaps in the plan. Maybe Orla's magic, so close to me, would make me too sick to do anything. Maybe Sianna wouldn't get there in time. Maybe Father wouldn't believe me or wouldn't banish Orla when the moment came. And I still needed to figure out how to get water and salt onto the harp.

I wished with all my heart I had the confidence in myself that Aren had in me.

FORTY-THREE

Late in the afternoon, I came to the foot of the dun. A pyre of dry wood stood just beyond where the slope started up, the top flat, ready to receive a body, and rolls of hot-burning firebark stuck all around the base. I'd gone out to find Orla's body, and here was her funeral all prepared. Who had ordered this done—my father or Adana? But it was wasted effort; there was no body to burn.

Dar was on the gate. "No luck, then?" he asked. "You didn't find her?"

"I did," I said, "but it's a long story and I haven't time now. How is Mother?"

"The queen keeps to her chambers. Word is she's mad with grief, but if so, she's quiet enough."

"And Father?"

"You'll find him changed, Lady. He's an older man than he was a few days gone," Dar said.

"Gil?"

"Determined to die, it seems, despite your sister's care."

"Have you seen Sianna?"

"No," he said. "Nobody's sent for her. I'll send a rider now, if you say."

"Too late tonight," I said.

"Prince Hafor came this morning," Dar said. "With Guthric and all. Said he'd had a message from Princess Orla. But we've sent nobody out, unless she conjured a messenger out of the air. And there's this: I'd swear on my sword he didn't know she'd died. He rode in here excited as a boy with his first horse. He wasn't happy to hear the news. We're keeping an eye on him."

"Thanks, Dar," I said.

"I'm glad to have you back, young Kiar—I mean, my lady."

"I'm glad to be back," I said, although my words rang hollow.

I took Kestrel to the stables, unsaddled her, and rubbed her down as quickly as I could. Out of the corner of my eye I saw movement at the stable door. When I looked up, Tuan was there. The sight of him, tall and quiet and familiar, lifted my heart more than I'd thought possible. All the strangeness of the past days fell away for a moment. I had never been so glad to see anyone.

I went to meet him, and he put his arms around me. I slid mine around his waist, resting my cheek on his shoulder. For a few moments, we stood together. I could feel his breath stirring my hair and wished I could stay here forever.

At that moment, Willow slipped through the stable door. Tuan and I stepped apart, but he held my hand.

"Hafor's here," Willow said. "Is Sianna coming?"

"No," I said. I hated lying to Willow, but I had to keep Sianna's secret. "I couldn't let you mention her before, because I think Orla can hear what we say—at least, when we're near the harp. Now it's too late to send for her."

"Do you have a plan?"

"Part of one. I've heard the harp speak. It sounded like a voice when the air moved over the strings. If Aren puts her on the hearthstone, the draft from the chimney will make the strings move, and she'll be able to speak."

"I wouldn't let her speak," Willow said.

"I have to make her tell the truth," I said, "so I need her to speak. If I could control the air somehow, I think it would be easier. But I don't know how."

"I do," said Willow. "I'll go up onto the roof. I can make the air move. You'll give me a signal, two taps on the chimney."

"That's clever. Thank you."

"And after you've made her tell the truth," she said, "will you burn the harp?"

"First, Father has to banish Orla," I said. "She's become an enemy of Valenia, and only the king can banish her."

Tuan and Willow exchanged a doubtful glance.

"What is it?"

"The king might not be able to do that," said Willow. "He's lost the light."

"Not lost completely," Tuan said, "but it's dimming."

"What do you mean, lost? What light?"

"The king-light, of course," Willow said.

"I don't know what that is."

"Do you remember when we flew back from Noermark?" Tuan asked.

I remembered lying on a bed of pine needles, covered by Tuan's wing and a shiver went up my back.

"When we came back into Valenia that last night," he said, "you chose the place to sleep. The next morning, you chose whether to eat or fly. "

"I remember," I said. "I wondered about that, because until then we'd been following you."

"It was because we were in your lands. There is a light around you here. Humans can't see it, but they feel it and know it's there. It's strongest in the rightful ruler, but you are the heir, so you have it, too. Swanfolk can see it. When we came back into Valenia, Willow and I knew."

"Your father's is fading," Willow said. "He left his people to go after the queen. You stayed to do what had to be done."

"But when I fought Hafor," I said, "Father left then, too. Did this king-light fade then?"

"He went to hunt the boar at Fellstead," Tuan said. "He was looking after his people."

"If the queen had flown farther," Willow said, "would he have turned back, or followed her? He didn't come back to his people. He brought the queen home."

"I don't understand. He still came back. But if he can't banish Orla, what do we do?"

"You'll do it," she said. "Your light used to be like starlight, or a new moon. Now it fills the stable. You banish Orla."

"It might not work," I said.

"If she's stuck in the harp," Willow said, "we could take it far away. But she might call Aren again, or maybe Hafor. If Sianna was here, how would she stop Orla?"

"I don't know," I said. "All the elements, but I don't know what to do."

"Bury her deep," Tuan said, "beyond the border. It might stop her. At least it'll make it harder to find her, if she does call Hafor."

"If we try, she'll kill Aren," I said.

He crossed his arms over his chest. "Because of her, the queen is mad, and the king looks like an old man. Gil is dying. She would have you marry Hafor and give Valenia to Noermark. Aren's life is not worth that price."

"And why Aren's life?" Willow asked. "He's doing what she wants. But you're trying to stop her, and she isn't doing anything to you."

"She'll make me marry Hafor."

"That's a threat. She hasn't done it."

"Because she can't!" Tuan exclaimed. "The iron necklace—somehow, it's made Kiar proof against magic."

"All that necklace did was stop me changing. And I haven't had it on for months."

"But you wore it for months, right against your skin."

"It explains why Orla hasn't attacked you," Willow said.

"There's still the spell she worked on Gil, two dolls bound together. That's blood magic, and she made one like it on me. I think she can make that spell work, necklace or not."

"But nothing else works on you," Willow said.

"It's not a lot," Tuan said. "But it's something on our side."

"And we'll be there," Willow added. "You aren't alone."

CHAPTER

FORTY-FOUR

The great hall was set up for a feast, and the smells from the kitchen made my stomach growl. I couldn't remember when I'd last eaten a proper meal. I threaded my way through the tables, past house folk carrying linens and setting benches in place.

Maybe it was only because I knew the purpose of the feast, but it seemed to me that under the bustle lurked a darkness. The few dogs in the hall milled among the people, their heads and tails low, sticking close to anyone who stood still for a moment and getting underfoot around those who were moving. People glanced at me and away again.

A guard stood at the door of Father's council chamber. Good. Father was there. I couldn't think of a time I'd needed to talk to him more or wanted to less.

"The king said he would see you as soon as you came back," the guard said. He caught the handle of the door before I could and swung it open.

"Lady Kiar is here, Sire," he said.

Father stood looking out the window of the chamber. There was grey in his hair—there must have been grey in his hair for years. When he turned around, the fading light made shadows in every line of his face. He looked much older than he'd looked before Orla died. Was it only a little over a week ago?

"Where is she?" he asked. "We've prepared the funeral fire."

"I'm sorry. I couldn't bring her body," I said.

"Was she too—" he paused, "damaged? By the water and the rocks?"

I wanted to tell him so. It was a simple answer, and one he would understand. But if things went badly tonight, I wanted my father to know I hadn't lied to him.

"I have a lot to tell you," I said, "and there's not much time."

Wordlessly, he sat down.

"First," I said, "we have a fight coming tonight."

"Hafor? He's in shock. He said Orla sent for him. You didn't see him when I told him she was dead. There'll be no trouble from him."

"Not Hafor," I said. "It's Orla we'll have to fight."

He rocked back in his chair. His mouth worked a moment. "Orla is dead," he said.

"Not as dead as you think. And she's going to make trouble."

"How can that be—not as dead as I think? I can't believe that."

"It's true. Shall I tell you what I've seen these last few days?"

He sighed and nodded.

"It started with the lung fever. She put a spell on Gil when she cured him. I saw her do it, but I didn't know what she was doing. And the morning she died, I saw her kissing Gil in the stables."

He looked at me. "Gil and Adana are betrothed."

"I know. But I saw her, and so did Willow. I didn't want to believe it. I told Adana, and that's why they fought. Orla admitted casting the spell."

"Easy to say now that she's dead."

His words stung. "I'm not lying! When it happened, when I first told you, I didn't tell you everything. That was wrong, and I'm trying to set it right."

I held my breath waiting for him to speak. He could stop us with a single command.

"You've always been truthful, Kiar," he said at last. "Go on."

"Orla said she saved Gil's life, so she had the right to him. When she and Adana were fighting, she slipped and fell into the river. We tried to catch her, we did! We searched and searched, all down the river, but only found her boot."

"I see."

"We thought the spell on Gil would come undone by itself. But it didn't, so I asked Sianna what to do. She said it was blood magic, and Orla was the only one who could break it."

"Even though she's dead."

"Yes. And Sianna needed some things to make Orla do it. She sent me to get them."

"Things. What things?"

"Some of her hair," I said. "A piece of rib, and a finger."

Father put his hand over his eyes. "Oh, gods. And you did this?"

"When I found her, it was already done. But that's not everything. She's made a spell against me, too, to make me marry Hafor. I'd be like Gil. And Noermark would have Valenia in the end."

"I am lost. Orla—why would she do such a thing?"

"I don't know. Maybe she's angry because Gil was the first thing she wanted that she couldn't have. As soon as she could, she stole him from Adana. She's angry at me because I saw what she was doing."

I'd never seen Father look so tired. I said the only thing I thought might comfort him. "I buried her. I sang the mourning song and did everything I could for her."

"Where?"

"Far downriver, east beyond our borders. Now we have to throw her spirit out, too."

"We, you say. Who else is on your side?"

"Aren, Tuan, Willow. You." I paused. "If you will help."

"I see. And what's the bard's apprentice got to do with this?"

"He found her first, took the things Sianna needs. Orla made him do it, Father, to put in his harp. She can speak through the harp—I've heard her once already."

There was another long silence.

"You'll break your mother's heart," he said.

"Her heart is already broken," I said, "and it was Orla who did it. I'm saving what I can."

I waited for his answer.

"I will not hinder you," he said finally, "at least until I see what is what."

"Thank you, Father," I said.

"When?" he asked.

"After supper, I think. Aren will sing—if she'll let him—and then whatever she does—"

"We must be ready. Go, then."

I ate some bread and cheese from the kitchen on my way to the bathhouse. I scrubbed as quickly as I could, dried, and dressed again in my riding clothes before running up to my room. I brushed out my hair for the first time in nearly a week, gritting my teeth as I did. Once it was freshly braided and I wore my dark green festival dress, I looked more like the princess Aren thought me.

I put my riding boots back on and slipped my long knife, sheath and all, into my right boot. Only the toes of my boots showed beneath the embroidered hem. It was a comfort to feel the knife against my calf.

When I entered the hall, the buzz of conversation paused for a second, then started up again. Adana left Gil and came to hug me.

"I'm glad you're back," she said, then whispered, "you know Hafor's here?"

"Yes," I said. "Adana, whatever happens tonight, I'm trying to get *her* to let go of Gil."

"How can I help?"

"We have to get salt and water on the harp somehow. Do you know a way?

She thought for a few seconds. "I think I do. Salt in a pitcher of water, and a little spill at the table."

"Good. Keep Gil safe. Near you, and away from her."

Mother and Father came in then. Her right hand was tucked into his left elbow, and he had laid his free hand over hers. Mother's eyes darted everywhere around the hall.

I'd never seen her hair loose except when she was going to fly, and she always braided it again right after. Now, her hair hung free down to her knees, the black streaked with wide bands of white. With her shoulders hunched forward, she looked smaller than ever, and her movements were sharp as a wary bird's.

Father and Mother sat in their usual chairs, and Elena, who would usually have stood behind Mother, sat on her other side. Beyond Elena, Adana's and Gil's chairs stood empty. They sat instead at a table off the dais. I didn't know if Adana had asked to sit aside, or if it was simply that Mother couldn't bear the sight of her. I was afraid of how she would react when I sat at Father's right.

As I was nerving myself to take my seat, Hafor approached me and offered his arm.

"Princess Kiar," he said, "We've all suffered a great loss. Shall we keep each other company at dinner?"

"Of course," I said, and laid my hand on his. As soon as I touched his skin, I wanted to snatch back my hand and wipe it on my skirt. Dar was in his place behind my chair. I wasn't alone. There were allies all around the room, and outside. I couldn't see Tuan anywhere.

Mother glanced around as I took my place beside Father. Once I was seated, she turned away again and seemed to take no more notice of me. She was so far away from us, in whatever place her grief had taken her, that she no longer seemed like my mother at all.

As we sat, the guard at the door stepped in.

"Sire, a harper has arrived, requesting food and a night's shelter in exchange for music."

FORTY-FIVE

"Send him in," Father said.

Aren had changed his clothes to something a little finer, but he still looked travel-worn. He bowed to the high table.

"You're welcome here, although we're in mourning," my father said. "After you eat, perhaps you'll give us a little music."

"It would be my honour, Sire," Aren said.

Adana waved Aren over to sit with her and Gil. I turned my attention back to Hafor.

"Your foster-sister isn't here," he said. Whatever he knew or suspected, he'd get nothing from me.

"Willow loves to fly," I answered. "She prefers it to being indoors."

"And your man, what is his name?"

"You mean Tuan? I don't know where he is. You take a great interest in the swanfolk, Prince Hafor."

"Only the ones in this household. That man of your sister's doesn't look well."

"He had the lung-fever. He's slow in recovering."

"And when he does, he will go back to the flock, am I right? With your sister?"

I looked down at my plate to hide my anger.

"I'm sorry," he said, "Perhaps you are fond of him. It was tactless of me to speak of death and parting when we've lost your sister and my intended bride."

I couldn't believe my luck. He had mistaken my anger for sadness about Gil and Orla. He didn't know what I knew, and somehow—my spirits rose—there was no way for Orla to tell him.

"That's quite all right," I said, smiling at him. "We're here, with the evening ahead of us. Who knows what it will bring?" I put my napkin back in my lap. As my hand rose above the table, he took it and pressed it to his lips.

"Good words, Princess Kiar," he said. "Or do I dare call you only 'Kiar'? Even if you will not be my sister?"

I smiled again. He took that as answer enough, as far as I could tell.

That dinner seemed to last forever. The main course came and went, and then platters of apple pastries and small seedcakes. I ate mine slowly, wondering how Adana would manage the salt and water.

I needn't have worried. As I put the last bite of cake in my mouth, there was a crash at Adana's table. A maidservant leaned on Aren's chair to catch her balance, the pitcher she'd been carrying in pieces on the floor. Water had splashed over the table, over Aren and Adana, and on the harp Aren held in his lap to tune.

"No harm done," he said, waving away the maid's offer of a napkin to wipe the harp. People moved their chairs back, relaxing to listen to the music, and I took the moment to slip out of my seat and over to the hearth. Holding out my hands as if to warm them, I put the pillar of one of the stonework arches between me and Hafor, then slipped my knife from my boot.

Aren came to the hearth. The belly of the harp was streaked with water, and droplets clung to the strings and the hairs among them. I glanced at Hafor; with the harp out in the open, freed of the case and its spells of protection, would Orla be able to talk to him as she'd talked to me that night? I hoped not. Hafor was speaking with my father and took no notice of Aren.

"A seat for the harper," I said.

As a servant came forward with a stool, Aren set the harp on the hearthstone and went to meet him.

Two raps on the chimney stones was my signal to Willow, but before I'd tapped, I saw the flames rise. An air I hadn't called was moving across the strings. The harp strings hummed, then wailed, and everyone in the room fell silent at the eerie sound. In the midst of it, I heard Orla's voice.

"Mmmmmmmmmoooooooootheeeeeeeeerrrr....."

Over the sudden babble of voices, Mother cried out "Orla! Orla!"

Hafor, sitting in the chair set for him next to my throne, bolted to his feet.

"Mmmmmmmmmmmotherrrrrrrrrrrrrrrrrr..." the harp said again, and Mother leapt up from her place, jerking away from Elena and stumbling towards the hearth.

"Hold her!" Father said.

Three of the guard hemmed her in, standing firm while she fought and twisted, crying Orla's name over and over. One dog began to howl, a low, moaning sound that rose until it was a thin, high keen.

Adana stood up, said something I couldn't hear, and pointed at the dog. Two of the maidservants dragged it away by the collar and shooed the others outside.

"Silence!" Father said. He looked at me. Perhaps this was all the help he'd give, but I took it gladly. Even Mother's voice fell, although she still strained against the guards who held her. I'd have to proceed before the water on the harp dried. Aren stood back, the small stool in his hands, and made no move towards the hearth.

"Who are you? Say your name!" I looked directly at the harp as I spoke and tried to put Father's tone of command into my voice. As I spoke, I rapped the pommel of my knife on the stones.

Once again, the flames stirred, and I felt the movement of air. This draft had a beat to it, the strong, rapid rhythm of Willow's wings.

At first, I thought the harp wouldn't speak, that Orla could keep silent at will. The silence lasted only a heartbeat, and then the harp wailed again.

"Orrrrrrrrrllllllllllllaaaaaaaaaa!" it wailed.

Mother shrieked again.

"My Orla!" she cried, "Come back, come back, swanling!"

I almost had to shout to make my voice heard over Mother's.

"Tell us why you died!" I said, tapping the stones again. As soon as the words were out of my mouth, I cursed myself for the leeway I'd given her.

"Mmmmmmmmmmmuurrrrrrrrrrrrdeerrrrrrrrrrrrred!" the harp cried, "Mmmmuurrderrrrred—Adaaaannnnnnnnnn-nnaaaa...."

"No!" I said, but the words were out.

Mother flung herself back, taking the guard completely by surprise, and broke free. She whirled and stumbled towards Adana, still standing where she'd been since she ordered the dogs out. The men caught Mother again before she reached my sister. A draft brushed the harp strings, and I heard a rippling sound like laughter.

"Stop it!" I shouted at the harp. "Tell the truth about the spell." Again, I hammered on the stones and felt the beat of Willow's wings dragging air up the chimney.

"Iiiiiiiiiiiii ssssssssssaaaaaavvvved," the harp wailed. "Iiiiiiiisss-saaavvvveed. Gillllllllllllll—mmmmiiiiiiiiinnnnnnnnneeeeeeeeee. Mmmmmmmmiiiiiiinnnnnnnnnnnnnne."

"You stole him! Admit it!" I struck the chimney stones again. A red haze clouded my vision, anger at Orla for her stubborn pride and her stupidity.

"Sssssspeelllllll—yessssssssssssssssssss," the harp said. "Sssssaaaavvve and keeeeep—mmmmiinnnee...."

The beat of Willow's wings at the edge of my hearing faltered for a moment. I thought of Willow, standing on the slippery slates of the roof, holding with feet never meant for perching and bracing with herself with her swan's legs against the powerful beat of her own wings. No wonder she'd paused. Air she hadn't moved touched the harp.

"Fffaaaaaaaaaaaaaatheerrrrrrrrrrrrrrrrrrr...."

Mother twisted back towards the hearth. Father glanced towards her, then stood and spoke directly to the harp.

"Who killed you?" he demanded. "Was it Adana?"

"Adanaaaaaaaaaaaa...Yessssssssss!" The harp voice sounded triumphant.

"For the reason Kiar says?"

"Yessssssssss....." The word died away. Then the laughter rippled again, and I saw how the strings shook off water.

I turned all around, looking for Sianna. If she was going to make Orla take the spell off, it would have to be soon. If she was here.

Father stood and took two steps towards the hearth. "Orla, I command you. Undo what you have done to Gil, and then leave here forever. Go into the otherworld, where you belong."

"No! No!" Mother shrieked. A harp string snapped, and the laughter rippled again.

Although I hadn't tapped the chimney, I heard Willow beat her wings again, more slowly now.

"Nnnnnnnooooo power, Fffffffaaaaaattthhherrrrrrrr." She laughed again. "Kiiiaaarrr to Hafoooooooorrrrr. Gillllll to meeeeeeeee."

For a heartbeat, I thought it had all gone wrong. Then Father asked the question that let me know he understood the danger. There was almost no water left on the harp at all.

"And Valenia?" Father said. "And Valenia, Orla?"

Before Orla could answer, Sianna was there, stepping out of the air, it seemed. A moment before, I'd have sworn there were only two maidservants staring, one frozen in the act of wiping her hands on her apron. They stumbled back as though they'd been shoved, and Sianna came forward, one hand palm-out towards the harp, the other towards the floor.

Her hair stood out, crackling with sparks. Her face, smooth and calm, might have been carved in stone, and the ripples of magic off her skin and clothing washed against me in waves. My stomach clenched, but I held my ground. Only a dozen steps separated her from Orla. I saw her body lean forward as she broke into a run.

For the first few steps, I thought she would be in time. Then Orla laughed again, a ripple of the harp strings. I glanced back at her and saw that the fire had dried up almost all of the water. Only a few drops remained on the highest notes of the harp, farthest away from the hearth. The laugh died into a sighing sound like a breath released before a great effort, and then the harp shuddered and exploded.

For a few terrible seconds, all I knew was the pressure of the air and the pieces of the harp flying, and a sound so loud it made my bones shudder. I'd heard trees split on a cold winter night. This was a hundred trees all splitting at once. The shock of all that power released, even with the stone-built pillar of the hearth between me and it, knocked me to my hands and knees, and I stayed down, trembling all over, my stomach roiling. Around me, people screamed or shouted wordlessly, and the shards of the harp pattered onto the stone floor.

I'd somehow hung onto my knife as I fell. As I rose, I switched it from my left hand to my right. My left knuckles were skinned and bloody, but my hand worked.

Every candle and torch was out. A dark red light, like a dying fire, spread from the hearth. The walls and corners of the hall were dark, as though all the shadows in the world had gathered there. In the red light I saw Aren scrabbling on the floor for the pieces of his harp. I didn't see Sianna anywhere.

Then I looked at the hearth. The fire was out, black and dead as though it hadn't been lit for years. The harp was gone. In its place, shimmering like the air above the forge, red as fire and blood and passion, Orla stood. It was she who cast the red light. I could see through her to the people beyond in the hall. The cut over her breastbone showed where Aren had taken the piece of her rib. Her right hand lacked the forefinger. She wore what I had buried her in, her trousers and one boot, and Hafor's bracelet.

"I told you not to meddle," she said. Her voice rose and fell, loud and soft, as though she were both near and very far away. "By head and hand and heart, I have bound Gil to me, and you have no power to make me give him up!"

She raised a hand and beckoned toward a corner of the hall. Gil came out of the shadows, dragging Adana behind him. She had her arms hooked through his and her feet planted, but even in his frail state, he made slow headway, leaning forward against her weight, taking one step and hauling. Two men grabbed Gil under the arms as he took another step, and their boots slid on the stones as he dragged them forward, too.

"He'll come to me," she said. "Whether he lives to do it or bursts his heart trying, he'll come to me in the end, sister!"

Orla's ghost whirled in place, laughing, and people flinched away, although she never stirred from the hearthstone. Aren gave up gathering the remains of his harp and backed into the shadows.

"Where is your wisewoman now?" Orla asked me. "Where are your allies, Kiar? Tuan, Sianna, your apprentice harper." She tilted her head as if listening up the chimney. "Even Willow. All gone." She shook her head and made a sad face at me. "Poor Kiar. All alone."

She turned again. "Come here, Hafor." Her voice was all sweetness. "I have a gift for you."

I truly admired Hafor then. He wore the closed expression of a man going into battle, and I could guess at the fear behind it. He walked forward, one step after another, as though every step would put his foot into a snare.

Father seized Hafor with an arm across his throat.

"No," Orla said, as though she was refusing a cup of wine. An invisible hand threw Father backwards. He slammed into Dar, already striding forward with his sword half-drawn, and landed hard on the floor. Dar swung with the impact and managed two more steps before Orla thrust him back, and he, too, stumbled and fell. Several of the guard came forward and stopped as though they'd hit a wall. Another, more cautious, put out a hand and leaned. After a few seconds, he put his other hand on the air and pushed with all his weight, and his legs braced hard. He might as well have been trying to push the castle over. Then he surged forward and fell hard, full-length on the floor. I heard his grunt as he hit.

Orla giggled. "Go back," she said.

He stood and backed past the invisible wall.

"Hafor," she said, sticking out her lip in a mock pout. "Aren't you eager for your bride? You seemed willing before."

She turned to me. I guessed what was coming. I set my feet hard and put my hand on the hearth pillar. She'd have to drag me by main force. Her hand came up, and she beckoned, a smile curling her lips.

I felt my gorge rise, but beyond that, nothing. No pull, no urge to step forward, not even an unsteadiness. Orla stopped smiling, then fixed me with a one-eyed look, a swan's look. Still nothing, and I knew that Tuan was right. I swallowed and looked her in the eye fixed on me.

"It doesn't work on me," I said.

"Not the little magic," she said, "but I have greater ones." She looked back to Hafor. "I can't force her to speak the betrothal pledge. I'm sure you have ways, Hafor. If pretty words won't do it, you can use a blade."

"I'd like to see him try," I said. I tossed my knife, flipping it and catching it again by the handle.

"You will," Orla said.

"Take the spell off Gil," I said, "and I won't kill Hafor."

She laughed.

"I don't care if you kill Hafor or not." She looked past me to where the two maids stood. They'd hardly moved from where they'd stopped when Sianna appeared. They were still as deer.

"You," she said to one, "Go to my house."

"I don't—Lady, I can't go in there."

"I give you leave," Orla said. "Go now." The maid stumbled backwards, caught herself, and fled into the night.

"She's biddable enough," Orla said. "She'll finish what I've started. We can all wait here until she returns. What a pity the harper has nothing to play on. A song would pass the time. Where are you, Aren?"

He walked out of the shadows, his hands empty at his sides.

"You promised me a song, Aren. Do you remember?"

"I remember," he said, and she smiled. For a moment, she looked like my sweet little sister again.

"Have you made it yet?" she asked.

"Not yet, Lady."

"I've been looking forward to it. Will you be my own harper, Aren?"

Ripples of magic shimmered in the air between them. Aren opened his mouth, closed it again, and then shook his head like someone shaking off a blow.

"How can I be harper to someone who is dead?" he asked.

I thought that she was going to throw him back, but instead she beckoned him forward. He came, one slow step at a time. Sweat broke out on his forehead. I risked a glance at Hafor, who had stopped. His feet were planted, and he leaned back, but he couldn't seem to take a step backwards.

Orla pulled Aren until he stood enveloped in the shimmer around her. She floated head and shoulders above him. Looking down into his eyes, she leaned to kiss his cheek.

He screamed and fell to his knees, one hand over the place she'd kissed. With a thrust of her hand, Orla sent him flying across the floor into the darkness.

"Whether I'm alive or dead, you are my harper," she said. "Look into a mirror if you doubt it." She turned back to Hafor, and he stepped forward again. Where before he walked upright, looking almost as though it was his own idea, now he pulled back against Orla's force. It did him little good.

"Come, now, Hafor," she said. "The spell will be done. We'll have what we want."

A gust of chilly air blew through the hall as the door swung open—the maid, back to say the spell was done. My heart sank. Then I heard Tuan's voice.

"Did you want this?" he asked from the doorway. In one hand, he held his knife, and in the other, two dolls joined by a cord. I recognized the dolls of Orla and Gil.

"Or this?" Willow asked, stepping from behind Tuan. She was naked, and her arms, breast and face were black with soot. Where the soot stopped her skin was red and blistered. She held the other two dolls of me and Hafor, and russet wool from the floor of Orla's house.

"Your messenger was too slow." She dropped the dolls on the floor and held the wool taut between her hands. Before anyone could speak, Tuan cut it in two with his knife.

Both Hafor and Orla cried out, and the red light around Orla pulsed like a heartbeat, or the throb of a wound.

"Cut the other one!" I said.

Tuan draped the cord between the Gil and Orla dolls over his knife, and Gil, still straining to reach Orla, gasped and staggered. Orla gasped, too, and bent double. Then she chuckled, a strangled sound.

"Cut it, then. You'll hurt me, but Gil will die. That spell's done, and even steel will not undo it."

Tuan glanced at me, and I looked at Adana, still holding onto Gil. There were tears on her face. She nodded. My heart sank; even now, she trusted me. But only Sianna could make Orla remove the spell, and she had disappeared. A quick death would be better for Gil than slow starvation.

I turned my head to nod to Tuan, and Sianna's voice rang out of the darkness.

"Stop!" Before I could work out where her voice came from, she limped into the pulsing red glow, holding her hands cupped before her. A snarl of black and brass curled between her fingers.

"By head and hand and heart," she said, holding her cupped hands out towards Orla. "I command you to remove every spell you have laid in this place, every charm and glamour, every word and bond."

Orla seemed to shrink and fade a little. She said nothing but shook her head, and then screamed as Sianna clenched her hands on whatever she held.

"Orla," she said, as though she were gently reproving a child. She moved her hands apart, stretching the wires and Orla's hair between them. Water, or blood, dripped from her fingers; in the ruddy light I couldn't tell which.

Orla curled into a ball, still floating, with her one booted and one bare foot almost touching the hearthstone. She raised her head and looked at Sianna, panting hard.

"I will undo it all. But you cannot stay. I still—" She stopped then, and I heard Mother moaning.

"Undo it, then," Sianna said, and pulled again on the wire and hair.

Again, Orla screamed. She sketched a shape in the air with the fingers of her maimed hand, then said a word and wiped downwards with her palm.

Gil collapsed onto the floor, and Adana fell to her knees beside him. Across the hall from me I heard Hafor fall hard. But Mother's shriek drowned out everything as Orla's flesh bloated, then sagged around her. In a few seconds, she changed from a lovely young woman to a week-old corpse. My gorge rose at the sight of her.

I expected her to disappear or fall to pieces on the hearth. Shockingly, in spite of what Sianna had just done, she spoke, her voice thick, bubbling, and raspy.

"Keep him, sister," she said to Adana. "I am free, and near my place of power. I can do what I will—what's one man more or less?" She turned her ruined face to Sianna. "You have no power to make me leave," she said.

I stepped close enough to touch her, if there had been anything to touch. My skin crawled at her nearness, but I slashed her with my knife. The blade passed through without leaving a mark, but she recoiled from the steel and shrank away from me.

"Get out," I said. "Out of this hall, out of this land. Go beyond the borders of Valenia and stay there forever. Never come here again. Never come near me or mine."

She rippled like water.

"Kiar!" she said, "Please, no, don't send—"

And she was gone, and the hall was dark.

CHAPTER

FORTY-SIX

The tick of flint and steel broke the silence, then tiny flames sprang up around the hall as people found and lit candles. Someone went slowly around the hall, lighting torches.

I sat down on the hearthstone, almost right below where Orla had stood. For a moment, the room spun around me, and I closed my eyes. Then someone dropped onto the hearth beside me, smelling of burned feathers and hair.

"You did it!" Willow said, flinging her arms around me. Then she said, "Ow," and let go. I opened my eyes. She was coated with soot from hairline to waist. Small blisters dotted the edge of the soot.

"You're hurt," I said.

She smiled, her teeth very white in a sooty face. "I'll heal."

"Well done," Sianna said. She limped forward and stood with her knee bent. Her hands and arms were burned and her

fingers bloody. "I'd sit, but I don't think I could get up again."
Aren came up behind her, two arcs of blistered flesh on the
place where Orla had kissed him.

"What happened?" I asked. "I thought she'd killed you when
the harp exploded. And the spells she cast—"

"All undone," she said. "Not only the one on Gil. There
were words of power everywhere in the castle. She must have
been setting them for years, places to stand hidden. They'll fade
now that she's gone. The ones on people will take longer. Seven
years, the teachings say, for the last of a spell to fade."

"That's how you hid," I said. "You used her own spells
against her."

Sianna nodded.

"She didn't notice I was hiding in one of her places. You
kept her busy for me." She touched Willow's hair and glanced
at Tuan and Aren. "All of you."

"We did it!" Willow said. "We beat her! And Kiar banished
her!"

Tuan looked towards the high table

"There's still Hafor," he said.

Hafor stood near the wall with my father and Guthric. From
the way my father stood, he had just told them something they
were going to do whether they wanted to or not.

"Go on," Sianna said to me. "Finish the job."

I caught the eye of one of the guard. "Get Prince Hafor's
horse, all their horses. Send someone for their things. All the
weapons stay here."

"Yes, Lady," said the guard. He left at a jog.

I pushed myself up and walked over to the little group. Tuan followed close behind.

Mother sat on the floor with her head in her hands. Two guards still hovered over her, unneeded, and Elena knelt beside her. I walked past, almost close enough to touch, and could think of nothing to say.

"...seen how powerful she was," Guthric was saying. "Small blame to Prince Hafor for falling under her control."

"You're leaving now," I told Hafor. "Your horse is being saddled, and my men are getting your things." He glanced down at my hand, and I realized I was still holding my knife. I handed it to Tuan to hold. I didn't need a knife to face Hafor down.

"I know what you planned," I said to Hafor. "Come into Valenia again, and I'll bury you here. Your knife." He hesitated and Tuan moved slightly beside me. Hafor pulled the knife from its sheath with two fingers and handed it to me, holding the blade on his palm.

"I'm not a fool," he said. "Better alive over the mountains than dead here."

"It's expensive for you to visit us," I said.

"Sire," Guthric said to Father, "can we not discuss this? Princess Kiar's courage and care are praiseworthy, but youth is hot-headed."

"Discuss?" Father said. "Prince Hafor has tried twice to take a foothold here."

Guthric sighed and removed three knives from belt, boot, and sleeve—all still in their sheaths.

"I will take my leave before you give it to me, Princess Kiar," he said, handing them to me.

"I hope we will see you again in happier times, Guthric," I said.

I looked past Guthric at Dar, who nodded and came forward.

"By the door," he said. "Never fear, we'll pack your things carefully."

"I'll give your regards to my brother," Hafor said as he passed me, "if he's still alive."

"Do that," I said.

I turned back to Father, unsure of what I should say.

"Well done," he said. "Well done from beginning to end."

"Orla's still dead and Mother's still—"

"I know." He looked past me to where she remained, still on the floor, drooped and silent. Sianna sat on a chair beside her, talking. I couldn't hear her voice, but Mother let Sianna take her hand.

"We can hope she might heal," he said. "What happened tonight?"

"I don't know," I said.

"She left when you told her to," Father said, "but not when I did."

I looked at the floor, and Father took my chin in his hand and raised my face.

"Don't," he said. "I wish it could have been me who banished her and protected us. I don't know why it wasn't. But Valenia will be in good hands."

"Valenia *is* in good hands!" I said.

"Well," Father said. "We all need rest, and some of us need doctoring. Once our guests are gone." He looked again at Mother.

"I'm going outside," I said. "Alone." I laid the Noermarkers' knives on the high table and crossed the hall. The men of Noermark stood by the door, and I passed them without a glance. Outside, three of the guard held horses., their harness fittings glinting in the light of a nearby torch. Another man led two more from the stables, saddled and bridled. They were beautiful animals; whatever else might come out of Noermark, they made good swords and good horses. Men of Father's guard stood by, ready to escort the Noermarkers to the border.

I slipped around the corner and leaned against the cool stone. Closing my eyes, I allowed myself to remember Orla as she had been, a little mouse of a girl, bright-eyed and clever. My tears spilled over, and I cried. I wept for losing her a second time, and for the pleading look on her ruined face as she begged me not to banish her.

When I finally finished, my chest ached. The courtyard was silent but for guards on the wall speaking to each other. I wiped the last of the tears from my face before returning to the door.

Willow waited for me in the torchlight near the hall doors. She wore trousers and a linen shirt, and salve glistened on her brow and cheeks.

"Better?" she asked.

I nodded. "How about you?"

"The salve helps the pain. Sianna says not to scratch."

"They always say that. Is she all right?"

"She says she will be. And Gil woke up. He's eating, at least, and he's talking."

"That's good. What about Aren?"

"His face will heal. He'll have the scar, though, all his life. And he'll be able to make several new songs from tonight, he says."

"He'll need a new harp to play them on."

"Yes. And the Noermarkers are gone. They weren't happy about leaving the weapons."

"I should have been here."

"The king saw them off."

"It sounds quiet in there. Has everyone gone to bed?"

"Some are waiting for you to come back. They're all proud of you. Maybe a little bit scared of you, too."

"I wasn't alone," I said. "I had you, and Aren, and Sianna, and Tuan." Saying his name reminded me. "At least he doesn't have to bury the harp. Orla's not in it anymore, wherever she is."

"Far away," Willow said. "Are you coming in?"

"In a few minutes. You go ahead." I heard voices from the hall, quiet and calm, as she opened the door. When it closed behind her, I let out a sigh.

"Princess Kiar."

I jumped and gave a startled squeak; I'd thought I was alone. On the walls the guard stopped talking.

"It's just me," Aren said. "I want to thank you."

"For what?" I asked. It came out more sharply than I'd intended. "You could have been killed."

"If you hadn't come along, when *she'd* done what she wanted, she'd have killed me. Or kept me around. I don't know which would be worse."

"Your harp is gone."

"But I'm still here. And we won. I nearly didn't find the rib. Even then it was only a part."

"That's what you were doing on the floor."

"Yes. Sianna sent me. We had a chance because there were still drops of water on the short strings, but she needed the other bits. We couldn't keep Orla in the harp when she wanted out—not so close to her place of power. But there was enough water, just barely, to force her to remove the spell."

"I can give you a harp, at least," I said. "We have a small one, not as fine as the one you had, but it's something."

"Thank you, Princess Kiar."

"Just Kiar. At least when we don't *have* to be formal. After the last few days we've had."

"Thank you, Kiar." He hesitated, then went on. "So my first song will be for you, not her."

"I'm not a fairytale swan princess, or a hero."

"I disagree."

"Not that I can stop you. Even a king can't tell a bard what to sing."

"Will you listen to them?" he asked.

"Do I have to?"

"I think you do. If you do heroic things, someone will sing about them. And you have to listen, at least once."

I sighed. "All right."

"Will you be in soon?"

"Soon," I said. The door opened and closed. In the sky above the castle wall, I saw the star at the tip of the Hunter's bow. A little while later, the door opened and closed again. I knew who was there before he took my hand. We stood in peaceful silence for a few minutes.

"Your personal harper," Tuan said. "He's sitting in the corner, counting on his fingers and muttering."

"I dread what we'll hear when he's done."

"I'm looking forward to it."

"Hells," I said.

Tuan laughed.

I turned and said, "Are you allowed—" and he kissed me.

Our noses and chins bumped, and our mouths glanced off each other. We both laughed.

"Gil and Adana make it look easy," I said.

Tuan pulled me around to face him. This time we didn't bump noses, and when we stopped, I felt breathless and dizzy, and not just from lack of air.

"Come back in, Princess Kiar," he said. "Your people are waiting to hear the tale from your own lips."

"If I must," I said.

He leaned down and we kissed again. Then we went back into the hall, hand in hand.

CHAPTER

FORTY-SEVEN

I told my story several times over the next few days, including once privately to Father in his council chamber, answering all his questions, leaving out nothing.

Sianna spent two days in Mother's solar while her leg mended. When she came back down to the hall for breakfast on the third day, Mother came, too.

Mother stood straighter than she had since Orla's death. Her hair was braided and the heavy plait, streaked white in the black, hung down her back. Her movements were less jerky and birdlike, and she looked at us straight with both eyes. Then she started across the hall towards us with quick steps, her chin up and mouth set.

I stood, heart pounding, remembering the last time she had touched me. She stopped, then held out her arms as she had when we were small children. I went to her, and she put her hands on my shoulders and pulled me close.

She felt so thin, and she trembled. I might have been holding a bird. After a few seconds, she let me go and went to Adana and gave her the same, brief embrace before releasing her and retreating across the hall to where Sianna sat.

"It's something," Adana said.

"She can't go back to the swans," Willow said. "She has to live here somehow." She looked up to see Adana frowning at her.

"What? It's true."

"Yes," I said, "but maybe she still loves us. Don't you think?"

Willow looked at me.

"Yes," she said, "I do. But she had choices before. Now she doesn't have as many."

"Grandmother told me a long time ago that kings and queens don't ever have as many choices," I said. "She could have flown away. She could still fly away. If she chooses to stay, I suppose she'd rather be with us."

"Maybe she'll get better," Gil said. "Even if she's not quite the same." I glanced at Adana. Gil, too, was not quite the same. Seven years, Sianna had said. Maybe he would be the same someday.

When I'd finished breakfast, I went to talk to Sianna. Mother stopped eating briefly as I approached, then continued. I sat down on Sianna's other side.

"How's your leg?" I asked.

"Better. I should be able to ride tomorrow. Your father and I will be in his chamber after breakfast. Will you join us? And Adana?"

"Yes," I said.

After breakfast Sianna, Adana, Father, and I went to the council chamber. When we were seated, with a guard on the door, Father said, "This is about Orla."

"What about her?" I asked. "She's gone."

"We need to remove everything she left," Sianna said. "She's banished, but not destroyed. She still has power, although I don't know how much. She'll gain more as she recovers from what we did. It would be best if everything that bound her to this place was destroyed. I want your leave to do this."

"Everything?" Father asked.

"I'm sorry," she said. "Any keepsake could give her a way back in."

"Kiar banished her."

"Yes, but, Sire, Kiar will not live forever. Orla may hold on to this world for many years. You need to think of the future of your people."

There was a long silence. I wanted to agree but held my tongue. Adana said nothing, but she glanced at me, and a crease appeared and disappeared between her brows. Sianna sat with her hands resting in her lap, patient as a tree. Finally, my father spoke.

"What do you need us to do?"

"Collect everything she owned and loved that is left here, and burn it," Sianna said. "Any gift she gave, that must also be burned. Bring it all together, and tomorrow morning, Kiar and I will take it down to her hut. We'll burn the hut with everything in it and scatter the ashes. I believe that will sever the bond."

"As you say," Father said. He sounded tired.

"We'll do it," Adana said.

"Yes," I said. "Today."

There was surprisingly little to collect. Her clothes, her hair ribbons, her doll and her toy lamb made of scraps of sheepskin, were all in her room. I pulled the embroidery she had been working on out of its frame and the blankets and sheets from her bed. Father sent two men with axes to destroy the furniture and bring it down to the courtyard, where a wagon stood waiting.

Willow brought the dolls Orla had made and the russet wool. Adana and I bundled everything into the wagon. Star stood saddled, and laden with food and blankets. Sianna asked for a hammer and a bucket and tied them to Star's saddle. When the pieces of Orla's furniture were on the wagon, Sianna took the reins, and I mounted Star.

When we reached the hut, we picketed the horses. Sianna laid the broken door aside and went inside. She brought out the brazier on its tripod of fire-hardened poles and started a small fire in it, then went back inside. I took the hammer and battered at the walls to break the clay covering, dropping pieces into the bucket and carrying them to the river. The unfired clay would soak up water and become only mud again to be swept downriver. Inside the hut I heard Sianna's voice rising and falling with words I didn't understand. When she emerged, she carried four plain dolls, without hair or clothes to mark them.

She threw the dolls on the fire. They twisted and writhed, and we watched until they fell to ash. When the brazier held only glowing coals, Sianna went back into the hut and came out with three large books and a smaller one.

"I hate to burn these," she said. "But she used them, and they bear her trace. And this small one is hers. She made it herself, and it holds spells she created. That is a great loss. A great loss."

She riffled through the pages of the small book, then sighed and set it in the brazier, propped up with covers open and pages fanning. It caught at once, the flames fluttering like wings as the parchment curled, writhed, and turned to ash. Then we cut the other books apart, covers from pages, pages from spines, burning them in pieces until they were gone. By the end, there were tears on Sianna's face, though she never made a sound.

After that, we took turns with the hammer, and both of us were sweating before we'd broken most of the clay away from the walls. We shook the framework and swept as much clay as we could into the river.

We took Orla's clothes into the hut, and all her bedding and toys, everything we could fit. I brought Star's saddle and bridle.

"Will we have to kill Star, too?" I asked. "And the golden mare Hafor gave Orla?"

"It might be better if we did," Sianna said. "The mare—did Orla name her?"

"No."

"A small bond, then. If she was given away, perhaps to that young minstrel, that would do."

"But Star," I said. It didn't seem fair to kill her for being Orla's horse.

"She could stay with me for the years she has left. If Orla is strong enough to come back, and has only Star to bind her here, she will at least come to me. You would have warning."

The relief of not having to kill Star was a weight off my shoulders. I tied her to the wagon with a piece of rope. When I came back to the hut, Sianna had set everything alight and thrown the brazier onto the pyre.

We rested and ate while we watched the burning, throwing the pieces of furniture on to feed the flames. Now and again, a shard of clay clinked and popped. It was after midnight when the last of the wood had burned. We took turns watching and sleeping until even the coals had burned down to a small glowing pile.

It was nearly midday when the ashes were cool enough to rake through. Nothing remained in them, but bits of clay smoked black and the darkened dish of the brazier. We threw the ashes and shards into the river and tossed the brazier in as well. We poured water everywhere the fire had burned. At dusk, we came back to the gate, smoke-smudged and weary from our two days' work. Someone took the horses and cart away. Tuan was there; he put his arms around me, and I leaned against him, weary to my bones and too tired to speak, or weep.

The next morning Sianna left. All of the family but Mother came to see her off. By Father's order, Star went with Sianna, tied with a new halter and lead to Night Wind's saddle. We had little to say. How could Father thank her for what we'd had to do to Orla? But even in his grief, he knew we had all done what was necessary. Sianna mounted Night Wind.

"You did well," she said to me, "There is something to swan magic, more than just wings. You have more of it than you know." She looked to Father. "I hope we don't see each other again for a long time, King Tir."

"I hope that, too," he said.

Then she rode away.

That night, Aren sang the song he had written for me. I wanted to run and hide.

"Play it again," Father said. I frowned at him, but he was the king, and my father. I didn't enjoy the song any more the second time through.

A few days later, Aren left, too, with new clothes and blankets, a harp and the golden mare. I was sorry to see him go, but glad as well.

Gil slowly regained his strength. He remained a quieter man than he had been. He and Adana married at midsummer and left with the swans after the harvest festival. The other festivals that year seemed sober and quiet. Only three people were gone, but those three were half our family. Mother was still silent, a shadow of the woman she had been. Father moved more slowly, too, and talked more softly.

At the festival of lights, there were now only three candles for our family. Father placed his first, as the king does, and Mother set hers next to it. I chose a spot farther away, where Tuan and I set ours together, and Willow put hers with ours.

Tuan sat next to me now, at court and at table. We hadn't talked about a betrothal, but when I thought of the future, Tuan was always in it.

The next spring, Aren came with his new master. My father had ordered a harp made for him, carved with a swan's head. It was a very fine harp for an apprentice, but his master made no objection. At Father's request, Aren sang the song he had made of our adventure, and his master let him sing several other songs as well.

Later, I spoke to Aren privately. Up close, with the light glancing over it, I could see the paler skin where Orla's kiss had scarred his cheek.

"Do you like your song any better?" he asked.

"No, but it's a good song," I said. "Even if it embroiders the truth a bit."

"Don't you bring out the embroidered clothes for a feast?" he asked. "Plain is for every day."

"Does a bard ever write a song for every day?" I asked.

He smiled, but his smile quickly faded. "I promised my first song would be about her," he said.

"It was," I answered. "She's all through it."

"But not what I wanted to write about her," he said. "Not when I first met her, when I made that promise."

"I know," I said, "Maybe you can write that one later."

They stayed for a week, and when they left, I watched them from the gate until they were out of sight. If Aren was going to sing about Orla again, I wanted it to be the song he'd hoped to write, for the beautiful young girl who had charmed him in my mother's solar. It was going to be a long time before we could forget our last sight of Orla, a red-lit corpse-spirit hovering over the hearth.

Tuan was waiting for me at the stable door, holding his bow and mine. He smiled and went in. I hurried to saddle Kestrel, thinking of green forests and brown plains showing tender new growth and blue, still lakes reflecting the sky. The deer were still winter-thin, but I knew we weren't going to hunt.

We were going to fly.

THE SWAN SISTERS (AREN'S SONG)

Melody is the traditional English tune "The Oak and the Ash"

1

There once was a man won a swan-woman's hand
and beautiful daughters they had one, two, three.
So valiant and fair, and wise beyond compare,
In Valenia's land where the swans fly free.

Where the ravens cry and the swan-maidens fly
by the banks where the river rolls swiftly by.

2

The eldest of three the Swan Queen would be,
the second the heir to her father's throne,
the youngest for her part knew well the magic art
and practised in secret, apart and alone.

Adana and Kiar and Orla were the three
princesses fair of the west country.

3

A certain young man had the heart and the hand
of Adana the eldest and loved her alone,
but Orla as well for the same young man fell,

and fashioned a charm that would make him her own.

And he pined and he sighed and his heart he turned to her
and abandoned the love that he did prefer.

4

The spell being set these two sisters met.
"Return me my lover," Adana did say.
Their anger was hot, by the river they fought,
and Orla fell in and was soon swept away.

She swam and she sank until drowned was she
and caught in the roots of a green willow tree.

5

Her spirit sought around, a passing harper found,
and called him to her with his knife keen and sharp
to cut a lock of hair and her forefinger fair
and a piece of her rib to put into his harp.

He did as she wished, set the harp upon a stone,
and the wind touched the strings and it played alone.

6

Adana then cried, "My love looks to die,
He pines just for Orla, no other will heed."
Kiar, brave and fair, said "Do not despair—
I will seek out the wisewoman, ask for her rede."

The wisewoman told her she must break the spell
and banish the ghost from the country as well.

7

Her sister she found, lying dead on the ground
where the green willow grows and the river roars.
and the harper stood by with madness in his eye,
and a harp that was speaking in Orla's words.

"I bid you to take me to my father's hall,
and I'll undo Adana before them all."

8

Kiar told her "No—to the wisewoman go
to take off the spell from Adana's man."
Said Orla, "Do my will, or this harper I will kill,
then take vengeance on you the best I can.

Though by magic's law I cannot tell a lie,
the whole truth I'll not tell, and so say I."

9

Upon the hearth stone the harp played alone
to all of the court who were gathered around.
"Here's my father and mother, my true love and another;
my sister Adana who left me to drown."

And Kiar then moved to make her break the spell
and tell all the truth of her death as well.

10

To forward her will a swan-maid stood still
on the roof by the chimney her signal to heed,
and the wind of her wings stirred the swan harp's strings

and forced it to say then what Kiar decreed.

Then Kiar spoke up and to the harp she said,
"I command you by heart and hand and head!

11

"The truth you must tell, and that is you fell
and nobody pushed you." The harp said, "It's so."
Said Kiar, "Hear me well! I command you, break the spell,
be banished and far from this country go!

Never come again within the borders of this land,
I command you by heart and head and hand!"

12

Her magic all dead, the dark spirit fled,
far over the border on exile wing.
And Valenia's land under Kiar's hand
is safe from all perils that magic can bring.
Where the ravens cry and the swan-maidens fly
by the banks where the river rolls swiftly by.

ACKNOWLEDGEMENTS

To write a book you have to sit quietly with the page and do the work. But no book is written in complete isolation. I'm indebted to so many people for late-night talks, book recommendations, information, ideas, feedback, and support. This book is richer for them.

People who read or listened to large parts of this story at various stages of its development gave me helpful suggestions and encouragement. Thanks to my fellow writers of To the Point writers' group, particularly Kevin Allen, Pauline Clark, Angie Gallop, and Gordon Graham, and also to David Kinraid, Ravi Nair, Larry Raney, and Ted Remington of the Bawdytalkers.

I've had great teachers who sparked my love of early history, technology, culture, and language, and who have influenced my work to this day. Keith Rossel first showed me the people behind the texts, and Dr Roberta Frank and Dr Lee Whitney introduced me to early English and the complex cultures of the early Iron Age.

My friends and mentors in the Society for Creative Anachronism taught me the rudiments of mediaeval armed combat, food and clothing. Particular thanks to Ian Hargrove, Joan Garay Hargrove, Jennifer Bulman and Henry Troup.

Thanks to Mary Vensel White for patiently shepherding me through the final preparation of the manuscript.

Thanks also to the Ontario Arts Council, which provided funding while I wrote.

Last but not least, thanks to David Syme for driving while I wrote in the car, for listening while I talked out plot points, for coffee and tea, and for always believing this day would come.

ABOUT THE AUTHOR

Elizabeth Creith has been a storyteller and visual artist for as long as she can remember. For a large part of her working life she made her living as a printmaker and potter. She first became a published writer with a humor piece, "A Loom with a Zoo" in September 1990. Her dream gig as a writer was to have a humor column; she has had four—two online, one on radio, and one in print.

She reads fantasy, folklore, history, paleontology, archaeology, science, poetry, and almost anything she can get her hands on about art. She writes humor, fantasy, poetry, and non-fiction, mostly pieces under 2000 words, and wrote her first novel-length draft in 2006 during the Three-Day Novel competition. She also practices bookmaking (with pages, not ponies), paper engineering, painting, and printmaking.

Elizabeth lives in a hundred-year-old farmhouse surrounded by roses and forest with her husband, cat, koi, and a lot of wildlife.